The Paranormal Powerwashers and the Missing Ghosts

Jules King

For my troupe:
You will echo in my words for eternity.
I am yours, always and forever.

1

Lilly

"I just wish I could kill the president and get away with it, y'know?"

Lillybelle rolled her eyes. *This again.*

With Venus, the subject of this exclamation was always one of two people. *Well, three, but it's not that one.* The first possibility was Yasmine, the snobbish sophomore class president who always picked the stupidest ways to spend the student body's money. *Something tells me it's not Miss queen B, though.*

"I mean, seriously," Venus continued, throwing her thick braid of brown hair over her shoulder. "Why does he have to be such a prick?"

Of course it's him. This time, Venus was talking about Alexander Mallen, and honestly, Lilly agreed. Alexander was smart, blonde, charismatic, and a massive misogynistic douchebag. He was the current president of the Paranormal and Supernatural club, although as soon as he had gotten more votes than Lillybelle, he had renamed the club something ridiculous.

The Paranormal, Supernatural, and Extraterrestrial Theorist and Investigative Adventurer Club, Lillybelle shuddered at the name. *Or PSETICAC, for short.* She sighed.

If the last president had put a limit on how many times a person could vote, Alex never would have gotten close to winning, she thought to herself, trying to wave away the part of her that was begging for a recount. *But I guess that's what happens when no one thinks ahead. Well, what's done is done.*

Lilly shot a look at Jeannie, who had taken the opportunity to retuck her short red hair behind her ear. She was shifting her weight from one foot to the other as she nodded in obvious agreement with Venus, who waved her arms around in an exaggerated manner.

"I'm not looking forward to the meeting today." Jeannie said, offering Lillybelle the stack of posters in her arms.

"Why not?" Lilly frowned, taking one off the top and using her prosthetic to press it against the white brick wall.

"Because," Venus pushed herself off the wall of green lockers and peeled a piece of tape off of the roll that she had slid up her arm. "The club president is an asshole who makes it feel like everything we do is a joke?"

"Kind of." Jeannie shot her friend an almost apologetic smile. "I mean, he used to genuinely care about this stuff in middle school, but now it's just a popularity contest for him."

She's right. Since Alex had become club president, there had been an influx of new attendees, but none of them took it seriously. The freshman girls would fawn over his nerdy jokes and goofy smile, which only fueled his massive ego. *It's like no one actually cares about what we're trying to do.*

"It does feel like all of our efforts at being taken seriously are kinda going down the drain." Lilly said softly, taking the offered pieces of tape.

"I'll say!" Venus was nearly shouting. "I mean, look at this poster!"

Lilly took a step back to look at the article that Venus found so offensive. A shiny purple ghost was smiling out at them, a camera flash taking up most of the background. Along the bottom, in a garish silver font it read: *Join us on our paranormal and extraterrestrial expeditions every Thursday! Beam on over!*

"It's ridiculous! It looks like the ghost is posing for the picture!"

Lillybelle grimaced. "You're right, you are completely right, V. It misrepresents what we as a club stand for. We don't want to capture the paranormal like it's all some circus attraction, we just want to prove it exists! This is a club about the science, the magical intellect behind it all. This poster makes it look like all we want to do is take selfies with ghosts."

"Exactly!" Jeannie stomped her foot, her usually soft voice rising in irritation. "It makes us all seem like crazy ghost hunters when we're not! We don't hunt ghosts, we don't want to hurt or trap anyone! We just want to prove that they're real!"

Stepping away from the now completely taped up poster, Lillybelle pulled the sleeves of her black sweater back down over her hands, bouncing back and forth on the balls of her feet. As she took the leftover posters from Jeannie, Jeannie smiled at her. Venus thrust a tape covered finger in the ghosts purple face, the smiling purple specter staring blankly out of his paper prison.

"Alex is the reason we're a complete joke! Everytime I talk to someone about my interests, they immediately respond in this patronizing tone. We have such a shitty reputation and it's his fault!"

"If only there was someone we knew who was a club officer," Jeannie's freckled face turned to Lillybelle, beaming. "Maybe then someone could stand up against his tyranny."

Lillybelle just shook her head as Venus whipped around, brandishing her masking tape talons as she stepped closer.

"Oh, miss club secretary!" Venus purred, voice sweet as she threw an arm over Lilly's shoulder. "You are the third most powerful person in the club. Why haven't you done anything against that treacherous, shit for brains-"

Her threats quickly transformed into a jumble of Spanglish insults that Lilly was partially thankful to not understand. The other half of her wished she hadn't taken Latin.

"You know I can't do much of anything! Because all of his friends got elected, I get outvoted at every turn. I mean, you see the kind of work I get stuck with," she brandished her pile of gaudy posters as she started down the hallway. "I never get told about the projects, but I have to do all of the research for them."

Something twisted in her chest. *That's not exactly true,* she thought, mind wandering to the manila folder tucked into her bag. Venus sniffed the air as she followed alongside Lillybelle, clearly suppressing more venomous words about Alexander.

"Wait for me!"

The pair stopped as Jeannie jogged the couple of yards they had crossed during their short conversation, holding each of their backpacks. Jeannie's gray pencil skirt had ridden up her pale legs, giving cause for Venus to tug it back down to where it was supposed to sit on her thighs before the trio continued down the hallway. A door slamming could be heard from somewhere in the building, the humming of the fluorescent lights filling the comfortable silence. The smell of old socks and some long forgotten disinfectant wafted through the air and Lilly tried not to gag as they passed the gross smelling janitor's closet. Jeannie's sneakers squeaked every other step and Lilly's boots were loud against the tiles of the floor, the laces slapping against each other every few seconds.

I love this, she thought, glancing between her friends. *The easy silence, the quiet moments. I never feel alone with them.* They made their way down the hall, feet slapping the floor loudly, but the sound was swallowed by the silence of the school. Most people had gone home already.

"Do you guys ever wonder why we haven't found anything

paranormal?" Jeannie asked, gaze going to Venus. "I mean, we're always looking, but we never seem to find any hard evidence."

"Are we actually looking, though?" Lilly laughed. "Outside of internet searches, I mean."

"Excuse me!" Venus protested. "I go out cryptid hunting, like, every weekend. And just because I haven't found anything doesn't mean I'm unsuccessful!"

"I don't think hiking and doing parkour in the forest behind your house counts as 'cryptid hunting'." Jeannie said, tucking her hair behind her ear with her nimble fingers.

"You're probably right." Venus sighed, folding her arms behind her head and leaning back. "But when do we have the time or opportunity to experience anything paranormal?"

Jeannie nodded knowingly. "Right? Between school, home-work, and clubs, I barely have enough time to breathe, let alone actually look for ghosts." For a moment, exhaustion slipped through the cracks of her calm, smiling mask and her face dropped.

The trio stopped in front of a set of double doors, a window sitting on either side. This was the main office, the center to the building. The three main hallways led towards it, the front doors making up the fourth 'wing' of the building. Over the office doors was a plaque that read *Springview High School*, and in one of the windows was a sports banner that said 'Go Cari-bou!' in bright green letters. Jeannie turned to the both of them, gesturing at the double doors with a smile on her face.

"I'll take the posters into the office and put them in Mr. Cole's mailbox. It'll be easier for him to hand them out that way."

Lillybelle nodded and very gladly unloaded the rest of the posters back into Jeannie's arms. *I should've done that at the start,* she thought to herself, but she ignored the bitter thought as her ginger friend danced to the door. Venus pulled it open and

Jeannie did a little bow of gratitude before ducking into the office. The two girls took a few steps away from the door as it swung shut and ended up leaning against one of the office windows, where the blinds were closed.

In the reflection of the darkened windows, Lilly saw a pale girl looking back at her, thin face, blue eyes, and twin black braids giving her an almost eerie look. Venus, reflected behind her, was taller, darker, stronger. Lilly gazed at her friend with an admiration that bubbled hot in her stomach as she turned away from the window. Her eyes were a muted green. *She's so pretty.*

Venus and Lillybelle exchanged a look, each smiling. Lilly pulled her prosthetic to her chest, letting her bag swing to the ground off her shoulder. There was a dull aching where her prosthetic met the stump below her shoulder, from a bruise gained earlier in the week. *Maybe I should take it off before the meeting? No,* she decided, *I can wait till I get home. I'll just take a hot shower later.*

Venus began to hum, swaying from side to side to an unheard tune, her thick braid swinging along with her. Just when she looked like she was about to burst into song, the lights began to flicker. Both their eyes went wide and Lillybelle felt her heart lift in her chest as a chill ran up her spine. As the lights continued to violently flicker, they both spoke at the same time, breathless:

"Adrienne!"

2

Jeannie

As soon as Jeannie saw the fluorescent lights of the front office flicker, she threw the posters into Mr. Cole's mailbox and ran. Her heart was pounding, her smile dropping from her face as she threw the doors open. Excitement was rising in her chest.

It's her, she thought, the door to the office slamming shut behind her as a chill wind blew up her skirt. *It has to be!* As the lights continued to violently flicker, Jeannie whipped around to her right, where Venus was scrambling with her phone. Venus swore several times as she hit her arm on the wall, but just as she got a handle on the device, the flickering stopped. Jeannie's heart sank and Venus sighed. Lilly began to jot something down in a notebook.

"Did you get it?" Jeannie asked, staring at Venus, shoulders lifting hopefully as she watched her friend.

Venus just shook her head, huffing air out of her mouth and sending a loose strand of hair flying back. "Everytime I am about to click record, it goes back to normal. It's like she is messing with us!" Venus violently shoved her phone back into her pocket as Lillybelle slid to the floor, flipping through her notebook.

Jeannie sucked in a breath of air, lungs shaking from the short run. *Details, Jeannie, details. What details do we have?* Closing her eyes, she thought back to the blinking analog clock that sat in the front office.

"It started at 2:29 and lasted about," she glanced at Venus's military-grade watch. "Thirty seconds."

Lillybelle just nodded, jotting the information down in the little notebook that Jeannie recognized. *She likes to keep track of things on paper. I wish I did that. I have my mental notes, but I know she has at least twelve pages in there. Not that it's exactly useful.* The only details they had managed to figure out so far were 'flickering lights,' 'missing objects,' and 'gets cold.' *What would Irsa say? That it's 'circumstantial at best?'*

Jeannie sighed, turning her thoughts to the page that was being filled with Lillybelle's scrawled handwriting. The black haired girl flipped to a new page, the top of which read the same as every page before: *Adrienne.*

That's what they called her, the ghost they knew haunted the school. The teachers and staff always dismissed their claims as faulty wiring or a bad back-up generator, but they knew the truth.

"Which entry is this?" Venus asked, pulling at the loose hair around her ears as she watched Lillybelle write.

"This would be number thirty-eight." Lilly said, checking the number she had written the previous time.

"She is getting more and more agitated these days." Jeannie said, glancing from the pages of the notebook up at the lights that had now returned to their regular, yellow state. "I wonder why."

Lilly shrugged. "It'll be the first thing I ask when we finally see her."

"Fuck!" Venus slammed her hand against the wall, making them jump. "I wish we could see her! I wish we could see anything! I just want to fucking do something for once! I'm tired of just sitting around, waiting for shit to happen!"

A gleam lit up in Lillybelle's eye and she tapped her foot on the ground, rapidly.

"What?" Jeannie asked, pulling at one of the loose red strands that had fallen in her eyes again. "Why do you look like you're ready to jump at us?"

Lilly swallowed and reached into her bag, pulling out a bulging manila folder. "So, remember when I said I don't get to know what the projects are?" Venus nodded and Lillybelle sighed. "That's not exactly true. Technically I'm not supposed to tell anyone, but I don't really care about Alexander anymore, so... Fuck it!"

Jeannie blinked as Lilly blew her bangs out of her eyes and flipped the manila folder open, the other side cradled in the crook of her prosthetic.

"It's a photography project," Lilly said, looking at Jeannie while seemingly biting back a smile. *She knows I love my camera.* "And each group is getting assigned a local legend to go investigate and document."

Venus sucked in a breath, grinning ear to ear. "Now we're fucking talking."

"And I already picked our location: The Abandoned Warehouse on 2nd street." Lillybelle smiled." They say that the warehouse burned down with 33 workers inside. None survived. Their angry spirits are said to haunt the building to this day." She seemed to look to a far off place, smile resting on her thin lips. "Some people think that the owner of the factory burnt it down on purpose, but no one really knows what caused the fire."

"We don't usually see people smiling when they talk about horrific work-related deaths, yet here we are?" Venus laughed.

Lilly smiled sheepishly. "Sorry."

Jeannie just shook her head, smiling just as wide as Lilly. *That's so fucking cool. I knew Lilly had something awesome up her sleeve, as always.*

"What made you choose this location?"

"Well," Lillybelle began, voice softer as she continued. "I told you how I did the research for all of the locations and their stories; well this location was one of the most promising I saw. Corporate espionage or careless working error? Who knows? Maybe we can find out."

"How would we find out?" Venus asked, leaning forward.

"Well, this place also didn't have as many sightings, which I took as a good sign, because if there are more than twenty, some of them are staged and some of them are mob mentality. But if there are just enough for them to stay similar and obscure, it has more validity."

"I'm not following." Venus shook her head.

Lilly looked giddy and the hairs on the back of Jeannie's neck rose, excitement bubbling in her chest. "There is a high chance of us actually finding a ghost at this site. They say dead men tell no tales, but I don't quite believe that. I think these ghosts have a lot to say." She grinned at her group, the light in their eyes telling her they would feel the same. "And I want to hear them talk."

"Now that's fucking cool." Venus whistled, leaning back.

"What's the address?" Jeannie asked, pulling out her phone and tapping her map app. "I wanna see if it's close enough to walk."

"I mean, we could definitely check it out after the meeting." Lillybelle handed her the first document.

"Fuck the meeting!" Venus said, zipping up her bag and throwing it over her shoulder. "Let's go right now!"

Jeannie frowned at the fully loaded GPS directions. *Damn.*

"We can't, it's an hour and a half walking."

Venus leaned over and pointed to a different number on the screen, one she hadn't bothered to look at. "Yeah, but a ten minute drive," she said, and then laughed when they both gave her a look. "You guys know I have a car, right?"

3

Jeannie

The drive over was nice, if Jeannie ignored the person who was driving. If she just stared out the window or closed her eyes, she could forget about it for a moment, but as soon as she opened them again, she would see Venus on top of the steering wheel, clutching onto it for dear life. Just looking at her made her nervous. *I don't even drive this cautiously, and I only just got my permit!* Glancing in the rear-view mirror, Lillybelle seemed to be smiling in the backseat. *No wonder she didn't even try to call shotgun.*

The windows were rolled down to let the breeze in, but it wasn't very consistent because as soon as they'd get at a steady speed, Venus would lift her foot off the gas and lose her mind. Jeannie was starting to think it would be easier to walk when the building came into view.

It peaked out from behind the trees, its once towering might now crumpled and decayed. The seventh floor looked like it had completely collapsed into the sixth, leaving the charred husk of a building teetering in on itself. The windows were gone or broken and the entire outside of the first floor was covered in colorful graffiti. More swear words than Jeannie had ever seen were scrawled on the side of the building in big, bold letters. *It's beautiful,* she thought, eyes roaming the piece of history and horror. *Terrifying. But beautiful.* Pulling out her camera, Jeannie took the shot.

Venus pulled into the almost grassy parking lot, tires of the Saturn struggling over the gravel and broken concrete. The parking brake turned on and the ignition turned off, Jeannie was safe to escape the car. The gravel and concrete were loud under her tennis shoes, crackling and groaning under her feet, as if they were the souls of the damned. Even before they approached the building, an eerie feeling began to set in. It almost felt as if the windows were eyes, watching to see what these intruders would do next.

Jeannie took a few steps towards the building, camera strap weighing on her neck as she held her signature Canon. The afternoon sun would usually be stronger, but the start of autumn had cut the hours of sunlight, dimming her shots. Hopefully her flash would be enough once they were inside. *If we can even get inside.*

She could hear Lilly's boots crunching as she came up behind her. A soft *beep* told her that Venus was on her way after locking the car. Together, they just stood and stared at the building. It towered above them, a melted metal and concrete framework holding up seven floors full of secrets. Jeannie took a deep breath.

"I guess, we should go inside?"

Venus half nodded, pulling on a sweatshirt emblazoned with a coffee shop logo over her t-shirt. "Did you get any pictures of the outside?"

Jeannie raised her camera, adjusted the exposure settings a little, and snapped a picture. Lilly glanced over at the camera.

"Are you using your wide angle?"

Jeannie shook her head, looking at the picture on the

camera's small screen, before lowering it. "No, I wanted it to look more natural. Wide angles can distort the image, and I don't want to distort evidence."

"We should look for an entrance." Venus sighed, bouncing from foot to foot, gravel crunching under her shoes. She started forward, but Jeannie grabbed her arm. *Always the impulsive one.*

"Well, wait," she laughed, glancing at the mangled warehouse. "Are we sure this building is even structurally sound? I mean, it caught fire how many years ago?"

"It burnt down about fifty years ago, but after the fire marshall did a thorough investigation, he decided it was stable enough to be used again if the company chose to." Lilly held up a folder that Jeannie hadn't noticed her holding and opened it, retrieving a sheet of paper.

Venus cocked her head. "Did the company choose to?"

"No," Lilly said, running a hand through her long black hair, having undone her braids in the car. "The company was sued by the workers' families and went bankrupt. The building was abandoned and hasn't been bought or used since. Another safety check was done about seven years ago and it was declared safe enough to move around in, but they said that attempting to go past the fifth floor was 'unsafe and dangerous'."

"Alright." Venus said, shrugging. "That just means no sixth or seventh floor. We didn't need to go up there anyway. I don't want to go up any more flights of stairs than I have to."

Jeannie laughed, but the small ball of anxiety that had been bubbling up in her chest seeped into her voice. Swallowing it all back, she followed Venus towards the decrepit building. Lilly trailed behind them both, folder still open, audibly tripping on a few roots and sticks as she walked.

The front of the building had a set of double doors with thick, rusted chains wrapped around the door handles. A large lock hung from the chain and no matter how much Venus kicked it, it did not budge. Venus suggested that they split up and go around the sides of the warehouse to find a back entrance or loading bay. Venus and Lillybelle would take the left side of the building, while Jeannie would take the right.

"Wait," Jeannie said, trying to swallow the hesitation that was making her voice tremor. "Do you have, like, a map of the building? If I get lost, I need to know where I am in reference to you."

The pair turned to Lillybelle, who pulled out a printed out blueprint from the folder.

"This is a layout of the building's first floor. These are the outer walls." She handed the picture to Jeannie, who held it out in front of her.

Looks like an ugly jigsaw piece, she thought, eyes tracing the crudely hewn walls that had more angles and turns than a hectogon. Lillybelle pointed at one of the weird enclaves on the right side of the building, Jeannie's side.

"There should be some kind of door here, if I remember correctly. If not, we'll meet at the back of the building here, where there is definitely a door." She put her finger on the back of the building, many, many turns and corners away from where they stood now. "If you can find an entrance that works, call one of us and vice versa."

Venus peaked over Lilly's shoulder. "Do we have a copy of that too?"

With a smile, Lilly produced another copy from her folder.

"You really did think of everything," Jeannie laughed, although she wasn't too fond of the idea of splitting up. "Make sure to take notes of things in your journal and to take pictures. I'll do the same."

Lilly nodded and Venus grinned.

"See you on the other side."

It didn't take much walking for her to be completely out of range of the conversation between the other two, leaving

Jeannie to listen to the silence and the trees. Slowly, she trekked alongside the building, trailing her fingertips along the outer wall. The texture of the rust and the layers of ash and dust combined with moss and decay made for an interesting exploration with her hands, fingers absentmindedly tracing the lines of different graffitied swear words.

The longer she walked, the more her anxiety weighed on her. The longer she walked, the more sure she was that the trees were hiding something. The longer she walked, the more she talked to herself.

"It's okay," she said, loudly, gripping the camera tightly. "Just pretend you're a detective in a silly holiday romcom. They never get hurt! They are silly, and almost always wrong, but they are always fine!"

Imagining herself as a silly detective in a silly hat, weirdly enough, helped a lot. *Silly detectives don't think they're being watched! They're stupidly confident!* Relaxing her shoulders, she strode onwards, ignoring the feeling of eyes on her that radiated from the shadowy trees and towering ruins.

For a majority of the walk, the windows were too high for her to see into, but gradually, the ground beneath her started to slope up the side of the factory warehouse, raising her to the windows a little bit more with each step. Finally, she came eye level with them, but layers of ash and grime made it hard to see. She sighed and continued alongside the building, sneakers sinking into the growing pile of rotting leaves that raised her to the windows.

The smell wafted up to her, but she took deep breaths in through her mouth to avoid vomiting her lunch onto her brightly patterned shoes. She just focused on squinting through the windows to try and see anything inside, although she refused to touch them for fear of breaking the ancient-looking glass.

One of the windows she came upon was already broken and gave her a view into one of the rooms of the warehouse. She peered into the window, but the lack of interior light meant there was little to see. Pulling out her camera, she set the flash to go off and snapped a picture in the dark. In the split-second it took for the flash to go off, something was illuminated in the dark room.

"Aaahh!"

Something flew at her face and she tumbled backwards, down the leaves and on to the ground. She hit the ground hard and heard a crash on the ground next to her.

"Shit, shit, shit!"

As she sat up, she immediately felt for her camera, making sure it wasn't broken or the lens wasn't cracked. She breathed out a sigh of relief and glanced around. Her phone had fallen out of her skirt pocket and smacked to the ground, face down. She held her breath as she picked it up and flipped it over, glad when she saw no cracks on her already scratched up screen. Jeannie stood up cautiously, brushing the leaf litter off of her short, gray skirt. As she managed to stand upright again, she picked up her camera to look at the beastly creature that had jumped out at her from the darkness. She flicked over to the picture and laughed.

Silly detectives might be stupidly confident, but they can be scared by birds!

It was just an owl! She laughed again, relief washing over her. *Must have scared it with my flash.* There was something in the background of the photo, though, she couldn't tell what it was on this small screen. She made a mental note to enlarge the photo on her laptop later.

She pulled out her phone and tapped out a message to the group chat.

Jumpscared by a bird. Poor owl just wanted some sleep, lol.- J

She sent the message, and followed it with a gif of an animatronic chicken, before turning off her phone, shoving it back in her pocket without checking for a response. Watching her step, she continued her path around the warehouse, searching for any entrance that didn't involve jumping through broken glass.

Jeannie found another window that had a good view into the warehouse, except this one was well lit. *Where's the light even coming from?* She snapped a picture anyway. A few times, a jazzy little tune played in her pocket, singing that she had received a new message. She ignored it, taking another long look through the glass. The room was an open layout with large pillars every couple of yards, rubble and burnt materials piled everywhere. Grime climbed the walls, eating at the ash stained concrete, slowly crumbling under the weight of the building.

She couldn't pinpoint why, but the room gave her an uneasy feeling. Maybe it was the way the light from the window highlighted the reddish-brown stains on the concrete or the scratches on the sheet metal propped up against the pillars. She made sure she took the picture and moved on, hoping the feeling creeping up her spine would fade as she walked.

After a minute, she remembered the blueprint Lilly had given her. *Wasn't there supposed to be a door around here?* The blueprint was soon unfolded in her hands and she frowned. *If I'm looking at this right, I should've seen that door by now. I guess there isn't one.* Sighing, she pulled out her phone, ready to send an update about the door when she froze. *What's that sound?*

She quieted her breathing, listening intently. *Voices?* Quiet, but there. She shoved her phone back in her pocket, starting towards the sounds.

As she began to approach the spot where the building turned, she smiled. *Maybe V and Lilly got there before me!* She sped up her walk, almost jogging to reach the corner, but when she reached it she froze. The voices she heard weren't familiar, weren't her friends. Her heart jumped into her throat as she shrunk back, against the warehouse wall. *I thought this place was supposed to be abandoned?*

There were two voices, but the feminine voice was loudest.

"Yes, I've been cleaning up after myself. Why don't you trust me to do this right?"

"Because you never do anything right." The deeper voice grumbled, irritated.

There was a stomp. "Fuck off, like you actually give a damn about that! You just want to know how I'm doing this so well because you're jealous, just like all of them."

"Jealous? Of what? The ability to be the only person in your group unable to accomplish anything? Just get it done and get out of here. We don't have much time left and you're on the verge of fucking it all up."

She huffed. "Fine. Go away!"

The other person started to say something, but was cut off, a sharp shift in atmosphere prickling the hairs on the back of Jeannie's neck. Now there was only an unsettling silence and the sighing of the woman. Jeannie strained her ears, but couldn't hear anything from the other person, no footsteps, no breathing. *Maybe he was on speaker?* She shook her head. *No, I heard him! Whoever they are, they're just... gone.*

The feminine voice had gone mostly quiet, only some grumbling could be heard. Jeannie focused on keeping her breathing quiet, barely sucking in enough air to breathe properly. She could hear the owner of the voice shuffling around, kicking and crunching through the leaves. Jeannie didn't know why, but she knew she did not want to be caught eavesdropping in that conversation. The woman's footsteps finally sounded like they were getting quieter, when Jeannie's phone went off.

The phone sprung to life in her pocket, singing a jazzy little tune as her blood ran cold. Jeannie shut it off in seconds, but it was too slow. The woman's footsteps stopped and Jeannie glanced around for somewhere to hide, but found nothing.

There were no hiding spaces and although she was desperate, she did not want a face-full of glass. The footsteps started again, rapidly getting closer to her. Crunching through the leaves, louder and louder, closer and closer. Jeannie pressed herself against the wall, hoping to disappear into the shadows as the woman was about to turn the corner.

A cold, hand grabbed Jeannie, fingers wrapping around her face and her stomach and an arm yanked her backwards. She tried to scream, but no sound escaped. She couldn't move, couldn't speak, couldn't do anything except watch. She couldn't even breathe. Her body was frozen still, only her eyes still working. But even with her eyes working, she couldn't see who had grabbed her. *The hands are invisible.* The woman arrived.

She had ratty blonde hair, pale blue eyes blown wild in a combination of fear and rage. But her appearance or ratty clothing was of no interest. Jeannie's eyes went straight to the blade she held in her hand, glistening silver in the light.

A knife! She's going to kill me!

But the woman didn't kill her. She didn't even lift the knife. She looked at Jeannie. She looked straight at Jeannie. *No,* she thought. *Not at. Through.* The woman's gaze looked right through her. As if she was part of the wall.

4

Venus

"Looks like Jeannie got scared!"

Lillybelle shot a look at her from over her shoulder, brows furrowed. "What do you mean?"

Venus held out her phone and Lillybelle turned around, squinting at the screen. A smile broke over her face.

"Ah, so that was the notification I just got."

"You don't check your messages?" Venus asked, her phone buzzing again in her hand. It was a reply from Berri.

Lillybelle shook her head. "My phone is always on silent, so I check them when I know I have the time."

Venus nodded as Lilly turned back to the building. *Makes sense.* She read over Berri's message.

> **BOO-BERRI**
>
> Where did you find an owl?

Venus smiled and tapped out a response.

> **YOU**
>
> Will tell @ meeting l8r

21

Glancing at the walls of the warehouse, a creeping feeling took hold of Venus and she couldn't shake the unease that the dark windows instilled. Her phone buzzed again.

Venus waited for a moment, hoping to see Jeannie's usual slew of heart emojis spill into the chat. But none came. The most recently viewed message from the redhead was her own. Exiting the group chat, Venus tapped on Jeannie's contact, labeled *Genie Beanie.*

Message was delivered, but not read. Not even after Venus sent her own slew of emojis. A small pit in Venus's stomach grew cold, pressing into her. She pressed the call icon and put her phone to her ear, chewing on her lip. *Pick up, pick up, pick up.*

After one ring, the line clicked.

"Hi, this is Jeannie! If you're hearing this, I can't make it to the phone right now, please leave me a message or call me back-"

Venus hung up. *She ignored my call? Weird.*

"Hey, Lilly, Jeannie just sent me straight to voice mail."

"Maybe she miss-clicked?" Lillybelle turned back, frowning. "Call again."

Venus did as she was told, sucking in a breath. Two rings, click.

"Hi, this is Jeannie! If you're hearing this-"

"Shit, straight to voicemail again. Can you call her?"

Lillybelle sighed, but pulled out her phone. "She's probably just caught up taking pictures."

Venus nodded as Lilly shifted her papers to her prosthetic and held the phone up to her ear. Even from a few feet away, Venus could hear Jeannie's voice from the phone.

"Hi, this is Jeannie! If you're hearing this, I can't make it to the phone right now. Please-"

Lillybelle ended the call and shook her head. "She's probably fine." A tremor in Lilly's voice said she thought otherwise, but Venus decided not to press it further.

She glanced at the map that lay in Lilly's arms. It looked as if they were near the back half, a couple of loose sketches and notes dotting the blueprint. Venus glanced in at the window and doubled back. Behind the smudged and mostly leaf covered glass, was nothing. No walls, or doors, or anything. Just darkness.

Frowning, she shone her phone flashlight in the window, as she had left her heavy duty flashlight in the car. The light, which had earlier revealed dank closets and a weirdly open room of pillars, now pierced the darkness to reveal nothing. The light shone into a void of black.

"What the fuck?" Venus muttered under her breath, leaning closer to the window with wide eyes.

A quiet sound hit her ears as she leaned forward, almost like whispering. Each tiny voice was soft, words indiscernible as the voices were from each other, a mesh of white noise as syllables. Heat emanated from the darkness, almost painful the closer she leaned forward. A gust of sharp heat blew in her face and she stumbled back.

She whipped around and jogged to catch up with Lillybelle, who had kept walking.

"You never told me this place was supposed to be some black void."

"What are you talking about?" Venus explained what she

had seen and Lilly frowned again. "That's not something any of the other encounters have described. Are you sure?"

Venus gaped.

"Yeah, I'm fucking sure, I felt it!"

"Sorry, sorry, just making sure." Lilly cracked a smile.

"I don't feel good about this, Lilly. We should get to the meeting point and then look for Jeannie."

"Okay, let's do that."

The rest of the walk around the building was uneventful, but with every step further, Venus felt more and more nervous. Each look through the windows seemed less and less inviting, blackness glaring back at her with every glance. The wind rustled through the trees and threw light shadows across the building, the dim light of the afternoon sun making them weak, yet sharp claws on the building.

They turned the final corner and Venus felt her heart drop. The back of the building- the meeting point- was completely empty. Heart pounding loudly in her chest, Venus glanced between the unread messages and the empty clearing behind the warehouse. *Where the fuck is Jeannie?*

5

Jeannie

Jeannie couldn't breathe. *Why can't she see me?* The woman's eyes darted back to the spot where Jeannie was supposed to be for just a moment, but she looked away. The woman paced for a minute, scanning the area where Jeannie had just been. Any fear that Jeannie had once had of being found was replaced by the opposite. *Why can't you see me? Look at me, please, look at me! I'm right here!* She felt like crying but no matter how much she tried to scream, cry, make any sound, nothing happened. The woman stalked around the corner and was gone, leaving Jeannie alone.

As the woman's footsteps faded to silence, Jeannie's thoughts ran wild, a tempest of emotions whirling through her brain. *Why can't she see me why can't I move why can't I do anything what is happening let me out let me out LET ME OUT.*

A shadow fell across her vision, but as she scanned her limited view, she saw that nothing had changed. She could feel the cold hands on her, holding her in place, but suddenly there was a different hand. The one covering her mouth and the one wrapped around her stomach tightened its grip, but she could feel her skin crawl as a third hand wrapped around her shoulder.

Unlike with the first two, she could feel warmth emanating from the palm as it pressed against her sweater- through her sweater. Another warm hand manifested at her waist, hot nails digging into the skin above her waist band. If she could have, she would have cried out in pain.

She could feel herself being jostled, one set of invisible hands pulling her one way while the other resisted. For a moment, the new hands released her, leaving her with the only original. The cold loosened, as if relieved or relaxed. Suddenly, the two burning hands slammed into her chest, sending her careening backwards. Her head spun as her vision came and went. In an instant, she had fallen back, stumbling and crashing onto the concrete floor of a dark room. The light from a broken window spilled in, dim. She blinked and took a deep breath, head spinning with information and questions.

Was I just inside the wall? It was the only thought that jumped into her mind, the only one that wasn't a question. She took another shaky breath and wrapped her arms around herself, closing her eyes. *Someone grabbed me and pulled me back against the wall- no. Not against the wall. That woman couldn't see me, even though I was standing right there. I was right there! And I couldn't move. Why couldn't I move? The woman left and there were more hands and someone pushed me and now-* Her heart stopped as she glanced around and realization hit her like a punch in the gut. *I'm inside the warehouse.*

6

Jeannie

She felt like she was going to be sick. Her skin was crawling, as though the hot and cold phantoms were still gripping her- even though they were gone. Whatever they were. The room was swimming so she shut her eyes, hard. It smelled like must and ash. She was covered in goosebumps and her hands wouldn't stop shaking. Her pockets felt lighter. *No!*

Her hands shot to her side and she began to pat, hands trembling uncontrollably as she tried to find her phone, her camera, anything. *It's gone, it's all gone. All of my shit is gone!* She opened her eyes in the dim room, panic tightening her chest as she tried to search for her belongings, but she couldn't find any of it. It was all gone.

Shaking, her hands roamed her skin, pressing and pinching to bring back sensation, pain feeling. *Anything to prove I'm still here.*

Her chest rising and falling rapidly, she tried to breathe- tried to do what she couldn't minutes earlier- she tried to scream. Her voice echoed off the walls, but was swallowed in

27

the black corners of the room, the destroyed rotten wood, the melted metal. The room was completely empty.

But the doorway wasn't.

Standing up, Jeannie steadied herself on the wall for a moment before stumbling towards the door. Her legs were like jelly and she prayed they wouldn't give out. Nearly collapsing to the floor as she bent down, her fingers wrapped around the crumpled piece of paper. For a moment, her heart lifted, but it immediately dropped again. *It's the map Lilly gave me. How did it get over here? Wait.* Something was scrawled on the paper, in what looked like charcoal. There was a little circle on the map with a word written in lopsided letters. *You.*

Another wave of nausea came over her and she sank to the floor in the doorway, crushing the paper in her fingers. She felt like crying. She felt like screaming. She felt like- She buried her palms in her eyes, pressing until bright colors flowered from the black of her eyelids.

What is happening?

It felt like an eternity before she could stand up again, though she couldn't how long it had actually been. Ten minutes, twenty minutes, three. So many thoughts were running through her head, few of them good. *Am I magic? No*, she thought, *not likely. The warehouse? It would make sense, if it's supposed to be haunted. Maybe it's cursed.* Maybe she was too. Her head was pounding, but she stood anyway, swaying on her feet as she uncrumpled the map and smoothed it against her thigh. *At least whatever it was left me my clothes.*

Jeannie stared at the map in the low light, turning it around a couple of times before she decided which way it was facing. Brushing her hair out of her face, she took a deep breath and stepped outside of the room.

The warehouse was dark, but some windows and a couple of large holes in the upper floors of the building let in some of the September sunlight. She wasn't sure if she should be grateful for a lack of structural integrity, but it didn't matter. *Does any of it matter anymore?*

Using the dim light, she slowly made her way towards what the map told her was the back of the building. The meeting point. The exit. *If the map is even right.* Most of the warehouse was an open layout, with tall stone pillars holding up a crumbling tower of floors. She tried not to think about the many layers of concrete and sheet metal over her head that could come crashing down at any minute, regardless of how safe the inspector had said it was seven years ago. Every once in a while, she could see doors that led into a stairwell or a closet and she kept her eye on the door as she passed it, though she wasn't 100% sure why.

Do I think something will be there? She asked herself, shaking her head as her eyes jumped from door frame to door frame. *There's no way anyone else is in here. Although,* she reconsidered. *I'm not supposed to be either. Who was that woman?*

With no flashlight or means of defense, Jeannie didn't have to try very hard to keep on edge, jumping at every shadow, stopping at every small sound in the building. Every door she passed, she made note of, not wanting to see what was behind it until she knew where the exit was.

"What happened to the silly detective?" She whispered to herself, almost laughing, but thinking better of it. Her voice felt impossibly loud in the silent place. "And her silly hat?"

After an eternity of wary searching and nervous walking, she spotted a sign in the distance. Heart lifting, she hurried towards it. The sign was scratched and old, but the letters were simple. *Loading Dock.* She almost cried out in relief, breaking into a sprint in the direction the sign pointed to. *That has to mean exit!* Her galaxy sneakers slapped loudly against the concrete as she ran through a set of barely open metal doors towards what must be the exit, but she skidded to a stop when she saw what lay ahead.

A mangled pile of melted metal and concrete rubble lay in her path, piled higher than she was tall. The metal was more sparse at the top, allowing her to see the loading bay door that lay past the mound. She groaned in despair, pulling at her red hair as she looked for a way around the pile. On one side was a collapsed pillar, the rubble pile so large that it reached the ceiling and completely cut off any way around. On the other was what *might* be an opening- but it was shrouded in shadows. Complete and total darkness.

Would I rather get impaled on a sharp spike than explore a dark corner in a haunted warehouse by myself?

Jeannie eyed the pile of tetanus and started to climb. The rubble was surprisingly sturdy as she scrambled up it, grabbing at the melted together scrap metal for handholds. It didn't take long to reach the top of the pile, but as she got to the top, she reached another obstacle.

The pile was too close to the ceiling to crawl over, leaving her with the only option of trying to slide through a gap between sheets of twisted scrap metal. She sucked in a breath and began to squeeze her way in between the metal, trying to push herself through the dangerously tight gap. The metal rods pressed against her skin, the cold of the metal seeping in through the tiny holes of her sweater. She paused to pull her sweater up over the metal.

The metal was uncomfortably icy against her skin, but she continued struggling through the gap, gasping and huffing as the metal rods scraped the skin on her back and her thighs. Jeannie bit down a cry as a sharp piece of metal nearly stabbed her stomach. She knew making a sound wouldn't end well. Carefully, she slid her hand between her stomach and the metal, cutting the back of her hand instead of the soft flesh of her midriff. *Did something just move?*

She pulled herself out of the gap, able to breathe freely again, but as she began to descend, her skirt caught on a piece of metal. She turned her head to unhook it and something in the shadows on the other side of the pile moved. Her head snapped up, eyes wide as she frantically pulled at her skirt, shaking as she scanned the still darkness. Nothing. She glanced down again, but as she pulled her eyes away, the black jumped towards her. Heart in her throat, she pulled on her skirt, hard. The sound of tearing filled her ears and she felt herself falling.

Jeannie slammed to the ground, ears ringing as she hit the concrete. Her forearms and elbows ached, but she scrambled to her feet quickly, backing away from the pile without taking her eyes away from it. Shadows all around her, in the corners of her eyes and in the corners of the room, were reaching, writhing, moving. Her gaze darted from the pile to the door on the far wall, and in a split second decision, she broke into a sprint.

Her fingers wrapped around the thick chain, scraping themselves raw as she pulled with all of her force. Rust stained her pink skin as it cut into her palm. Her feet slid on the ground as her body weight pulled the chain, pulling towards the ground. Hand over hand, full body pull after full body pull, the chain moved.

The door slowly raised, a grinding sound filling the room as she heaved it open inch by inch. In her peripheral vision, she could see the shadows reaching out for her, but the light spilling from the door kept some shadows at bay. Soon, the door was up over her head, but she kept pulling until it slammed against the ceiling. As soon as it did, she let go of the chain and bolted, not looking back as she ran from the building. As she ran, heat brushed the side of her face, tugged her hair, but she was gone.

The concrete under her feet turned to grass as she burst into the open, sucking in the crisp autumn air. She collapsed onto her knees in the grass, grabbing the grass in her fists to ground herself as the giant metal door slammed shut behind her. Every cell in her body screamed that she was safe in the open air. Screamed that she was safe in the sunlight. She was safe.

7

Lilly

Lillybelle bounced her leg as she leaned against the warehouse wall, staring down at her phone as a now painfully familiar voicemail played in her hand before stopping. She tapped redial again, and waited, knowing what would happen before it even stopped. She let out a sigh and Venus looked up at her from the floor. Her prosthetic was aching again.

"She declined again." Lilly said, shaking her head and staring up at the swaying trees. "Why isn't she picking up our calls?"

Venus kept her eye on the garage door that covered the back of the building. "I don't know. We told her we'd call when we found a way in. She should have been here ten minutes ago."

"Maybe she got in and ran out of service?" Lillybelle said, leaning her head back against the wall. Even as she said the words, she didn't believe them.

"Yeah, I just want to make sure she's okay."

After a moment, Venus started to say something else, but Lillybelle shushed her. Her blood was loud in her ears, but something drew her to the wall. A sound. She pressed herself against the concrete and motioned for Venus to join her. The industrial walls didn't allow much through, but she heard something. It was soft, like words being spoken directly on the other side.

The whispering.

She pushed herself up and Venus jumped back. Her heart was pounding in her chest, but a chill ran through her when she heard loud footsteps slapping against the concrete, coming towards the wall. And fast.

"Someone's inside," Lillybelle said, eyes blown wide.

Venus took a few steps back, eyes on the giant metal door.

"They're trying to get out."

The footsteps stopped and a loud grinding sound started. Lillybelle and Venus watched in horror as the door began to creak up, opening. They both stepped back, unsure of what to do. Lilly could see something moving in the darkness, slinking back with every inch of sunlight that bled onto the concrete. The door slowly ground upwards and when it stopped, something came flying out, red hair swinging behind her.

Jeannie shot out of the building, but she wasn't alone; she was closely followed by what looked like a shadow. *No. A person.* Made of the black shadows the person lunged. Its fingers were outstretched, grabbing onto her hair for a moment, before letting go. It didn't follow her far, staying inside the darkness of the warehouse. It watched Jeannie's escape into the light for a moment, before slinking away into the black. The door slammed shut and the ground shook. Lillybelle's eyes were wide. She glanced at Venus. *Did she see that too?* Venus was staring at Jeannie, a look of relief covering her features. *I guess not.*

"Jesus, Jeannie, you scared the crap out of-"

"Are you okay?"

Lillybelle cut Venus off, mouth dry as Jeannie flung herself onto the ground. Her hair was a mess, there were scratches along her legs and stomach, and her skirt had been torn. There were deep scrapes across her knees and elbows, and blood was running down her leg: she had cut her knee. Her bag and her camera were nowhere to be seen.

Jeannie just lay in the grass, breathing heavily and staring up at the autumn sky, a small smile of relief appearing on her face. Her fingers were curled around the blades of grass and the red leaf litter, clutching it tightly.

"I will be now."

After chugging a waterbottle that Venus had in her bag and taking several minutes to breathe, Jeannie seemed to collect herself. Venus and Lillybelle sat in the grass next to her, extremely concerned.

"What the hell happened?"

Slowly, Jeannie began telling her story as Venus rummaged around in her bag for some bandaids, recounting the situation with the owl and how she had dropped her phone, and then how she had heard voices from behind the corner. This was where Lillybelle interrupted.

"What was this woman talking about?"

Venus poured some water over Jeannie's knees, blowing on them a bit and making her hiss in pain, but Jeannie just shook her head through it.

"I don't even know. The other person didn't seem to be too happy with her."

"Who was the other person?" Venus asked, cocking her head to the side as she peeled the wrapper off the first bandaid. It was princess themed.

"That's the weird part; well, one of them." Jeannie said, cracking her fingers in her lap, even when they stopped making any sound. She didn't seem to notice the blood on her knuckles. "This other voice sounded like they were standing outside with her, but when she told them to leave her alone, they cut out completely. No breathing, no movement, no sound. They were just gone."

"Are you sure it wasn't just a phone call?" Lilly frowned.

Venus smoothed out the bandaid on her leg and Jeannie shook her head.

"I mean, maybe, but it felt different. Like one second, they were there, next to her behind that corner, but the next they were completely gone. It was weird."

Venus flashed a wry smile as she smoothed out the other bandaid and jokingly said, "Maybe it was a ghost."

Jeannie didn't laugh. Her expression was hard to read, fear and intrigue among the swirling emotions that painted her features.

"I mean, that would track. It might explain how I got away from her."

"Wait," Lilly asked, blinking as more questions filled her mind. "What do you mean, 'Got away from her?' Did she see you?"

Jeannie's expression was one near hysteria as she gripped Venus's hand tightly, knuckles whitening under the drying blood as she explained how she had been dragged through the wall. There was a beat of silence as Lillybelle and Venus sat, processing. Lilly's thoughts went back to the shadow person, the void windows, the whispering. *Could those be connected?*

"Why didn't you call us for help?" Venus interrupted, brows furrowed as frustration tinged her voice when she spoke. "And why were you ignoring our calls?"

Jeannie blinked, confusion joining the whirl of emotions on her freckled face.

"What?"

"I tried to call you after you messaged the group, but you sent me straight to voice mail." She said, smoothing out a bandaid on the back of Jeannie's hand. "Lilly tried too, but same thing."

"We tried calling you for like ten minutes when we got over

here," Lillybelle continued for Venus, "but every time it just went straight to voicemail."

Jeannie stiffened when she said that, eyes wide. "Wait. My phone went *straight* to voicemail? No ringing, just voicemail?"

"Why are you talking as if you weren't the one declining our calls?" A knot began to form in Lilly's stomach as she laughed nervously. "You were the one declining our calls, right?"

Jeannie shook her head. Her eyes were wide in fear and her voice trembled.

"When I went through the wall, all of my stuff was gone. My phone, my camera, my bag, everything. Everything except this." She reached in her pocket and pulled out a crumpled piece of paper. "This was laid out on the floor of the room I ended up in, sitting in the doorway."

She flattened out the paper for Lillybelle and Venus to see. It was the layout of the map that Lilly had given her earlier, except something was written on part of it. Lilly turned the map around to get a better look at it. *You?*

"That's not your handwriting."

"That was written on it when I found it." Jeannie said, nodding.

"So whatever brought you through the wall left you a map telling you where you were after rescuing you?" Venus said, adding the last bandaid and kissing her knee.

Jeannie squinted at Venus, expression softening for a moment.

"Was it rescuing me? Or was it trading one shit situation for another?"

"And on top of all that, whatever stole your shit has been using your phone." Venus dragged her hands down her face. "Holy fuck."

Lilly tapped Jeannie's foot with her finger. "Keep going."

Jeannie continued her harrowing tale, telling about how she felt the shadows were watching her and then how they started to follow her. The scrap pile and the panic. The fall and the sheer fear that, as she explained, was the only reason she could have had the strength to open that door. Lilly closed her eyes, still confused by the information circling her mind. The entire time Jeannie had been talking, the whispering and the shadows hadn't been far from her thoughts.

"Wait, why didn't you mention the person who was chasing you?"

"What?" Jeannie gave her a look that said she wanted her to be joking.

"When you ran out of the warehouse, there was someone behind you."

Jeannie shook her head, leaning back in the grass, obviously done. Slowly, Lillybelle explained what had happened up until when they started listening. She talked about how they must have heard Jeannie falling, but that they also heard whispering, which Jeannie had not included in her story. When they asked her about it, she just shook her head.

"I didn't hear anything. I might have been too panicked, but I didn't hear any whispering."

Lillybelle continued, recounting the moving shadows she saw and how she saw someone or something chasing Jeannie, almost grabbing her as she ran from the warehouse.

"You saw the shadows moving, meaning I'm not crazy." Jeannie shuddered.

"But the person you saw," Venus said, brows furrowed in concern. "That's different. The shadows might just be, like, haunted, but the thing chasing you must have some degree of sentience. And it was different than the other sentient thing that saved you, to some degree."

"What does that mean?"

Venus shook her head.

"It means we are dealing with more than two kinds of paranormal activity. We're going to need more hands on deck for this."

Lillybelle nodded absentmindedly, before checking her phone. *Fuck!* She stood up quickly as the other two frowned at her.

"The meeting! It starts in four minutes!"

Venus jumped up as well.

"Shit, we have to go!" Venus gave Jeannie a hand and helped her off the ground. "Can't be late to the first meeting of the year!"

"Especially because we're doing the project that we aren't supposed to know about yet," Lilly said, leading the way around the side of the building she had come up on.

"But then everyone will know about the project!" Jeannie said, arm tightly hooked through Venus's. "And we can tell them all what happened!"

Lillybelle nodded. "And we can come back afterwards!"

"Our own little army," Venus laughed. "Let's go get the gang."

8

Venus

Venus's tennis shoes loudly slapped the tile floor of the school as the three of them thundered down the hallway and skidded to a stop in front of the classroom door. She and Lilly had left their bags in the car, so they had been able to run a little faster from the parking lot. *But was it fast enough?* Heart pounding in her chest, she glanced down at her black watch, green numbers glowing up at her. 3:31. *Shit.* Lillybelle was breathing heavily next to her as she shoved her sleeve back up her arm and put a shaking hand on the door. *We're late.*

Lilly pushed the door open and the quiet hallway immediately echoed with the peals of laughter emerging from within. A familiar voice, throwing around the words 'Bigfoot' and 'trap,' made Venus roll her eyes. *Does he ever shut up?*

Even though the meeting was supposed to start six minutes ago, Alexander was droning on and on about his Sasquatch trap to a posse of wide-eyed freshman girls. Lilly strode right up to him, crossing confidently through the brightly lit English classroom after rearranging her curtain bangs. Venus hung back, just behind Jeannie, who was still standing inside the doorway.

40

Alex was lounging on the table at the front of the classroom, where Mr. Cole would typically have grammar worksheets stacked high. His messy black hair was always in his eyes, gangly limbs waving in the air the longer he talked. An old class ring hung around his neck, weighing heavily against the thin fabric of his shirt and constantly clacking against the shiny *President* pin dangling from his shirt. Venus could feel her blood start to boil as the egotistical brat barely looked at Lilly before waving her off to a blonde boy with a clipboard.

Que cabron, she thought to herself, eyes gliding over the faces of the other officers, who either ignored Lilly or leered at her. All Alex's friends, of course. *At least Caleb isn't a jackass pendejo, like them.*

Caleb, the blonde with the clipboard, had simply smiled at Lilly. Setting down his clipboard, he escorted her to a corner desk next to the door, where several stacks of papers and files were laying. A *Vice President* pin gleamed on his superhero t-shirt as he began to explain something to her quietly, Lilly nodding along.

His seat now empty, a freshman girl moved to fill it, and Venus noticed that the entire front of the class was filled with them. They surrounded Alex, each one fawning over his nerdy charisma and laughing in all the right places to boost his ego. Venus just rolled her eyes.

Behind him and his posse of fans was a white board. Usually, it would be covered with grammar lessons or character analysis, but it had been erased and replaced with a theorist's daydream. Pinned up with various colored magnets were grainy pictures of ghosts and specters, connected to various printed articles with red string. Names and coordinates were scrawled on the board in various colors, with a drawing of what looked like a sad Sasquatch taking up a large corner of the board.

All that's missing is a tinfoil hat.

Jeannie groaned and turned to look at Venus. "This really doesn't help with the crazy theorist stereotype."

Venus leaned against the doorframe and tugged on her braid as she scanned the board, before turning her eyes on the lanky teen that was stretched across the desk.

"His shirt doesn't help."

Lillybelle snorted, eyes on the papers as her hands ran over them. "People in glass houses shouldn't throw stones." Venus just stared at Lilly, who jerked her head at her. "You're wearing the same shirt, idiot."

She looked down at herself. *Mierda.* Her shirt was smaller, full of holes and covered in paint splatters, but it was still the same shirt.

Venus huffed and Caleb, who had been standing next to Lilly and pretending not to listen, shot her a smile. *At least he's nice.* The blonde seemed to realize something and he crossed over to Alex. Venus narrowed her eyes as Alex stopped his story to hand him a pin labeled *Secretary,* in messy handwriting. Caleb held it out to Jeannie, who was closer than Lilly.

As Jeannie leaned across the doorway to set the pin down, Venus could feel eyes on her.

"Nice shirt."

Seriously? Venus instinctively rolled her eyes as she turned to see Alex giving her a once over, arms crossed over his knee. *He always has to go after me first.*

"Thanks," she said, hoisting her backpack up higher on her shoulder. "I got it from your mom last night."

"So that's why you were late enough to hold up our meeting?" He continued, glancing at the girls that watched him readily. "To make juvenile jokes?" He lazily turned his attention to Jeannie, giving her a once over before laughing harshly. "And how have you been, Joanna? Oh, you look like shit. Did your trip home to hell not go as planned?"

Venus cringed, glancing at her friend. The trip to the warehouse *had* left her a little worse for wear, her short skirt torn at the edge and her legs covered in bandaids and bruises. Something black glistened in her hair. Jeannie just smiled sweetly, gaze hard.

"Call me the right name, and maybe I'll dignify you with a response, shithead."

A few people laughed and Alex just smiled.

"Fiery temper to match the fiery hair, but, we all know you love me."

Venus smiled as Jeannie seemed to straighten next to her.

"Oh yeah," she said, voice sharp. "I do! But only chopped up in a stew."

Alex let out a short laugh, but his smile was tight. Venus fought off a laugh. *That makes him nervous? He would never survive what she just went through.*

"Hey!" Mr. Cole called out from the back of the classroom, where he was lounging casually. "No violent implications! You guys know I can't be hearing this stuff from students."

Venus smiled at Mr. Cole. *And that's why he's my favorite teacher.*

"Sorry Mr. Cole," She piped up, hooking her arm in Jeannie's. "It won't happen again within earshot."

He nodded, face solemn, but a smile hiding in his eyebrows. "It better not! I need to be at least ten feet away for my plausible deniability."

Everyone who had been listening to the mini-fight laughed. Venus pushed past what she had deemed the 'Alex fan-club' and made her way to the back of the room, where a colorful hijab had caught her eye. As Venus pulled out a chair at the cluster of desks, Jeannie collapsed into a desk, all bravado dissipating like a mist.

An auburn haired boy wearing a badminton shirt who sat at the desk next to her nodded in acknowledgement of their existence, his tongue peeking out as he focused on the task at hand.

He was playing thumb war with a girl in a leopard print hijab, with flare pants to match. Her neatly kept nails dodged his chewed thumb, her black eyes, nearly the same as his, darting back and forth behind her turquoise glasses.

Venus smiled at the familiar faces as she sat down and shot a look over at the other person who sat at the cluster. A pale face poked out of a striped mint green button down, a host of silver necklaces slipping under the neckline. They kept brushing their dark brown hair out of their face as they popped colorful chocolates into their mouth. As they intently watched the game, a blink would reveal green glitter that had been hidden on their mono-lidded eyes, a grin on their face.

"Who's winning?" Venus asked.

"Well," they popped another candy in their mouth, not taking their eyes off the match. "Jaimie had the upper hand when they started, but through a combination of skill and cheating, Irsa is currently winning."

"I am not cheating, Berri!" Irsa said, straightening as she smiled. "I am just better than him in every way."

"Hey!" Jaimie cried out, still very focused on his thumb match.

Berri crunched on a candy and chuckled, neon green acrylics tapping on the desk. *When did they get those done?*

"I heard the argument." They said, hazel eyes darting up to meet Venus's gaze.

Venus just sighed, slumping down a little further in her chair. "I fucking hate Alex."

Jeannie nodded, head in her arms. Berri grinned widely, candy-stained teeth shining out at the group. "You say that as if we weren't friends with him, like, two years ago."

"Yeah" Venus said, gesturing as she spoke. "But he's completely changed! He used to be half decent, but now? He's a spineless, misogynistic *mierda* who thinks every word he says is gold!"

Jeannie lifted her head from her arms. "He used to be a lot nicer."

Irsa made a sound that sounded as if she doubted that assessment. Berri nodded, popping another candy in their mouth.

"I'm going to have to agree with Irsa; he still sucked."

"Looking back on it," Jaimie said, shifting in his seat to get some height on Irsa, which was hard, as almost everyone in the group was taller than him. "We were pretty sucky, too. Middle school?"

Berri shuddered at the thought. "We weren't that much better. Not as bad as he is now, obviously, but we weren't saints."

Venus sighed, digging her fingers as far into her scalp as her braid allowed, as she thought back to everything she regretted in middle school. *It's not like I could forget. It's all I can think about everytime I go to sleep. How I let everyone down...*

"I guess you're right," she said, shaking her head violently. "He still pisses me off, though."

Everyone else in the group murmured in agreement. Berri brushed their hair back from their face again, revealing neon green acrylics. *Pretty.*

"So, why were you guys late?" Berri asked, giving Jeannie a once-over. "Also, are you okay?"

Jeannie just waved a hand, chin resting on her forearm. "It's a long story."

Berri cocked a pierced eyebrow. "Would it have anything to do with the odd series of messages in the group chat?"

Venus nodded, but Jeannie shrugged. "I wouldn't know, I lost my phone."

"Dammit!" Jaimie cried out, slamming his desk and making them all jump.

Venus looked over and saw Irsa sitting back proudly in her

chair while looking at a dejected Jaimie, his thumb trapped under hers. *Not like this doesn't happen every week.*

"How do you always win?" He wailed, forlornly staring at his conquered finger, trapped under her pale brown thumb and pink nails.

Irsa just smiled at him. "Maybe you just suck at thumb war?"

Berri held up a finger and swallowed a chocolate before speaking. "Maybe there's a psychological reason?"

Jaimie's eyes widened and he began to nod. "You're right, I could just be stupid."

Berri stammered in protest at this misinterpretation of their words, but everyone just laughed. Venus rolled her eyes. *Drama queen.* She glanced up towards the front of the room, seeking her twin-braided friend, and saw Lilly making her way over. Her eyes looked to be in a far-off place as she wandered over, a folder cradled tightly to her chest along with a clipboard. As she reached the table, she shot a smile at everyone in the group and settled into a chair.

"Alex said he would start soon."

Venus nodded and stretched, muscles vibrating as she reached towards the yellow fluorescent lights above her. She lazily ran her eyes over the group and stopped. *One, two, three, four, five, six. Who are we missing?* She furrowed her brows. *Berri, Irsa, Jaimie, Jeannie, Lilly, Me. Ohhhh.* She swallowed.

"Does anyone know where Theo or Acacia are?"

"I was wondering where they were." Jeannie sat up and began rubbing her arms, a frown forming across her pink, freckled cheeks. "I know Theo was here today, I saw them in fourth period."

"Acia had an Honors Society meeting after school today." Lilly added. "I only remember because she was telling me about how tired she was from hauling all those cans in for the food drive."

"Yeah, I remember that!" Irsa nodded, finally removing her thumb from Jaimie's. "She said she was doing that to get more hours in before the quarter deadline."

Jeannie sighed, cracking her knuckles on the table. Venus's eyes went to her hands, which were stained blue. *Has she been drawing on them again?* A smiley face on a knuckle gave the answer.

"For someone who is always preaching about communication, Theo sucks at it. She probably had to go pick up Bayani and Yalina from school, since their mama is probably working." Berri squinted at the ceiling, as if something was only just escaping them. "I think his other mom is also away on a business trip or something, but don't quote me on that."

The group of sophomores all nodded with different degrees of exasperation and humor, but before a conversation could be struck up again, a throat loudly clearing interrupted. A side glance showed the ever irritating, and ever charming, Alex standing up.

All conversations died down to a silence and all eyes turned to him one by one. A soft, barely audible sigh at her side told her Lilly was pulling out the club notebook. *Of course she gets stuck with the menial tasks. Keeping track of hours, the research.* She shook herself slightly, returning her thoughts to the trembling person in front of her. *Never mind. It's time for the torture to begin.*

9

Lilly

Lillybelle shifted in her seat, tapping the top of her notebook with her pen. *Let's see which way this will go.*

"Hi everyone." Alexander smiled, running a hand through his unruly hair. He had an air of charm about him that masked how much of a tool he was, but at least he was a good spokesperson. "Welcome to the first official meeting for the Paranormal, Supernatural, and Extraterrestrial Theorist and Investigative Adventurer Club."

Lilly could hear as Jeannie sucked in a breath. "God, I hate that name!"

"No wonder no one takes us seriously, we sound like lunatics." Berri whispered.

Lilly ignored them, though she agreed. Jaimie exhaled a quiet laugh, but she saw Irsa pinch him as Alexander continued.

"Welcome, all new theorists. Welcome back, theorist veterans. We've already met, but I'm Alex, the club president. I'll get right to business, because I want to jump right in to exploring the unknown," He continued, taking a stack of papers off the

"

table and shuffling them. "So, I will be giving you an assignment. I want you to form groups of 2 to 3 people, and when you've done that, one of the club officers will give you a list of locations to choose from. My Vice President, Caleb, will explain the assignment."

Alex took a seat, shoulders tense as the attention shifted away from him. The boy with blonde hair stood up, holding the clipboard that Lilly had been holding earlier. He smiled at the audience, ready to tell the club everything he had already told her. *And told me not to tell.* Exhaustion tugged at her features. *I was so ready for this earlier. I wonder how they'll feel about it now.*

"Hi, I'm Caleb, but you already knew that. In the past, we've relegated assignments to research projects and different in person activities, but we wanted to take a different approach this year. This will be a photo project."

There was a murmur of confusion that went through the students, but Caleb just continued to smile. Jeannie stiffened next to Lilly. *She lost her camera, didn't she.*

"Once you have formed your groups, you will choose a location off of this list," He held up the clipboard. Even from this far away, she could tell which one she had marked off-limits. "Each of these locations is rumored to be haunted, cursed, or have claims of extraterrestrial activity. We have no way of knowing if these claims are true, which is where you come in. Your group will be assigned to take pictures of this specific location."

Another round of whispers filled the room, but as Lillybelle looked around, she felt eyes on her. Berri was glancing between the three of them, eyes flicking from Jeannie's band-aid to Venus's averted gaze. *Do they know already?*

"This assignment was chosen to help us eliminate some of these claims and focus our attention on the sites that are the most promising. If you have any concerns, you can come to me,

Alex, or our club secretary, Lillybelle, who is sitting there in the back."

She raised her hand as some of the club members turned to look at her. There was a mix of confusion, apprehension, and appreciation in their eyes, but she didn't really care. She managed a smile.

"The pictures are due by the next meeting," Caleb continued after the attention returned to him. "Which is next week, same day and time. You have the rest of the meeting to decide on groups and on which location you want to document, but you might want to choose fast. Some locations are better than others and each location can only have one group."

And with that, the club erupted into chatter.

"Is this why you are all late?" Berri asked, turning around to face Lilly. "The text, the band aids. You three started the project already."

Jeannie nodded.

"And that must be what Caleb was just reminding you about?"

Lilly sighed. *I should've known Berri would figure it all out immediately.* "Alex and Caleb had me do research on all of these local legends and ghost stories and I finally got Caleb to tell me the project. He made me promise not to tell, but..." She glanced at Venus. "Anyway, I was excited, so we went to the location."

"And that's what the texts were about?" Irsa asked, crossing her long-sleeved arms over her chest. "Scared by a bird?"

"That's not all I got scared by." Jeannie said under her breath.

Jaimie's eyes went wide.

"That's part of the reason we came back," Venus continued, meeting Lilly's gaze. "For the meeting, obviously, but we also need your help."

"Did something happen?" Jaimie asked, sitting up straight and leaning across the table. "Something real?"

Lillybelle swallowed, Jaimie's barely suppressed excitement spilling over to her and bubbling up in anticipation. "Something's special about this place. It's a long story, so it's better if we can tell everyone at once." Her voice was quiet as she leaned across the table, a twinge of pain at the base of her prosthetic socket caused her to wince. "After you get your locations, can you meet us at the warehouse in thirty minutes?"

Irsa's face lit up. "Of course! You three are a group, so Jaimie, how about you, me and Theo?"

Jaimie nodded.

"I'll text Acia to team up, so we'll meet you guys there?" Berri said, turning to tap away on their phone.

"I'll text and ask Theo right now. I'm sure she won't mind." Irsa paused and frowned, staring at her fingers as they hovered over the keyboard. "Is 'she' okay?"

When she looked up at the rest of the group, there was panic in her eyes. Berri smiled.

"I think 'she' is fine. Last time I checked, Theo uses she, he and they with varying love for each. You can always ask, I don't think they'll mind."

"Thanks. I think I'll be good without asking, though." Irsa said, resuming tapping away at her phone. "Thanks again."

Pronoun crisis resolved, Lilly settled back in her chair, still rubbing at the place her arm met the socket. *Why does this hurt so much? It isn't usually this bad.*

"Thank you for agreeing to come back with us." Lilly said softly.

Jeannie nodded.

"I know you don't know why yet, but I promise, it's not for nothing. I don't think I could go back to that place with anything less than an army."

. . .

A loud whistling rang out loudly in her ears as a cold swept over her. She shuddered and her eyes went wide as something brushed her prosthetic. *No, I must have imagined that.* That, of course, was when everything went dark.

10

Jeannie

Jeannie sat up straight in her chair as a couple of the freshmen girls shrieked, heart pounding loudly in her chest. Blinds shut, the room was nearly pitch black. It made her skin crawl. Trembling, she closed her eyes as a rustling of papers could be heard across the desks, mouth going dry. *I never was afraid of the dark as a kid. Why now, of all times?* Jeannie opened her eyes very slowly, fingernails digging into her own forearm. The forms of her friends were outlining themselves in the shadows as her eyes adjusted.

"Do you think this counts as activity?" Venus asked in the darkness.

Lillybelle's voice could be heard behind the rustling of papers. "I don't know, but I'll write it down anyway." Her pen light went on and Jeannie could see her scribbling away in one notebook and then the other.

This is the first time it's more than flickering. I wonder what's got her so upset? She shook her head, shooting a look at the front of the room as she tried to swallow her nerves down. Before the lights had gone out, a ceiling lamp above Alex had

53

been flickering on and off. Another chill ran-down her spine and she shuddered, cold prickling the skin beneath her sweater. "Everyone relax," Mr. Cole said, pulling a pro-grade flashlight seemingly out of nowhere. "The lights should be back on in a few minutes. Until then just sit tight and theorize or something."

Alex stood. "It's probably just a busted generator, so there's nothing to worry about."

Jeannie squinted at him in the darkness, biting on the inside of her cheek as she shifted in her seat. She tried not to roll her eyes as the club president sat back down, shoving her hands under her thighs to stop them from shaking.

"Where's his paranormal curiosity? How is that theory at all helpful to the advancement of paranormal research?"

Berri smiled at her in the darkness, their hazel eyes glittering conspiratorially. "He's probably too scared of our ghost. What was the name we gave her again? It started with an A, something like Adelaide or Aerilyn..." Their words trailed off as they looked at Jeannie.

'Are you okay?' they mouthed.

Jeannie shook her head, mouthing back *'I'm fine.'* Even though the dark made her feel as if there were layers of dirt on her skin.

"It was Adrienne. We didn't give her that name, that's who we think it is." Lilly said, looking up from her many papers. *Typical Lilly. Neck deep in paperwork.* "We believe she is the spirit of a student who went missing many years ago. She went missing and was never seen again. Officially, the case is still open, and still a missing persons. But most people think she is dead."

"Her body was never found," Irsa added. "Leading some forums to believe that the person who killed her hid her body somewhere in the school building, as that's where she was last seen." When she was given a weird look, she explained. "I did a project on her in my forensics class."

Venus was nodding in the dim light of the cellphone's flash. "And that would be why she's still here. She's pretty harmless, just messing around with the lights and stealing people's shit from time to time. I mean, I get it, it gets boring being trapped in this hellhole. For eternity? No thank you."

Irsa and Jaimie laughed.

"Do we have any solid proof of her yet, or are we still just in the 'collect and analyze' phase?" Asked Jaimie, lacing his fingers with Berri's.

Lilly closed her notebooks and sighed. "Sadly, we still only have these recordings of the lights and missing items so far. There isn't much real proof; only speculation."

I wish we knew what happened to her.

The lights flickered back to life, illuminating the crowded classroom once again. Jaimie dramatically hissed at the light, to which Jeannie sighed in relief, smiling. Venus stretched back in her chair, her braid looser then before. Everyone clicked off their phone flashlights and Alex turned to the class again.

"I think we should end today's meeting here. Make sure to sign up for a location before you leave and if you aren't sure if you want to do this project, talk to me or Caleb about it and we can give you an alternate project. Thank you for coming, and we hope to see you next week!"

As soon as he had said the word 'end', people had stopped listening and started packing. Jeannie stood, straightening her skirt. Her fingers brushed the goosebumps that had appeared on her thighs through the fresh slit in her skirt, the cold chill having dissipated. Lillybelle tucked her notebook in her bag and made her way to the front of the room. *Probably to confirm something with the rest of the club officers.* Jeannie turned to Berri, who was pulling on a sweatshirt, trying to come up with something to distract herself from the anxiety rising in waves in her mind.

"Did Acacia confirm the team up?"

Berri nodded, pulling the sweatshirt down past their hips. "Yeah, she said she would pick me up at my house in twenty. I'm going to head out, my mom is waiting out front and has my brother in the car, so I'll tell her about the meet up when I see her."

Jeannie's heart lifted at the mention of Berri's baby brother and she smiled softly. "Tell Mikey I said hi."

"I will!" Berri said, smiling. "Sometimes I think you like him more than me."

"You know that's not true!" A pang of guilt, slightly over-shadowed by the thought that Berri could be right, ran through her. "I just love kids, and your little brother is so sweet!"

Berri wrinkled their nose. "Maybe to you! See you soon, J."

Jeannie waved as the rest of the group chorused their good-byes. She turned back just as Venus stood up, rolling her head back to crack her neck. Jeannie shuddered at the sound. *Hate, hate, hate.* Jaimie visibly cringed and Irsa just grinned, cracking her own knuckles and torturing Jaimie further. He shot Jeannie a look for help. *It must be so much worse for him, I know that just makes his skin crawl.*

"Do you guys mind if we head out?" She asked, squeezing his shoulder. "Venus texted my mom to pick me up, since I lost my phone at the warehouse."

He wailed dramatically. *Oh, Jaimie. Forever the thespian.* "You want to leave us? I can't believe you! You aren't the woman I thought you were! You aren't the woman I love!" He lay back in his chair with a flourish, eyes closed and face twisted in a faux sadness.

He should be on a stage.

Irsa smacked his arm. "You really have to stop watching those telenovelas." He stuck his tongue out at her and winked at Jeannie, who chuckled.

"I'll take that as yes."

Jaimie sat up and laughed. "Yeah, go ahead. Irsa and I were thinking about calling Theo, so we'll see you later, alligators. Well, not later," he amended. "In thirty minutes!"

Jeannie waved and Irsa waved back. Lillybelle was standing by the doorway, humming and smiling as Venus led the way across the classroom.

"Ready to go?" Venus asked, holding out an arm.

Jeannie nodded, chewing on her lip as Venus led her towards the carpool lot where her mom would be waiting, loaded up with unanswerable questions. *Am I ready to go back?* Her hand brushed the tear in her skirt and a shudder ran over her as the feeling of the burning hands on her skin washed over her again. *Do I have a choice?*

11

Lilly

Several calls, two arguments, a bargain, and thirty minutes later, Lillybelle watched four cars pull into the parking lot next to Venus's beat up old silver Saturn. The pair had arrived ten minutes early. *Why wait?* The first two cars that arrived came together. Irsa and Jaimie came out of one, arguing about pizza crusts. Jeannie trailed out of the second car, smiling sheepishly as her mom got out of the driver's side of the first. Her mom just shook her head and handed her the keys.

"Thanks, mom."

"Yeah," Jaimie chirped. "Thank you for the ride, Mrs. Smyth!"

Jeannie's mom kissed her on the cheek and smiled at Jaimie as she pulled open the passenger side of one of the other cars. Lilly could see Jeannie's dad leaning out of the driver's seat, beaming.

"Don't come home too late!" Her mom called, smiling widely. *Jeannie looks just like her.*

Jeannie nodded and smiled, watching them drive off. As soon as they were out of sight, her smile dropped and she pressed the heels of her hands to her forehead. *Guilt.* Lilly couldn't help but smile.

"She's going to be so pissed when I tell her about the camera." Jeannie groaned.

Irsa leaned against the hood of Jeannie's car. "What did you tell her about your phone?"

"I said it died."

She had borrowed Lilly's phone to ask for a ride from her parents after Venus's text hadn't gone through. Lilly had over-heard her dad saying that he was coming straight from a job, but he would be there ASAP. *Her parents are so awesome.*

Out of the next car that parked, hopped Berri, who was wrapped in a familiar oversized sweatshirt. From the driver's side, came a very pretty girl with dark brown skin and electric blue hair, falling straight past her shoulders. Her hair was tucked behind her ears, which held her hearing aids, the silver and white plastic contrasting against her bright blue hair. She was wearing black ripped jeans and a gray sweater that was full of holes, neon pink high-tops shining in the weakening autumn light. She smiled when she saw Lilly.

"Hi Acacia."

"Hey Lilly. I hear that this is the prime locale?"

She nodded with a smile as Berri locked the car and Acacia brushed her hair out of her gray eyes.

Acacia jerked her head at Jeannie as she scanned the bruised girl. "What happened to her?"

Lillybelle chuckled nervously. "It's a long story that involves a mysterious stranger, going through walls, moving shadows, and several sentient entities. Jeannie can brief you when everyone gets here."

Acacia nodded as if what Lilly said was a completely normal sentence and they both turned their heads when they heard the last car pull into the parking lot. *I'd recognize that blaring radio anywhere.* It was a familiarly scratched blue minivan with many school and sports stickers on the back and sides, old boy-bands blaring from the cracked windows. Out of the driver's seat hopped a gangly, brown-skinned teenager with their shaved undercut pulled up into a ponytail, black hair swinging behind them as they sauntered over to the group. He was wearing black jeans with random sequins sewn into them and a silver halter top, a patch jacket thrown on top.

Venus patted them on the back and laughed. "Glad you made it, Theo."

Theodora grinned around at the group, rainbow braces glittering. "We're all here? Great! Now the party can really get started!"

"Oh!" Lilly said, approaching the group with Acacia trailing behind. "Did you bring the bolt cutters?"

Theo's face lit up and they ducked under Venus's arm, opening his trunk and rummaging around for something.

Berri's eyebrows scrunched. "Why do we need bolt cutters?" They asked, resting their head on Irsa's shoulder.

Jeannie shuddered. "Because I really do not want to go back through the back entrance, and the front door is chained shut."

"That reminds me!" Irsa exclaimed. "What the heck happened? We only got a vague explanation earlier."

As Theo searched their trunk for the bolt cutters, Jeannie recounted her tale for a second time, with Lilly and Venus jumping in when she got tired. The story finally fully told, everyone stood around, dumbfounded. *That's how I felt.* Jeannie exhaled a shaky breath and squeezed Venus's hand, as Venus had thrown her arm over Jeannie's shoulder in an attempt to be comforting.

"Do you guys believe me?"

"Are you kidding?" Jaimie looked incredulous. "Of course we believe you! That sounds terrifying!"

"Yet also thrilling." Irsa interrupted, smiling. "Were you really worried we wouldn't believe you?"

Jeannie nodded, eyes darting from face to face.

"Well, don't worry. We'll find the perv ghost that chased you and that asshole who stole your stuff." Acacia said, reaching over and squeezing Jeannie's other hand.

"Yeah!" Theo said, finally finding the bolt cutters. "And we'll kick their asses!"

"Yeah!" Berri and Venus chorused.

"Maybe not the guy who took your stuff. Are we sure that they're really a villain here?" Irsa said, contemplatively looking at the warehouse. "I mean, it made sure that crazy lady didn't see you. And it labeled your map so you would know where the exit was. Sure he stole your stuff, which isn't cool, but does he deserve to be beaten up?"

Jeannie nodded again. "I'm not convinced that it had negative intentions, but still, they didn't feel completely positive either."

Everyone nodded as Theo led the way to the front of the warehouse, holding the bolt cutters triumphantly over their head. The conversations queued up again as Theo began to work on the thick, rusted lock that held the front door shut. Lillybelle watched as Theodora tried to break the chains, tuning out the conversations of her friends rehashing the same questions she and Venus had already asked. One question Jaimie asked caught them all off guard.

"What happened to your hair?"

Jeannie stared at him, confusion evident on her face. Lillybelle looked at Jeannie's hair and squinted. Stuck in her pretty red hair was some black goop, sticking her tangled strands of hair together in a knotted, sticky mess.

"Oh, ew!" Venus exclaimed. "When did that happen?"

Jeannie demanded to know what they were talking about and Irsa snapped a picture of it with her phone and showed her. The expression on her face told them that she didn't know where it came from either. Suddenly a thought popped into Lilly's head.

"The shadow man!" She blurted, making everyone look at her. Acacia looked amused. "When I saw the shadow person reach out after Jeannie, he touched her hair. That must be what's left from him touching her."

Jaimie looked amazed and reached out to touch it, getting the sticky substance on his fingers and rubbing it between his thumb and forefinger. "Maybe it's ectoplasm. Like from a ghost!"

Berri leaned over and gave it a sniff before gagging. "Smells like motor oil."

Theodora grunted as she pushed the bolt cutter down, pressing with all her weight. "If you're right, that would mean that the shadow thing isn't pure ghost."

"Those are a lot of ifs." Irsa reminded, crossing her arms.

Lillybelle sighed, nodding. *I'm glad someone here has some logical sense.* Everyone in the group knew that Irsa was the one who was most skeptical of the paranormal- well, anything that came out of Venus's mouth, anyway- and for good reason; her insights were usually necessary to help ground them in reality when any one of them started off on a bs tangent.

"You're right." Acacia said, drawing everyone's attention to her. "We need to figure out what these things are before we just assume they're ghosts or demons or whatever."

A big clang made everyone jump and they turned to see Theodora standing victoriously over the cut chain. He smiled at Jeannie. "Ready to get back in there and hunt some ghosts?"

Jeannie grinned back and met Lilly's eyes. *She looks different.* Her eyes didn't quite finish the smile as she spoke.

"Let's do this."

12

Jeannie

It took a good deal of pushing to get the rusted-over doors to open, but eventually, it was done. The light of the autumn afternoon spilled into the warehouse, revealing the grimy floors and ash stained, rotting walls of the front room. Jeannie was nervous when she stepped inside the warehouse again, this time of her own volition. She was surrounded by her friends, but something about the warehouse's atmosphere made her feel naked and alone, as if it could see through her. See through her facade.

I told them I was fine, but I lied. Fear was gnawing her insides, like a rabid dog on a meaty bone. Something in the back of her mind whispered that all was not safe and that she should turn around and escape while she still had the chance, but a louder voice told her to push on. She decided to listen to the louder voice, but she still hooked arms with Jaimie for some layer of protection. He smiled at her and squeezed her arm. *At least I know they've always got my back.*

The group slowly looked around the front room, Acacia taking the pictures since Jeannie's camera had been lost to the walls. A time card machine hung off the wall, one of its screws missing and the other melted to the wall. Whatever wallpaper was left was peeling, mold and rust crawling up to the roof, where the cracked concrete revealed a partially caved-in ceiling covered in cobwebs. It was eerie, especially when they saw the handprints that had been singed into the walls.

"This must have been one of the rooms where they were trapped." Lillybelle said, her voice sounding small in the unsettling room.

The hairs on the back of her neck prickled up. *Right. People died here.*

"What are you talking about?" Berri asked.

It occurred to Jeannie that they hadn't been given a briefing on the history of the building, but Lilly happily obliged.

"Fifty years ago, this was a warehouse full of workers. It was on a holiday weekend when not many workers were present, but a fire broke out. Because of shoddy business practices and awful safety precautions, all of the workers that were here were trapped inside. All of them died."

"Weren't some of them teenagers?" Venus asked. "I remember hearing about working conditions in history, so weren't most of them young?"

"Yeah, most of them were around our age or older."

Jeannie shuddered at the thought of the teenage workers banging on the doors, screaming as the fire raged and melted their skin to their bones.

"Some of them would have suffocated to death on the smoke before even feeling the heat of the fire." Acacia said, sadness tinging her voice. "Same as the Triangle Shirtwaist Factory Fire."

A wave of nausea came over Jeannie and a chill ran down her spine. "Let's not talk about that right now."

Everyone agreed and silence fell over them. Jeannie ran her hand along the ash painted wood pile that might have been a desk, tracing the angles of the char with her fingers. She could tell there was something in the corner of the room behind the pile, but couldn't make it out. She felt in her pockets, panicking for a moment before remembering she didn't have her phone. Jeannie nudged Jaimie.

"Can you turn on your phone flashlight? I want to see what's in the corner."

Jaimie gave her an odd look, but he started to pull out his phone anyway. She didn't know how, but she could sense that he knew she just didn't want to risk any moving shadows. Venus murmured something as Jaimie flicked on his light. When asked to clarify, she just shook her head and slung her bag over her shoulder. Venus unzipped her backpack and pulled out a flashlight, flicking on the thick beam of light. She clicked it off and held it out to Jeannie.

"Since you lost your phone, you need this more than I do." She flipped it around in her hand and held it by the head. "And if you ever get into a pickle, you can use it as a weapon."

Venus mimicked swinging the flashlight down on someone a few times before putting it in Jeannie's hands. *The silly detective from the holiday romcom is no more. Now, it is time for the heist movie security guard.*

"Thanks." Jeannie said, squeezing it tightly in her hands.

Jaimie nudged her shoulder and she turned to see what had been glinting in the corner. It was a chip bag that had been ripped open and turned inside out, the empty silver lining shining out into the room. Jeannie's brows furrowed as she reached to pick it up, but Acacia smacked her hand away.

"Let me take a picture of that before you touch it."

Acacia snapped a quick photo with her phone, flash blinding them all momentarily. Once the picture was confirmed and they had blinked themselves back to sight, Jeannie picked up the bag, turning it over in her hands.

"What the hell is this doing here?" Jeannie asked no one in particular, staring at the blue logo on the front of the chip bag.

Jaimie inhaled deeply and squinted at the bag. "It smells fresh. It can't be more than a few days old."

"That's not possible," Jeannie protested. "How would it have gotten in here? The front door was rusted shut and the back door was closed."

Jaimie just shook his head, baffled. "Someone else has been here lately."

"Maybe the woman who you over heard earlier?" Irsa suggested, taking the bag from Jeannie and looking it over.

Acacia just shook her head at the three of them. "Let's just hang onto it and move on. Remember, we're here to take pictures and get Jeannie's shit back, not pick through the trash of any random delinquent who wants to trespass."

We're trespassing, Jeannie wanted to say, but she thought better of it. Irsa tucked the chip bag into her leopard print pant pocket and walked back over to wear Berri was standing, talking to Lillybelle. Jaimie hooked arms with Jeannie again, standing on her left so that she could hold the flashlight with her right hand.

Behind the destroyed desk was a door, but it was blocked by the mangled furniture. Theo and Venus got on one side of it to pull while Irsa and Acacia got on the other side to push. With much heaving and hoeing, the desk was moved out of the way enough for them to get past. Before they left the room, Jeannie gave it one last once over.

"Should we leave the door open?"

Theo glanced over at the double doors that they had wedged open with some debris. "Probably. I think it would be a good idea to let the light in, air out the place."

Jeannie shrugged, giving the door a forlorn look. "I don't know, it feels kinda rude."

"I don't know." Lilly glanced back at them, smiling. "If I

were a ghost who had been locked in the same place for fifty years, I'd be relieved that someone left the door open."

Jeannie wrapped her arms around herself. *Did it get colder in here?*

"Maybe. Let's just go."

In single file, each person squeezed past the desk and through the door. Jeannie tried not to think about the implications of the chip bag as they made their way into the next room, lost in thought. She almost ran into Jaimie, who had stopped after entering the next room.

"What's the hold up?" She walked around him and stopped dead in her tracks, a wave of nausea washing over her. "Well," Jeannie said, her voice finding its way back to her. "That's a lot of dark space."

The entire section of the warehouse was empty of machinery, but the ground and pillars were stained with blood and ash. There was little light from the windows covered in dirt and leaves, leaving the warehouse floor shrouded in shadows. Thick, black, wriggling shadows. Jeannie could feel her skin crawl as her brain brought back the flashing images of the shadows moving towards her, racing after her as she ran for the exit. She could feel the blood drain from her face as the rest of the group filed into the main warehouse.

Jaimie put a hand on her shoulder and she jumped. "Sorry. Are you okay?"

No. Jeannie nodded. "Yeah, I'm fine." She let out a shaky breath. "It's just a lot darker than I thought it would be."

Jaimie squeezed her hand and gave her a reassuring smile. She took a deep breath and looked over the room. *I'll be okay,* she thought. *I have my friends around me, I am safe. There are witnesses. If I die, my sacrifice will not go unnoticed. Besides, the security guards in heist movies never die.*

"God, this place is filthy." Venus said, mournfully looking down at her now stained green Converse that had once been shiny and clean. They were smeared with ash, dust, and leaves, the grime obscuring their canvas beauty.

A memory popped into Jeannie's mind and a small smile crept onto her face. A memory of rushing water and laughing. "This place could use a good power wash."

Everyone chuckled, but Berri gave her an odd look. "It's funny that you mention that," they said, a look of amused awe painted across their features. "I actually have one in my car right now."

Theo raised an eyebrow. "Question: why the fuck?"

Berri laughed. "Mikey likes to do chalk paintings on the driveway, but he will fill it up super quick, so it's become a tradition where I'll just use my powerwasher to clear it so he can start again. The garage is super crowded with shit, so I just keep it in my car." They shrugged. "It's never come in handy before now."

Irsa waved her hands in front of her. "Wait, are you suggesting that we power wash the spooky, haunted warehouse?"

Lilly smiled. "I mean, it's not a terrible idea."

"Let's just finish exploring first." Acacia brandished her phone. "We still need to take photos of this place before we give it a makeover."

Berri shrugged at Jeannie. "I'm guessing you've pressure washed before, so we can just think of it as our once over before we get started."

Jeannie nodded, mind drifting off to her days of washing the car and driveway with her dad's pressure washer. "Yeah, we need to know how big this place is before we even think of getting started. Or we'll run out of water or soap or extension hose."

They agreed to split into two groups, not wanting to take any chances with an ambush of any sorts. Because Berri had pressure washing 'expertise,' as they called it, and Jeannie had been in the building before, they became 'team leaders.' Theo, Venus, and Jaimie all joined Jeannie, while the rest went with Berri.

As they slowly made their way through the large room, there wasn't much need for teams, as there wasn't any room to exactly split up. There were several doors to the sides, but few of them opened, as they were either locked or something blocked the entrance, whether inside or out. The few rooms they could access had nothing of interest, just old vandalism and fire damaged furniture.

Their teams finally came into use when they reached the first stairwell. Because Jeannie had done it before, her team would stay on the ground floor and make their way towards the back of the building. Berri's group would go to the second floor, look around, and take pictures while also heading to the back. No one was exactly excited when they realized they would have to go up the stairs to get to the second floor.

As Venus was the most nimble and the most athletic, Venus was sent up the stairs to test if they were stable as everyone watched from the bottom. *Please don't get hurt, please don't get hurt.* The steel stair case creaked and heaved under her weight as she went up and out of sight. She came down moments later with a thumbs up. *Thank god.*

"The last step before the platform has started to fold in on itself, but other than that, you should be good."

"Make sure to go single file." Jeannie suggested, nervously watching as Acacia put her weight on the steps.

She had been trying not to think about it, but she knew that a fifty year old building with fire damage and collapsed rooms was not exactly safe to move around in, especially in groups.

Lillybelle nodded in agreement. "We don't want to put too much weight on it if we aren't sure of the stability."

The two groups said their quick goodbyes and after a chorus of 'good-lucks' on both sides, the two split apart, Berri confidently leading the line of teenagers up the rusted and slowly collapsing metal stairs. The creaking footsteps faded to silence and after a minute, the group of four was left to themselves.

Jeannie flicked on the beam of her flashlight, sweeping it around to her to better see as she lead the group forward. Her eyes darted to every shadowed corner, her flashlight following her gaze so quickly that no shadow had the chance to escape her eye, let alone move. Every so often, she would glance over at the map which Jaimie held in his hands, who was tracing the path they took with a pencil and marking off each spot they had already visited.

After several minutes of slow searching and idle chatter, Jeannie stopped in the doorway of one of the rooms. *What... No. No, no, no.* Her heartbeat was loud in her ears and her vision was starting to tilt.

"What?" Theodora asked. "What is it?"

Jaimie pointed at the map and offered it to Theo. "This is the room where Jeannie was forced through the wall."

Theo made a sound in response, but Jeannie barely heard, eyes glued to the wall that connected to the outside of the building. Venus came up behind her and put a hand on her shoulder, but she didn't feel it. She heard her words through a haze.

"Are you okay? What's wrong?"

Jeannie just wordlessly pointed at the wall. Outlined on the concrete wall in a sticky black substance, was Jeannie's body. It was if it had been traced in tar. And in the center of the chest were two hand prints, exactly in the spots where she had been pushed through the wall. *He's taunting me.*

13

Lilly

Lillybelle hated everything about going up the stairs. The way they creaked, the way they looked, the fact that the steel pillars holding them up were slowly crumpling under their own weight. What she hated the most was the fact that she had to go last, following Irsa, whose leopard print flare pants kept catching on the nails and curling scrap that stuck up all around them, giving Lilly a miniature heart attack everytime Irsa stumbled.

Why did I choose to be in this group? She thought to herself, heart pounding. *I love these guys, but this sucks.*

Every time she put her weight onto the steel steps, it groaned under the collective weight of their little exploration party and she cringed. *If I trip, I can't catch myself like they can.* She tried not to think about how long it had been since these steps had been traversed by something other than dust or wind. Along the far wall of the concrete pillar that was the stairwell, were windows that went up vertically. All the glass in the windows was either destroyed or warped by the weather or the heat of the fire from fifty years ago.

There wasn't much sound to distract her thoughts as each of them was too focused on not tripping and dying to speak. Her heart pounded in her throat with every step, trying her hardest to not look straight down through the stairs and to the concrete floor that seemed to pulse under her focus. If she stopped breathing for a moment, she could hear Irsa humming nervously. That was when she remembered Irsa's fear of heights.

Just one more step. She thought to herself. *Just one more step closer to the destination.*

She glanced up to see how many more steps were ahead of her as she mounted the first metal landing and internally cried out in dismay. She was on the first of three platforms, meaning there were two flights of rickety stairs left for her to cautiously climb. *Fuck.* She could hear Irsa suck in a breath as she realized the same thing.

Berri was at the head of the group and they glanced back at the other three, eyes going to Irsa's face before meeting Lilly-belle's gaze.

"Hey Lilly," Berri said, voice shaky as they went up the first two steps, slowly putting one foot in front of the other. "Do you know the nursery rhyme 'Down By The Bay?'"

A smile tugged at her lips as a memory of a haunting tune sang out in her mind. "The really old one that's going viral right now?"

Berri laughed and it ricocheted quietly off of the concrete walls, warping like a broken record. "Yeah, that one. Remember how we used to harmonize in Honors Chorus?"

It was Lillybelle's turn to laugh. "Where you take the low and I take the high?"

"Yeah. Let's do that."

"What if we did it in rounds?" Acacia interjected, a smile evident in her voice. *She loves music, even when she takes out her hearing aids. I bet the vibrations in here would be pretty nice.*

"Except the first and third do the version with the growing and the second and last person does the version with the rot. We all harmonize at the end."

Berri stopped on the middle step, turned, and smiled at the group. Irsa tapped her foot on the step, impatient out of fear.

"Would you be down?"

Lillybelle smiled. "Sure. Irsa, do you want to take the middle one?"

Irsa nodded nervously, eyes focused on the back of Acacia's sweater. Her fingers were wrapped tightly around the handrail. Berri inhaled deeply.

"I'll start, just repeat after."

After a deep breath, Berri began to sing in a smooth tenor. Acacia's sweet soprano followed, starting the next round in the pause Berri took to start the next line. As Berri sang the next line in the verse, Irsa chimed in with the start of her round, cutting through the reverberations of the previous keys with her shaky alto. Acacia's hands trailed the rusted and jagged rail as Lillybelle sweetly borrowed her key to sing the next line. After reaching nearly the end, Berri and Acacia both paused so that Irsa and Lillybelle would catch up to them in the song.

The verse closed harmoniously, each voice mixing together perfectly to create a sweet melody as Lillybelle mounted the second platform. *Just one flight left.* A smile split across Lilly-belle's face as Berri started again, their melodious baritone distracting from negative thoughts. When Acacia's honeyed soprano joined the song, filling the air with a twinkling tune heavy with dark implications, Lillybelle somehow felt her spirits lift.

As they finished out the song a second time, Berri reached the top of the stairs. They were about to take a step onto the second floor platform, when they froze. Irsa protested for a moment, but was harshly hushed by Berri, who turned to reveal an expression of pure fear, eyes wild as they stood at the top of the stairs. Lillybelle strained her ears to listen, but when she heard it, a wave of horror washed over her.

A loud sound could be heard echoing through the second floor, bouncing off of the concrete and reverberating through the shaft of the stairwell. Someone was applauding them.

14

Lilly

Lillybelle's blood ran cold as the sound bounced around them, louder and louder, her mind racing. *No one else is supposed to be here. Jeannie's group couldn't have gotten up here so fast, the next stairwell is halfway across the warehouse and the elevator doesn't work.*

Irsa said what they were all thinking. "Who the fuck is clapping?" She hissed, trying to take a step back, but almost knocking Lilly over.

"Careful!"

After a quick apology, Irsa urged Berri forward. As Berri took the step forward, Lilly remembered something. *The top step!*

"Wait!"

It was too late; Berri's foot went through the step and they fell forward, arms flailing for something to grab onto. The clapping was drowned out by screaming. Acacia grabbed onto their hoodie so that they didn't fall too far through the crumpled metal step. Berri wheezed, the hoodie catching at the neck.

Fuck! With the help of Irsa, Berri was heaved out of the stairs, shouting every swear word in the book the whole way.

"Did you have to fucking strangle me?"

Acacia began to apologize, but Berri just waved it away, rubbing at their throat. They leaned back on her as they winced and Lilly could finally see what had happened.

The stair had broken and when Berri's foot had gone through it, the second step crumpling away completely. Berri had gone falling forward, scraping their palms on the metal edge of the platform connecting to the last platform. A deep cut ran the length of their calf, Berri's swearing telling them that it hurt like a 'son of a bitch'. Blood dripped down their leg, staining their jeans a bright scarlet. Berri exhaled shakily.

"Alright. So, we'll have to jump the gap." They shakily brushed their brown hair out of their eyes. "Acacia, you go first."

"What? Why me??"

Berri grit their teeth and gestured with their neon green nails, which, miraculously, remained unbroken. Their palms were bleeding. "Because, I need you to help me across because of my leg, and Irsa is scared of heights. We need Lilly to stay on this side to make sure Irsa gets across safely after me."

"Why do we have to keep going?" Irsa piped up, voice loud and squeaky over the clapping that continued to ricochet through the concrete stairwell. "Why can't we just go back the way we came?"

"Don't you want to find out who the hell is clapping so damn loud?" Berri almost shouted this last part at the doorway, which did not cease the almost thundering applause.

Irsa groaned."Not really!."

"Where's your sense of adventure?" Berri asked, looking between the three of them.

"Bleeding right in front of us." Acacia bit back. "But fine, we'll keep going."

"So I have to go last?" Lillybelle protested, her internal calculations telling her that this wasn't quite fair.

Irsa nodded.

"Hello! Prosthetic arm, anyone?" Lilly said, holding up her prosthetic arm.

"Me too!" Acacia said, pointing out her hearing aids.

Berri rolled their eyes. "Oh, put the disability card away. If you can go zip-lining and trampolining, you can jump a gap and hold Irsa's hand."

Lillybelle frowned and exchanged a look with Acacia, but a voice in her head told her that Berri was right.

"Fine." Irsa said, retucking the ends of her hijab with shaky fingers. "I'll go last."

Lilly met her gaze, and nodded. "Thank you."

Irsa just nodded rapidly, closing her eyes. Berri patted her shoulder before thumping Acacia on the back. "Good luck."

Acacia shot Berri a dirty look and took Irsa's hand, taking a look down through the broken stairs. She closed her eyes for a moment and hummed the tune to 'Down by the bay'. The new top stair screamed as she jumped, crashing hard onto the rusted steel of the second floor stair platform. The entire stairwell swayed and shook, making Irsa shriek and clutch onto Lilly as Acacia groaned.

"Fucking ow!"

Berri tilted their head and frowned as the stairs settled. "The clapping stopped."

Lilly stopped. *They're right. It's completely quiet.*

"Well, that's just fucking perfect." Acacia spat, pushing herself off the floor and checking to make sure that her hearing aids were still secure.

Berri grabbed Acacia's hand and immediately hopped the gap, banging their leg into the side of it. Swearing again, they turned to Lilly.

"Make sure to grab my shoulder, not the arm," Lilly said,

passing Irsa her papers. "I'll hop sideways and you have to pull me, okay?"

"Got it."

Acacia stood on their other side, hands outstretched. "I'll catch you."

Lilly nodded. She took a deep breath, and leapt. Hands grabbed her right arm and an arm wrapped around her back. Time felt slow as her heart rose in her chest. For a moment, she was falling. Then, her foot connected with the platform and her friends dragged her up onto the platform. Her left limb ached from the pressure that had been put on it, but she shook away the tears that had sprung into her eyes. The stairwell shook again and her knees nearly buckled beneath her. Now she understood why Acacia and Berri had sworn so loudly.

Berri and Acacia turned back to Irsa, hands outstretched, a grin on Berri's face. Irsa was cradling the papers tightly to her chest.

"You're up."

Irsa backed up a few steps, fear sparking in her eyes."No, I'm good actually."

Lillybelle outstretched her hand. "We got you."

Irsa took a deep breath, closing her eyes to try and center herself. Nodding, she handed the papers to Lillybelle, who backed up to make room for Irsa. She stood atop the step, tightly clutching both Berri and Acacia's hands. A quick hop, and she slammed down onto the platform. She immediately ran towards the wall, staying as far away from the stairs as possible and breathing heavily.

Lilly glanced behind her at the stairs. "We have to find a different way down."

The other three agreed, and when Lillybelle decided to go into the second floor first, no one protested. The door had been ripped from its hinges and she decided to believe it was by the

Fire Marshal, shutting down her theoretical thoughts that bordered on fantasy.

The first thing she noticed about the second floor when she went through the doorway was that the lighting was better, more light spilling into the broken windows. These windows were much cleaner too, less graffiti and dirt than the ones they had seen below. The warehouse floor was much more cluttered, however, covered in destroyed machinery and rotting piles of who-knows-what.

There was a gaping hole in the ceiling, a slightly smaller hole mirrored on the floor, debris and light spilling down from floor to floor. Lilly decided not to look at the black abyss of what lay beneath the hole and decided to focus her attention above her, looking up to where the hole came from. It seemed to have started from a collapse on a higher level, but before she could get any closer to inspect it, Acacia called out to her.

"Are we just going to pretend that the clapping thing didn't happen, or what?"

Berri leaned against one of the crumbling pillars, steering clear of the hole in the floor. They had a hand pressed to the growing stain on their calf. "Oh it happened. We just need to talk about who the fuck was clapping and why."

This section of the warehouse was a completely open floor plan, meaning they could see from one side of the building to the other with only mild obstruction. With one glance, Lilly could see that there was no one else here.

"Well," Irsa started, wrapping her arms around herself. "It can't have been a homeless person taking shelter here, because the doors were locked. Also the stairs wouldn't have been so easily broken."

Acacia nodded. "Yep, and animals are out because they can't clap. I can't have been hallucinating, because all of you heard it too."

Acacia looked a little hesitant about her last claim, but Berri chimed in.

"Yeah, we all heard it. This means it can be two things: A ghost, or Theo playing a wicked, but very mean, prank."

Irsa pulled out her phone. "I'll text the group chat and ask where they are."

Berri nodded at her before turning to look at Lilly. "What else do we need to know about the warehouse? So we can be prepared for vengeful ghosts or whatever the fuck we're dealing with."

Lilly untucked the folder from under her arm and flipped through a couple of pages before she got to the page she had been looking for. "This warehouse used to be for some shitty textile company and a lot of their product was stored here, but after the fire, it was revealed that they also had people working on sewing on the upper floors. This was a major shock to the public, as it let them get away with paying these immigrant teenagers basically nothing."

Acacia slid down to sit on the floor next to Berri as Lilly continued.

"The fire is thought to have been started by a cigarette in a scrap box. It set the inner walls on fire and it spread across the building. The workers inside tried to escape by the stairs, but the doors were locked. The supervisors took the elevator and escaped. Another group came down, but couldn't escape because the front doors wouldn't open. But on the third trip, when the elevator was carrying the last of the workers down, the fire made it stop between floors. The workers were trapped."

Berri looked as if they were about to be sick.

"Sorry to interrupt your absolutely joyful tale," Interjected Irsa, holding up her phone. "But I texted them and they're still downstairs. I told them to meet us up here."

"That can only mean one thing!" Berri said firmly, nodding

to themself. "This building is haunted by the ghosts of the dead workers."

Lilly nodded. *That's what I thought. But, why do I have a bad feeling about this?*

Acacia shook her head. "But why? What gives them unfinished business?"

Lillybelle clicked her tongue at them both. "If you would let me finish, I would have told you." They apologized and she laughed. "The reason this warehouse is believed to be haunted is because the supervisors escaped, but when the fire department arrived, the doors were all locked."

Irsa's eyes widened in horror. "They locked the workers inside to die?"

"The supervisors said that the doors jammed, but the workers families thought that it was on purpose. Nothing was proved."

Berri shook their head. "That's fucked up."

"It gets worse." They looked as if they didn't believe her, so she continued. "It's believed that the fire wasn't actually an accident; some people think that the owners set the building on fire so as to get the insurance money. The business on the verge of bankruptcy and they owed the workers back pay. Some think that the owners did it all on purpose, and that's why this place is haunted."

"Because they want revenge?" Berri looked confused, but Lillybelle just shrugged.

"Maybe just closure? Maybe justice."

Acacia shook her head. "Wait, wait, wait. Why do people think this place is haunted? Like, what makes them think there are ghosts? Did someone experience an event, or something?"

Lillybelle walked over to the window and smiled, looking out over the broken glass and into the molting trees. "Yeah, a journalist wanted to know what happened, like, ten years later, so she came to explore, but she left the building screaming. She claims to have heard wailing and screaming, as if the workers were being tortured by the eternal flames of their deaths."

"Wow, that's..." Acacia couldn't seem to find the right word. "Dark."

Lilly laughed quietly. *That's one way to describe it.*

"A few months after that, she came back. Her story was different that time, all she heard were some conversations, before something like a shadow chased her out of the building. She never went back after that. Only a few people have come here since, all with similar stories."

"So, Jeannie's shadow isn't new?" Irsa looked surprised. "Why didn't you say anything about it earlier?"

"I guess I had brushed over it because it didn't seem important at the time."

"So what does that mean for this investigation?" Irsa asked, brows furrowed and head tilted.

Berri's face split into a smile. "It means it's time to find some ghosts."

15

Venus

Venus checked her phone, eyes scanning the new messages quickly before turning her gaze back to Jeannie. After seeing the handprints on the wall, she had sunk to the floor, refusing to speak. Theo, forever the mom-friend, immediately stepped into his role, giving their jacket to Jeannie to wear and helping her back up from where she crashed. Jaimie was running around in circles, looking like a chicken with his head cut off. *I mean, what is there to do?*

The fear in Jeannie's eyes was something Venus hated seeing and yet something she had seen more times in the past hour than in the past three years. When Jeannie had told her story, Venus knew that there was something that she was holding back, something that scared her even more than what she had described. *But, if I ask, all she's going to say is that she's fine. Which is a load of crap, but whatever.*

They had continued through the building after a couple of minutes of breathing and pep talks, and a lot of threatened ass kicking by Theo (to the shadows). Jeannie had the jacket tied around her waist and was now leading the way towards the back of the warehouse, slowly, but steadily. Now they stood in front of yet another door, waiting for Jaimie to finish checking it so that Venus could go in and take the pictures. The only reason he needed to check it was because the first door they tried had held a surprise for them. *That poor raccoon.*

This room was a lot like every other: a small storage closet that held boxes and ancient looking machinery that had been ravaged by the years, rot ripping open the crates and spilling their mold-covered, burnt contents onto the already gross floor. There was no window in this room, the only light coming from Jaimie's phone and Venus's wide beam flashlight which Jeannie clutched as if her life depended on it. Trash lay scattered on the floor.

"Isn't it kinda weird how there is so much modern trash in here?" Jaimie asked, exiting the room and giving a thumbs up to Venus to show that it was all clear.

"Thrown in through windows maybe?" Theo said, arms folded as they leaned against the wall, shooting a glance at the rest of the group.

Jaimie cocked his head.

"Maybe out here," He gestured at the open warehouse space. "But that room doesn't have any windows."

Venus stepped into the room as Jaimie continued, snapping a photo of the room with her phone's flash on its brightest setting.

"Someone else has been here."

A shudder ran down her spine as Jaimie said that, but she tried to ignore it. *There's no way. The doors were all locked.* She picked up a piece of trash and flipped it over to look at the label.

"I don't know about you guys, but I'm pretty sure that ghosts don't eat 'extra cheesy, extra processed' chips and 'super party stuffed' cookies." She said, exiting the room with one of each bag in hand, phone safely tucked in her back pocket.

Theodora snatched one of the bags from Venus's hands.

"These expiration dates are for three years from now, these bags are definitely recent."

They can't be! There's no way in. She shot a look at Jeannie. *Unless... I mean... What if she wasn't the first to get in like that?* She pushed the thought away. Venus looked in the bag and waved it in front of Jaimie's face.

"Want any, Jaimie? I know you want some."

He backed away, disgustedly throwing his hands up in front of him. "No thanks. I'm a vegetarian, remember?"

Venus grinned even wider and pointed at some blurred out fine print. "Even better; they're vegan!"

He was starting to look green around the edges as he looked to the other two for help. "I think I'll pass on the haunted floor cookies."

Jeannie snorted and Venus shot a smile at her. *Mission accomplished.* Venus turned back to Theodora and Jeannie, throwing down the trash and wiping her hands on her pants. The pair were just laughing and having a good time, and Venus was relieved that the mood had lightened, if just for a moment.

"Let's keep going?"

Slowly, the silly procession continued, checking each room for crazy wildlife before taking pictures and making jokes about what was inside so that they could move on to the next. It was easy to forget why they were here and what had happened to make them do this, but it was fun to just exist for a bit.

They eventually reached a large metal doorway that went into what looked like it could have been a stairwell but it was smaller. There was a panel on the wall next to it and in front of the door was a metal lattice. Jaimie voiced Venus's thoughts before she could.

"Why is there an elevator in a warehouse built over seventy years ago?"

Jeannie took a step closer to it, looking down the elevator

shaft. "I guess they needed a way to transport machinery and stuff between floors without having to take the stairs."

Venus tapped at the battered button panel, the metal buttons stained and rusted over. The lower button seemed to be stuck down. "I wonder if it still works?"

She pressed on the top button, peering into the dark elevator shaft. She sucked in a breath and started coughing. It strongly smelled of metal and smoke. Jaimie looked skeptical.

"After fifty years of no use and a fire? I doubt it. Even then, there's no electricity."

Venus jabbed at the button again, mashing it with her thumb a couple of times before taking a step back and sighing. "Was worth a shot."

As she turned back to the group, Theo tapped Jeannie's shoulder.

"Lead the way to the infamous pile."

Jeannie nodded and they continued through the building, no longer stopping to search the rooms, instead just sticking their heads and flashlights in to confirm Jeannie's stuff weren't in them. *Like a security guard, making her rounds.* Occasionally, Venus would snap a picture of the rooms, sometimes of Jeannie, Theodora, and Jaimie, messing around and having fun.

As they made their way through the building, Venus's pocket vibrated. She pulled her phone out of her back pocket and glanced at the screen as everyone else's phones started buzzing and singing. She scanned the message and when Jeannie gave her a look, explained.

"Irsa wants to know where we are, for some reason."

Jeannie's brows furrowed. "Ask her why."

Theo nodded and started tapping away phone magically in hand. "On it."

"I'll tell them we're on our way to the rubble pile in the back of the building. I wonder why they need to know?" Venus asked, confusion etched into her features.

Jaimie shrugged. "Maybe they just want to meet up."

Venus cocked her head at Jeannie. "Let's keep going. I wanna check out the pile before we meet up with them."

They continued walking and Venus slipped her phone in her pocket, but Theodora kept looking at his phone while they walked. He laughed as his phone dinged with a notification.

"She said she'll tell us what happened when we get up there. They made it to the second floor and got spooked by something I guess."

Venus followed Jeannie as she lead the way to the back of the building, hooking her arm with Jaimie's quite aggressively. Venus saw Jaimie stifle his laugh, as the look on Jeannie's face was a combination of fear and determination that looked almost fierce. She swept the flashlight beam across the warehouse, pointing it into every semi-dark corner as if someone was waiting to jump out at her. Venus knew that her fear was not unfounded, yet she still found it humorous.

They knew they were approaching the back of the building when Jeannie pointed at a rusted over sign that hung on the wall. Venus could barely make out what it said, but Jeannie clearly knew what it meant.

"How can you even read that?" She asked, squinting at the almost scratched out words and various arrows.

"What are you talking about? It's pretty clear that the loading bay is this way. Just read the sign-" Jeannie stopped, staring at the sign, dumbstruck. "That's not what it said."

Venus put a hand on Jeannie's shoulder. Jeannie's expression was unreadable.

"What did it say?"

Jeannie shook her head, closing her eyes in what seemed to be frustration. "The warehouse is gaslighting me, I swear to god. The sign very clearly said 'Loading Bay' with an arrow pointing this way." She gestured through the metal doors, and then shook her head. "Maybe I was just seeing things."

"Maybe the shadow man was making you see what it wanted you to see." Venus suggested.

Jeannie just nodded. "Yeah, let's say it's that. I'd rather it be that then it be me just going crazy because of some ghosts we haven't even seen yet."

Jaimie squeezed her arm. "You're not crazy, you're just being gaslighted. It's not your fault, so let's just forget about it and keep going."

Theodora nodded and dramatically pointed towards the doors. "Onward!"

Jeannie smiled weakly and followed Theodora through the open metal doors. Venus stayed back for just a moment, snapping a picture of the sign before following. As they continued through the doors into the new room, the pile came into view. Jeannie had not been exaggerating when she had talked about the sheer size of the pile; it was almost touching the ceiling, barely leaving any room for someone to squeeze through.

The pillar to the right of the pile was almost completely collapsed, part of the building having crumpled in on itself in this part. Past the tall and formidable pile of sharp scrap, unstable concrete, mangled steel, and melted sheets of metal, the now open loading bay door revealed the yellowing grass of the outdoors. The light let in through the open doors lit up the far side of the room, creating perfect pockets of shadows in the corners of the room. When Venus wasn't directly looking at them, they seemed to writhe.

She turned her attention to the unobstructed side of the pile, and saw that, what should have been the easy way through, was an unnaturally black abyss. Just looking at it made her stomach turn over, as if something was hidden deep in the shadows, ready to attack. *I get it now.* The first thing Jeannie did was turn her weaponized flashlight on the shadowed corner, soaking it in white light. It was just an empty corner, created by a pillar. It was an empty space that lead to the other side of the loading bay, but even with the light on it, Venus was scared to go near it.

Something about it felt hungry. Venus felt that if she were to go stand in the corner, it would be equivalent to covering yourself in honey and walking into a bear's den; it would be suicide.

She could tell that Jaimie and Theodora felt similarly as neither of them made a move to give it a better look. The flashlight beam shook and Venus saw that Jeannie was shaking. *She's terrified, even when nothing is there.* Venus trembled with restrained anger. Something that was hidden within shadows like a coward dared to terrify someone she cared about without even showing its face.

"If I ever meet the thing that chased you," Venus said to Jeannie, jaw set. "I'll make it regret even looking at you, let alone scaring you."

A tense moment passed before everyone burst out laughing. Even Jeannie smiled, biting back laughter. Venus's anger deflated into dismayed disbelief as she looked around at her so called friends.

"Well, fuck you guys! I can be scary!"

Theodora nodded, still laughing. "No, no, I believe you! I know you can kick ass. Just, your face was so fucking funny!" Theo dissolved into laughter once again, doubling over and slapping his knees.

Jaimie nodded, wiping imaginary tears from his eyes. "You looked so serious, it's just really funny."

Even Jeannie nodded, lips pursed in a restrained smile. Venus scowled. "Screw you guys, I'm pissed off! This fucker has the audacity to basically scar Jeannie for life, and yet he hides in the dark like a fucking coward."

Jeannie's eyes widened, but her smile didn't fade. "Don't say that! What if it can hear you?"

"Well, good then! I want it to hear me. Maybe it'll get mad and show itself."

Theodora wheezed and started coughing.

"I love how you refuse to refer to it with any pronouns." Jaimie said, smiling wide.

"That's because it doesn't deserve pronouns, right?" Venus said indignantly. "Not because we don't know it's pronouns, it doesn't get to be referred to as anything other than 'it' because I have no respect for it."

"That's not why I'm calling you 'it,'" Jaimie called out, glancing around as if it was listening. "I just don't know how to refer to you, you creepy bitch."

Now Jeannie burst out laughing. Venus pouted and turned towards the stair well that was tucked to the side, light spilling from the doorway to illuminate a path for them to walk.

"Screw you guys, I'm going upstairs."

Venus began to walk to the stairs and she could hear the rest of the group laughing as they followed, one of them jogging to keep up. When she got inside the stairwell, her heart dropped. *Well, fuck.* The first five steps were completely gone, either broken to the point of collapse or destroyed by rust and flames that had damaged the overall structure. Behind her, Jeannie and Jaimie groaned.

Venus cracked her neck to the side and shook out her limbs, backing up a few steps as she eyed the gap in the stairs. *I bet I could jump it.* Before Jeannie could say anything in protest, Venus was running, leaping into the air and slamming her hands on the edge of the metal stairs to propel herself forward. She shot through the air before landing hard on the stairs platform. Glancing back, she had completely jumped over the last step. Venus turned and grinned at the group, who just stood looking dumbfounded. *See! Parkour fucking works!*

Theo's ascension up the stairs was much less impressive, yet much smoother. He used his hands to push himself up as if he was getting out of a pool. Their arms didn't tremble once, as if they were actually good at push-ups. They sat up very smoothly and straightened their outfit, smiling widely.

Jeannie opted for a more traditional approach. Jaimie laced his hands together and gave her a boost, helping her to easily climb onto the stairs. Jaimie jumped up after she moved to the platform, straddling the stair to pull himself up. He got up very jerkily, steadying himself on the wall.

"Sorry that not all of us can be so graceful." He said when Theo gave him a look. "Some of us don't play sports."

Jeannie rolled her eyes. "Says the Badminton player."

He shot her a sad look. "You and I both know that barely qualifies."

After a laugh, they started up the stairs, Venus leading the way up and taking them two at a time to avoid the broken steps. Jeannie and Jaimie followed behind her gingerly, trying to avoid putting too much weight on the aged metal. Theo brought up the back of the group, audibly not caring too much one way or another about tripping or falling. Which they did multiple times. *What happened to that grace?*

By the time they got to the top of the stairs, Jeannie and Jaimie were wheezing and even Theodora was attempting to conceal their heavy breathing. Venus was doing fine breathing wise, but her calves were burning. She was just glad to be off of the rickety old stairs and on the unstable concrete of the second floor. She could see that the second floor was entirely open, the only closed doors being the stairwells and the elevator. Any walls that had once stood had been burnt to only the foundations, leaving charred husk-like patterns in the floor.

As they got out of the stairwell, Venus easily spotted Lilly and Berri's group, Irsa sitting on the floor next to Acacia and leaning against the wall next to the first stairwell, all the way across the building. Glancing back to make sure everyone was out of the stairwell, Venus wrapped an arm around Jeannie and followed Theo, who very gladly led the way, maneuvering through the maze of broken machinery and melted supplies.

It took a surprisingly long time for them to get through the massive room, as the floor was absolutely covered with debris and piled with decimated boxes of who knows what. If there wasn't an impassable pile, there was a glass covered spot of floor or a section of ground that was just completely missing. More than once did they have to double back because a section of the building was collapsing in on itself.

Eventually, they made it to where Lillybelle stood leaning against a window sill, Berri rifling through the papers with their long, neon nails. Jaimie squeezed Jeannie's hand and went to go sit next to Irsa, who smiled at their approach.

"I'm glad you guys made it through safely."

Venus smiled back at her. "Me too. What happened to you guys?" She asked, giving Berri's bleeding leg and Acacia's scraped hands a once over.

Berri's eyes glinted with irritated mirth as they smiled. "Funny story."

As Venus rinsed and bandaged Berri's leg and applied band-aids to Acacia's hands, Berri and Lillybelle slowly told them the story of what happened, specifically the mysterious clapping and how the step had collapsed under them. Once Berri has finished, Jaimie started explaining the little that had happened on their end.

"So the two things I have gathered from this," Acacia said, scooting over to the rest of the group, who were now all sitting on the floor. "Is that one, this place is haunted, and two, someone other than ghosts has been coming here. I'm willing to bet it's that woman from before, but why she's here is a different question entirely."

Venus felt as if her head was spinning with all of this information, each thought pounding against her skull.

What have we gotten ourselves into?

16

Jeannie

They made the decision to go back to the cars and grab the power washing equipment so as to avoid any further injuries. Jeannie had stolen Acacia's spare beanie and used it to keep her hair out of her face as she thought about everything that had been happening over the last few hours. *Has it really only been two hours?*

Venus shot a look at Jeannie as she leaned against her car. "Are you totally sure you're okay with going back in again? Even I'm having second thoughts, and I wasn't the one pushed through a wall."

Jeannie smiled at Venus, but shook her head. "I'll be fine. I have you guys to protect me." She watched as Berri opened their trunk and started unloading the equipment. "Honestly? I feel like I can't leave without finding answers. It's still early enough to get out, but I need to know what's happening here."

Venus nodded sympathetically. "Also, you need to find your stuff."

She laughed. "Yeah, that is a bonus."

Berri huffed as they unloaded the equipment, setting the motor and the tank on the overgrown gravel of the parking lot.

"Alright!" They called out, reaching back into their trunk. "I have two hand held pressure washers and one of the ones on wheels. Who wants one?"

Acacia, Venus, Theodora, and Irsa all raised their hands.

"I'm sensing that the math here won't quite work out." Lilly said with a laugh.

Jeannie smiled too, stretching her arms above her head before something caught her eye in the trunk of her car. She immediately started laughing, not explaining when everyone else looked at her questioningly. *This can't be real.* She fished her car keys out of the pocket in her skirt and clicked the button to unlock it, wrenching open her trunk as the beep went off.

Laying in the back of her car was her dad's old pressure washing equipment, complete with two professional pressure washers on wheels, one professional handheld and one cheaper handheld. *That can't be a coincidence, can it?* She handed one of the handhelds to Venus and the other one to Acacia. Lilly helped her carry the first washer with wheels out of the car, setting it down next to Berri's equipment. Berri gaped.

"How do you have so much equipment? Why is it good quality???"

Jeannie smiled, pushing the beanie back on her head.

"My dad got laid off for a little bit, so he took up power washing as a means of getting by. He got a better job, but once in a while he'll do a bit of freelance work for some extra cash."

Lilly chuckled. "I overheard him saying he was on his way back from a job. Can I assume this is what he meant?"

Berri just shook their head. "And here I was thinking I was the hottest bitch around."

"Oh, that hasn't changed." Lillybelle said, smiling wide. "You're still hot. Jeannie just has more equipment."

Berri stuck their tongue out, but smiled. "Alright, who wants what?"

Soon, all of the equipment was dealt out, the only person not holding something being Jaimie, who insisted he was fine with nothing. Berri glanced around.

"I am sensing a flaw in our wonderful plan."

"What would that be?" Venus asked, pointing the handheld as if it were a sniper rifle.

Berri lifted the power-washer. "We have no water."

With a look around the parking lot, Jeannie realized they were right.

"There goes our plan to clean the haunted ghost factory." Irsa sighed, slumping her shoulders.

"Haunted ghost warehouse." Jaimie corrected, poking her with the wand of her own pressure washer.

"There has to be something," Lilly glanced around. "There's no way this place would have been built with no water access. Let's look around. That's a kinda big fire hazard if they didn't."

Maybe that's part of why the fire raged so long. Jeannie cringed. *Let's hope that's not the case.*

Splitting off, everyone began to search the overgrown grounds. After a couple of minutes, a hysterical, high-pitched shriek announced to the group that something had been found. Theo had walked directly into a pole sticking out of the ground, flipped over it and landed on his ass. Everyone rushed over and Venus arrived first, laughing her ass off before helping a grumbling Theo off of the ground.

As Irsa helped to smack all of the leaves and dirt off of the back of Theo's top and pants, Jeannie looked at the pole that Theo had tripped over. She scraped away the ivy that had grown up all around it, parting the thorny leaves that engulfed the pole. As she pulled away the moss and vegetation, she saw what it was.

"I found our water source."

Lilly looked at her, confused. Jeannie pulled aside the greenery and revealed a rusty old water pump, the metal of the pump rough and tired. Acacia grinned and clapped her hands.

"Alright, now all we need are the hoses."

Everyone turned to Berri expectantly, but Berri just put up their hands defensively.

"Don't look at me like that! I only have fifty feet of hose, and then maybe twenty feet for each washer."

Everyone's eyes switched to Jeannie, who sighed.

"I have some hose, but we only have one water pump, and like seven washers." She turned to Berri. "Would you happen to have any hose splitters?"

Berri shook their head and Jeannie sighed again, but Venus grinned. "I think I have some in my car."

Jaimie looked confused by this statement. "Why the hell would you have hose splitters, just, in your car?"

Venus started walking back towards her car. "Got to be prepared for situations like this."

He trailed after her, expression still confused. "Why are you prepared for a situation such as this?? This," He said, wildly gesturing at the warehouse and the rest of the group. "Is not something any sane person should be prepared for."

Venus retorted something, but Jeannie just laughed as the pair argued all the way to the car. *She always says that she's not a prepper. She's a liar.* After collecting all of the necessary supplies, Berri screwed the longest hose up to the opening of the pump. By some magic miracle, the hose screwed on correctly. Berri tried to move the lever of the pump, but it didn't budge. Irsa tried and failed. Theodora tried and failed. Acacia tried and failed. Irsa and Jaimie tried together and both failed. It wouldn't budge.

"You should give it a try Jeannie." Irsa said, panting.

Yeah right, she thought to herself, glancing at her flabby arms and weak fingers as the hairs on the back of her neck prickled up. *If Venus, the resident gym rat and parkour expert, and Irsa, our resident swimmer, can't move it, there's no way I can.*

Jeannie decided to humor her and took hold of the handle, neat fingers wrapping around the rough metal of the lever. As she tried to pull up, she felt a wave of heat run up her spine. The lever moved up. There was a deep groaning sound from inside the pump and the hose fattened, grayish water spraying out from the end of the hose. *Oh. I guess they loosened it.*

Smiling at her gawking friends, she tried to let go of it, but her fingers refused to let go. A familiar feeling washed through her, one that turned her hands into stone, smile falling away as nausea washed over her. *NO NO No no no no no not again no no no.* She pulled again, panic rising in her throat. She tried to call out, but it was as if her tongue had been glued to the roof of her mouth. A tickling heat began to rise from the pump and she watched in horror as a hot, black shadow slowly started to make its way up her forearms, licking at her skin and inching farther up.

Irsa shrieked and Lillybelle jumped back about a foot. Acacia scrambled with her phone while Venus grabbed the handle and tried to pull it down again, but it wouldn't budge. Venus released the handle, but Jeannie couldn't, her hands glued to the lever as the shadows crept past her elbows, seeping under her sweater. The shadows on her fingers were seeping into her skin, a painful warmth spreading deep into her bones.

Jeannie couldn't move and she couldn't speak, her breath was caught in her throat. She couldn't scream. She couldn't let go. It was as if she was in the wall again. *Help me help me help me help heLP HELP HELP ME PLEASE.* Out of the corner of her eye, she could see Jaimie fumbling with something, but she couldn't see what. Lilly wrapped her arms under Jeannie's armpits and started pulling, but to no use.

"Let go of the handle!" Lilly cried.

Jeannie couldn't even open her mouth to respond as she felt the shadow permeate up to her elbows, the surface shadow creeping up to her shoulders. Lillybelle cried out as Jeannie felt the shadow spread onto her armpit. Suddenly, a cold spray of water slapped Jeannie's arms, shocking her back into reality. The shadow shrunk back, retreating down her arms and with a jolt, Jeannie let go of the lever, falling back onto Lilly, who crashed to the ground.

Her head was spinning and she looked up at the person who had sprayed her. Jaimie stood over her, a look of shock on his face as he brandished the pressure washer, staring at the pump. *When did he manage to hook it up?* Venus shakily pointed at Jeannie's hands.

"Is it still there?"

Jeannie looked down at her hands and a wave of nausea came over her. A shadow stayed under her skin all the way up to her elbow, but even though it looked like it was still there, the painful warmth was gone.

"No," she said quietly, finding her voice again. "It left its mark, though." She looked up at Jaimie in awe. "How did you know what to do?"

When he met her eyes, she saw his fear. "I didn't, it was Irsa's idea to wash it off."

Irsa nodded eyes wide. "It looked like ash," she said softly. "You can wash off ash."

Jeannie nodded. Lillybelle groaned and Jeannie immediately got up, apologizing. She held her hand out to help Lilly up and when she took her hand they all froze. Lilly's fingers had the same shadow stains that Jeannie's arms had, streaking down her palm.

"Must be because I touched you through the sweater." Lilly said, awe evident in her voice.

Acacia tapped her phone and handed it to Lilly. "I recorded what happened. Are you guys okay?"

Shakily, Jeannie nodded. Lilly was much less hesitant.

"It felt weird, like some slick warmth grabbed hold of me. I couldn't let go of Jeannie until Jaimie sprayed her."

"What the hell was that?" Venus asked.

"Maybe the shadows from before?" Lillybelle said, flexing her fingers experimentally.

Jeannie shook her head, cutting anyone else off. "It doesn't matter. Now we know that water hurts it." She turned towards the warehouse, eyes set on the open doors that showed the shadowed and grimy inside of the building. "Let's go clean that fucker up."

17

Lilly

Lillybelle flexed her newly colored fingers, staring at them. *What the hell was that thing?* She shook her head. Theodora had said that it looked like a black out tattoo and Lilly had to agree. She sure hoped it wasn't as permanent as one, though.

Her eyes shifted over to her other hand, her prosthetic. What was really baffling was the fact that it had not only stained her skin, it had stained the plastic case of her prosthetic fingers as well. It was just her finger tips, but still. *How was it powerful enough to stain our skin? Why only where it touched deepest?* She glanced over at Jeannie, who stood at the water pump, calmed down from her earlier excitement. Jaimie had unscrewed the pressure washer and the pump ran clean, clear water. She watched Jeannie's face as she roughly scrubbed her fingers against her skin, nails scraping at the shadows that seemed to sit beneath the surface.

"It won't come off, " She said quietly, her face blank. Her eyes were tinged with sadness, but her eyebrows were furrowed with frustration.

Venus kicked the pump, making Lilly jump. "When we find that fucker, we'll make it take back whatever the fuck it did to you. Both of you." She met Lilly's eye for a tense moment before turning to Berri. "How do we do this?"

"Well," Berri said, eyes flicking to each person as they spoke. "We'll need to connect your hose connector to the end of the fifty foot hose after we shut off the water. Then we connect your other hose connector to your first one so that we make seven spots for hoses to connect to."

"Will there be enough water?" Irsa asked, crossing her arms in front of her chest.

Berri cocked their head. "Why wouldn't there be?"

"I don't know," Irsa shrugged. "I don't know how this stuff works!"

Jaimie chuckled and patted her on the back. "None of us do."

She stuck her tongue out at him and he just laughed. Venus and Berri got to work on screwing in the different hoses, with Acacia helping wherever she could. Lilly walked over to Jeannie, who had leaned back against the warehouse wall a couple of feet away. Jeannie looked and met her gaze before glancing down at Lilly's hands.

"Sorry I got your hands all stained."

Lilly shrugged, leaning next to Jeannie. "You're my friend, I'd have a lot worse happen to me for you." She paused and then laughed. "I was about to say I would have my fingers cut off for you, but that's not true. It already happened once, I'd rather keep the ones I have left, y'know?"

Jeannie laughed too, lacing her fingers with Lilly's. "I like your fingers."

Lilly chuckled, looking down at their intertwined fingers, squeezing and gently rocking them. *I like you.* She cleared her throat. "Thanks. So do I."

Jeannie smiled, then let out a deep breath. "I'm kinda conflicted."

"About what?"

"About all of this. I mean, come on. We came here for a club project. It's not like we have a grade riding on it, so why am I so determined to find out the truth behind all of this? But also, it would be weird if I didn't want to know after all of this, right?" She sucked in a breath before exhaling harshly and squeezing Lillybelle's hand. "What do you think I should do?"

Lilly blinked at her. "Whatever feels right. I can't tell you what you're feeling. I mean, I can't even imagine what you're feeling. You had a strange run in with some random woman with a knife, you were sucked into the wall, your shit got stolen, the shadows chased you, a shadow man grabbed your hair, you're being gaslit by some haunted warehouse, and now some shadow goop has stained your skin. I'd be pretty mad. I am mad, and I've only had, like, one thing happen to me!"

Jeannie chuckled and stared down at her shoes. "Yeah," she said. "I should be more upset. And I do want to find out what the deal is. Are there even ghosts here? Or are they demons?"

Lilly felt a smile spread across her face, though a pang ran through her heart.

"I can't wait to find out with you. Because we'll find out together."

"Yeah," Jeannie said firmly, beaming back at her. "Together."

"Guys!" Theo called, stepping towards them. "Stop being gay and get over here!"

"Never!" Jeannie called back, lifting up their joined hands in defiance.

"Yeah!" Lilly called, making the motions to flip her off with her prosthetic. "See how much effort I went through to do that?"

"Yep!" Theo said, posing dramatically. "It's because you love me!"

Jeannie and Lillybelle started laughing, releasing hands to walk over. Lilly punched Theo on the shoulder and they dramatically stumbled back.

"I've been wounded!" She cried, falling back against Irsa, who quickly swept their legs out from under them into a bridal lift. "Oh shit! You're strong!"

Irsa laughed. "I kinda have to be. I'm a swimmer, remember?"

Theo flailed for a moment before realizing they couldn't escape Irsa's grip.

Acacia nodded thoughtfully. "It's those swimmer shoulders and upper arms. I envy those muscles."

Irsa laughed again, dropping Theo on the ground. "Thanks, although, I don't agree."

Venus laughed and picked up one of the handheld power-washers. "We're all set up. Let's get cleaning."

Each of them grabbed one of the washers except Jaimie, who insisted that it would be better if he didn't have one. Instead, he grabbed the main hose and carried it towards the front doors while everyone else lugged their pressure washers, each attached to a heavy hose of their own. He set it down just outside of the front doors and peaked inside.

"We might have to move some of this stuff before we start." Jaimie sighed.

Lilly stuck her head inside and saw that he was right. She set down the washer with wheels she had been rolling across the gravel, rolling up her sleeves. "Let's get started."

Piece by piece, the group slowly removed every piece of mangled furniture and movable rubble outside the front room and onto the leaves. The trash and small pieces of rubble were the easiest to remove and soon the room was empty except for the grime and ash that hung thick in the air. With everything removed, the room felt much lighter, much safer to be in. They designated that Jeannie and Jaimie hold the lights and that Berri be the first to show how to power-wash, as they had the most experience.

"Alright so here's what you do." Berri said, holding the pressure washing wand in their left hand, right pointer finger on the trigger. "You point it at the wall, and you spray."

Berri demonstrated by pointing the pressure washer nozzle at the wall and holding down the trigger. Water shot out of the nozzle in a concentrated blast, spearing through the years of ash and grime to reveal the pale gray of the concrete. Using the pressure washer, Berri carved out a star onto the wall, letting the stream cut through the dirt and drip down.

The group stood in awe, blown away by this new power they had achieved. Within minutes all of them were testing out their washers on various surfaces, with Berri and Jeannie giving tips and telling them what not to do. Berri also demonstrated the use of various nozzle heads, including the flat horizontal sprayer and the flat vertical sprayer. In no time at all, the walls were washed of their ancient dust and dirt, showing the rough bare concrete for the first time in fifty years.

While most of the group sprayed the room itself, Lilly took her pressure washer and began to wash down the furniture they had removed, washing the destroyed desk and the melted supplies of their accrued dust and ash. The almost decimated wood seemed to soak in the water, a foul stench releasing into the crisp autumn air. Lilly almost gagged. It was as if a campfire had gone horribly wrong.

Please don't let me be smelling dead people, please just let it be a bad sandwich.

She bit her tongue as she felt bile rising in her throat, but she swallowed the bitter taste back down and kept spraying, hoping that the water would take the smell away with it.

Why are we doing this, she asked herself, the power washer heavy in her hands. *If we wanted to get rid of the shadows, why would we start here? Why don't we just go straight to the back of the building?* She shot a glance at Jeannie through the open door, her red eyebrows knit together in concentration, hands relaxed. *It's not about that, is it? It's about the shadows. Shadows of the past, maybe? In the ash, in the grime. The shadows will still be there, but if there's no dirt, the shadows look a hell of a lot more manageable. And that's something we can control.* Lillybelle shook her head.

Quickly, she moved on to a different piece of furniture, the metal shelf that had melted into a crumpled ball. The ash easily washed away, running in dirty rivulets between the red and yellow leaves that coated the ground. The rush of the water was a relaxing sound and Lilly started to feel herself relax as she passed the hose over it rhythmically, spraying line by line.

A shout from inside the building snapped her out of her pressure washing trance, calling her attention to the others. Acacia had called her name, beckoning her inside. "We're done in here, we're going to move on to the next room."

Lilly glanced at the dripping old furniture that lay in the leaves. "What about this stuff?"

Acacia shrugged. "We'll just let it dry out while we clean everything else."

Lillybelle shot a glance back at the desk once more before following Acacia into the building, where Theo, Venus, Irsa, and Jaimie were all pushing the shelf out of the way of the door. After a couple of minutes of grunting and groaning, the doorway was completely clear of the shelf and the group slowly filed into the big, dark room that was draped in shadows and grime.

Each person split off into their section as everyone started spraying down the walls and the pillars. The room was mostly silent except for the hissing water until a loud crack made everyone jump. *What's happening this time? A ghost, a demon, what-* Theo was standing next to a window, shock on their face. The glass was shattered. *Oh.*

They had accidentally switched the washer to a higher pressure and broken one of the few untouched windows. Reluctantly, Theo gave the pressure washer to Jaimie and announced that she was going to clean the leaves from the windows. Venus left with him to go find a washcloth that he could use to wipe down the windows.

Washing the flat concrete was much easier than the curled nooks and crannies of the mangled furniture, the sweeps much more even and neat. *This is kinda relaxing.* It was easy to get lost in the rhythm of the hose and watching the ash melt away in seconds was a type of euphoria that Lillybelle couldn't even describe. The pain in her left arm had gone away, so nothing was stopping her bliss.

She started from the top of the wall, sweeping the stream of water from left to right, and then from right to left. The slow, but steady repetition of the pattern was soothing, the liquid dirt trickling down the wall and cutting through the rest of the grime to make an easier path for the pressure washer later.

Out of the corner of her eye, she could see Venus going in a steady circle around one of the pillars, using a wrapping approach, as if it were a candy cane or a spool of ribbon. She seemed to be smiling at her handy work. On the other wall, Berri started from the top, keeping a steady stream all the way to the bottom before starting on top again, a focused expression fixed on their face. Jaimie seemed to just be having fun with it, not having a focused approach.

Lilly could see Jeannie's style too, next to Berri, but it was much different than the others. She didn't use the flat stream like they did, instead she used the narrow one usually reserved for details. She would trace an image in the dirt, like a heart or a smile, and then she would fill it in. As soon as it would fill in, she would draw a bigger version around it and fill that drawing in. *Like Russian nesting dolls.* Unlike Jaimie, her drawings were very methodical and she was very focused on the shape of what she drew. Jeannie had a thoughtful look on her face, but her eyes were a little sad. *I wonder what she's thinking about.*

Lilly decided to focus on her own work, watching the strokes of clean surface as if they were paint strokes on a canvas, each one erasing decades of grime. She wondered if this would count as historical restoration or as vandalism. She wasn't sure if she wanted to be accused of either.

Irsa was the first to reach a door. "Should we clean out each room too? Or are we just doing the main area?"

Lillybelle took a look down the hall and tried to tally up how many doors there were. She quickly lost count.

"Nope." Venus said. "Let's just do this main stretch and then the rest of the floors if we have time."

"We can always come back if we want to." Theo nodded.

Everyone agreed and as Lilly looked towards Theo, she noticed that more light seemed to be spilling into the room. The windows had been cleared of leaves and dirt, letting them share the sunlight once again. As the light filtered in through the now clean glass, the shadows began to melt away, relegated to the farthest corners. *Jeannie doesn't seem to care how clean it is. The corners are a no go.*

It was peaceful as they washed the room, each person keeping to their own thoughts as each focused on the task at hand. Lilly didn't know how much time had passed, but she knew that they had reached the elevator when she felt a tug on the hose and turned to see what the issue was.

"Is it caught on something?" Jaimie asked, who was also tugging at his hose.

Venus set down her pressure washer, carefully avoiding the puddles that covered the floor. She followed the hose a little ways down and sighed.

"No," She set her hands on her hips and turned around, looking irritated. "It looks like we ran out of hose."

"Well," Berri said, setting their machine to the side. "I guess that's the end of this wash-through."

Irsa sighed and tugged at the hem of her hijab. "That sucks, I was actually getting into that."

"Yeah, we should def come back later with more hose to finish off the building." Theo kicked at the hose, foot swinging past it. "Should we just leave this here and head upstairs?"

Lillybelle glanced around.

"Well, it's your stuff," She said, looking to Jeannie and Berri. "Wanna just drop and go?"

Jeannie nodded. "It should be safe; I mean, who would come in and steal it? And why?"

Jaimie nodded in muted agreement and Berri shrugged.

"I'm down." Berri turned towards the front door. "Let me just run to turn off the pump."

As Berri headed back through the dripping building, Lilly set down her washer and turned to admire the work they had all put in. The walls were clear of dirt and someone had tried to wash part of the ceiling, but had decided it was a bad idea for obvious reasons. The pillars on the way towards the elevator were clean and the windows had been cleared of any gunk, letting the slowly setting sun shine its rays into the large room.

As Berri reentered the main room and the stream of water from Acacia's pressure washer finally died out, she sighed.

"Which set of stairs?" Jaimie asked, leaning against the quickly drying concrete pillar that Venus had finished minutes earlier.

Almost in unison, Irsa and Berri said: "The far ones."

Lilly nodded in agreement, knowing that whatever was wrong with the far stairs couldn't compare with the ones they had braved earlier. The rest of the group just gave them a weird look, but agreed and started to lead the way towards the far stairwell. As Lillybelle was walking, she cast a glance at the wall which Jeannie was working on and stopped dead in her tracks.

An almost perfectly symmetrical heart had been carved out of the grime and displayed on the cracking concrete of the warehouse wall. It was bigger than the windows that sat on either side of it, yet it still felt small in comparison to the rest of the room. When looking at it, Lillybelle couldn't help but feel that Jeannie hadn't been done with her heart when she had stopped drawing.

After a beat, Lillybelle broke away from the heart, following the rest of the group towards the back stairwell. It only felt like a moment to reach the staircase and Lilly couldn't recall ascending the stairs either, only vaguely remembering needing help up a gap. Acacia told the other group that they had already searched the second floor, and so they passed it to head to the third floor. The third floor looked a lot like the second, but there was obviously more fire damage. *Closer to the source of the fire.* The weather had also taken much more of a toll, the concrete more worn and cracked.

Piles of melted rubble and machinery dotted the ground, taking up spaces as small as trash cans to spots as big as cars. The windows on this floor were almost all whole, very few of them clogged with leaves or covered with graffiti. It would have taken a lot of effort to get up here and few were determined to do such a thing just to write their name in spray paint. Next to each stairwell was a small room that could be assumed to be a closet by its size, but it wasn't on any of the blueprints that Lillybelle had tucked in her jacket pocket.

Ignoring it, she gave another look around the place, stepping onto the third floor after Venus, Jaimie, and Jeannie. There weren't many dark crevices, as much of the light was let in through a massive hole in the ceiling, one which seemed to rip through the entire building, as you could see the sky looking up and the dirt looking down.

There was a clear cut path into the center of the third level, seeming to meet with another path to the other stair case, all of the unsalvageable scraps and rubble seemingly moved out of the way. Theo said they were going to poke around the rubble to look for stuff and the rest of the group agreed to split off in groups of two or by themselves, promising to not go out of sight of the others. Lilly decided to go alone, letting everyone else pair off before she started down the pathway.

Out of the corner of her eye, she thought she could see something squirming in the shadows of the piled rubble. *Is something in the darkness or is it the darkness itself?* She shook her head and kept walking, trying to keep the thoughts out of her mind as she continued down the curving aisle. She decided to focus on the piled rubble that was slowly sloping upwards around her, reaching her waist at its highest point. Now that she was paying attention, the piles seemed to be meticulously placed, but the scrap and melted machinery looked like it was too heavy to move. *And who would want to move it?*

Unease weighed on her and a chill ran up her spine. The aisle began to widen out as she approached the center merge point. She squinted at the center point. *What is that?*

There seemed to be a bowl shaped indentation in the ground, around the size of a dinner plate, with some black substance burnt into the floor. Kneeling down, she rubbed at it with her fingers and found it to be sticky, turning into slimy threads of the substance as she pulled her hand away, the molasses like material staying on her fingers as she waved her hand about. *It's the same shade as my fingertips.*

"You should lick it."

Lillybelle jumped and turned to see Berri standing behind her with Jaimie, both grinning.

"You scared the shit out of me!" Lilly made to put her hand on her chest, but stopped when she looked at the substance. She gave the clean, white Badminton shirt that Jaimie was wearing a forlorn look.

"Oh, hell no." He said, immediately taking several steps back. "This is my new badminton shirt! I just fucking got it!"

Lillybelle laughed at his panic, as he jumped behind Berri, who stood unfazed.

"Fine! I'll just get a tissue from my bag."

He stuck his tongue out at her as she slung her bag off of her shoulder and opened it, gingerly rifling through her folders to look for her small tissue package. Berri leaned over her shoulder and peered into the bag.

"Can I see one of the building blueprints?" They asked.

"Sure." Lilly said, using her prosthetic to grab the blueprint out of her pocket.

Berri took the papers with their nimble fingers and began to study the map as Lilly cleaned her fingers of the sticky substance.

"What are these two towers for?" Berri lowered the map and pointed at the two towers that sat directly across from the stairwells.

"Ah," Lilybelle said, squinting at the blueprint. "Those are the delivery chutes."

"Delivery chutes?" Jaimie asked, squatting next to the weird dip in the floor and poking it with a piece of metal. *When did he find that?*

"Yeah, it's these big metal tubes that they have so they can send down boxes and materials to the other floors and to the ground floor for transport."

"How come we haven't even seen them?" Berri asked, brows furrowed in a look of disbelief.

"Yeah," said Jaimie, tilting his head. "We haven't even seen another door for that chute thing, let alone any chutes."

Lillybelle just shrugged. "Maybe they bricked it off after the fire? I don't know, it doesn't show the entrance to any room on any of the blueprints."

"That's kinda weird." Berri said, leaning back against one of the melted machines, blueprint still in hand.

"It sure is suspicious." Jaimie said, a grin on his face.

"Agreed." Lillybelle stood up and pulled out her phone, poking Jaimie in the back with her prosthetic. "Move, I need to take a picture."

A look of dramatized offense came across his face. "How dare you!"

Sighing, Lillybelle snapped a photo of his 'outrage' and then zoomed in on the floor dip.

"What do you think this is?" She asked.

Jaimie got out of her frame and looked at it, standing up. "I don't know. It looks symmetrical and it doesn't belong in this warehouse, so it has to be younger than fifty years."

Lillybelle's eyebrows knitted together. "No shit, Sherlock, whatever that sticky stuff is, it's fresh. Second, what does symmetry have to do with anything?"

He shrugged and Berri just repeated the word 'Symmetry' in a mystified and gremlin-like tone. Lilly burst out laughing. Jaimie laughed with her and Berri just shrugged.

"Maybe it's an altar to the ghosts."

"Like, as in worship?"

"Maybe, or, like, a seance or something. What if someone is feeding the ghosts, or talking to them?"

Lilly considered it for a moment. "Maybe. Whatever it is, let's just keep moving. We should probably look for Jeannie's stuff because the sun sets in," She checked the time on her phone. "An hour at most."

Berri waved off the thought nonchalantly. "We'll be gone before it even gets dark!"

They lead the way down the other aisle, leaving Jaimie and Lillybelle no choice but to follow. They began checking behind rubble and they searched every corner, but couldn't find Jeannie's stuff. Jaimie tried calling Jeannie's phone as they all listened for the catchy ringtone, or even the buzzing of the vibration, but nothing could be heard.

Lillybelle searched the area near the stairs, but with no luck, she turned back around and saw Berri pressed up against the wall where the transportation chutes were said to be.

"Any luck?"

Berri shook their head. "Let's head back to the elevator to meet up with the rest of the group."

The three quickly made their way to the elevator, where Theo stood next to Venus, discussing piercings while Irsa and Jeannie stood with Acacia, arms all linked up like three peaceful peas in a pod.

"Nothing?" Jeannie asked, her voice not very hopeful.

Lillybelle shook her head as Jaimie answered. "No, sorry."

Jeannie let out a sigh. *Looks like she was expecting us to say that.*

"It's fine. We'll just check the last two accessible floors and then go home, because I'm really tired." She said, rubbing her eyes with her stained hands. Lillybelle hadn't noticed before, but the stain went all the way past Jeannie's elbows.

"Which stairs do we want to go up?" Theo asked, hands in their pockets as they looked at the group.

A cold rush of air *whooshed* past and they all exchanged looks. Before anyone could respond, there was a loud, brassy chime, and Lillybelle turned to see the elevator doors slide open.

18

Que carajo?!? Venus's jaw dropped as the elevator's lattice doors clunkily slid open and revealed a dimly lit elevator interior. She blinked a couple of times to ensure she wasn't just seeing things, but the elevator was still there, doors open wide in some kind of eerie welcome. She turned to the rest of the group, their eyes as wide as she imagined hers were.

"The elevator isn't supposed to be working, is it?"

Irsa's eyes were wide as she turned to Lilly, clutching her arm. "You said the elevator was trapped between floors as the fire burnt."

Lilly nodded, a look of pure fear plastered on her face. "Yeah, it was. Floors three and four. The firefighters managed to get the bodies out, but the elevator stayed stuck."

"Maybe they fixed it? I mean, didn't you say they were planning on restoring the factory or something?" Jaimie asked, shifting nervously from foot to foot, but Venus just shook her head.

"Even if they did, we tried the elevator earlier, remember?"

Theo groaned. "I was hoping you wouldn't bring that up! We know that it doesn't work, so how the fuck is it working?" Their voice was on the verge of hysterics.

Venus swallowed, her mouth suddenly dry. "Well... Do we want to get on?"

"Are you shitting me?" Theo spluttered, waving their arms around violently, nearly smacking Berri upside the head. "This isn't Scooby-Doo, we aren't going to get on the rusty ass ghost elevator!"

Irsa tilted her head, eyes seemingly analyzing the elevator. "Why not?"

Venus had to bite back a laugh as Theo gaped at her. *Irsa's supposed to be the logical one, not Theo.*

"'Why not?' I don't know, maybe because there is no reasonable explanation for this elevator to fucking be here?"

Irsa shrugged. "I think it's a sign that we're supposed to go up."

Theo's response was more unintelligible spluttering. Jeannie took a deep breath and shakily blew out the air, wrapping her arms around herself. "Yeah, okay."

Theo's eyes were cartoonishly bulging out of their sockets.

"Okay?" Venus laughed as she looked at the others, most of whom were nodding in agreement. "Let's do it then."

Venus stepped out of the group, cautiously putting her foot on the metal elevator platform. It was surprisingly solid, holding her weight as she fully entered into the dimly lit box. The room swayed a little as she moved around, but no more than a usual elevator did. The walls were thin sheets of steel and the black paint was peeling from the lattice windows that ringed the elevator. The lattice started at waist level and stopped at the sunken metal ceiling, a single glass lantern hanging from the center of it. The candle's flame flickered as she stared up at it.

The wall that held the door was simple, a folding lattice door sandwiched between two steel walls. A large brass button panel stuck out of the right wall, but all of the buttons were rusted over, or, at least covered with something that Venus hoped was rust. None of the numbers were distinguishable, and even if they were, there was no way Venus was going to try and press on them.

"Well?" Acacia asked, glancing inside the elevator at her. "Is it safe?"

Venus nodded, looking around. "Seems safe enough."

"Good enough for me." Irsa shrugged.

It didn't take long for them to file in, as there was ample room in the massive elevator. It was obviously designed to hold machinery more than people, but it fit their need well enough. Jaimie and Theo hung back, Theo still baffled that they were even considering using an unsafe and most likely haunted elevator. Jaimie seemed to hold off for a different reason.

"Come on, Jaimie," Berri called. "This elevator is fine."

He hesitated, swallowing as he looked down the space between the elevator and the ground, eyes glued to the darkness below.

"I don't know. You know how I feel about elevators."

"I know, I hate them too." Acacia nodded. "But really, this one's not that bad."

"Yeah!" Berri added. "This one honestly feels safer than the one at the airport. By a lot!"

Jaimie laughed nervously. "And now I'm never going on the airport's elevator."

Acacia chuckled and outstretched her hand.

"It's not that bad."

Lillybelle nodded. "This elevator was created to carry machinery weighing way more than our combined weight, so we'll be fine."

Venus bit her lip, trying to ignore the information that Lilly was intentionally leaving out: the fact that this elevator hadn't been used in over fifty years probably countered any security they would have gotten from that information in a normal circumstance.

Jaimie let out a shaky breath. "Okay, fine," He stretched out a finger towards the group. "But if we die, I get to say I told you so."

Theo watched in awe and shock as Jaimie cautiously stepped onto the elevator.

"Come on, Theo." Irsa called, beckoning him. Theo stood still, almost turning up his nose to them so as not to look at them. Lilly sighed.

"I'll give you one of the prettiest rocks in my collection if you get on the elevator."

Theo shot a glare at her and then sighed, running his hands frustratedly through his hair. "I guess we're really doing this!" They groaned into their hands. "Fuck it! I'm not letting you dumbasses die without me." And with her hands still in her hair, she hopped onto the elevator, shooting a glare at Jaimie, who just feebly smiled in response. "You were my only hope, you know? To talk some sense into them."

He smiled. "Sorry, Theo."

Theodora just shrugged and waved their hands at him. Almost as if on cue, the elevator doors slid shut, the creaky lattice door slamming against the wall. Theo hooked their fingers in the lattice and shook it. It rattled, but did nothing else.

"Yep," Theo released the door and swung her arms back and forth. "This is definitely haunted."

The elevator jolted and Venus's heart beat against her ribs as she felt the elevator lurch upwards. Jaimie clutched onto Theo's arm as Berri leaned on the wall, nervously pulling at their sleeves. Out of the corner of her eye, Venus could see Jeannie's hands were laced together, knuckles going gray from squeezing. The third floor had sunk completely out of view before Acacia cleared her throat.

"Did you know that some buildings don't have a 13th floor

because they think it's bad luck? And in Japan, that number is four." Acacia swallowed, fiddling with one of the holes in her sweater. "It's funny how superstitious people are, right?"

Venus knit her eyebrows together, the steel walls vibrating and the lattice rattling. *Why does it feel like I'm sinking?* They approached and began to pass the fourth floor much more quickly. "Is it just me, or is the elevator speeding up?"

As soon as she had said that, the elevator decided to lurch again and the fourth floor was gone in a second. Jaimie closed his eyes and began muttering something as Theo wrapped his arm around him. Berri grabbed on to the elevator's window sill as Acacia braced against one of the corners. The fifth and sixth floors were just a flash of dim light as they passed.

The elevator slammed to a stop, sending all of them flying up, and then crashing to the ground. Venus tried to steady her breathing as the palms of her hands ached. Blood was pounding in her ears, to the point where she didn't even hear the lattice slide open. The smell of ash and metal was overpowering. Slowly, she lifted her eyes to the wall that was visible through the now open elevator doors, the dimming sunlight shining onto a faded black number. *Seven.*

Venus shakily stood up, careful not to cross the elevator's doorway as she wobbled. She closed her eyes, shaking her head violently before opening them. The chipped black paint was still staring at her from the crumbling wall.

"I don't understand," she said, turning to look at Lilly, who was trembling as she straightened up, leaning on a frazzled Irsa. "The seventh floor is supposed to be inaccessible. You said it was destroyed!"

Lilly nodded slowly, wincing as she did. "The elevator wasn't supposed to work either." She gestured at the elevator.

Berri gestured at the group from the floor, head against the wall. "I'm guessing it's safe to assume that logic need not apply.

What with the shadow demons, miracle goo, and an invisible audience."

Venus brought her hands up to her temples, but stopped short of touching her face. Her palms were red and raw, but there wasn't any blood. Bits of dirt and gravel were pressed into her flesh, the skin stinging when she blew on it.

"So are we just going to assume that because this haunted elevator took us here, that it's safe to get off on this apparently destroyed seventh floor?" Venus looked around at the seven of her friends, each in some state of disarray or injury. They were all looking at someone else to answer. "Okay, I love you guys, but that wasn't a rhetorical question!"

"Let's just get off this elevator," Acacia said, wrapping her arms around herself. "I'd like the safety of solid ground."

Lillybelle looked as if she might counter the 'solid ground' bit, but she was interrupted by Jaimie, whose voice was two octaves too high.

"Yes, please."

Venus turned back towards the elevator's doorway and stepped towards the door. As her boot hit the concrete of the infamous seventh floor, a glowing white figure rose from the ground, startling Venus backwards. She bumped into someone, but was too distracted to check who.

The silhouette of a teenage girl was hovering over the ground, her dark hair hanging loosely around her ears. A gray apron floated around her as she slowly raised her eyes to meet Venus. They were strikingly brown, gold rings shining out at her. The woman smiled.

"Hello. My name's Lori. What are yours?"

19

Jeannie

Jeannie didn't know how to react as she stared past Venus and at the dark haired girl hovering in the doorway. *I don't know if I should be shocked a ghost just showed up or shocked she didn't show up earlier.* The smell of iron filled her nostrils and something hot and wet told her she had cut her leg worse than before. *Great.* Her fingers stung as she tightly clutched the rough lattice of the windows. Her head was spinning and she could taste bile on the back of her tongue, but she swallowed it back.

But none of it mattered because a ghost had just appeared out of the ground and asked what their names were. Venus, standing firmly at the head, was just staring at her. Jeannie had to swallow six or seven times before she could speak.

"Uh, hi."

Venus breathed out a sigh of relief, as if she was glad someone else could see her too. The ghostly girl now known as Lori shifted her beautifully brown eyes to look at Jeannie and as Lori smiled, Jeannie felt her mouth go dry again.

"Hello, Jeannie."

Jeannie blinked several times. *How-*

"How do you know her name?" Irsa asked.

Whipping her gaze to Irsa, Jeannie could see that she was trembling, leaning on Lilly for support. Lori tilted her head. She looked completely unbothered. "Her name has been circulating the factory floors for a while now."

Jeannie turned back to the ghost. "How long?" She asked hesitantly, the sinking feeling in her stomach growing.

The spirit seemed to ponder it for a moment. "I would have to say... Two hours?"

Oh. There were multiple sighs of relief.

"Lori, get away from there!" A sharper voice rang out, firm.

Lori glanced over her shoulder and sighed. Her gaze lingered on Jeanie for a moment longer. "Alright."

With a small wave to the group, the ghostly figure faded out of sight, leaving just a pale cloud of mist hanging in the air. Venus rubbed her eyes in frustration, but Jeannie found herself sighing in relief. Lori's presence had a different weight than the shadows did, almost refreshing. *Mist instead of sludge.* Before anyone could say anything, another head popped out from the side of the elevator doors, light hair falling over pale eyes. Theo flinched hard as the new ghost spoke.

"Are you just going to stand there all day? Come on!" Her eyes sparkled at the group as she came fully into view and she stretched out a hand. "Everyone can't wait to meet you!"

With that, the girl disappeared to the side, leaving Jeannie's head spinning. *What the hell is happening?* Jeannie gave Jaimie a look and he immediately hooked elbows with her, still clutching onto Theo. Theo had bent down and was wiping what looked like blood off of a fresh rip in their jeans. They met Jeannie's eyes and smiled, but it didn't reach their eyes all the way.

"I'll just add a new patch, it's fine."

Jeannie nodded, but as Theo turned towards the door, pain flashed across their face.

"We should get on solid ground," Lilly shot her a look as she said that. "Well, more solid ground, so that we can fix up all these cuts and scrapes."

There were mumbles of agreement and nods from the group. Taking a deep breath, Jeannie stepped past Irsa, who seemed to be hanging back, hands on her hijab. Jaimie almost pushed her off of the elevator, eager to get onto the concrete ground. It felt good to be on something solid, but a voice in the back of her head nagged her.

This is the most unstable floor of the building. This is where the fire started. Why do you think it's safe to be up here?

She just shook her head and refused to think about it. Turning back to the group, she watched as Venus stepped off, her green eyes glimmering brightly as she eyed the ghost that hovered nearby. This new ghost was smaller, only slightly bigger than a child. She simply floated there, watching them patiently disembark from the rusted elevator.

Berri and Acacia followed Venus out, both looking surprisingly composed, but Jeannie couldn't help but notice that two of Berri's nails were chipped, one snapped in half. Lilly hung back, standing with her back to Irsa, who was standing behind her as she readjusted her hijab. Jeannie quickly averted her eyes to look at the seventh floor instead.

To her left, the roof had mostly caved in, leaving the floor covered in rubble and the building open to the rapidly darkening sky. What remained of the walls were covered in dark stains, as rain and weather from the past fifty years had washed most of the ash and char to the ground, caking it in a charcoal mud. Where too much weight had piled, holes in the ground had been created, gaping pits into the darkness of the other floors. Windows were just warped mats of blackened glass and ragged gashes in the collapsing building. Any machinery that had once been up here was buried under the rubble. About halfway down the factory floor stood the tower of the stairwell that had once led to the roof.

Well, that's a death trap, she thought, but she shook her head. *This whole place is a death trap.* Moving on from the charred and entirely ruined roof-access, she turned her attention closer to them. Across from the stairwell, the one closest to the 'loading bay,' was a completely clean and uncovered section of wall. Set in the wall were four large metal gaps, almost like vents.

Those must be the delivery chutes Lilly mentioned earlier, she thought to herself. *I wonder if they go all the way down.*

On the right side, the roof was mostly intact, though there was still a large gap in the ceiling near the farthest wall. It was almost a perfectly circular indent, the rubble from the ceiling strewn in various chunks in the area. The floor was mostly empty as well, leaving it as a perfect space for all of the ghosts to congregate. The feeling of eyes on her was bad enough, but knowing they were all standing there, watching?

Lori stood in the front of the group, talking to a taller woman, whose hair was pulled back into a bun, gray streaks running through her dark hair. She looked severe, but not cruel. A woman who was used to being in charge. *Used to the burden.*

Venus took over the bandaging of scrapes while Theo began the distributing of granola bars and water. *I'm surprised everyone's taking this so well.* Jeannie wasn't the only one a bit scratched up, but, at this point, she didn't mind. The s'mores granola bar was all that she needed, but as she ate, she noticed the spritely ghost from before hovering closer. She was eying the granola bar.

Can ghosts get hungry?

She offered part of the bar to the gray girl. "Want some?"

The girl shook her head. "I'm not hungry." *Should have*

known. "With all of the half-eaten food and wrappers being left around lately, we've been eating pretty well!"

Jeannie frowned. *Wait, what?* Before she could ask what she was talking about, Jaimie called out.

"Why are you talking to us when everyone else is over there?"

The ghost tilted her head at Jaimie and grinned widely. "I'm not like everyone else."

That was true enough. This ghost was different from Lori; where Lori was tall and ethereal, this spirit was small and chaotic. There was a mischievous gleam in her eye that wasn't mean, but it was definitely trouble.

"I'm Giorgia. The others like to listen to Fiadh, but I would rather just do as I please. It's not like they'll punish me. Besides, Fiadh thinks you need some time to adjust, but I think you're all adjusting fine." There was a slight accent in her voice, but it didn't feel as if Giorgia was trying to hide it. "I'll take you over there."

Having finished up their granola bars and packed away their trash, Theo followed Giorgia as the lead, Jeannie right behind and Venus coming up at the rear. The path was a bit treacherous for a larger group, but not as terrible as it would have been to be on the roof, judging by the state of the ceiling.

Giorgia floated above a pile of rubble as Jeannie maneuvered over a mound or melted scrap. Jaimie almost tripped, but Theo helped hold him up as they both stumbled.

"No offense," Giorgia turned to look at Theo as he spoke. "But why exactly are you escorting us? I'm not ungrateful, really, I'm not. I'm just wondering."

"Oh! It's because humans might have a hard time maneuvering this floor without dying!" She laughed, her skirts floating up around her. "You lot wouldn't have been able to even get up here had we not used our energy to get the elevator working."

"That was you guys?" Acacia stepped in front of Venus, who stopped, staring at Giorgia.

"Yeah. We pretty much died in there, so we have some amount of control over it with our very limited, but still pretty impressive powers!"

As Theo helped Jeannie over the last large piece of ash covered equipment, she couldn't help but glance over at the ghosts that watched them. They were gathered in smaller groups within the larger group, each careful to sit under the giant missing part of the ceiling. *That's where the light comes through,* she realized.

Giorgia danced around Jeannie and towards the center of the group, where a woman in a long sleeved dress and long apron was sitting, legs folded under her. Giorgia smiled at Jeannie.

"Someone wants to meet 'ya."

Jeannie was led past the ghost now known as Fiadh, who had stopped her conversation with Lori to watch them pass. The girl sitting on the floor looked up at Jeannie and her breath caught in her throat. She was very pretty, a lovely face peaking out from dark curls, her skin a similar brown to Theo, if not a little grayer. Her eyes, however, were striking, a brilliant warmth in her gaze. *She feels familiar.* Jeannie sank into a sitting position in front of her.

"You're-"

"I'm Quinn." She cut Jeannie off. *Even her voice is pretty.* "It's nice to meet you."

Jeannie's eyes widened as the ghost rose up a bit. Sitting on the concrete behind Quinn were Jeannie's belongings. Her brightly colored phone case sat leaning against her camera, both very carefully piled on top of her backpack.

"I'm sorry for taking your things, I just... I couldn't let you leave without asking for help and I knew you would come looking for your things."

Quinn very carefully put her hands on the backpack, fingers almost going through the fabric as it lifted into the air. Slowly, she floated it onto Jeannie's lap.

"You were the one who hid me?"

The ghost nodded, eyes in her lap as she pulled at the seams of her skirt. "When I saw her coming, I knew only bad things would happen if you were caught, so I used all of my strength to pull you into the wall. But, I'm not the one who pushed you through it."

"Then who did?" Venus asked, crossing her arms and scanning the faces of the ghosts. *She looks kinda scary.*

Quinn shrank back from Venus a bit before shrugging, avoiding looking directly at either of them. "We aren't the only beings in this building. But that isn't important! The reason I took your belongings is because we need your help: Something has been happening to us."

Irsa sat down next to Jeannie, tilting her head at Quinn. "How do you mean?"

Quinn looked up at the three of them. Her eyes were bright, a streak of amber being the only color in her otherwise crystal gray eyes.

"Whatever is doing this has teamed up with the shadows and now-" She cut herself off.

Jeannie shifted in the prickly silence. "What?"

"Doing what?" Irsa asked, leaning forward. "What's happening?"

Quinn just shook her head. "I wish I could say more, but even telling you this is risky."

"Risky?" Irsa furrowed her brows. "Why?"

"Because the shadowy presences hunt us through the building. They stalk us from the darkness, so we stay up here most of the time."

"I'm sorry," Venus said, pressing the bridge of her nose. "But I'm still trying to wrap my head around the fact that you're all real. The shadows hunt you?"

Irsa shook her head. "I don't understand. Do you mean you're safe here?"

"This is where the rain comes in." The look on Quinn's face was almost melancholic.

Jeannie suddenly realized that it had been over fifty years since any of the ghosts had felt rain. That made her chest hurt.

"They're scared of it!" Giorgia was almost buzzing with energy as she hovered between the four of them. "The rain, the water! They hate the stuff. So when it rains, we spend our time here, in the rain. It stops them from getting to us!"

Jeannie was almost regretful as she asked. "What happens if they get to you?

Both Quinn and Giorgia shivered before Quinn spoke again, quiet.

"The shadows consume you. As a living human, you have a body to keep the shadows at bay, meaning the worst they can do is scare you, maybe make you tired. But as a spirit, it literally drains everything from you."

Jeannie's throat was suddenly dry, her heart pounding in her chest.

"Then why not leave?" Irsa asked, crossing her arms as she sank down next to Jeannie. "I mean, you're ghosts. You can just go through the walls an escape, can't you?"

Quinn shook her head. "We can't. The shadows, they are contained within the walls, but there are more outside. We would be captured within moments and destroyed."

Jeannie furrowed her brows. *That must've been the eyes I felt earlier. Coming from the trees.* Lilly stepped up behind the four of them, making Jeannie and Irsa jump when she spoke, a burning question escaping her tongue.

"But what keeps you here, as ghosts? Why not move on into the final afterlife, if there is one? Do you want revenge, justice?"

Lori settled behind Giorgia and Quinn, smiling.

"It's nothing like that. We used to be angry about what happened. We wept and screamed for a long time."

"Nearly a decade," Quinn added.

"Yes, we nearly scared that lady to death." Giorgia laughed.

"The journalist, forty years ago?" Lilly continued.

Giorgia scratched her head. "Was it that long ago? Yes, some lady who wanted to ask us questions. We scared her, accidentally, but she came back later. This time, we were fine, but something else chased her out."

"But it's not that we don't want justice," Lori intervened, attempting to steer the conversation back to Lilly's question. Once in a while, she would look over to Fiadh. *For approval?* "We do. But, most of us are just too afraid of dying again to move on. We've decided to make the best out of our situation."

"Some girls couldn't take it, so they passed on." Quinn said, hands knotted in her skirt. "They were too angry, too sad. They couldn't stand the injustice."

Irsa leaned forward. "So it's true? They locked the doors on purpose?"

Quinn and Giorgia exchanged a look, but Lori looked back at Fiadh.

"I heard whispers that the owners weren't makin' enough money. We hadn't been payed in weeks," Giorgia said, in hushed tones. "And I don't care what those papers said, none of us girls smoked."

Quinn nodded. "That's what we told that woman. Only the managers smoked."

"So they started the fire on purpose?" Jeannie reiterated, her head spinning.

"There's no proof of that," Fiadh cut in, voice crisp.

"But none of us started it, that's for sure." Giorgia said, indignant.

"Wait," Jeannie said, thinking back to what Giorgia had said earlier. "Something else chased the journalist out of the building?"

Giorgia nodded.

"And earlier, you were describing what the shadows do to you." Venus continued. Jeannie could feel the tension in her dropping away. "How do you know that?"

No one spoke. Irsa's eyes went wide. "Has it happened to one of you?"

After exchanging a look, the three nodded. Jeannie's voice hitched. "I'm so sorry."

Quinn shakily shrugged. "It happened so many years ago."

"Is that why there aren't as many of you as the report says?" Lilly asked.

Jeannie shook her head, confused. "What do you mean?"

"The report says over 30 girls died in the f-" she caught herself. "accident. But there's only ten of you here."

Jeannie blinked and did a mental head count. Lillybelle was right. There were only ten ghosts in the room. Fiadh appeared next to Lilly, a look of irritation and exhaustion on her sharp features.

"The shadows are the least of our problems right now. This is why we decided to ask for your help!"

"What do you mean?"

Fiadh exchanged a look with Quinn, who just looked back into her lap. "Girls have been going missing."

20

Lillybelle was taken aback. "What do you mean 'going missing'?"

Fiadh shook her head, wringing her hands as she kept her gaze on the sinking sun. "We become weaker when the sun sets, more susceptible to the influence of the shadows. We go into something similar to sleep at night, but every few nights we will all awake to find someone missing, no trace of them anywhere in the building."

Lilly ran her fingers nervously across the tops of her notebook, twisting the pen between her knuckles as she flipped to a fresh page. "Do you have any idea what's happening?"

"Well, we do know it isn't the shadows," Giorgia chimed in, ignoring the look Fiadh shot her. "They are very obvious in their attacks. When they attack, it's always someone who's alone and someone who is loud. We always spend the night in the group and none of us make any noise!"

Lilly wrote quickly, pen going in sweeping movements across the page as she jotted everything down. Fiadh came around the side of her, peering at the notebook.

"At first, it happened unexpectedly. We assumed it was a tragedy or a mistake, but we were so busy mourning that we didn't realize it was a pattern until the next of us disappeared."

Quinn shuddered. "And it was different than when someone was taken by a shadow, because we could still feel part of them in the building. But this... They are just gone!"

"And things are changing." Fiadh twisted her ring around her finger. "It's happening faster and faster."

"Two days ago, we lost Clara!" Giorgia cried.

"And as our ranks grow fewer, the shadows grow stronger. Something is organizing them. At this rate, none of us are going to be left by the end of the month."

Quinn looked up at Lilly, her eyes heavy with what looked to be fear. It was as if she wanted to cry, but couldn't. "Please, you have to help us!"

Lilly stopped writing. "How would we be able to help?" She spluttered, panic rising in her chest. "We're just teenagers!"

Fiadh put a hand on Lillybelle's prosthetic, probably attempting to comfort her, but Lilly recoiled, heart pounding in her chest. *What... no, that can't be...* Theo sprang up, jumping to her side.

"Are you okay? What's wrong?"

Lilly could barely respond, bile rising in her throat. "I felt her touch me."

Theo shook his head, clearly not understanding. "What?"

"I felt her touch me!" Lilly's voice was rising hysterically. "She touched my prosthetic and I felt her touch me! I can not feel you touching my prosthetic, but I felt her touch me."

"Are you sure?" Acacia asked, glancing between her and her prosthetic.

"I'm pretty damn, sure," She said loudly. "This happened earlier, too, but I thought I imagined it! Do it again!"

Fiadh was startled but reached her hand out again. Where her prosthetic met the ghost's hand, Lilly felt a flutter. A tingling of nerves, in a place she hadn't been able to feel for seven years. After a moment, it was gone. The flutter, faint, disappeared.

"It's gone!"

Berri's eyes widened. "Take it off!"

Lillybelle shook her head, eyebrows knit together as she trembled.

"What?"

"Take it off!" They repeated, jumping to their feet. "Maybe you can feel her better without the prosthetic being in the way!"

After a moment of hesitation, Lilly began to take off her prosthetic, unhooking it from the the socket. She very carefully, handed off the limb to Theo, who cradled it to their chest like a baby. The ghosts all watched her in a mix of horror and awe as she peeled off the sock and handed it to Berri. The air that hit what was left of her arm was piercingly cold, as sweat had drenched the space. *What if it doesn't work again? What if I just imagined it?*

A few deep breaths. A few words of encouragement. A few minutes. She nodded to Fiadh.

Very slowly, Fiadh stretched out her hand, laying her finger on what looked to be empty air. Both of them gasped as Lillybelle felt a tingling sensation run up her arm. *Her hands are cold.* Even with the coldness of her touch, Lilly had never felt warmer in her life, warmth spreading from a place that hadn't been warm since that awful night in the hospital.

"I can feel you," She choked out. "I can feel."

Acacia gaped. Lilly's breath hitched as Fiadh moved her fingers down through the air, reaching where her wrist would have been.

"Please help us," She whispered, lacing her fingers with the air that was once Lilly's left hand. "You're the only ones who can."

Tears welling in her eyes, Lilly nodded.

"What can we do?" Jaimie asked, eyes darting between Lilly and the ghosts.

Lori kept her eyes on Lilly's 'arm' as she spoke. "What you did earlier with the water was helpful. Now, we are safer going down there, but we need you to find out what's happening to us."

Lilly could see Jaimie nodding out of the corner of her eye as the rest of the group began to gather and discuss.

"Fiadh," She said, voice hushed and shaking. "Can we just stay like this, a little bit longer?"

Without a word, Fiadh squeezed her hand. Sinking to the ground, hand in hand with a ghost, tears streamed down her face, hot on her cold skin. A wave of shock rocked through her body and she gripped Fiadh tightly. Lillybelle could feel again. And so she could cry.

21

Jeannie

When Jeannie arrived home, night had set in. The lights from her parents bedroom were off, but the hallway light was still on, the yellow glare seeping through the front windows of the house. She turned the key and removed it from the ignition, letting the ringing silence fill the air as she stepped out of the car. The coolness bit into her skin, the open cuts on her legs stinging in the nipping breeze. The porch lights were on, so it only took her a few moments to unlock the door, but in those few moments, she tried to ignore the feeling that something was just over her shoulder.

Every movement she made, something in the corner of her eye moved too. The entire drive home, she could have sworn something in the darkness of her trunk was moving. That someone or something was hiding in the shadows. Even when she had checked that there was no one in the trunk about a dozen times before even unlocking the car.

She stepped over the threshold and closed the door firmly behind her, only turning around to look out the window when she heard the lock click. *Nothing.* The porch was empty, the bland suburban street beyond filled with only minivans and swirling leaves. *Why do I feel like someone's watching me?*

The inside of her house was dark, the yellow light from the upstairs hallway spilling down the walls and dimly lighting the doorways around the stairs. She could smell something rich from the kitchen doorway.

They probably left my dinner out. She wasn't hungry. *I'll put it away later.*

She felt guilty for a moment- about the food, about being home so late- but something else won the struggle. Jeannie stepped on the ankle of her shoe, kicking it off to the side before yanking her foot out of the other one. The stairs creaked as she raced up them, landing lightly at the top. Only when she reached her bedroom and closed the door quietly behind her did she exhale. She pressed down on the lock, but after a moment, she dragged the desk chair in front of her door, setting it below the handle. Looking at it, she just laughed. Well, tried to.

Why am I being so paranoid? It's not like anything followed me home. The ghosts are trapped, so the shadows probably are too. I'm fine. I'm safe.

Why can't I believe that?

She ran a hand through her sweat streaked hair, slinging her bag to the floor as she strolled past her bed, yanking open the drawers in her dresser. The clock sitting on her desk blinked the time at her, telling her what she didn't want to know. She didn't even bother to look at which pajamas she pulled out of the drawer, tossing them onto the bed behind her. She glanced over at the clock again, but caught her eye on something else. Jeannie slowly stepped in front of the mirror that hung next to her bathroom door, eyes trapped on her reflection. *I look like shit.*

The girl reflected would have to agree. Dirt was caked into her hair, leaves sticking out of the tangled red strands, her bangs plastered to her skin. Her hazel eyes were a dull green, exhaustion lining her features. The gray beanie she had accidentally stolen from Acacia sat askew and the jacket Theo had leant her was hanging limply around her waist, covering the rip in her skirt that Jeannie could feel. Dried blood was crusted on her knees and a cut ran along her thigh. Her sweater sleeves were a darker shade of green than the rest of the fabric, the hems damp.

Her hands were what caught her attention the most. Sticking out from the damp sleeves was skin stained black, a color deeper than any tattoo she had ever seen. It was as if instead of blood running through her veins, it was oil. Slowly, she rolled up her sleeves, watching for where it ended, just above her elbows. The ends were jagged, almost looking like roots, digging into her flesh and reaching to go deeper. The longest root reached her shoulder, the shortest tapering off at her inner elbow. *What kind of movie character looks like this?*

Not one that survives.

She felt her chest tighten as her breathing sped up and she quickly darted into the bathroom, closing the door loudly behind her. It was a blur, but in moments the water streaming from the shower head was scalding and she was standing under it, her sweater, skirt and socks in a ball on the bathroom floor. Something stopped her from stripping further, but she could barely think, fingers scraping at her skin incessantly.

Jeannie was almost choking on her sobs as hot tears streamed down her face, cold compared to the boiling water pouring down her back. She wished she could scream. She could feel the eyes on her, the hot shadows licking at her skin. She wanted it gone, wanted it away from her. The shadows were blinking in the corners of her vision, but she violently spun around, almost slamming into the shower door.

It felt like hours had passed when she finally turned off the water. She had rubbed the skin raw and was almost relieved to see that her blood was still red. *At least I'm still human.* She refused to look at herself as she exited the bathroom, not bothering to put on her pajamas as she crawled under the covers. She couldn't pin point when she fell asleep, but of course, she would regret that. As soon as she began to dream.

22

Lilly

illybelle was in what felt like a void. She was standing, but as she glanced around, the void melted from her sight, revealing a very familiar set of surroundings. The warehouse. It was dark in the warehouse, and it was completely empty of life.

'Oh', she thought. 'I must be dreaming. But why don't I feel like I have any control?'

There was a sound in the distance, like muffled voices. She reached out her hands, but froze. Only one hand would stretch out, the other only being air. She never went to sleep with her prosthetic on, but she almost always dreamt that she had both her hands. The fingers she could see were stained black at the tips, nearly vanishing from view when against the darkness. The arm was there, it was just invisible- almost ghostlike.

Slowly, she began to walk- if you could call it that- towards the voices, a light appearing around some far corner. The more she walked, the louder the voices got, but she didn't seem to be getting any closer.

Suddenly, she could hear the voices all around her, pounding in her ears as the words stung her skin. Her heartbeat was being drowned out by the volume, each sound pulsating in her ribs and rattling her heart like a clap of thunder. They were right in front of her now, yet she could barely make them out. A cacophony of treble tones and deep timbres assaulted her ears, rising and falling in volume like an ebbing tide until a word finally jumped out at her.

"-plan!"

It was a woman's voice, her word almost a shriek that scraped against Lillybelle's ear drums. It was higher pitched, yet heavy and grating. The second voice chimed in, more masculine, smooth and almost velvety.

"Don't complain about your plan when I've been holding up my end of the bargain so far. You are the only one who seems to be lacking! How ironic."

There was a huff of frustration, and the outline of a woman began to materialize in front of her, shaky and wavering in the abyss of dark corners. The outline's arms were crossed over its chest, foot tapping in aggressive silence on the concrete.

"Don't you dare act like you're better than me! None of this would even be happening if it weren't for me, so maybe show a little gratitude-"

She was cut off by a harsh laugh and the outline recoiled. The deep laugh echoed cruelly around, bouncing off of the ground and ceiling out into the nothingness. The darkness in front of the outline seemed to get thicker, deeper, blacker. It was exuding hot energy; energy that felt chillingly familiar. Lillybelle reflexively glanced at her fingertips and the stain on her skin: it was the same feeling as when she had tried to help Jeannie.

"You came to me. I made the offer, you took the deal. Don't you dare forget which of us is in control here."

"You need me!" The woman cried, clawing at her chest and gesturing wildly at the slowly growing pit of darkness. It towered over her, dwarfing everything around it, humming with power yet absorbing all sound near it simultaneously.

"You aren't the only one willing to take a deal. You didn't think you were the only one who could do this, were you?"

The outline froze, unnaturally still. When she spoke again, her voice was quiet, almost a whisper in the ringing void.

"That's impossible."

"I never really needed you." Lilly could almost hear the sneer in his voice as the honeyed words hung in the void. **"Isn't that right?"**

A gasp broke the air behind Lillybelle, and she whipped around, her feet un-sticking themselves from the floor. On a piece of ground almost tens yards away, Jeannie sat kneeling, tears running down her expression of desperation as shadowy tendrils wrapped around her arms, forking up her skin like tree roots.

'This isn't my dream,' Lillybelle thought, her hands going limp by her side. 'Its hers.'

23

Venus

Venus winced as Berri slammed their cardboard chocolate milk carton down next to their styrofoam lunch tray. *Why does everything have to be so loud today?* The cafeteria was already crowded, the voices of hundreds of students all droning on around her with their mindless chatter. Berri's brown patch sweater sleeve slid up their arm as they ran their fingers through their brown hair, silver necklaces clacking softly against the bronze dragonfly brooch that had been pinned to the sweater's slightly worn collar.

Theo glanced at them, grease from a slice of pizza dripping onto his chunky silver rings. As he shifted to make room for Berri, the glittery rhinestone ribs on his shirt glinted in the cafeteria lights, contrasting against the rest of the loose fabric and the black mesh under shirt that stretched up to his wrists. Acacia smiled through her sandwich, pushing her lunch box out of the way as Berri groaned.

"Really, Acia?" They gestured towards her shirt, which had a black cat outline sitting on a grinning Jack-o-lantern. "It's not even October yet!"

Acacia shrugged as she swallowed a bit of sandwich, a little piece of tomato dripping down her chin as she raised her hand to cover her mouth. "So? Theo's wearing a skeleton on his shirt!"

"Theo's always dressed like that!" Theo nodded in agreement as Berri took a sip of chocolate milk. They continued, "And you are wearing matching pumpkin earrings and a necklace. I'm willing to bet your socks match too."

Acacia opened her mouth before smiling. "I can't even defend myself, because you're right."

Irsa tugged at her hijab, readjusting the pale blue fabric around her face. Her dark blue turtleneck had been rolled up her forearms, revealing some jotted down formulas as she picked up an apple slice and bit into it.

"Where's Jeannie?" Irsa asked. "Wasn't she right behind you?"

Berri nodded, poking at something on their tray with a plastic fork. "Yeah, she wanted to buy a cookie so she had to add money to her lunch account."

There was a murmur of understanding and a couple of nods as Venus took a sip out of her water bottle. She had rolled her red flannel up to her elbows and had left it unbuttoned over her neon mothman shirt, only the front part tucked into her high-waisted, acid wash jeans.

"So," Venus started, setting her black aluminum water bottle down next to her backpack. "What are we going to do about the whole warehouse situation?"

Theo sucked in a breath and Irsa began to over dramatically rub her face.

"I was hoping that that whole thing was, like, a dream." Irsa said, eyes closed. "Was that really a thing that happened? Like, actually?"

Berri nodded. "Yeah, the giant bandaged cut on my leg is kinda a big reminder for me." They pulled out their phone. "It's also a reminder to go get a tetanus shot."

"Well, we have to do something!" Venus sighed. "We can't exactly leave them hanging. They asked for our help!"

"Well," Theo interjected, wiping the pizza grease from his fingers with a napkin. "Do we have to help them? I mean, no one else knows that they are there. And this is really none of our business. It's not like we have any obligation to go back."

He's right, she thought to herself, gaze sinking to the spaghetti Kristina had packed her. *But I don't think I'd ever be able to sleep again if I ignored them.*

Acacia put a hand on Theo's mesh covered arm. "Maybe we have no obligation, but would your moral compass let you rest easily knowing that they suffer and you could have done something?"

Theo threw his head back and whistled. "No, of course not. My moms raised me better than that." A strangled laugh escaped his throat as his head snapped back forward. "It was just an idea."

"And it's not a bad suggestion." Irsa said. "It's a fair perspective to consider."

"What perspective?" Someone said from behind them.

Venus jumped in her seat and turned. *People have really got to stop doing that.* Jeannie was wearing a brown-plaid overall dress that fell past her calves over a white sweater, thick black boots laced up her calf and under the folds of the dress. Her stained hands were hidden beneath a flowery pair of gardening gloves, fingers curled tightly around the styrofoam tray.. Her hair hung in limp, slightly damp knots around her face, a thick glob of black substance glaring at them from the red strands. A bruise was starting to form on her cheek.

Standing behind her was Lillybelle, arms piled with books and papers. She was wearing a black turtleneck with red corduroy pants, a wine red trench coat billowing out behind her with embroidered pomegranate pockets crammed full of paper scraps and pencils. Her hand was shaking and dark circles seemed to be forming under her eyes. *I guess she didn't get much sleep either. Not like she ever does.*

"Theo mentioned how we don't actually have to go back."

Jeannie nodded, sliding her bag down her arm and setting down her tray as Lilly piled her miscellaneous stack onto the table, either not noticing or not caring about the large sticky spots on the surface.

"He's right, this is a really big deal. I don't want to force anything on any of you that you aren't up for, or don't want to deal with. It makes total sense to bail while you're ahead and fairly safe." Her eyes flitted to her own hands for a moment, then Lillybelle's fingers. "I wouldn't judge any one of you if you didn't want to keep going."

Did she practice this speech?

Acacia nodded. "I agree, this is a lot of pressure for us to take on with everything else going on. I personally want to keep going, but if you don't want to, you don't have to."

Berri waved a hand in the air. "No need to even ask, losers: I'm in."

Irsa smiled and nodded along.

Theo took a deep breath. "I'm going to momentarily be the voice of reason and say, 'but what if we get hurt? Isn't this super irresponsible?'" After he finished with his pantomime of the school principal, he continued. "Having said that, I'm 100% going with you. I just wanted to make sure we thought this through before getting traumatized."

"Right." Irsa rubbed her hands together, and turned to Lillybelle, who had sat down on the uneven bench by now. "You probably have a plan for us, Ms. Secretary?"

"Where's Jaimie?" Lilly asked, looking around.

"He's making up a math test," Jeannie said. "He said we could start without him."

Lilly nodded, pushing her hand across her face as her prosthetic rested lightly on the pile of papers. "Right. I didn't sleep very well last night, so when I inevitably woke up at 2, I started to do some research. I couldn't find much online that was genuine, just a bunch of shitty twelve year old vampire transformation guides, so I went to the library."

"What time does the library open for you to do that much research?" Theo asked, using a pencil to lift one of the many, thick stapled piles of paper up off the gross lunch-room table.

"Our local library is open 24 hours," Acacia said sheepishly. "My mom said that they get too many visitors after hours for them to close."

Venus laughed and shook her head. "Of course, you two would know that."

Lillybelle smiled as she opened the tote bag that had been hiding behind her backpack. It was bulging with books, hardcover, paperback, and leather bound.

"Yeah, speaking of, you know how they have a twenty book checkout limit? Well, I'm overdrawn by twelve books at both that library and the school library, so I used your library card to check out the other six."

Acacia buried her face in her hands and started laughing as Berri gawked. "Why did you even have her card?"

Lilly pulled the library card in question out of her back pocket and put it on Acacia's sandwich bag before unpacking multiple stacks of paper-filled folders. The card looked wellworn and the Acacia that smiled up at her from the whiteplastic still had braces. *She must have gotten her card in sixth grade.* "Because I needed to pay back the late fees that I owed her."

Venus picked up the book that was on top of the pile. It was bound in brown leather and the title was scratched into it and painted white. The title read *The Pathway to The Paranormal: A Guide Book for Beginners.* "Where did you even find this?"

"Our local library has a surprisingly large paranormalnonfiction section. Like, it's bigger than the paranormal fiction section." Lilly looked slightly concerned by this fact. "I thought it might be a good place to start, so I was scanning some of the books during my first classes, and I think we should visit one of the other haunted sites so that we can get some more information."

Venus began to thumb through *The Pathway to The Paranormal: A Guide Book for Beginners*, mindlessly scanning the pages as Lillybelle started to talk about the use of another site. A chill ran down her spine and she could feel the hair raising on the back of her neck. The pages of the book slipped from her fingers and before her eyes the pages flew to the side, slamming open onto a page in the middle of the book. The table went silent. When Venus looked up, everyone was staring at her and the book.

Quickly, she glanced down and read the title of the page: *Photographic Evidence*.

"Jeannie, do you have your camera with you right now?"

"Uh, yeah, I think so," she began to rummage in her bag. "Why?"

Venus just shook her head, scanning the paragraphs beneath the title.

"Can I see it please?"

Wordlessly, Jeannie handed over the camera. Trying to remember what they had taught her in her Freshman Newspaper class, Venus fiddled with the dials, scrolling back through the most recent pictures. There was a picture of the warehouse from a passenger seat window, the tall gray building almost collapsing in on itself as the bold and colorful graffiti creeped up the sides of the building like a choking vine. She scrolled to the next photo.

This was also of the building, but from just below it. The colors were brighter, the light softer, the shadows deeper. The sunlight reflected sharply off of the broken windows, casting long and strangling shadows that dripped from the unnaturally dark abysses of the windows. Even in the places where the window panes were clear and unblocked, only darkness swallowed the light, masking the truth of the warehouse's innards.

Venus clearly remembered being able to see the outlines of things through the upper windows, but in the photo that was able to perfectly recreate the lines and values of the graffiti on the wall, the windows were empty shadows, gaping maws that gave nothing. *Just like when I shined my flashlight inside.* A knot began to form in her throat, but she swallowed and scrolled to the next photo.

She couldn't help but laugh, the anxiety dissipating momentarily. At first glance, it was a blurry photo of a frightened owl throwing itself out of a rotting window. Behind the owl, the flash illuminated a small concrete room, with a doorway that barely stood out of the darkness. Venus remembered the silly, startled text that Jeannie had sent about the owl.

"You have to send me this photo later."

Jeannie managed a laugh as Venus scrolled to the next photo.

The uneasiness returned immediately as she stared at the picture. It was almost surreal; it was a brightly lit shot of the warehouse floor, but something felt off. It was almost too bright- it definitely hadn't been that bright when they were inside- and there were unfamiliar reddish-brown stains across the concrete and metal. What caught her off guard was the smile. Tucked behind the pillars were inky black shadows and one of them was smiling. Venus swallowed, blinking a few times to see if her mind was playing tricks on her. The smile remained.

She scrolled to the next photo and before she could even look at it, Jeannie sucked in a breath. Venus looked up at her. Jeannie's ginger brows were furrowed, cheek sucked in as she chewed on her lip.

"What's wrong?"

Jeannie wrung her gloved hands in front of her, hazel eyes glued to the camera screen. "I didn't take that photo."

Venus turned back to the image that sat on the screen. It was taken from a low spot, probably on the floor, but it was angled upwards, towards a crumbling, ash covered doorway. In the corner of the frame was a burst of bright red hair, laying piled up.

That must've been Jeannie after she fell.

Standing in the doorway, was a woman, pretty and partially transparent. Venus was able to recognize the startled features as Quinn, the ghost girl that had rescued Jeannie. Her gray and amber eyes were wide with fear, one brown hand knotted in her apron folds as the other stretched towards the camera. Only one of her feet was on the ground, shadows seeping towards her. The edges of the photo had matching distortions, the darkness seeming to drip along the sides of the image.

Venus tried to scroll to the next photo, but there were no more. She frowned. "I don't understand."

A violent chill ran up her spine and she shuddered. The lights began to flicker across the cafeteria and teenaged screams filled the air. Her hair stood on end and papers lifted up out of Lilly's many folders, scattering across the table. A whisper behind her ear made her jump.

"Snap."

The lights shut off, plunging the windowless room into darkness and screaming chaos. Goosebumps started rising on her arms and legs as a chill settled over the table, like a mist. Quickly, Venus flipped the dial out of the gallery and raised the camera to her eye, aligning the shot in the darkness and snapping the picture. As soon as the exposure finished loading and the flash went off, the chaos stopped and the lights came back on, row by row.

Theo's hair was a mess and Irsa was quickly readjusting her hijab, pulling off papers that had settled on her head. Acacia had taken off her hearing aids and closed her eyes, only opening them when Berri tapped her arm. Lilly's distress at the mess was evident and Jeannie was gripping the edge of the table tightly, stained knuckles going gray.

"So, Adrienne definitely is trying to tell us something." Berri said, staring at the mess of papers that had resettled across the lunch table.

Lilly nodded, taking a deep breath before rummaging through her bag and pulling out the evidence log-book. "What did you get a picture of, V?"

Venus scrolled to the gallery and pulled up the most recent photo. The flash illuminated Theo grabbing at their floating hair while Irsa held onto her hijab, but someone was standing behind them. She had long, pale hair and was wearing a black plaid shirt. Her eyes were a deep brown and she stared into the camera. She was also completely translucent. *Holy shit.*

"Oh my god." Jeannie was staring at the photo. "Is that-"

"Adrienne." Lilly finished, eyes wide as she quickly started scribbling in her notebook.

As the rest of the group immediately began questioning what that meant, Venus turned her attention to the rest of the picture. Along the bottom of the image, several words were traced in a gray substance. *Lievas Avenue.*

"There's a street name on the picture."

Lillybelle straightened beside her. "What's the street?

Venus repeated the street to her and Lilly immediately began searching through the papers that had been scattered across the table.

"I'm pretty sure that's one of the locations for the club, one of the one's mentioned in one of the ghost story books." Theo shot Lilly a look of concern, but she ignored it, hand digging through the piles. "Adrienne has to be telling us to go there, right? I mean why else would she tell us a street?" Lilly seemed to be talking more to herself than any of them, but Venus didn't mind. "Or maybe the history of the location is what she wants us to look into? It could be- ha!"

She snatched the manila folder off the table; it had been sitting right in front of her. Lilly flipped the folder open and stopped dead. Venus leaned over and stared down at the file. Scrawled across the document, in some green substance, was one word.

Help.

Lillybelle looked up at Venus, her blue eyes big and confused. Acacia made a noise in the back of her throat and Venus rotated the document for each of them to see. After a moment of dumbstruck silence, Theo was the first to speak.

"So... What does that mean?" He looked at each of his friends in turn. "Does it mean that this place needs help? This place has help? Maybe she's asking us for help with this place? What if Adrienne needs help!"

Irsa shook her head. "So many questions, but Theo makes a good point." She turned to Venus, eyebrows hunched together. "How do we answer all of these questions?"

Venus looked back at the paper. "Well, if we all agree, there is only one way to find out."

Jeannie nodded and Acacia smiled. "To Lievas Avenue!

24

Lilly

Lillybelle had politely declined Venus's offer to drive and instead found herself piled into Theo's cramped and messy minivan with Berri, Acacia, and Irsa. Twenty minutes into the ride, and she wasn't quite sure if her choice was an improvement.

Where Venus was an overly cautious driver, Theo was very much not; windows down, wind blowing their hair across their sunglasses as they sped down the empty roads. Music was blasting from the nearly broken stereo -- the name of the boy band proudly displayed at the top of their phone -- and was being periodically interrupted by a set of directions. Lilly sat between Irsa and Acacia, Berri having claimed the front passenger seat; their feet were now proudly propped up against the dashboard.

Candy wrappers and crumpled up school assignments rolled across the floor, empty energy drink cans and crushed soda bottles decorating every crevice. All of their backpacks had been slung in the trunk, so every sharp turn made them wince at the sound of their bags crashing to the other side of the vehicle.

Irsa sat with her feet together, knees leaning towards the door as she stared out the window, her hands in her lap. Lilly watched as she mindlessly mouthed the words to the song and bobbed her head, her eyes trying to trace something out the window. Acacia was leaning forward, elbows on her knees as she bent her head over her phone. Tilting her head forward, Lilly could see that she was watching Star Wars edits with the sound off.

Theo was loudly singing along to the peppy boyband, hands drumming out a beat on the steering wheel. Their ponytail had been coiled up into a bun to let their undercut breathe, but locks of hair were wiggling free, dangling and bouncing in the wind. Some of it was blowing in front of their sunglasses, the lines of the road reflected in the bronze rims.

Berri's feet were up on the dashboard, but their hand was hanging out of the open window, weaving up and down in the rushing air. Their fingers rose and fell as the music crescendoed, abruptly dropping off into silence before the next song began playing. Slowly, their palm flitted up again, higher and higher. When Berri's arm was stretched as far as it would reach, their hand was blown back and it dropped down.

"Did you guys ever fantasize in the car?" Berri said abruptly, dialing the music down until it was quiet in comparison to their words. "Just, stare out the window on long car trips, your mind not even registering the trees outside? The horizon is the least of your concerns, and your mind just, like, makes up stories to keep you entertained?"

Irsa broke her concentration and turned smiling to Berri, whose neck was craning over the side of the seat. "Yeah, all the time. Sometimes it's stories to match the music, but a lot of the time I just start overthinking everything."

"Me too." Lilly cast a glance towards Irsa, whose gaze had lowered to her clasped hands. "Is there anything in particular you are worried about?"

Irsa shrugged. "It's just weird. I always knew about spirits, and I knew they existed. I mean, my whole childhood was full of stories about jinns and spirits and angels, so I shouldn't be surprised about all of this. But I still find myself in constant disbelief. I mean, yes, spirits being real is not surprising. And the shadows are like jinns, in a way, but... I don't know." She trailed off and Acacia jumped in.

"I know how you feel, I'm having a hard time coming to terms with it. I mean, it's pretty surreal," she turned her phone over in her fingers, her bright blue hair falling in front of her face. "Seeing this stuff in slashers and horror movies is one thing, but experiencing it in real life? Having it all right in front of your face?"

Irsa nodded. "I just have a bad feeling about this."

A knot had formed in the pit of Lilly's stomach and it curled, gnawing on her. *They aren't wrong. I never thought my obsession with ghost stories would turn into this.* She glanced at her prosthetic. *But that feeling was worth it. And if this is the price...* Her fingers tightened on the manila folders in her lap, a glossy black and white photo peeking out from beneath a document. The glowing green word had faded from the page, but she couldn't help but trace it over in her mind.

Help.

Theo coughed from the front seat as a robotic voice read out a map direction over the car speakers. "But, this is still really cool, right?" Their voice shook at first, but stabilized after a deep breath. "Like, even if all of this is scary as shit, and probably faith shaking, it's kinda cool? Like, ghosts are real! I cannot focus on that enough. Ghosts. Are. Real!"

Berri chuckled and Acacia managed a laugh.

"Yeah," Berri said, straightening up and pulling their feet from the dash. "I mean, we've seen more shit in the past twenty four hours than most people have seen in a lifetime! That's dope as hell!"

Irsa laughed at Berri's enthusiasm and something popped into Lilly's mind.

"We've seen more than Alexander!" Acacia gave her a weird look, but she continued anyway. "That pompous, arrogant, asshat can't even dream of seeing and experiencing what we have!"

"Yeah!" Theo added. "And we can remember that when he says stupid ass, dumb fucking-"

Acacia drowned out the rest of his sentence, eyes wide as she laughed. Irsa smiled and cracked her fingers, shoulders relaxing as Berri did a cringy little happy dance as Theo took a sharp turn. The three in the back fake screamed as the car lurched to the side violently and then broke down laughing.

The silence that followed was warmer and filled with the volume of the pitchy, yet peppy boyband love songs. The wind rustled her papers, but most of them were left untouched. One slipped from her pile and a gust floated it to the ground, next to Acacia's fuzzy gray boots. It was the photograph that had been peeking out from the pile and Lillybelle bent down to pick it up.

"I think we're here." Theo said.

Lilly could feel the car start to slow and she snatched up the image, careful not to crease the picture. As she straightened, Berri and Acacia gasped, leaning towards the windows. A quick glance at the picture showed a building, but as she peered around Acacia to see where they were, she realized that it was a picture of where they were.

Had they not been looking straight at it, they would have missed it completely. The small brick house was almost entirely consumed by plants, prickly bushes and winding greenery pulling the building back into the woods, like hungry hands. Trees towered above it, branches creating a net over the roof. Low hanging limbs rested on the dull tin roof, the metal crumpling under the slowly crushing weight. Any windows that still had glass were misty and thorns wound around the front path where a driveway had once been.

Acacia turned away from the window to look at Lilly. "So, what is this place?"

The black and white image, Lillybelle now recognized, was of the building currently cloaked in red and brown verdure. It was the same brick house with its tin roof, but back then, the foliage was hidden behind a stone wall that lined the back of the grounds. The windows had seemed almost new, with pale painted shudders sitting proudly on either side. A worn dirt pathway led from the house through a trimmed garden with a flowering hedge and lattice arch and to the road. A date was penned along the top in faded blue ink. 1937.

"Well, from what I've read about this place, it was abandoned in early 1947 after a mysterious death." Theo groaned under their breath, but Lilly continued, leafing through the folder to find the details. "The house was originally built back in 1910 but was bought by a Mr. and Mrs. James Gornelle in 1935. They were a newly wed couple who came to settle down here after, and I quote, 'family drama back north.' At least, those are the realtor notes."

Acacia leaned over her shoulder to look at the documents with her. "Who died?"

"Well," she said, handing the property page and photograph to Acacia and picking up the police report. "According to this photocopy, it was Mrs. Cordelia Gornelle, at the ripe old age of... 36."

Irsa frowned. "What happened to her?"

"Their twelve year old son, Joseph, came home from school and found his mother on the floor, her head bashed in. Laying next to her, they found a bloody sock. They later matched it to her, but they couldn't figure out how it came off, why it was there, etc. It was treated as a murder investigation at first, but when no evidence came up, they closed it as an undetermined death."

Berri huffed as Theo slowed the car down to a crawl. "She was obviously murdered! Why didn't they question her husband?"

Lillybelle shrugged, turning to the next page. "I'm not sure, they just say no other evidence was found."

"It says here that Mr. James Gornelle and his son Joseph Gornelle moved out six weeks later, but never sold the property." Acacia had flipped to a different page of the property documents, but now she looked up to meet Lilly's eyes. "Why would he leave, but not sell the house? If he wanted to get rid of bad memories or something, why not just get rid of it entirely?"

"I had the same question." Lilly said, passing Berri the police report after they beckoned for it. "So I did some research, and I dug up this newspaper clipping!" She pulled a photocopied newspaper article from the folder and brandished it in front of her. "This was a much smaller town than it is now, so for someone to only move across town after such a violent death, the Daily Arrow couldn't come up with a better story. Luckily enough, they actually got an interview out of Mr. Gornelle."

"Ooh!" Irsa's head shot up, her warm black eyes shining. "Can I please read it?"

Lilly laughed and handed it over. Irsa clutched at it greedily, barely able to contain her excitement. *I forgot she wants to be a journalist. But who doesn't love a good interview article?* Irsa cleared her throat and began to read.

"In a personal interview with the tragic widower, Mr. James Gornelle, we get to see into the mind of the man who moved away from the site of his loving wife's heartbreaking death. When asked why he moved, he said, quote, 'I couldn't stand being in those walls anymore, knowing that that was where she took her last breaths. I couldn't trust those walls to protect my family anymore and I didn't want to force my son to relive that every time he came home from school.'"

Theo sighed. "Okay, that's honestly sad. And kinda sweet, y'know? He wanted to protect his son."

Berri gestured for Irsa to continue.

"We noted that he had yet to sell the house, even though he and his son have been comfortably moved into a different home across town for around a month. Gornelle said, quote, 'I can't let go of her just yet. I need to keep my family safe, but I don't want to leave her behind. I know she is still there and we had so many good memories that I can't bear to give up.'" Irsa flipped the page and frowned. "That's it? That was a pretty short article."

"Yeah, but it gave us some pretty important information," Acacia said. "Mr. Gornelle, while being super suspicious otherwise, hinted at the fact that Cordelia's spirit may be restless and still in the house."

"That could be why Adrienne sent us here." Berri jumped in, turning to face the back seat, face squished on the side of their headrest. "Maybe we can figure out how to help her, and in turn, figure out how to help everyone at the warehouse?"

Lilly nodded, but the gnawing pit in her stomach returned. *It can't be that simple, can it?*

A little silver car that was easily recognized was parked just off the road near the house, out of reach of the outstretched bushes, waiting to fold them into its tight, wooden embrace.

Theo pulled up behind Venus's car as she hopped out of the driver's side, waving at them as she popped her trunk. The five of them piled out of the messy minivan as soon as Theo threw it into park and Lilly caught Jeannie's eye as she hopped out of the back seat. Jeannie had been avoiding her gaze all day. *Does she remember me from the dream? Does she know that I know?*

Jaimie had disembarked from Venus's passenger seat, eyes wide, and Lilly couldn't help but smile, shifting all of the papers she had regathered into the crook of her prosthetic. *I remember my first drive with Venus. It was terrifying.*

"Alright, Madam Secretary," Venus said, smiling ear to ear as she ducked under the top of her trunk. "What will we need for this mission to be successful?"

The air felt different this time around; even though they all knew the risks much better now, it didn't weigh as heavily on her as it had. The jokes and the smiles eased the anxiety that tugged at her chest and she felt her shoulders dropping. Very quickly, Lillybelle gave Jaimie, Jeannie, and Venus a run down of what she had told the others about in the car.

"Regardless of who owns the property now, it is still an abandoned building and therefore it is illegal to trespass." Lilly said, brushing a loose strand of hair behind her ear that had fallen out of her braid.

"It is illegal to be caught trespassing," amended Theo, leaning against the front of their car. "So let's take care not to get caught and not to destroy shit that we don't need to disturb."

There was a round of nods and murmurs of agreement.

"So, which of my prep bags will I need?" Venus asked, pulling a basket towards the edge of the trunk, inside of which were various backpacks. "Do I need my hiking bag, my parkour bag, or my survival bag?"

Berri tilted their head and peered into the box. "Do you have a light survival bag? Like, a mix of hiking and survival?"

Venus nodded, as if this was an entirely normal question. "Yeah, that's tucked under the driver's seat, can you grab it for me?"

Berri skipped around the group. "Mhm. Brb, babes."

As Berri went to grab the bag, Venus rummaged around in the basket and started assigning people gear. "Jeannie, here's your flashlight for dual-wielding against shadow demons and knife wielding people. I added new batteries when you gave it back to me in homeroom." Jeannie accepted it easily, her stained fingers tightening around it. Venus grabbed a handful of metal objects and handed one to each person. "You get a pocket knife, you get a pocket knife, everyone gets a pocket knife!'

Acacia chuckled. "How do they even let you into the building with this many knives on you?"

Venus just shrugged, picking up a rusty looking crowbar as Berri returned with her 'light survival bag'. It was a camouflage drawstring bag that seemed to be bulging with stuff.

"What do you even have in there?" Lilly asked, holding the blocky Swiss army knife that she had been handed tightly against the manila folder. Venus smiled at her.

"Don't worry about it."

After Venus had successfully locked her car, they decided to split into pairs. *The Buddy System only fails when there aren't enough buddies. We should be fine.*

Venus was with Theo, Jeannie paired with Jaimie, and Irsa hooked arms with Berri, leaving Lilly and Acacia together. Acacia caught her eye and nodded and Lilly nodded back. *She knows the drill.*

Lillybelle led the way, Swiss army knife in one hand, paper documents cradled in the other. Glancing back, she saw that Acacia was dual wielding the knife and one of Venus's folding tactical tools. It looked like a shovel, but it had a serrated edge. She had tied a brown plaid shirt around her waist, a pumpkin patterned beanie contrasting against the blue shades of her hair. Her black boots crunched on the fallen leaves as she followed Lilly towards the towering trees.

A wave of nostalgia washed over her as she turned back to the house. Lilly's childhood had been spent with Acacia and Jaimie, running through forested backyards in search of adventures and monsters. The three of them would stay out for hours, only coming back when their skin was glowing with cold and their shoes were soaking wet from jumping over the creek, always unsuccessfully. Lilly would always lead the 'hunt',

Jaimie would stay in the middle out of fear, and Acacia would take up the rear, ready to fight off anyone or anything who would dare attack them. *But that was before Acacia's dad got sick. Before Jaimie's family moved across town. Before my accident.*

She shook her head. There was no point in remembering any of that right now; they had a ghost to save.

The trees loomed over them, the tangled branches reaching towards them like fingers. Rotting vines and dying leaves dangled towards them, swinging in the biting breeze like strands of matted hair. It seemed like everyone had gone silent; all that could be heard was the whistling of the wind as it picked up, the rustling of dry branches, and the crunching of twigs and leaves as they were crushed. There was the occasional cough or laugh, but after a moment, the sound would be whisked away by the wind, or suppressed by the woods.

Each of them had chosen a different route to approach the building; of course they had. Lilly had decided to advance from the right, deciding it would be safer to avoid the woods as much as possible, but not to get too close to the house itself either. Neither gave off a particularly inviting vibe.

The house seemed darker the closer they got, but was a beacon of light compared to the shades that lurked in the tangled and overgrown decay of the surrounding woods. The bricks were covered in a layer of dying moss, but there was little dirt on them; they seemed worn and crumbling, but not grimy. Thorn bushes curled around the side of the house, their brambles and barbs knocking against the glass.

The shudders depicted in the photograph were still there, but one of them had fallen down and another was barely hanging on. The pale paint had once been a pretty lilac color, but now it was a faded gray and chipping. Pieces of it were peeling and curling like grimy finger nails, outstretched and sharp. A piece of destroyed lattice lay tangled in one of the dying rose bushes, several yards from where the arch had been photographed. The wood was thin and flaky, as if it would disintegrate if touched.

A sharp crackle sounded to her right and Lillybelle's head snapped towards the woods. The wind shook the gangly branches, raining brown and orange leaves down on them, specks of rotting wood floating through the air.

The old trees overshadowed them, their heavy branches stretching towards them like greedy talons. One branch brushed her arm and she reflexively pulled back, almost bumping into Acacia. Acacia was also on edge, fingers tightly wrapped around the base of the tactical shovel. *She must have decided the shovel would be a better defense than the knife.* The shadows seemed to grow darker, and the trees larger, the longer Lillybelle stared at the encroaching foliage.

The more she stared, the more she noticed, and the more she noticed, the more unsettled she became. The bark on some of the trees was unnaturally smooth, no curve, no grains, no line, just smooth, pale tree. On a tree just behind it, however, the bark was unnaturally detailed. It looked as if each inch of the bark had been meticulously engraved in the wood. Words started jumping out at her, one after the other.

Blood. Die. Guilty. James. Blood. Help. Head. Brick. Die. Cry. Hurt. Killed. James. Bones. Die. Help. Hurt. Trapped. Murder. Head. James. Guilty. Scream. Brick. Hurt. Murder. Help. Cry. Trapped. Murder. Murder. MURDER.

It was as if the woods were whispering the words as she read them, each word echoing in her mind. Quickly, she turned to Acacia, but found her staring at something else entirely, eyes wide in horror. Lillybelle followed her gaze and when her eyes landed upon it, she gagged.

Not even five feet away from them, an animal of some sort was trapped in a cage of thorns, dark shadows surrounding it from all sides. Its skin had been stripped from its body, leaving only a mass of meat and guts. She could taste the bile rising in her throat as the creature pulsated, not yet dead in its impenetrable cage of spikes.

A loud crash to their left made them both jump and Lilly turned to see Venus and Theo standing in front of the front door. Theo was less standing in front of the door as their foot was *through* the door. Venus had her face in her hands, but the movement of her shoulders hinted that it was less disappointment than laughter. Acacia and Lillybelle exchanged a look before starting towards the front of the house, not saying a word. She tried her best not to look back at the creature, as its squirming image was reliving itself in her mind, but as she reached Venus and Theo, she shot one last glance at the animal. The shadows had closed in on it hungrily.

Shuddering, she turned to the group. Berri and Irsa had returned from the other side of the building, Jaimie and Jeannie trailing slowly behind them. Jeannie had her eyes on her camera, which was cradled in her hands. She was scrolling through some photos, but before she could ask about them, Berri spoke.

"I hate to be a party pooper, but this place is fucking scary as hell." Irsa nodded heartily as Berri pushed their hair back. "Like, the woods seem high-key, I don't know, evil?"

Lilly felt the tension in her chest lift slightly. "I thought it was just us."

Acacia nodded, loosening her grip on the shovel. "Yeah, I wasn't going to say anything, but we saw something really weird out in the woods. There was an animal, with no skin, trapped in thorns."

"And it was still alive." Lilly jumped in. "Like, wiggling on the ground and everything."

"But there was no smell of rot or blood or anything. And it was only a couple of feet away."

Lillybelle opened her mouth to interject, but closed it. *She's right. There had been no smell.* The air had tasted the same next to a dying, rotting animal as it did where she was standing right now. *Something is wrong with these woods.*

Irsa shuddered. "We didn't see anything that bad, but we saw into one of the windows. The windows are covered in dust right? Well, we looked back at them after a minute and there were fresh handprints across the windows."

Venus's eyes went wide. "This place is no joke. Do we still want to go in?"

Jeannie and Jaimie exchanged a look that Lilly couldn't quite place.

"I'd say we should decide sooner, rather than later." Theo said, pulling their leg out of the door. "As we probably don't want to stay here longer than we have to regardless."

Lilly nodded and stepped forward. "Let's do this."

25

Jeannie

As Theo pushed the slightly destroyed front door open, Jeannie took a deep breath in. The air was thick with dust and she coughed, covering her face with the sleeve of her sweater. When she blinked the dust out of her eyes, she saw the room as it was.

The house was small on the inside, which was to be expected; as was the dim light streaming in through the cloudy windows. Most of the group had entered in front of her, leaving her standing in the doorway, Jaimie a few feet in front of her. His pale blue tennis shoes has already been dulled by the leaves and inexplicable red mud near the edge of the woods, but the dust in the air made their contrast even more stark.

There were only a few pieces of furniture dotted around the room, with a closed door to the left and a doorway to the back of the house in the center of the back wall. On the right, a low table sat between a gray brick fireplace and a low couch with a matching chair, both of which were draped in sheets. Between the two doors was a taller, long piece of furniture, obscured by a sheet like everything else. There was a groove in the wooden floor boards where a carpet once was, but now dust layered over the rotting boards instead, creating a puff of dramatic 'smoke' with every step.

Shadows hung in the corners of the room, under sheets and in doorways; yet none of it bothered her. Instead of immediately making her heart beat faster and her mouth go dry, her mind was calm and her throat clear. *These shadows are different.* She couldn't place her finger on why, but she just knew. They were lighter, cleaner; they weren't dangerous.

The presence of the shadows was familiar, but their weight was a sharp contrast to the ones that haunted her. Her thoughts flickered back to her dream: the helplessness she had felt, frozen and wrapped in inky tendrils. She couldn't move in that dream, she couldn't breathe; it was just like when she had been in the wall, except it felt as if it would never end. The dream had kept going as she was forced to listen to a conversation. She had barely understood it, but she had been forced to sit through it nonetheless, unable to process her thoughts, let alone someone else's.

Someone else coughed and Jeannie's gaze shot up. Lilly was standing by one of the windows, her prosthetic cradling the documents that she tended to carry while she ran her finger along the dusty sill. *Lilly was there too.* She was in the dream, but she hadn't just been a spectator or a visage; she remembered it.

Lilly hadn't said anything, of course she didn't. But she didn't need to. It was obvious in the way that she had looked at her first thing in the morning; a look of fear, pity, sadness. A look of confusion. *A look that could only be given by someone who's seen you at your lowest. A look that remembers.* Jeannie swallowed and looked around the room again. *Focus on the now, Jeannie. There is no point focusing on that stuff right now.*

She felt a hand on her arm and she flinched, but once she saw that it was just Jaimie, she relaxed. He gave her arm a little squeeze and he smiled, reassuringly. Jeannie couldn't help but smile back. *My best friend, til the end.*

Turning her gaze to the room at hand, Jeannie decided to investigate the tall, cloaked piece of furniture. Her fingertips brushed the grubby sheet and she had to physically stop herself from recoiling. *It's just a piece of fabric,* she thought to herself. *A little dirt never hurt anybody.*

She caught sight of her fingers as soon as she thought that. The skin that now more closely resembled her pen drawings than the rest of her skin, so dark that it was evidently unnatural. If she unfocused her eyes, it almost disappeared in the shadows. With as much purpose and focus as she could muster, she closed her hand on the sheet and tugged it aside.

It fluttered to the ground like a silken bird, sending up a puff of dust as it settled on the floorboards. It was a piano-the piece of furniture- and it was untouched by dust. The deep brown wood glistened as if it had never been abandoned. A little wooden stool was tucked beneath it and very slowly, Jeannie drew it out beside her and sat down. Her stained hands hung over the keys as if held up by wires.

Her fingertips tingled, aching to tap one of the keys stretched out before her. She didn't know how to play, but somehow that didn't matter. There was a flurry of footsteps around her as the group gathered on all sides. Irsa hovered by her shoulder, the pianist of the batch.

With a painful finality, her finger dropped, landing heavily on a key in the center. A soft *plink* rang through the room. It felt as if her skull reverberated with the note. Her blood hissed and for a moment, the silence was louder than her heartbeat.

"It's been a while since I've had visitors."

Jeannie spun around, almost falling off the piano stool as she did so. The rest of the group followed suit and they quickly found themselves face to face with a ghost.

She had small features, her face dwarfed by the large crown

of pale reddish curls held back from her face with a simple, but pretty headband. A thin dress with long sleeves and glittering buttons down the front swept to the ground, ending right at her feet. Black slippers peeked out from the hem of her dark patterned dress, the puffy shoulders almost distracting from the blood that was dripping down the side of her face.

Theo was the first to speak. "You are really pretty," they blurted, eyes wide.

The ghostly specter blinked several times before her face abruptly flushed. *Can ghosts blush?* "I'm sorry?"

Before Theo could respond, Lilly jumped in, obviously frazzled, but eager to shut Theo up. "Are you Cordelia Gornelle?"

The woman folded her olive hands in front of her, straightening the front of her dress. "Yes, I am. I do have to say, it has been quite a while since I've had visitors. And such," She glanced at Theo. "Bold ones, at that." Cordelia wandered towards the piano, her hand brushing the top of it. "I've missed the sound of the piano. Can any of you play, chance? I would but..." She held up her hands and smiled.

Irsa raised her hand. "I can play." Her voice came out a bit higher than usual. "But, do you mind answering some questions for us?"

"We have a lot." Berri jumped in, punching Theo in the arm hard as they spoke.

Cordelia nodded. "Do you mind?"

Jeannie stood up immediately, backing away from the piano to leave room for Irsa and Cordelia. The rest of the group instinctively stepped back, leaving Irsa wringing her hands next to the ghost. Her shoulders were tense and as she lowered herself onto the stool, Jeannie could see her hands were shaking.

"Any requests?"

The ghost shook her head, smiling still.

The room was quiet as she placed her hands on the keys. Irsa took a shuddering breath in and began to play. The melody was sweet, filling the air with high notes to pair with the arch of the song. Cordelia smiled, closing her eyes as she seemed to sink into the music. Irsa too relaxed, her expression changing and her brows knitting together as she tried to remember how the tune was supposed to go.

By the time the song ended, the air was lighter and when Jeannie released her breath, it was crisp. *Cold.* Cordelia straightened, as if awakening from a dream, as she unfolded her hands.

"Thank you. It has been so long since... Well, I will not dwell on the past." She smiled prettily at the group. "Before I answer any questions, may I ask you one?"

"Of course." Venus jumped in, her voice choking up.

"Why did you come here?"

They exchanged a few looks and nodded to Lilly, who took a deep breath.

"Our school has a spirit that we believe is named Adrienne. We were looking through some photos of a different haunted location and she wrote this address on one of the pictures. On it, she put the word 'Help'. We weren't sure whether or not you needed help, so we came to find out."

Jeannie noticed that Lillybelle had left out how they thought Cordelia might be able to help them, but she said nothing.

Cordelia just smiled. "Yes, I know Adrienne. Sweet girl, but lonely."

Jeannie's eyes went wide, but Acacia took the words out of her mouth. "You know her? How?"

"Well," Cordelia settled on top of the piano, the hem of her dress swinging as she kicked her feet out. "Neither of us are trapped in our 'death spots', as they are called, so we met at the Night Market." Seeing their confusion, she elaborated. "The Night Market is a place in what we call the 'Underworld,' where beings and spirits can meet and do business."

"I wasn't aware ghosts could even leave their death location." Jaimie said. "Wait, is ghosts an offensive term? Should I say spirits? Ghouls?"

Cordelia laughed. "Ghosts or spirits is fine. Ghouls are something different entirely. Now, about your first assumption: we can leave our location if we haven't been trapped in by the shades. By what you assumed, I'm guessing you've met someone who is trapped. Am I correct?"

Lillybelle nodded. "Yes, at the old warehouse on 2nd Street. There are about ten spirits there, but they are trapped by the shadows and can barely move around their own building."

Cordelia frowned. "I didn't even know anyone was there. Poor souls."

"Yeah, some of them are disappearing." Venus said. "Do you have any idea why something like that would happen?"

"Shadows are always a threat." Cordelia said, but Venus shook her head. "Sometimes ghosts just disappear. Especially after fighting with one another."

Jeannie frowned. *What is that supposed to mean?*

"Why is it that some ghosts are trapped by shadows, but others, like you and Adrienne, aren't?" Berri asked, crossing their arms in front of them.

"That has to do with the nature of the shades. I can't explain it to you perfectly, but here is what I know: they love dirt. The reason I am not trapped is because my husband came back and cleaned the house once a year, on the anniversary of my death." She scoffed. "Seems to be the only anniversary he remembered. And after he passed, my son did the same. My grand-daughter as well. This continued for years and years. I even got to meet my great-granddaughter!"

Jeannie bit her lip for a moment, not wanting to ruin the smile on Cordelia's face, but curiosity got the better of her. "You don't have to answer this if you don't want to, but what happened to you? The reports say that you died under myste-rious circumstances."

Cordelia's features didn't move, but something flickered in her eyes. "Ah. I thought you might ask that," she sighed. "It was my husband. We had an argument when he came home for lunch. He was in the garden, I went inside and he threw a brick at my head. I died."

Jeannie could feel her heart speeding up in her chest. Cordelia continued.

"He didn't do it on purpose-kill me, I mean-but he covered it up anyway. He threw the brick away into the woods and got rid of everything that proved he did it. It helped that his best friend was an officer. But he felt guilty. So I decided to get back at him. I was going to haunt his dreams for the rest of his life."

Jeannie swallowed hard. "Oh."

"He couldn't take it after twenty years of my torment and so when he came to clean the house on the twentieth anniversary of my death, he stabbed himself."

Theo blew air out of their mouth, eyes wide and firmly staring at a spot on the ground.

"I felt a bit guilty," Cordelia said, biting her thumb. "So, to put him out of his misery, I consumed his life force."

"I'm sorry?" Berri sputtered. "You what?"

Cordelia sighed. "I'm not the best at explaining these things, but I know someone who is! There is a woman at the Night Market, she goes by the name of Frances, she can tell you more about it. I can give you the address if you'd like?"

Jeannie nodded and Lilly held out one of the documents and a pen, blinking rapidly.

"Do you mind elaborating on energy consuming? I'm a bit curious." Acacia said, rubbing her chin with her fingers.

"Well," she started. "I consumed his energy, letting him die quicker. Ghosts don't exactly eat, but we can consume energy from living or dying things to recover energy faster. Once he died, I forgave him for killing me and his spirit moved on peacefully."

"Oh," Jeannie said, relief washing over her. "Do you need help moving on?"

Cordelia smiled at them and pushed off of the piano.

"A ghost does not need to move on to be happy. We can be happy simply existing, as long as we are safe from the shades." She handed the paper back to Lilly. "You should talk to Frances, she can answer your questions better than I can. Tell her I sent you."

Lillybelle nodded, eyes glued to the paper.

"How will we get in?" Theo asked. "You know, if it's for beings like you?"

"You have all been touched by the Underworld." Her gaze hovered over Jeannie. "Some of you more than others."

"Okay." Venus said. "Well, thank you for your help. Is there anything we can do for you while we're there?"

"Yes, actually!" She said, clapping her hands together. "Do you mind getting me a pack of cigarettes?"

"Um, none of us are old enough to buy cigarettes." Theo said, rubbing the back of their neck. "Sorry."

"No, no," She laughed. "Ghost cigarettes. Anyone is old enough to buy those because only ghosts can smoke them. Don't buy them from Tommy, though. He sells trick cigarettes!"

Jeannie nodded. "Thank you, Mrs. Gornelle. You've helped us a lot."

"It's actually Ms. Gornelle, although my maiden name is Mills." She winked. "'Til death do us part' and all that. Stay safe and come back to visit me!"

As the rest of the group said their goodbyes, Jeannie stepped outside. The air was crisp and the wind was blowing through the rattling branches.

We're one step closer to figuring this out, she thought to herself, sucking in the fresh air. *To the Night Market!*

26

Venus

This can't be it.

Venus had parked her car and gotten out before even getting a proper look at the building, but only after checking to make sure her gps was accurate. When she did, she double checked the directions that Lilly had texted the group chat. She glanced at the street signs and sighed. This was the place.

A dingy brick building stared down at her, the aging brick standing tall on the outskirts of downtown Springview Falls, similarly dingy brick buildings lining the streets on either side. The street lamps had turned on automatically, even though the sun had only started setting a couple minutes ago. Venus shot a glance at her phone to check the time. It was only 6:30. She had already texted her mom, her dad, and Kristina in a group chat called *'Guardians of the Planet'* to ask if she could sleep over at Theo's. All three of them had said yes.

The store out front had large glass windows and showed off the inside of a pretty boutique. An equally pretty name was emblazoned in messy cursive on the sign that hung above the front door. Above the shop were curtained windows, most likely containing an apartment or studio. There was a 'for lease' sign in the second window. *Oh, gentrification, how we love you so.*

Jutting out from the wall directly in front of her was a glowing neon sign, one she had never seen before in the sixteen years she had been living there. The sign lit up one purple letter at a time before flashing the entire word and restarting: *Hades.*

The sign blinked the letters over and over. A large blinking arrow curved beneath it, pointed down a set of brick stairs in the side street that descended into darkness next to the building. Jaimie and Jeannie stood next to her, Jeannie rubbing her knuckles nervously while Jaimie tapped on his phone. A buzzing in her back pocket told her that he was messaging the group chat.

"I mean, I've walked down this street every week for over a decade. How have I never seen this sign?" Jaimie asked, crossing his arms as he slid his phone in his back pocket. *Finally someone said it.*

Jeannie shrugged. "Maybe we haven't been able to see it because weren't looking."

Venus sighed. *Maybe.* Theo's car arrived within two minutes, but in the two minutes before they arrived, Venus had plans.

She kicked Jeannie's shoe. Lightly, but enough to get her attention. Jeannie looked up at her, confused at first, but that melted into a smile when she met her gaze. *She has beautiful eyes.* Jeannie kicked her back and Venus returned the favor. After a kick, there would be a beat of stillness before a tap would be returned on her converse. This continued until Jeannie kicked her in the shin and they broke down laughing. The ache in her leg couldn't help but make Venus smile.

Since this started, Jeannie hasn't seemed like herself. I hope we can fix this and she can come back to us.

Theo's car pulled up and the rest of the entourage piled out, each of them doing the same double take that Venus did when she first arrived. Berri whistled and crossed their arms behind their head.

"So, do we just go in?"

Venus nodded. "What took you guys so long?"

Theo rolled his neck and sighed. "We had to grab some stuff from people's houses since we confirmed the sleepover."

"It's a lot easier to attend something called the 'Night Market' when your parents are okay with you being somewhere else for the night." Acacia said, gesturing towards the car. "Though, when my mom asked if we were going to be doing any 'fun sleepover activities,' I did not tell her this."

"Yeah, I wanted to make sure we were all set with our stuff." Lilly nodded. "Did it not take you guys as long to stop?"

Venus shook her head, shooting a look at her car. "Jaimie took the longest, convincing his mom and his siblings that he had everything and that he didn't need anymore food for the road."

He smiled sheepishly. "By the way, anyone want some empanadas? Or some bunuelos?" He laughed. "You know my dad, can't let me leave the house without feeding the whole group." Jaimie glanced at Theo. "My parents wanted to make sure that we didn't drain your house of food with our 'teenage appetite.'"

Theo just smiled. "Jaimie, from one immigrant family to another, I think we'll be fine."

Venus smiled to herself, knowing that her grandmother was the exact same way. Irsa and Berri both nodded along. Every time the three of them talked about their families, it felt as if they had the same grandparents.

'Are you eating enough?' 'Are you dating anyone?' 'Have you found a good Mexican/Egyptian/Chinese boy?' 'Why can't you speak better Spanish/Arabic/Cantonese? 'Why don't you visit more?' 'Are you going to become a doctor or a lawyer or join the family business?' She shuddered. *I can't even imagine what it*

must be like for Theo or Jaimie, having a culturally mixed house-hold with twice as much cultural obligation.

"I guess we should go in then, right?" Berri pushed off the car they were leaning on and crossed their arms tightly across their chest. "Like, do we need a game plan, or what?"

Venus shot another look at the slowly flashing neon sign and the dark staircase behind it.

"We won't know until we go in, will we?"

Venus stepped forward, letting the group fall behind her as she approached the steps. There was a handrail on the brick wall, which she wouldn't usually use, but having experienced the stairs in the warehouse and having heard Berri's horror story, she opted to grab it. The metal was cold against her palm, some parts of it sticky. The stairs themselves were a creaking black metal, as if they had been put in as a second thought to the basement shop.

As she hit the landing at the bottom, a sign stared at her from the brick wall. It was etched metal, whatever paint once there, scratched off. *Welcome, Orpheus.*

The door to get in was crimson, chimes ringing through the air as Venus pushed the brass handle and stepped inside. It was small, like the lobby of a hole-in-the-wall psychic shop. Incense was burning in a holder to the left, a shelf holding various gumball and temporary tattoo quarter machines. A double doorway sat directly across from the front door, hidden by tattered violet curtains covered in golden tassels. Immediately to her right was a wooden reception desk, and sitting behind it, a tired teenage receptionist.

She had short, spiky brown hair that curled around her variety of brightly colored ear piercings, neat black eyebrows, a thin scar on her lip, and, when she looked up at Venus from her phone, it was clear that she had a septum piercing. She glanced up at them through thick lower lashes, heavy eyeliner making her brilliantly green eyes pop against her golden brown skin. She was wearing a long sleeve black sweater under a wine red crop top. The name tag that sat on her chest read 'Erina.'

Erina looked the group over, setting her polaroid phone case down on the reception desk.

"You're new," she said, tilting her head to the side before giving them a once over.

"How did you know that?" Lilly asked, her voice coming out tighter than usual. Venus shot her a glance and she looked flushed.

"I'm a psychic," Erina said, rolling her eyes before smiling at them. "You need to be touched by the Underworld to even see that this place exists, let alone come down the stairs, and you all look 100% unsure about what to do."

Venus nodded. *Of course,* she thought. *It must be easy to spot outsiders or 'newbies.'* Erina narrowed her eyes at Jeannie and held her hands out. They were covered in multicolored, chunky rings and bracelets. One ring had an evil-eye set into it.

"It's plain as night that all of you were introduced to this fairly recently, but some of you have definitely dipped your toes in a little deeper than the others," she beckoned to Jeannie and, unsure of what to do, Jeannie gave her hands to her. "Fascinating," she said, almost under her breath as she ran her fingers over the stains in Jeannie's skin.

Then, to the rest of them: "You all are in a very particular situation. Shadows and ghosts for your first time? That must be rough."

She released Jeannie's hands. "I'd be careful in there; not many people are going to be so willing to touch your hands in that condition."

Venus watched as Jeannie's features contorted, confusion and fear flitting across her face. A deep rage bubbled somewhere inside of Venus, but she pushed it down. *She means well,* she reassured herself. *It's a warning, not a threat.*

"How were you touched by the Underworld?" Irsa asked, putting a hand on Jeannie's arm, almost protectively.

Erina's eyes wrinkled as she smiled at them, mouth closed. She leaned forward, as if telling them a secret, and as she did, Venus noticed a pointed tattoo on her collar, peeking out of her sweater.

"My dad's a witch."

Venus sucked in a breath, her mind reeling. The silence that followed showed that she wasn't the only one not expecting those words to exit her mouth.

"Witches are real?" Lilly asked, her voice lifting.

Erina nodded. "Yep. And so are a bunch of other beings that your parents probably told you aren't real when you were a kid."

Before Venus could ask about what she meant, Berri jumped in. "What's with the sign outside?"

Erina frowned and leaned to the side, trying to catch a glimpse of it out the window.

"Hmm? Oh! You mean 'Welcome, Orpheus'?" Berri nodded and Erina sighed. "Well, it's a metaphor. Anyone who enters here is called 'Orpheus' because all of you are entering the Underworld, driven by your need for... something. Knowledge, candles, cake, conversation-whatever it is that you need. Orpheus came for love. *You* are here for the Night Market, but this is one of the many entrances into the Underworld. This is the Hades entrance."

Venus shook her head, trying to wrap her mind around what was being said. "What even is the Underworld?"

Erina raised her hands in front of her, defensively. "That," she laughed. "Is above my paygrade."

Venus sighed.

"Thanks for the help, Erina." Theo said, sticking a dollar in the paint-splattered tip jar that had seemingly appeared out of nowhere.

Erina nodded, somewhat hesitant. "Anytime, folks."

Venus smiled at her, before turning towards the ominous violet curtains.

"Orpheus is also a warning." Erina called out, making Venus turn to her for just a moment. "Don't look back."

Venus's heart beat a bit harder in her chest as she turned away from Erina this time. *What does she mean by that?*

The floorboards creaked as she crossed the lobby, reaching out her hands to push aside the curtains. The fabric was thick, layers and layers of varying shades creating an ombre the further she pushed in. From the violet burlap to a lilac wool in three or four layers, the wool shifting to orchid linens as she stepped deeper into the wall of colors. Between each shade and texture of purple was a layer of the same texture, in bright white. Her hands stayed outstretched in front of her, parting the silk periwinkles and the tulle wisteria to reveal a sea of baby blue sheer. The layers didn't stop and began to close in behind her, the thick pressure making it harder and harder to breathe until-

A hand landed on her shoulder and she jumped, almost turning her head to see who had grabbed her. *Don't turn back* echoed in her head. Instead, she grabbed the hand and pulled it further forward, right next to her face. Theo's brown, ring covered fingers clutched onto hers and she could only pray that the rest of the group was following behind them. Closing her eyes for a brief moment, Venus took a deep breath in, squeezing Theo's fingers between hers.

Her eyes opened for her to reach farther in, pushing past the thick yards of denim and through the cerulean cottons. There was stumbling and shouting from the rest of the group behind her, shoving her away from the Persian blue tweed and navy toned corduroy. Midnight blue fleece hung in layers, each length thicker and darker than the last. As the last of the group filed loudly into the curtain behind her, darkness began to wrap around them, hot and stiff. The curtains obviously went deeper than they appeared, but to encapsulate eight people and still have layers left to go?

As the space seemed to go pitch black as the curtains closed behind the last person, she felt her fingertips push through the last layers of black chiffon, her skin gasping for light the same way she gasped for air. Grabbing tightly onto Theo with her other hand, Venus leapt forward, breaking free from the fabric embrace.

The hallway she emerged into was dark and, in the moment her eyes took to adjust, the rest of the group burst from the curtain. Some were sweating, panting, hair and clothing askew. Venus smiled at her friends and turned her eyes on the room before her.

The walls and ceiling were washed in a deep blue and black ombre, colors sinking and rising like violent ocean waves in a slow-motion storm. White and silver lights and rhinestones were scattered across the hall, making it glitter like the night sky. The thick carpet was a deep purple, thin golden designs carved into the darkness of the room. Venus turned, jaw dropped in awe as she took it in. Something shined to her right and turning her attention upon it, she realized it was a plaque. There was one word inscribed in a faint, matte gold.

Styx.

Berri straightened after catching their breath. "Okay, what the hell was that?"

Venus shrugged. Berri scoffed in response.

"It must be part of the illusion?" Lillybelle pondered, more to herself than the group, but Venus heard her regardless.

"Maybe to show darkness before we gain metaphorical light through enlightenment?" Irsa said, readjusting her hijab. They all stared at her for a moment before she shrugged. "Or maybe it's just a weirdly structured curtain-hallway to make sure that people really want to be here? I don't know, I'm just spitballing here."

Jaimie put a hand on Venus's shoulder and made eye contact. "Do we go in?"

He gestured behind her and as she turned, she saw that there was yellow light spilling through a doorway on the left, at the very end of the hallway. She took another deep breath.

"I guess so."

Acacia stretched her arms out in front of her before dramatically gesturing forward. "After you."

Venus rolled her eyes, but stepped forward anyway. She would gladly be the first person through, the first line of defense. *As long as it's me and not them,* she thought to herself, clenching her fist in her opposite palm as her feet carried her closer to the doorway. *In case anything goes wrong, they've already gone through enough. It should always be me first.*

Reaching the doorway, she was relieved to see only a beaded curtain standing between them and the 'Night Market.' Glancing back, she caught the eye of Jeannie. Her hands were tightly clenched and it looked like she was chewing on the inside of her lip. *Something's wrong.*

Venus opened her mouth to say something, but Jeannie shook her head quickly.

'I'm fine,' She mouthed.

Something cold rose into her chest, but she pushed it down. Though it didn't feel right, her mind raced, reminding her not to pry. *If she wanted to tell you, she would.* Venus turned back around and pushed through the beaded curtain.

The space on the other side seemed incomprehensible.

It was a grass street, stretching as far as the eye could see, surrounded on either side by buildings. Whatever roof had been there in the other room either didn't exist or was so high up that it was hidden by smoke and darkness, a dark 'sky' hanging overhead. Market stalls lined the streets, the clamor of a market rising up in her ears. Lanterns were hung outside buildings, candles and string lanterns hung everywhere to give the Night Market an orange glow.

Flavored smoke was rising from every building, roofs made of thatches and of grass, of metal and of stone, of gems and of wood. Aromas of every kind were wafting through the air: animal, sweet, blood, savory, sawdust, flowers, body odor, bread. The air was thick, yet crisp to breathe in, sitting on her skin in a way that was not unsettling but not comforting. Whatever space was not crowded with stalls was crowded with people; or what looked like people.

A pang of fear and confusion ran through her chest. Theo leaned over to her, pressing against her shoulder. "Is it just me, or does this place feel like it was not meant for people like us?"

Venus said nothing. She just turned to the group, squeezing in so as not to bump in to anyone unfamiliar.

"Ok," Jaimie said, scrunching his shoulders together. "What's the plan?"

Venus instinctively turned to Lillybelle. Lilly looked a little paler than usual, her french braids hanging limply over her shoulders as she clutched her papers to her chest. She swallowed, blinked a few times and scanned the market. Shifting the papers to her prosthetic, she pointed over Theo's head.

"I think that could be a good place to start."

Turning, Venus saw that she was pointing to a building a block to the left, with a sign that read 'The Flying F-pan.'

"What makes you say that?" Acacia tilted her head to the side, squinting at the sign. "I'm not doubting you, just curious."

Lilly smiled for a moment and Venus saw her prosthetic twitch. "Just a hunch."

The road, or more accurately, the grass path to the shop was crowded with all sorts of people and creatures, but as they made their way towards the sign that acted as their beacon, they began to meander further from the main pathway. The buildings grew closer together, the space around and overhead becoming tighter as the amount of people became fewer and fewer. Very soon, Venus found herself standing in front of a gray building up a flight of stone steps, large windows shrouded with curtains peering down at them like large eyes. The sign swung in a breeze that she couldn't feel, and as she looked around, she realized that, save their group and a handful of others, the area was empty.

Some people were laughing and chattering in the distance, an earthy smell whisking through the air. Venus inhaled it, holding the scent in her nostrils for as long as she could before ascending the stone steps. The door handle was made of wood and pressed firmly into her palm as she pushed the door open, chimes jangling softly as she stepped inside.

It was a shop, a dark wood floor holding up a dimly lit room, various corners and wooden beams draped in curtains and beads. A crystal chandelier hung in the center, towering shelves and display tables filling the cluttered space. A check out desk sat to the left of the door, an ancient looking cash register sinking on to the wood counter top like a rusty anchor at the bottom of the ocean. As she stepped further into the room, she saw skulls from different animals, lined up on the wall by size. Candles, sticks, feathers, totems, flasks, and crystals covered every surface, each with an affixed label and price tag.

Lilly stepped ahead of Venus, turning in wonder at the expansive shop, eyes wide. Venus couldn't help but smile. Jaimie bent over one of the tables, looking at a selection of what seemed to be jars of slime. Acacia laughed and pointed at a sign behind the cash register. It read *Frances is Out, Be Back Soon*.

"Okay, Lilly, how did you know this would be the place?"

Lillybelle smiled. "It's kinda silly, but I think the sign is a pun. It says Flying F-pan, so like frying pan, but flying, because ghosts can fly? Also, F-pan is a play on the name Fran, short for Frances."

"That's pretty smart, Lilly." Berri said, punching her shoulder.

She just smiled and looked around the shop.

"What even is this stuff?" Jaimie asked, picking up a small jar of goopy green stuff.

"It's ectoplasmic essence." A voice said.

Jaimie stumbled back from the table as someone stepped out from behind a shelf. As the jar went flying out of his hands, there was a clamor of noise above their heads and a large bird swooped overhead, forcing them to duck as it caught the little jar in its talons. It cut through the air, over their heads again, before landing on the shoulder of the new person. Without anyone making a sound, the bird opened its talon and dropped the bottle in the person's weathered palm.

"And you, Lilly, was it? You're very clever. That is indeed why I named my shop this, except for one part. The pun does not reference spirits. It references witches." The middle-aged woman smiled, flashing glittering white teeth. "Because I'm a witch, not a ghost."

The witch was wearing a long, tattered brown coat over a thick green apron, layered under several other aprons, each with bulging pockets, long white sleeves peeking from under the coat. On one hand, was a heavy duty falconry glove, and on the other was a wooden bracelet with glittery accents and acorns dangling from it like charms. Thick, violet goddess braids were wrapped in a bun on top of her head, a glittering green headscarf holding it back from her face. Her black breeches were tucked into tall brown boots, the bottoms of which were covered in leaf litter.

"Dr. Frances Martins. How can I help you?"

27

Jeannie

Jeannie swallowed, but her mouth had gone dry. Each deep breath in filled her lungs with the thick smell of incense and flower petals, probably due to the dried herbs dangling overhead. The witch standing in front of them looked comfortable, as if she already knew everything about all of them. Shaking her head at the thought, she stepped forward.

"Witches are actually real?"

Dr. Frances Martins eyes darted to Jeannie, the emerald green and glittering violet orbs piercing her soul as the witch's features broke into a dry smile. "Yes. And many more, too."

"What else all exists?" Lilly asked, having pulled out a notebook at some point in the silence.

Dr. Martins rolled her shoulders and the bird of prey shifted its talons, its feathers shimmering in the low light. "It would be easier to say what doesn't exist on this plane."

"Okay, what doesn't exist?" Lilly asked, her pen hovering over the page, unfazed.

Dr. Martins just laughed and clicked her tongue. The bird

launched itself from her wrist and disappeared into the rafters of the shop.

"What can I do for you bunch?" Dr. Martins asked, crossing through the group and behind the cashier's counter and flipping the sign to say *The Doctor Is In.*

Jeannie shot a glance at Venus, who had untied her hair and let it fall thickly around her shoulders.

"Well," Venus said, following the witch to the front of the store, Jeannie trailing behind. "Cordelia said that you could tell us more about this world than she could. We wanted to know if you would."

Dr. Frances shrugged, as if she was unfazed by their acquaintance with Ms. Gornelle. "Sure, what do you want to know?"

As Jeannie stepped forward, a burst of hot air rushed across her back, her skin crawling as the skin on her arms constricted. A sharp pain ran through Jeannie's arms and she looked down at her forearms, but nothing was there. She shifted them in front of her, squinting at her hands. The light wasn't reflecting the same way it was off of Venus's skin, or Acacia's skin, or Theo's skin. It wasn't even reflecting, the ink under her flesh absorbing all of the light.

What is happening to me?

She swallowed the taste of bitter bile that had risen in the back of her throat, eyes darting around the shop room to see if anyone had noticed. Venus was looking over at her out of the corner of her eyes, mouth open as if she was about to say something. Before anything else could happen, Lilly stepped up to the counter, face set in a familiar determination.

"Why is this place called the Underworld?"

Dr. Frances let out a sigh as she pulled up a stool and pushed herself onto it. "You really jump straight into the big questions, don't you?" The witch started to pull herbs and plants from her myriad of pockets. "Well, this is called the

Underworld because we are an entire world that operates, not separately, but alongside the human world. We aren't two different worlds, we just don't work on quite the same planes."

"But, isn't the Underworld in reference to, like, the Greek mythological afterlife?" Lilly asked, her dark brows furrowing. Seeing her react so familiarly squeezed Jeannie's heart and she couldn't help but smile, even as her skin twisted painfully.

"Yes, but no," Frances said, leaning forward onto the wooden counter with a twinge of exasperation. "The Greek afterlife is referred to as the Underworld, which this is not, so I understand the confusion. None of us know much about the actual afterlife, not even the ghosts or those who claim to know. We just call it the Underworld because most of us in the Underworld are considered 'others' to humans. They call us unnatural or a fantasy, and so we claim the mantle of the Underworld, because they understand that just as much as they understand us."

Jeannie kept her gaze on Frances as she spoke, watching the lines around her eyes tighten the more she talked about humans. As if it pained her.

"I have a question, if you don't mind my asking," Acacia said, leaning against one of the decorated wooden pillars. After a nod of confirmation from Frances, she continued. "How do you know Ms. Gornelle?"

Dr. Martins' lips twitched to a smile. "I gather my materials from all over. A few years back, I was picking moss from a graveyard and she happened to be lingering around her son's headstone. She likes chatting and smoking, so I showed her around the market. We've been good friends since."

"Why was Ms. Cordelia bleeding?" Theo stepped forward, concern painting his features.

As Theo stepped forward, Jeannie felt her attention tugging to the left as another flash of heat coursed through her veins and her eyes wandered to the window that faced the street. The grass of the street was longer than grass normally was, but what really caught her eye was the color. At a glance, it seemed to be a soft green, but the longer she focused, the more she noticed. Each blade glittered in the lantern light, some patches with a shimmering gold tip, others with sleek blue edges. Some of it was round clover, the green fading into a soft pink each time someone stepped over it. A breeze rustled the turf, swishing it in patterns she had only ever seen embroidered.

"Well," she could hear Frances start, but it was almost muffled in her mind, eyes glued to the grass through the warped window glass. "She bled to death due to the blunt force trauma, so the blood on her head is from her death."

Jeannie's mind was filling with the patterns of the grass in an attempt to distract from the pain, when someone stepped in front of the window. Their hair was a shimmering gold color and as they bent under the paper lantern string to light a translucent cigarette, pointed blue ears stuck out from their patchy, velvet hat. The smoke rose up in tiny blue rivulets, and, quickly, they raised a jar up to catch the swirling indigo smoke in the glass, corking it and holding it up to the light.

"But not all ghosts look the way they did when they died. Fiadh and Lori and the others definitely didn't. Why is that?" Theo said, a wooden shelf creaking as they probably leaned on it.

The deep blue mist wriggled in the jar, almost as if it was squirming to get out. It shook violently, smacking against the sides of the glass. The person clutched the cigarette in their teeth and rattled the jar, seemingly subduing the shadowy smoke. They had turned towards the window and, catching sight of their face, Jeannie took an inadvertent step back.

"You've met other ghosts?"

The face in the window was almost a skull, skin shrunken against the bones. And their eyes were gone. All that stared at Jeannie were black chasms, too deep and dark to show the caverns of skin or bone that should have been there. The skull grinned at her and she could feel her heart beating against her throat.

"There's a warehouse," Jeannie could hear herself saying, eyes still transfixed on the face. "It was abandoned a while back due to a fire and there are the ghosts of the girls who were killed still there."

"What are you looking at?" Venus's voice came from behind her, loud enough to break her away from the window and Jeannie turned to look her in the eye.

Concern was creeping over her features as Jeannie took an inadvertent step towards her. Venus glanced over Jeannie's shoulder and Jeannie turned to follow her gaze. The person with the smoke had disappeared, taking their haunting face with them.

"Nothing."

"I had heard that there were spirits still there," Frances said, wiping down the counter with her gloved hand. "No one has been able to reach them to prove it because of the shadows around the building."

"We're the first?" Berri asked, crossing their arms as their brows furrowed. They didn't look pleased.

"I'm not sure whether I should be impressed or worried." The witch said, confirming Berri's expression. "About your original question, they typically choose not to look like their deaths if it was especially traumatic.

"Such as burning to death in a crowded elevator?" Lilly asked, cradling her prosthetic and her papers to her chest.

"Yes."

"Why aren't the shadows inside Ms. Cordelia's house evil?" Jeannie asked, eyes hovering over the doctor. "She said that the nature of her shades and the fact that they were clean had something to do with it, but she didn't explain."

Dr. Frances Martins said nothing for a moment, simply

looking at Jeannie. When a minute-long eternity had passed, she spoke. "I was waiting for *you* to ask that question." She smiled. "Shadows are a delicate subject around Underworld folk because they are one of our biggest threats, especially to ghosts and other creatures susceptible to the shades, but only under certain circumstances. I call it the 'corruption' of darkness."

Jeannie crossed towards Dr. Martins, situating herself on the other side of Venus and against a shelf opposite of Theo as the witch continued.

"Shadows start out as just that, shadows. But in a place with a large part in the circle of life, such as a place where many people have died or a hospital maternity ward, energy spills out into shadows. These shadows personify, becoming creatures that can move through darkness and function as animals, on a basic level. The corruption comes with dirt, or any build up of filth. For example, a maternity ward will have many shadows that are typically good and helpful or just don't do much because it stays clean."

Lilly's pencil was scratching away again as Irsa nodded, as if this made sense to her.

"An abandoned building, however, will gain lots and lots of grime over years and decades and after wallowing in muck and dirt for so long, these shadows become starved. The mix of filth and constant darkness starves and corrupts these shadows. They congregate, become aggressive, hungry, feral. They will eat anything and everything they can. They will even possess or embody the dying of inanimate things to better trap what they can. Once they do that, humans and many creatures are at risk, so it must never get to that point."

"That must've been what happened to the forest outside her house." Acacia said, glancing towards Lilly, who shuddered. "The forest felt possessed and there were rotting animals trapped in the thorns."

Dr. Frances nodded. "That section of the forest has been wholly claimed. I would suggest not going there but to visit Cordelia. It's dangerous, even for humans."

The pain sparked again and Jeannie watched as her skin constricted, something almost writhing underneath. A choked breath escaped her lips as she froze. It felt as if something had wrapped around her arms and tightened, like a corset inside her skin. She looked down at her hands and felt her chest constrict as the dark stains seemed to writhe under the surface. Quickly, she shoved her hands into the pockets of her brown plaid pinafore, tugging the sleeves of her sweater farther over her hands.

"Why do the shadows need to eat?" She asked, voice coming out higher than she intended as she winced. Venus gave her a look, but she shook her head.

A screech rang out and a flutter of wings filled the air. The large bird swooped over her head and dropped something that didn't register in Jeannie's mind until it was splashing down on top of her. She jumped as the cold water hit her skin, most of it sinking into her sweater. Venus swore and Theo rushed forward, offering a dish towel they had pulled from some pocket somewhere.

"Sorry about that," Dr. Frances said, the bird landing on her shoulder. "You looked like you were in pain."

Jeannie froze as Theo patted her sweater and forearms. The pain had stopped.

"How did you know that would work?" Jeannie asked, staring at the now empty water bottle on the floor.

"Shadows hate the stuff."

"What was that?" Lilly asked, eyes wide and pencil at the ready. "Moon water, Venus water, holy water?"

"Tap." Frances smiled at them. "Not the first time water has worked to make it back off?"

"No, not the first time." Jaimie said.

"Shadows need to eat because the dirt drains their energy. Simply existing drains their energy, just like with any of us. But all of that anger, spite, aggression, it drains them faster, their hunger becoming more acute. Ever been in a filthy place for a long time and gotten irritable? It's the same for them."

"Do ghosts need to eat?" Acacia asked, flipping the loose sleeve of her plaid shirt between her fingers.

Frances nodded. "Yes, they are a lot like shadows. They too need to gain energy."

"That's what Cordelia was saying, but she said you could explain it better than she could." Theodora said, rubbing Jeannie's hands. *Theo always has warm palms.*

"Well, I have spent many, many years researching things of this world. You could almost say it was a family tradition. All these books you see around you?" She gestured to the many shelves. "They are the result of generations of witches researching, doing rituals, experiments, writing papers, casting spells, doing many, many things to learn the truth about our worlds. And we have only begun to scratch the surface!"

"Generations of witches? Is magic like, a genetic thing?" Theo asked.

"Yes and no. I am a woman of science by trade, woman of magic by blood."

"Science?" Berri perked up. "What kind of science?"

Dr. Martin smiled at them, her eyes twinkling and face softening as she spoke. "I have a PhD in biomedical engineering, I just do this on the side."

"How can you do magic and science? Aren't they contradictory?" Theo asked, glancing between Berri and Dr. Frances.

"Magic is simply science that can't be explained to a majority of the world yet."

Irsa nodded knowingly as Lilly's continued her notes on another page. Berri's eyes were wide in awe and they looked as if they were going to ask her more when Acacia cut in, smiling at Berri.

"Sorry to interrupt, but why do ghosts need to eat?"

"Right," Dr. Frances sighed, still smiling. "Ghosts are like shadows in that simply existing is very draining and so they need to absorb life from plants and animals, dead or alive, similar to how we eat food. If they don't eat, they won't fade, but they won't be able to use any of those famous ghosty gifts, like possession of objects and invisibility. Like how witches need energy sources for spells, such as dead animals, offerings, or other such power sources. Everything needs energy."

"So it doesn't get any easier after we die?" Jaimie asked, seemingly tired at the thought.

"Not as a ghost, no." Frances chuckled. "But in the afterlife, who knows! Ghosts typically go the 'vegan' route, only absorbing energy from deceased plants and animals, sometimes old food scraps or specific sacrifices to allow them to eat our food. Dia de los muertos, for example, like a buffet. But, when starved, they can and will absorb it from living things. The larger the animal or plant, the more energy they gain. Hell, they can even absorb other ghosts!"

Jeannie frowned. "Other ghosts? What would happen if a ghost absorbed another ghost? Would it be obvious?" Jeannie could feel the eyes of her friends on her, but she kept her gaze on Dr. Frances.

"I mean, no, probably not. When a corrupted shadow absorbs something, it doesn't just take its life force or energy, it consumes it, often torturing it before it is destroyed. A piece of that life force, however, will always remain within the shadow. A ghost will only consume the life force, leaving the shell of the plant or animal to wither if dead, to weaken if still alive. This is because there is something physical tying it to the material world. If a ghost consumes another ghost, however, the consumed ghost simply ceases to exist."

All of the air in the room seemed to go still as Jeannie stiffened, heartbeat growing loud in her ears. *I feel like throwing up.*

"Why would a ghost want to consume another ghost?" Venus asked, shifting closer to Jeannie, voice dry.

"Desperation, mostly. When trapped in by shadows, it's a bit difficult to find anything to eat, so they might turn to cannibalism as a last resort. However, some ghosts crave power. By consuming a life force similar to their own, they become more powerful."

"Powerful enough to, say, overpower any shadows that may be trapping them in?" Lilly asked, meeting Jeannie's gaze.

Dr. Frances eyebrows furrowed together. "In theory. But it would take a lot of ghost cannibalism to become that powerful, depending on the strength of the shadows."

The group went silent, everyone looking at one another. Jeannie shuddered, glancing from Venus to Dr. Frances. "Do you mind if we look around for a bit?"

The witch shrugged. "Go crazy."

28

Jeannie

Jeannie wandered in between a set of bookshelves, hands trailing along the leather wrapped covers, eyes absently scanning the labels under each book. Lillybelle and Acacia had also immediately set off searching through the shelves, bookworms as they are, but Theo and Venus stayed by Dr. Frances, still having some questions weighing on their minds.

"So, is the Night Market only open at night?" She could hear Theo ask.

Dr. Martins chuckled as Jeannie looked up at the top of the shelf, checking to see if there was a sorting system of any sort. "Ironically, no. It's only called that because most of us inhabitants of the Underworld get called 'creatures of the night.' There are a good deal of people who can only come at night, due to sunlight and various human issues, so the biggest business hours are after the sun has set. You arrived at our rush-hour."

Theo and Venus could be heard responding in mumbles, but Jeannie focused on the words scratched on plaques, each barely visible behind various hanging herbs. To her left, the plaque read 'Otherworlds and Overworlds', something Jeannie had a feeling didn't quite apply to her interests. She turned to face the other shelf.

"Can ghosts eat human food?" Venus asked in the distance.

The plaque on top of this shelf, half obscured by a large hanging piece of what looked like a branch of mustard leaf, read *Possessions: Objects, Ghosts, and More!*

Dr. Martins laughed. "Definitely not. They can consume the spirit of the food, though. Like I said, Dia de los Muertos is the best night of the year for them."

Jeannie's heart pounded in her chest as she found herself searching the shelves of *Possessions*, not knowing what she was looking for. Over the tops of the spines, she could see Lilly searching just as fervently, moving surprisingly quickly.

"So, no junk food for ghosts?"

Her finger stung as it hit a green spine, the leather almost scaly as her blackened fingers wrapped around the edge subconsciously. A burning sensation ran up her fingers, become more severe the longer it went on, crawling all the way up to her elbows. A fluttering next to her made her spin to her left, where she saw Dr. Martins bird, staring at her.

"No, no junk food for ghosts. Witches do love junk food though, so if you're offering-"

A patter of laughter rang out, but it was dim against the ringing that accompanied the burning under Jeannie's skin. Taking a step towards the bird, she saw it was standing next to a cauldron full of water, crisp and clear. A small wooden sign above it read: *For hand washing before handling spell compo-nents.* Without a second though, she plunged her arms into the water.

Instantly, the pain and the ringing dissipated, but there was a loud hiss behind her. She turned to see who had made the sound, but there was no one behind her. The birds black eyes watched her, and, seeming to be pleased, began to pull at its feathers. The hiss rang out again and her eyes flew to the green, scale-covered spine that she had left unattended.

"You said earlier that people had heard that the warehouse was haunted, but no one had been successful in finding out." Theo continued with their line of questioning, voice quieter at a distance. "What did you mean by that?"

Jeannie felt for the worn leather tag that hung off of the book, squinting down at it. The title was one word. *Possession.*

"Well," Dr. Martins started, setting something loudly down on the counter and making Jeannie jump, even though she was on the other side of the shop. "We witches tend to want to know what is happening in our circles. We go to different locations, some psychics or mediums reach out, we try to find out who is there. It's like a system."

The book was heavy in Jeannie's hand and without much thought, she unhooked the cord that bound it and began to flip through the pages. An image on one of the pages made her stop cold, eyes going wide as her blackened skin twitched.

"Are you saying witches are like some kind of organized society of magical people?" Theo asked, flabbergasted tone carrying across the shop.

It was a drawing, a sketch almost, of a man curled up in a ball. His hands were stretched out towards a black scribble, almost as if the artist had spilled their ink on the page. The man's arms and legs had black ooze shooting up them, like forking branches. The page burned in her hands, and she almost dropped the book. *He looks just like me.* The man in the page had been drawn screaming.

"A bit. We have our own local rules, our own covens, our own national and international conventions. It's like anything, you have to reach out to be connected. Some witches freelance, some become corporations. It's a spectrum of magic ingenuity."

Something had been scrawled under the image in messy, but curling font, a paragraph of details that made Jeannie's blood run cold. In the distance, she could hear Venus ask how people get involved in these societies, but her mind drowned out the Doctor's response. The haunting passage read as follows:

'*Possessions of this kind are very dangerous, and if left unchecked, can turn fatal. Shade and corruption possessions are caused by the physical or mental connection of something/someone to a powerful shade. The darkness will consume the flesh, eating into the bone until it permanently stains. It is a marking of corrupt possession.*

'*This victim, drawn above, described the pain of the markings as hot, searing, and twisting. As if he was being repeatedly branded and tortured by flesh he could no longer control.*'

Jeannie dropped the book, hands shaking as she stared down at the skin that plagued her. *No. It can't happen like this, it can't...* Heart pounding in her ears, she picked the book back up and flipped to the index, eyes quickly scanning the alphabetized list. Her heart beat a sigh of relief when she found it. *Cures.*

"If one is involved in a coven, they can easily be involved in the organizing departments of governmental witchcraft." Dr. Martins voice came back into range. "Many young witches reach their potential through coven learning, but it is equally possible and achievable to do it individually. Each route has its pros and cons, as does anything."

"Can anyone become a witch?" Venus asked.

Jeannie quickly thumbed to the page of the book that was attached to her desired heading and scanned the list of cures. At the top of the list, was it's own index.

'*The type of cure is wholly dependent on the type of possession. With so many types of possession, there are just as many cures or methods of preventing progression.*'

She scanned the list, eyes flicking from symptoms to cures quickly, anxiety mounting as, the farther she went down the list, the less she saw about her symptoms. Frustration growing, she flipped back to the picture and her eyes went to the bottom of the page. There was one simple sentence.

'*Cursed possessions have no cure.*'

It felt as if she had been punched in the stomach. Tears stung her eyes and she couldn't breathe, her lungs pressing against her ribs like overinflated balloons. She stared down at her fingers, knuckles graying as the corrupted digits clutched the page. *No, please.* A whisper from behind her made her turn, the words unintelligible. *Who said that?*

Through the shelf, she could see Acacia browsing and Lilly-belle frantically flipping through the pages of a heavy tome, eyes wide. Berri and Jaimie were smelling candles to her left while Irsa wandered around, staring at the herbs suspended from the air. Jeannie pressed the end of her sweater sleeve to her eyes, wiping away the hot tears that had formed. None of them seemed to notice her panic. *Good.*

"Anyone can be a witch, with varying degrees of effort." Dr. Martins finally replied, though Jeannie hadn't noticed her silence. "Some take to it easily, due to talent or blood magic. Some struggle and work very hard to accomplish even simple magic, but anyone can become one."

The whisper repeated itself, quietly, but growing louder in her ears. Turning in circles, Jeannie realized no one else could hear it, but it wasn't just in her head. It was coming from another shelf, one tucked farther in the back of the shop.

Learn the truth, *learn the cure,* **learn the truth,** *learn the cure,* the whispers repeated, a familiar voice overlapping as it grew louder. She could almost place it, but not quite. The skin on her hands squeezed, but not painfully. **Learn the truth,** *learn the cure,* the whispers urged again and Jeannie felt herself being led forwards, towards the far shelf.

"Interesting," Venus replied in the distance.

"Interested in joining our ranks?" Frances inquired softly. "There are always covens looking for new members."

The whispers emanated both from her skin and a thick white tome, the book itself wrapped in thin white paper. The tag that hung off of it was delicate under her fingertips. *Demons and Their Corrupt Origins*, it read. Jeannie could feel her heart skip a beat and her mouth went dry. *Demons?* She thought to herself, panic rising in her chest. *This can't be real.*

The book seemed to open in her hands, and without much of her own input, flipped to a page whose title read, *Shades and Demons: How One Begets The Other*. There was one main passage that seemed to jump out at her. Each time she tried to read anything else, the familiar whispering drowned out her thoughts.

'When shades have been corrupted for over a decade, and their hunger has rarely been sated, they adapt; evolve. They subsist off of less, become stronger off of excess. If, after decades of nothing, something large is consumed, these animalistic instincts coalesce into something more tangible, and more sinister. Consciousness develops and the strongest shades merge into one, strong form. This is what many creatures and cultures have called Demons.'

"No," She could hear Venus say. "I was just curious."

'Demons control shadows, as an extension of themselves, yet can let them roam freely if they desire. They can extend to anywhere and have certain abilities, but being darkness incarnate is limiting. Only through connection with a host, a human or other creature with enough sentience to survive possession, can Demons reach their full power, and what they often crave most: freedom.'

"Well, in case you change your mind, take this. It's a flyer for one of the more open-minded covens. They are always happy to teach new members."

The book shut before she could read more, closing and wrapping the cord tightly around itself in her hands. She blinked. *Demons. Is that what this all is?* Shaking her head, she crossed back towards the front of the store, where Venus stood holding a brightly colored flyer next to Theo, who was messing with a small skull. *I need to tell Venus about this.*

"Why is it that abandoned buildings are more likely to be haunted?" Venus asked, pocketing the flyer as she shot a glance at Jeannie, who had stopped just behind her. "I mean, we never hear about these horrific, dangerous hauntings at like, hospitals, even though life and death happens there a lot."

Jeannie opened her mouth, ready to interrupt Venus. But when she tried to speak, she couldn't. *What is happening?* She tried to form the words, but her mouth just froze, vocal chords refusing to make a sound as her throat ached around the words. *Why can't I speak?*

Dr. Martins nodded at Venus, and flashed a smile at her, seemingly finishing her task of sorting her daily forage.

"Abandoned buildings are not more likely to be haunted, they are more likely to be dangerously haunted. Graveyards and hospitals, for example, the final resting places and place of death for many people, yet no dangerous ghosts. Why? Because they are kept very clean. No dirt, no shadows get corrupted. No corrupted shadows, no danger for ghosts. No danger, no fear. No fear, no aggression. It's a cycle. No aggression, no need for abandonment."

Jeannie felt herself nodding as Dr. Martins' gaze settled on the books in her arms. Her eyes flashed for a moment, something unreadable in them before she met Jeannie's gaze. It looked as if she wanted to say something, but as she opened her mouth, Irsa gasped behind her.

"Oh, Berri look!" As they all looked over at her, she seemed to be holding up a brass bell with a trident shaped handle. "You've shown me one of these before, remember?"

Berri lit up and crossed over to her.

"This is a Tao bell! I've always loved seeing the different designs of these, especially in how they're used in temples."

Dr. Martins smiled. "We do get our resources from all over the globe."

Jaimie frowned, crossing behind Berri and Irsa. "So witches don't only use pagan symbolism?"

Dr. Martins laughed. "No, not at all! Specific religion has little to do with witchcraft. Some rely heavily on their religion or their deities to perform, but some don't at all. None of it matters under the wide berth of magic."

"You mean that witches believe that all religions, like Christianity, Tao, and Islam are the same? Or are you saying you think they are all part of a bigger tapestry, like a pantheon?" Irsa asked, frowning.

Dr. Martin laughed and shook her head. "I would answer that complicated question with a similarly complicated answer, but it seems that you all are on your way out." A jingling rang out as her eyes darted to the door, several bills fluttering down onto the counter.

Jeannie turned and saw Lilly dashing down the store steps and around the corner. Theo started out after her, leaning off the stoop to call after her. By the time the rest of them made it to the doorway, Lillybelle had turned around, a guilty look on her face.

"Sorry," she called out, clutching a large tome to her chest. "There's something I need to check, I'll meet you back at the house!"

And without another word, she disappeared down the grassy street.

29

Lilly

As soon as Lillybelle picked up the book, she knew what she had to do. The title, *Communicating with the Unseen,* had called to her and as she struggled to unhook her bike from the back of Theo's car with a book tucked in her waistband, she could feel the leather carved cover pressing into her back like a stamp in her skin. It had been a miracle that she had remembered the way back through the market, pushing through crowds of what weren't people and bursting back through the set of curtains, although they hadn't been as deep as she remembered them to be.

The sky was dark already, orange street lights the only thing lighting the way as she pedaled, damp black hair blown from her face. The wind caught in her trenchcoat, billowing dramatically behind her as she stood on her bike pedals, soaring through the nearly empty streets. Her heart was pounding in her chest, eyes stinging, but she couldn't care less. All that was on her mind was the excerpt she had read in the book.

It had been the first page that she had landed on when randomly flipping through, but she immediately knew this is what she had been looking for. The cool fall air was crisp, moonlight reflecting off of the schools dark windows as she screeched to a stop in the high school staff parking lot, the white brick building staring down at her. The parking lot was completely empty, and the Friday night janitor's van was nowhere to be seen.

Very carefully, Lillybelle lay her lavender bike against the school wall, and clutching the thick leather tome to her chest and her patterned tote to her side, she began her trek around the school. The path was familiar to her, a path her older brothers had taken her many, many times before. *I could do this blindfolded.*

She snuck around the left side of the school, past the second floor chemistry classrooms. In the darkness, she could barely see the mad scientist stickers that had been stuck all over them, which was the only section of the glass that didn't reflect the moonlight.

Lillybelle turned right when she saw the old beech tree, its winding branches shaking with yellowing leaves in the fall breeze. She skirted behind it, staying out of sight of the security cameras. She traced with her free hand the many, many names roughly carved into the bark. Vincent had carved his name into it with his first girlfriend, five years ago. *And then again with his third girlfriend, two years ago.*

As soon as she could see the glass tiles of the beat up old greenhouse in the distance, she knew she was almost there. The northernmost tile on the bottom had two missing screws and two loose screws, and once those were removed, it was easy to squirm through the gap.

The warm air in the greenhouse was thick with dew, a slight smell of decay and pollen. *Nothing has changed since they've left, not even the smell.* The careful steps she took across the tile floor so as not to creak was almost muscle memory by now, only the occasional misstep to avoid footprints in the dirt. Feeling the handle, she knew it wasn't locked; It rattled as it turned, but it was as familiar to her as her brothers' ringtones.

The cool air of the school hallway hit her hard as she stepped out of the humid greenhouse. Moonlight shone through the small glass windows which lined the outer wall, blue shadows painting the empty corners, echoing with the silent chatter of teenagers gone for the weekend.

Her heartbeat was loud in her ears, the stiff air settling under her sweater in an uncomfortable layer of silence. She had never actually been alone in the school, truly alone. Night's like these, Vincent was always on her right, Cyril six steps ahead. In daylight, Venus or Jeannie or Acacia always by her side. Or the empty halls of a school day, but even then she could feel that someone else, staff or student, was in the building. *Just in case.*

But there was no one in these cavernous halls, every step she took ricocheting impossibly loud all around, her breathing too quiet for the long corridors of empty lockers. Taking a deep breath, she pushed the book into her tote and pulled out her phone, flicking the flashlight on to comfort her, but it only cast more shadows.

Where should I do this? Lilly thought to herself, turning and looking down the two hallways that led away from the office. She squeezed her eyes closed and tried to imagine where she would go if she were a ghost. *Here. Out in the open. It's not like anyone could see me as a ghost.*

Tucking her boots under her, she sat with a *fthump* on the ground, crossing her legs as she opened her eyes. The leather bound tome was heavy in her hands, the red dyed words carved into the cover staring up at her, waiting. She placed it on the floor in front of her, and hesitated for a moment, before anxiety got the better of her.

Sighing, she reached into the bag and pulled out a hand mirror her parents had bought for her when she was six, as part of a fairy princess set. It's cheap pink-plastic crystals had fallen out and been lost years ago, but the plastic mirror was still clean and clear. Lilly opened it and set it down next to the book, angling it so she could see down the hallway behind her. It was blurry, but it was enough. She fumbled with her phone for a moment and something glimmered in the corner of her eye. Flipping around to see what it was, she breathed a sigh of relief.

It's just the security camera. At least no one can see me right now.

Having made all of her preparations and stalled as long as she could muster, she lifted the cover of the book. Without any effort, the book opened up to the page that had jumped out at her in the witch's shop.

How to See The Unseen: A spell for hearing the voices of the dead.

Her breath caught in her throat, hand shaking as she held her phone flashlight over the words of the spell, tracing them in her mind as her prosthetic rested on the open page.

'When trying to contact a spirit, you need as many physical representations of the spirit as you can find. If you have any items of theirs or pictures, those will strengthen the bond to the physical plane and to your ability to see and hear this person.'

She searched her bag for a moment and pulled out the notebook that contained all of the entries of Adrienne's activity. She flipped to the back page, where she had taped a yearbook photo of Adrienne, one that had been attached to the article about her disappearance. Lilly had read the article so many times, she had it practically memorized.

"Adrienne Mills, 17, has been declared missing by the Springview Falls Police Department. Adrienne was last seen two days ago, at Springview High School, by the school's janitor, Richard Trabazo, 32.

'Yeah, Adrienne was a good kid, staying late every Tuesday to tutor some trouble-makers in math. A good kid. Last I saw her, she was getting ready to leave after tutoring was over She always

said hi to me. Nice girl, always paid attention to the little guy like me, y'know?'

Her parents say that she has no reason to run away and that she is a 'good girl who always comes home on time'. They reported her missing when she didn't come home from school after her tutoring session. The search for her is ongoing."

In the photo, a girl wearing a white turtleneck and denim overalls smiled at the camera, her pretty blonde hair pulled into two scrunchy space buns. *Mills, Adrienne.* Across the top of the photo, Lilly's own red pen handwriting read *March 12th, 1993.* The day she went missing.

Lillybelle placed the notebook on the ground, next to the book, open to the picture. After checking the mirror and confirming the hallway behind her looked the same, she turned back to the spell book.

'Ensure there is a light source nearby, preferably a candle, and have on you something with which the spirit can sustain itself, such as food or a small sacrifice. These will encourage a spirit to show itself, as light and energy are good for protection and safety.'

Lilly frowned and checked her bag. Her hand closed on a squished plastic wrapper, which she lay next to the photo. *I have my phone flashlight and this probably expired candy bar.* She thought. *That has to count for something, right?*

Her boot creaked loudly as she readjusted and she froze, the volume of her presence sending a chill down her spine. *When did it get colder?* She shook her head and turned her attention back to the spell at hand. One thing to worry about at a time.

'Now recite the following passage out loud three times, inserting the name of your chosen spirit into the appropriate places as you do. Disclaimer: if this spell fails, it means the spirit does not wish for you to see or hear them at this time. Wait a moon cycle and try again.'

"Great," Lillybelle said, voice softly echoing in the school atrium. "If this fails, I have to wait a whole month to try again. I hope for both of our sakes that you want to be found." She took a deep breath, her entire body shaking. "Okay," she said louder, "Here goes."

"Adrienne Mills, answer my call, let me see into the veil. Adrienne Mills, I am your thrall, let me hear into the veil." A soft ringing filled her ears and she could feel a tingling at the tips of her fingers and where her arm met her prosthetic.

"Adrienne Mills, answer my call, let me see into the veil. Adrienne Mills, I am your thrall, let me hear into the veil." The ringing became louder and the tingling turned to stinging. Her eyes began to burn and she closed them, her breath hitching.

"Adrienne Mills, answer my call, let me see into the veil." She was near shouting now. "Adrienne Mills, I am your thrall, let me hear into the veil!"

A blast of wind blew her hair from her face and her ears popped. The stinging sensation stopped and her eyes felt fresh. Slowly, she blinked her eyes open. The book had slammed shut and her phone flashlight was off. Blood was pounding in her ears and her mouth had gone dry. She started to reach for her phone when she caught sight of her hand mirror and froze.

A blonde girl was smiling in the reflection, just over her shoulder.

"Hi, Lillybelle. It's nice to finally meet you."

30

Venus

The page she had snatched from the store was icy cold in her fingers, but Venus didn't care. Just glancing at it had shot a chill down her spine, so she knew it had to be important. *It just has to be.* Standing underneath the 'Flying F-Pan' sign, the flickering lantern light illuminated the scrawls that covered the page, writing jagged, as if it had been hastily written. *I'd feel bad about stealing it if the page hadn't just regenerated in the book, so why do I feel so shitty holding it?*

The hair on her arms was standing on end as she ran her fingertips across the sharp edge of the paper. It was the necklace that had caught her eye; the majority of the page was covered with a drawing of it, a large black stone, roughly hewn and strung on a thin piece of leather. Every part of it looked rough, from the sketch to the writing. Yet gazing at it made her feel uneasy. Called the 'Pendant of Resilience,' it didn't sound like it was something that might seep into her nightmares, but everything about it screamed that it would. She didn't even have to look at the scrawled descriptor to remember what it said.

'*Artifact dates back centuries. Found in the ruins of a*

gravesite. *Said to be a beacon of dark magic, natural and demonic. Powered through the consumption of human souls. Used to concentrate dark energy for destructive purposes. Lost by the National council of witches fifty years ago, usually surface in places of great tragedy.'*

Underneath the description was a black ink drawing, presumably of someone using the pendant. She was floating in the air, pendant glowing and darkness surrounding her. Venus touched a finger to the drawing. It stung like ice.

Venus ran a hand through her hair, having finally undone her braid from stress. *Places of great tragedy? The warehouse definitely qualifies.* She took a deep breath, leaning against the window of the shop she had stolen the page from. Through the glass, she could hear Jeannie and Acacia pay for their books, snippets of conversation. *If whoever's doing this has this pendant, then it would make sense why the shadows are being weird. Plus, it could be her way out.*

Theo was standing across the street with Irsa, buying ghost cigarettes from a guy in a moss ballgown who called himself 'Petera the Great.' He had verified that he was, in fact, not Tommy, and so they felt safe buying the ghost cigarettes from him. *I'll have to show them this later.* As she folded up the stolen page and shoved it in her pocket, she found another paper stuffed into her pocket.

It was the flyer Dr. Martins had given her. It was surprisingly thick, the paper itself oddly coarse. It had large letters across the top, penned in swirling green calligraphy. *'Looking for new coven recruits!'* Read the top of the flyer, the ink glittering in the low light. Across the bottom, *'If interested in joining a group of intelligent, welcoming witches, contact us below!'* Underneath was a myriad of phone numbers, some for recruitment and some for HR and magic satisfaction.

What Venus was really interested in was the giant symbol that shone from the page. It seemed to be a seven pointed star, inside of a large, looming triangle. It was stamped on both sides of the flyer, even when the writing was only on one side. *Must be the covens symbol,* she thought to herself, folding up the flyer and tucking it into her back pocket.

Twisting her loose hair tightly around her finger, Venus glanced through the store window at Jeannie, who was talking to Dr. Martins. She was cradling several large tomes to her chest, her fingers peeking out from the hem of her sweater. The skin looked tight, as if ink had poisoned her blood stream. If she stared hard enough, it seemed to squirm.

A jingling bell pulled her attention away from Jeannie as Jaimie descended the store steps.

"Hey, V! What's up?" His dark eyes glittered warmly in the lantern light as he looked at her, a smile permanently etched on to his tan skin.

"Not much," She said, kicking a clump of clovers with her converse, watching it turn pink as she moved her foot over it. "I just feel kinda uneasy."

Jaimie tilted his head as he looked at her, hands in the pockets of his coffee stained blue jeans, only his paint stained thumbs hanging out.

"What specifically is bothering you? I know all of this is kinda crazy, but I feel like you've adjusted pretty well to all of this weird stuff. What's really getting to you?"

She chewed the inside of her lip before answering. "I think Jeannie and Lilly are hiding something."

He frowned. "What, like, from us?"

"No, not together. I think each of them are hiding something. I think what the shadow did to Jeannie is bothering her more than she is telling us. Every time I ask her about it, she says she's fine, but I know her! She doesn't go silent unless something is really wrong."

Jaimie nodded. "Yeah, I've noticed that too. We shouldn't

pressure her, I don't think. I'm sure she'll tell us when she feels safe enough to."

"I guess."

"What about Lilly, why do you think she's hiding something?" Venus gave him a look, to which he laughed. "Dumb question, sure. I wouldn't worry about Lilly too much, though. This is how she gets when she thinks she has a lead, whether or not she actually does. I think she gets it from her brother."

Venus frowned, searching her memory for the black haired teens she had met way back, when they themselves were high school students. "Which one, Vincent?"

Jaimie shook his head. "No, Cyril. He seems like the calm and collected one, but in reality? He was always silently calculating risks and how far he could go before getting caught. Lilly and I realized that the first time Vincent went to the hospital. Both he and Cyril did the exact same thing, but Cyril hung back and got his timing right, so that when he failed, he didn't break his leg."

Venus laughed, untwirling her hair. "So you're saying Lilly is calculating her risks and should be fine?"

"Yep. That's how she's always been, cards held close to her chest. She knows when she needs help and when she can do things by herself. Sometimes she's wrong, but she learns from her mistakes. Most of the time, anyway." Jaimie smiled. "And that's where we come in."

A warmth spread in Venus's chest, remembering how many times Lilly had given her the support she needed. "Give her that shoulder to lean on?"

"Yep. And sometimes, someone to hold her back."

A second set of jingling made Jaimie and Venus turn to see Jeannie, Acacia, and Berri coming down the stairs, Berri with a small paper bag and Jeannie with an arm full of books.

"So apparently, and I thought this was pretty cool" Acacia said, grinning ear to ear. "even if you remove one of the books from the shelf, she'll never run out of copies because of the way the bookshelves are enchanted. So, when you pull out a book, you hold one copy and another materializes, but if you want to put it back, you simply push it back into the book currently there and they merge! How cool is that!"

Venus smiled at Acacia, who was holding a book herself. It was small and wrapped in cords, which were sealed with wax.

"I got an antique copy of Dracula, with notations from a real vampire!"

"Another for the collection?" Irsa asked, crossing back to them with Theo trailing behind.

Acacia nodded excitedly. Jaimie tried to peek into Berri's bag. "What did you get?"

Berri shook their bag, a jangling and clacking sound muffled. "A couple of crystals, some buttons, a couple other shiny doodads that I thought were cool. Y'know, the usual."

Jaimie nodded gravely, as if this was obvious. Venus glanced over at Jeannie, who had crossed next to her and was staring down at the cover of one of her books. Venus nudged her arm.

"They look kinda heavy, want a hand?"

Jeannie froze for a moment, seemingly hesitating as she looked from her hands to Venus's. Finally, her shoulders fell and she nodded. "Thanks." She handed Venus the books, which weren't very heavy, but Jeannie looked as if a dozen weights had been lifted off of her. "Sorry, I've been kinda out of it."

"It's okay." Venus said, smiling at the freckled ginger she found so pretty. "What did you get?"

Jeannie flinched again, but as she met Venus's eyes her face softened. "A couple of books about ghosts and shadows that I thought might help"

Venus nodded. "Good thinking."

"Alright, is everyone here?" Theo said, tucking his packet of what Venus assumed where ghost cigarettes into a pocket. "Besides Lilly, of course?"

There was a round of 'yep's.

"Alrighty, let's head back home to eat something bad for us and then stay up watching movies to forget that our world views are being shattered! Woo!"

Venus laughed and held out her arm to Jeannie, who after a moment, looped her arm with Venus.

"What do you think Lillybelle is doing?" Jeannie asked.

Venus smiled again, thinking back to what Jaimie had said. "Getting her timing right."

31

Lilly

Lillybelle whipped around to stare at the teenage ghost who had appeared behind her. *I'm never gonna get used to this.*

"Adrienne?"

The ghost grinned. "The one and only!" She said, voice lifting as she floated higher into the air.

"Wow. I can't believe that worked."

Adrienne nodded. "I know right? Usually, a ghost can choose whether or not people can see her, but a spell like that one makes it so that you can see and hear me all the time."

"Is that a violation of your privacy? I'm sorry."

Adrienne just waved her away with her hand, crossing her legs and letting her denim skirt ride up, revealing black underwear. Lilly averted her eyes to her book, her cheeks heating up.

"Don't worry about it, I wouldn't have let you do the spell if I had an issue with it. I mean, I wouldn't have helped you at all if I didn't want your help, but I do."

Lillybelle swallowed. "Sorry, to interrupt, Ms. Mills, but you're kinda flashing me."

Adrienne laughed. "Sorry! See anything you like?" Lilly could feel herself turning redder as Adrienne laughed again and continued in a sing-songy voice: "I'm just messing! You're a minor~"

"Aren't you also a minor?" Lilly asked, glancing back up to see that Adrienne's skirt had been pulled back down.

"After 30 years, I don't think I can claim that title anymore." She said, lounging in the air. "I mean, physically, sure I'm 17. I mean, I'm also dead physically. But mentally? Well, its debated. In theory, because I'm dead, my brain never finished developing and therefore I still have, like, the brain function of a 17 year old. But also, I have 30 years of knowledge and experience, because I'm a ghost. So, it's really a tossup."

"Right." Lilly blinked a couple of times. "Sorry, you just look... different then I imagined," she managed to say.

Adrienne's blonde hair was pulled away from her face with colorful butterfly clips that contrasted with her pearl studs and lace choker. Instead of the overalls Lilly had become accustomed to seeing her in, she was wearing a red flannel shirt and a denim mini skirt, one buckled boot and one white sock adorning her feet.

"What, then the yearbook photo from a year before I died?" Adrienne laughed, and twirled in the air. "Yeah, just a bit. This is what I was wearing when I died!"

"Right." Lillybelle frowned, her voice getting quieter. "You died here."

"Major bummer, right?"

"And they never found your body."

Adrienne nodded, lips pressed together in an expression that wasn't discomfort, but wasn't confusion either. "I wish I could tell you where it was, but I actually don't know. See, when a person dies and becomes a ghost, it actually takes a minute for our non-lives to settle and I wasn't cognizant when my body was hidden. Sorry."

"It's not your fault," Lilly said, partially in disbelief that she was reassuring a ghost that her murder wasn't her fault. "Sorry if this is an uncomfortable question, but, who killed you? Or, were you even killed?"

"Oh, I was, but I don't actually know that either. Terror, blunt force trauma, and death do a number on your memory. I just remember getting chased down the hallway by a blank face and then waking up dead, two days later."

"Wow, that sucks."

Adrienne sank to her level behind the book, forcing Lilly to turn back around. "Yeah, kinda. But that's not why you're here."

Lilly's eyes widened as she stared at Adrienne. "Why are you helping us?"

The ghost's eyes darkened and she settled herself on the ground, folding her hands in her lap. "It doesn't benefit me at all if you help them, so it's hard for me to come up with a reason, but there isn't one. I like to explore. I have the freedom to leave because the janitor, who honestly creeps me out a bit, makes sure the school is clean so there are no good or bad shadows. So when I saw you researching in the library last week, I thought 'what could the girl obsessed with finding me be looking at?' So I saw the different locations and decided to check them out myself."

Lilly watched Adrienne as a myriad of emotions jumped across her face: sadness, guilt. Fear.

"I went to the warehouse that night. And I heard screaming. I couldn't get close to the warehouse because of the shadows, but I heard the screaming of a spirit and then silence. And it brought back this memory. A memory of my death." Adrienne bit her thumb. "I thought it was weird how Cordelia remembers her death and her murderer, and so do other ghosts, but I couldn't. And so I asked Dr. Frances. She said it was because they know where their bodies ended up and they know how they looked when they died, but since I don't know either, I can't remember any of it. But when I heard the screaming of a ghost being..." She stood up and Lilly stood too. "It's easier if I just show you what happened."

Closing her brown eyes, Adrienne stepped back. Lilly watched in muted horror as bruises appeared like butterflies on her skin, red fingers on her legs, black and blue hands on her neck. Cuts opened up on her arms and bled through to the flannel and her neck threw itself to the side, her blonde hair matting with blood as something invisible tore her apart. When she opened her eyes again, they were cloudy and one had burst blood vessels.

"This," she said, voice coming out strangled. "Is what happened when I heard her screaming that night. I remembered being strangled and beaten in a dark room until I couldn't breathe." With a snap of her fingers, her body reverted to how it had first looked, bloodless. "That's how I died."

Lillybelle was silent, her mouth going dry as it hung open. Her stomach rose into her throat and she quickly covered her mouth, swallowing it back down.

"Sorry. I know that was really graphic, but I needed you to understand what I went through. I know those girls died in a graphic way too, and I hated imagining dying again. Once was enough. So when I heard you and your group talking about how the girls were going missing and that you were going to help, I knew I could send you in the right direction."

"How can I help?" Lilly finally choked out, putting her hand on her chest, which was quickly rising and falling.

"I don't know how you can help them. But now I know that you can help me. There's a spell, in the book," she said, sinking down onto her knees and flipping the pages quickly, without touching them. "A spell that lets you see the last moments of the dead. It needs to be performed on the night of a full moon. Tomorrow night is a full moon. I would do it myself, but I need someone who actually has a body to do the spell."

Lilly frowned. "Why the sudden urgency? You were calm for months, why now?"

Adrienne lifted the book and placed it in Lilly's hands, eyes growing fierce.

"Because I feel that my killer is nearby. Since that night where I remembered my death, I've been able to tell if he's close. And he is here, every school day." She leaned close to Lilly. "He still works here." Lilly shuddered. "And I fear he might kill again. Come back tomorrow. Do the spell. Find my corpse. And justice will finally be served."

Lilly nodded, quickly gathering her things, throwing them into the tote. "Okay, I will. I promise."

"Wait! That's not all. Tomorrow is the first full moon of fall."

Lilly shook her head, mind spinning with all of the information that had just been thrust upon her. "What does that mean?"

"It means that any magic that is done tomorrow is twice as powerful. Including the consumption of energy by ghosts."

Lilly's eyes went wide. "So if a ghost was consuming the others, tomorrow would be the day to finish it off! Gain the rest of her power, finally break free!"

"Exactly! You have to stop that from happening."

"But how? What are we supposed to do?"

"I don't know, but I know someone who might." Adrienne waved her hand and a file came flying out of Lilly's tote bag. "He goes by the name of Tommy. He's sorta sketchy, but he won't harm any of you and he's the type that you go to if you need to know anyone or anything. If anybody knows how to save those ghosts, its him. He's at this location, the one Berri picked out for your project."

Lillybelle put a hand to her temples, trying to wrap her mind around what Adrienne was saying. "How do you-"

"I sit in on all of your club meetings. I know that your dorky club president thinks no one is here, but there is." After a moment, she tucked the paper back into the tote bag and met Lilly's gaze. "Being invisible lets me see a lot of things people don't want me to. Some of them aren't as bad as you think they are. Now go."

Adrienne turned to gaze out the far window, eyes landing on the front doors of the school. "You have work to do."

32

Venus rubbed her eyes and yawned, stumbling as she reached the bottom stair, socked feet slipping on the unfamiliar wood flooring. She turned right, into the open kitchen, where the smell of eggs, sausages, garlic rice, and pancakes wafted through the air in an odd, but not unpleasant mixture. Mrs. Lexie, Theo's mom, was standing at the island, drinking coffee out of an absurdly large purple mug.

"Good morning, Venus," she said, looking over at her with a smile. "There's a bunch of stuff for breakfast so that you guys could have some options. There are some fried eggs on that plate, there's rice in the pot, pancakes over there- Oh, make sure you leave a couple of chicken nuggets, because that is all Bayani can stand right now."

Venus nodded, smiling at the thought of Theo's eight year-old brother pushing away delicious plates of Laotian food in favor of chicken nuggets. Theo's mom just shook her head.

"How are Mala and Yalina doing?"

Mrs. Lexie sighed. "Preteens are mean."

Venus laughed. "Yeah, I remember not being super nice at that age. What is Mala in, eighth grade?"

"Yes, eighth and sixth. They go to the same school and can't stand it, but that's a whole other story."

"I'm sure." Venus looked around and grabbed a paper plate off the counter. "Thank you for the food, it looks delicious."

"Oh, don't thank me, thank Mrs. Liyana. She cooked before she left for work, you know how she loves having you kids over." Mrs. Lexie glanced at her watch. "Alright, you kids enjoy, I've got to go wake up Bayani for his hockey practice."

Venus nodded. "Have fun!"

Mrs. Lexie nodded back and disappeared up the stairs, leaving Venus alone in the warm kitchen. The well worn calendar that hung off the fridge showed that hockey practice wasn't for another four hours, but Venus wasn't going to rob Theo's mom of her quiet time.

She filled a plate with hot and cold foods before settling down at the beat-up wooden table against the window. Sunlight was streaming in through the giant window panes, a gentle warmth in the early morning as plastic sun-catchers cast rainbows across the room. Catching sight of her reflection in the glass, she winced. Her hair was a mess, her crumpled Bigfoot pajama-set not boosting her self esteem as it hung loosely from her frame. *I need to get back on the weight rack.* As she lifted the first forkful of fruit to her lips, she couldn't help but recall the night before.

Lilly had rung the doorbell of the Nguyen house at 11:30, only two packs of cookie-dough into Acacia's chosen slasher, soaked in sweat and carrying quite the story. As soon as she had finished apologizing to Theo's moms and eaten all of the food they had forced onto her plate, she told them everything, from how she felt about the book to what Adrienne said about the location Berri had picked out. There were hours of pointless plan making, all of which were incoherent, until Acacia reminded them that they couldn't do anything planned unless sleep was had.

According to the Nguyen house rules, and Irsa's promise to her parents, Theo, Berri, and Jaimie all slept in Theo's room while the rest of the group got the various floors and couches in the game room. Venus wasn't sure how the trio of he's and they's slept, but it was kinda hard for the rest of them to fall asleep with such a close deadline hanging over their heads. The whispers of worries continued until Lilly finally passed out, leaving Venus alone with her thoughts. Jeannie had been constantly tossing and turning all night, but she never woke up, as if having some endless nightmare.

Something about all of this still felt off. She couldn't pinpoint what it was, but there was more to the story that they weren't seeing.

Well, whatever is off, it sure isn't Mrs. Liyana's cooking, because these are the best pancakes I've ever had in my entire life.

She dug into her plate, shoveling the syrup soaked hotcakes into her mouth. She heard the creaking of the stairs behind her and she looked to see Berri stretching on the last step, brown hair clouding their eyes from view. They were wearing an oversized band t-shirt over boxers and rainbow knee socks.

"Mornin' B."

"Mornin' V," they yawned, crossing behind the island, obviously in search of the coffee.

"How'd you sleep?"

They shrugged, grabbing a mug from a cupboard and rinsing it out. "Was the last asleep."

"Me too." Venus said, shoveling some crispy tater tots into her mouth.

"What time?"

"3:30."

Berri raised their eyebrows, looking over at her as they

pressed a button on the coffee machine. They kind of reminded Venus of those sheepdogs in the old cartoons, the ones that always were drawn with hair over their eyes until shit got serious.

"Lilly?" Venus nodded and Berri just shook their head. "She should really go to a doctor for that."

"I agree."

As the sound of coffee trickling into the ceramic mug filled the air, Venus gave Berri another once over.

"Are those the compression boxers you were telling me about? Y'know, the ones for-"

"No, they're not. All these ones do is make my ass look great."

They struck a pose and Venus laughed, turning her attention back to her plate. When her plate was almost clean, she heard Berri gasp and looked up to see Berri gawking at a pancake they had speared on a steak knife.

"Venus..."

"What?" she asked, immediately smiling and on the verge of laughter.

"This is the best fucking pancake I have ever tasted in my entire life."

She held her tongue and nodded. "Yeah, buddy, it is."

Venus shook her head and took a sip of the orange juice she had poured during Berri's pancake euphoria. A few moments later, Berri's paper plate thunked onto the table, overflowing with pancakes and sausages, all of which had been doused in strawberry syrup. The smell of coffee and syrupy sweetness filled the air and the sound of Berri's delighted chewing was all Venus could hear.

When half of Berri's pancakes had been dunked in the syrup pool and devoured, Venus decided to interrupt them.

"I think we should go meet Tommy."

Berri nodded, politely wiping the corner of their mouth

with a paper elephant napkin that read 'Happy Sixth Birthday, Yalina!'

"I agree."

"I think we should go without the others."

Berri met her eyes, the hazel shifting closer to amber and reflecting her own green as they searched her gaze. Finally their lips lifted in a smile. "When do we leave?"

Venus smiled back, glancing at the clock which read 8:10. "Twenty minutes?"

"Perfect, see you at the car in twenty minutes." And with that, Berri shoved a sausage, pancake combo in their mouth, downing several swigs of black coffee as Venus stood up.

In twenty minutes, Venus was able to get dressed, brush her teeth, pack her stuff without bothering the sleeping ladies, and leave a written note on the counter explaining their absence. Yet, even as she closed the front door behind her at 8:29, Berri was already leaning against the passenger side door, poptart in mouth and muffin in hand, wearing the outfit from the day before.

"How do you manage to do this every time?"

Berri shrugged, wrenching the handle and opening the door of the car as she unlocked it. "Dunno, maybe I'm just better? Can we swing by my house, I need to change and get my stuff."

"Why didn't you pack an outfit for today?"

"I did, but the vibe changed since then."

"What does that even mean?"

The drive to Berri's house to pickup the equipment from the back of their car was short, but full of fun facts about coffee beans and their unsustainability. By the time they had arrived, Venus had learned about how jam could be made from the fruit of the coffee plant. While Berri went inside to change, Venus decided to fix her hair in the side mirror. *I don't even drink coffee!*

She had decided a princess pony would look best, having

selected a wonderfully shitty quality black ribbon from her glovebox, to match her black 'Sasquatch Crossing' t-shirt that she had tucked into her dark blue jeans. Her brown flannel was tied around her waist, as it felt much too warm for a fall morning to be wearing long sleeves.

Hearing a door closing to her left, Venus turned to see how Berri was doing when she felt her heart drop in horror.

"Nuh uh, turn around! Berri, I swear to god, you are not getting into my car looking like that! Are those jorts?"

Sure enough, Berri was standing in their driveway wearing denim shorts. There were little mushrooms painted along the bottoms, but it did nothing to detract from the fact that they were jorts.

"What? Do you not like my outfit?"

Tucked into the offending jorts was a green turtleneck sweater vest, puffy red button-up sleeves sticking out. A brown corduroy jacket was thrown over their arm and checkered yellow socks were peeking out of the top of their thick work boots, an ugly bandage very obvious on their leg. A tote bag hung off their other arm, a gift from Acacia's recent crochet phase.

"Yeah, the 80s called, they want their jorts back!"

"Denim shorts were popularized in the 60s, smartass! Now get out here and help me load up the gear!"

Venus shook her head violently. "Nuh uh, I will not be seen in public with someone wearing jean shorts. No way!"

"Will you stop bitching about my excellent taste and help me?"

Many complaints and a lot of heaving later, all of the pressure washers and Berri's jorts were safely strapped into Venus's car. Soon enough, the location was typed out into the gps and they were cautiously soaring down the road, never veering above ten below the speed limit.

The windows were rolled down and Venus could see Berri's

hands out the window in the corner of her eye. The winding back roads were fairly empty, warm sunlight spilling through the canopy of red and orange leaves, yellow fluttering down around the car as they drove past a railroad crossing. The 70s station was blaring on the radio, Fleetwood Mac filling the fall air with notes of love and shadows, breaking silence and breaking chains.

By the time the song was winding down, they were turning into the six-space parking lot of a graveyard. A rusty metal sign on a fence post read out *Jane Truth Cemetery*. As she parked the car in one of the empty gravel spaces, Venus stretched her neck to get a better look at the location.

There was a collection of a dozen mausoleums and maybe thirty graves, all surrounded with a rusty old fence. A semi-paved path led straight through to a gate on the other side, a dirt path leading up a little hill to an old, wooden house. The gps had a blinking message and a smiley face emoji.

"Is this the place?" Berri asked, glancing from the cemetery to the gps.

You have arrived! Said the gps, the emoji unblinking and unforgiving.

"I guess so." Venus sighed. "Do you still have the pocket knife I gave you yesterday?"

Berri responded by pulling it out of their pocket and opening it. It was rainbow chrome.

"Let's go."

The pair quickly got out of the car, locking it soundly behind them. The gravel was loud beneath their feet, a crunchy leaf or two getting trampled as they hesitantly made their way to the gate. A deep breath in carried the smell of wet leaves, even though it hadn't rained the night before. Venus tentatively placed her hand on the top of the gate, her mind replaying Jeannie's panic when she had grabbed onto the pump. *Was that only two days ago?* Somehow it felt like more time had passed, but at the same time like it was just yesterday.

She shook the thoughts out of her head and pushed the gate, the creak as it swung open almost making her jump. As soon as it was open she yanked her hand away, rubbing it roughly on her jeans, leaving red and brown streaks across the blue denim. Berri laughed and stepped around her.

"That's why I brought gloves."

Berri wiggled their fingers and Venus saw that they were wearing black fingerless gloves, green acrylics like talons free to the air. Berri strode ahead, skipping past the graves that were either too covered in grime and plant life to see the names, or were too faded to read. Though the headstones themselves were old, the dirt in front of one of them looked disturbingly fresh.

"Should we knock on the door of the house?" Berri asked, pointing their acrylics over their shoulder and up the hill.

"I guess," Venus said, kinda dreading approaching the creepy old building. "Maybe Tommy is like, the caretaker?"

"I mean, why else would you live next to a graveyard?" Berri said, pushing open the gate on the other side of the small cemetery, holding it for Venus to pass through. "Unless graveyard real estate is undervalued and dirt cheap, I guess. But, still."

"You've got a point." Venus said, squinting up at the house.

The windows were dark, and the wood of the porch looked worn. The closer they got to the house and the higher up the hill, the more felt off about the whole building. It looked fairly clean, but the brick foundation was splattered with long dried mud and the railing was splintering in places. Berri reached the bottom of the porch stairs first, a look on their face that said 'nah, I'm good.'

"What if we just called from here?" Berri said, laughing nervously. "I mean, there's a window right there, he should be able to hear us."

Venus nodded, eager to not climb any more sets of questionable stairs. "Hello? We're looking for someone named Tommy!" Venus shouted, glancing from the distant front door to the window that sat above them. "We were told he would have some information for us?"

"We come in peace!" Berri called out, giving Venus a thumbs up.

Silence. There was no movement in the house, no creaking floorboards, no shuffling, no one peeking out from behind a curtain. No wind whistling through eaves. Birds chattered overhead, but the house above the graveyard was dead still.

"Hello?" Venus tried again, leaning farther towards the front door. "Is anyone there?"

Nothing.

"Maybe we should try the graveyard again?" Berri said, inching away from the house. "Adrienne never said Tommy would be alive. Maybe he's a resident down there?"

Venus took a long look at the house. There was a layer of dust on the door mat. It didn't smell like anything. "Yeah, that's probably a good idea."

Berri bounded down the dirt path almost gleefully, but Venus lingered. *Something's off.* The house was still. Too still. She reached out to touch the railing, but her hand froze. It wouldn't move forward, no matter how much she tried. She yanked it away, heart beat spiking. Shaking her head, she quickly followed Berri down the hill, glancing back every few steps as the house receded into the trees.

The creaking gate slammed behind them and Berri doubled over laughing, eyes wide. "Dude, that was fucking freaky."

"Yeah," Venus said, glancing over her shoulder, out of breath somehow. "Like, it didn't feel real."

Berri nodded violently. "I felt the same way! Like, it was a dollhouse instead of a real house. Uncanny valley up the wazoo."

"Let's just find this Tommy so we can get out of here!"

Venus decided to take the path farthest left, Berri close behind as they tried to read each of the tags on the mausoleums. About halfway down the row, Venus noticed a groove in the otherwise undisturbed dirt. Following it led to the door of a large mausoleum, taller than even Berri, who, at 5'11, was no shorty. A plaque was welded into the door. The last name was scratched off, but the first name was as bright and bold as ever. *Tommy.*

Venus turned to Berri, who shrugged. "Do we just knock?"

"I don't know, I've never had to see if the owner of a mausoleum was at home and available before!"

"Just, do it!"

"Fine, I'll knock!" Berri gently tapped the mausoleum with their knuckles, quickly pulling their hand away from the stone. "Hello? Mr. Tommy? We have a couple of questions for you, if you have the time. We're kinda on a deadline, though."

Silence. Venus knocked a little harder than Berri had, peering around the side to see if there were any other ways in. There weren't.

"We sort of really need your help!" she said.

Nothing.

"Adrienne sent us!" Berri called.

"Why did Adrienne send you knocking on my mausoleum?"

Venus and Berri whipped around. Sitting on top of the opposite mausoleum was a person, although, it was hard to call him that. Where a face should have been, there was just a skull, blue skin pulled tight across the bones. A patchy red velvet hat sat askew on his head, shimmering gold hair hanging in oily strands around his pointed ears. All of his teeth were sharp, a deep violet cigarette hanging between smiling ghostly lips. He had no eyes, just pits of void, never ending. When Berri spoke, Venus was surprised to hear their voice shaking.

"Are you Mr. Tommy?"

Blue fingers, surprisingly human looking, appeared from the

hems of long black coat sleeves, straightening a wrinkled gray dress shirt, only the left half tucked into his pinstripe pants. He wasn't wearing shoes, his blue toes wiggling freely against the stone mausoleum.

"It's just Tommy, no mister. Do I look like a mister to you?" Tommy said, leaning forward on the mausoleum that did not have his name on it. His voice had a slight Brooklyn accent, but it went in and out.

"Kinda?" Venus said, which earned a punch in the arm from Berri.

Whatever smile Tommy had, dropped. "Is it the hat? It's the hat isn't it?" Tommy threw the hat into the air and it transformed into a handkerchief by the time it landed back on his head. "I'm not a mister, but a he, for those wondering. Today, at least. Yesterday, no. Today, yes. Capiche?"

Berri nodded.

"You're Tommy?" Venus asked, eyes still wide in disbelief.

He spat his cigarette onto the ground, where it became an indigo flower. "Who's asking?"

Berri curled into Venus, uneven acrylics digging into her arms. "Us?"

Tommy sighed and hopped off the mausoleum, landing lightly in front of them. When he straightened his legs, he towered more than a foot over them, dark pits staring down at them.

"I saw you yesterday," he said, poking his sharp black nails in Venus's face. "You were standing next to that redhead in Dr. Martin's shop. You should tell your friend not to stare; it does wonders for my ego!" Venus sputtered, but he moved his blue finger into Berri's face. "I know what you're here for."

His blue fingers crept down his shirt like a spider and he gripped the hem as he squinted his eye sockets at them. *Is he about to... Oh, god!* Venus felt her eyes go wide.

"Wait!"

33

Venus

Before she could finish, he had pulled his shirt high, and Venus averted her eyes instinctively, but not without getting an eyeful.

"Okay, wow. Um, yeah, that's a ribcage."

Underneath his shirt was a gleaming white ribcage. No organs, no blood, none of it, just a painfully clean ribcage connected to a similarly clean spine. Berri's eyes were wide, open mouth gawking.

"Well, duh, how else would I resource my barbecue spare ribs?" He said, indignantly.

Venus could only shake her head at the amalgamation standing in front of her, bewildered. "What?"

Tommy frowned. "Are you not here for my world famous barbecue ribs?"

"No."

"Do you, like, take the bones back after the customer is finished eating?" Berri asked, any terror they once had gone.

"Of course, I have a business to run here!"

Venus took several steps back, pressing her palms into her

eyes to try and unsee the situation. "Ew, just, ew."

"Well, they get cleaned every time I deep fry 'em, so they're actually pretty sanitary." He laughed. "I gotta stay above the health code, y'know."

What the hell is happening? Venus opened her eyes again, staring between Tommy and Berri, who nodded, almost knowingly.

"Honestly, I'd try em."

"Berri!"

Tommy dropped the hem of his shirt, crossing his arms in front of him. "So if you're not here for my ribs, what do you want?"

Venus sighed. *Finally, we can get back on track.* "We were told you had some information for us?"

He squinted at them again, his lack of eyes somehow making his stare more intense. "You cops?"

Berri made a face of disgust. "No."

"Census takers?"

Venus exchanged a look with Berri, this time confused. "No?"

"Okay, what do you want to know?" Tommy leaned back against the mausoleum. "You get three questions before I start charging you." After Venus gave him a look, "What? Knowledge is power and power don't come cheap."

Venus looked at Berri who just shrugged again. "Okay, um, what exactly are you?"

"Genderfluid," he said, looking at his nails.

"No, we gathered that much," Berri said, rolling their eyes. "We meant, like, supernatural Underworld wise. Because you're not a ghost."

"No, I'm not a ghost." He smiled. "I'm a ghoul."

"Oh," Berri said, voice two or three octaves higher than normal. "Like a jiangshi?"

Venus frowned. *A what?* Tommy nodded. "Similar, not the

same."

"Okay." Berri nodded back, paling considerably. "So, you, like, eat people."

Venus recoiled, taking a few involuntary steps away from Tommy, who scoffed.

"That is a reductionist stereotype!" He exclaimed, putting his hand on his chest. Venus sighed in relief. "It does happen to apply to me. However-"

"Excuse me?" Venus said, eyes wide. Her heart was beating a little faster in her chest.

"Oh, calm down. One, ghoul is a general category that refers to anything that is undead and eats. Two, ghouls eat dead people, ie, not you. Three, only some ghouls eat people, most don't. And four, one corpse can hold me for well over ten years, and my last meal was three years ago, so take a breath, sweetheart. I happen to be a vampire ghoul, meaning I need human meat and blood to live because I am undead, but I am perfectly capable of getting what I need from graveyards such as these, where I've already gotten permission to eat their bodies. From the spirits themselves, so there!"

Venus blinked several times, nodding as her brain processed what was being said. She took several deep breaths. "Sorry, it's just not everyday you come face to face with someone who has the ability to eat you."

If he had eyes to roll, he would've rolled them. "You know humans can eat you too, right? So can dogs, cats, pigs, birds, mice- the list really goes on."

Berri nodded. "He makes a good point."

"Okay so, you're a ghoul, a vampire ghoul." Venus said, taking several mental notes. "Not a ghost or a witch."

Tommy nodded. "Not a witch, but ghouls do have our own magical abilities."

"So we've noticed," she said as Berri picked up the indigo flower that had once been a cigarette.

"So, you're like a zombie wizard." Berri said, watching the flower turn translucent in the sunlight.

"I resent that classification." Tommy glared at the flower.

Berri pointed at the house on the hill. "Who lives up there? The house kinda seemed deserted."

Tommy flashed a toothy smile. "What house?"

Venus looked back up to the hill. *What the-* The house was gone, the path leading up to it now simply grass and fallen leaves. Berri sputtered and Venus turned to see that the flower had turned into vines, binding Berri's wrists together and winding up their arms. Before either of them could say anything, Tommy burst out laughing, now sitting on top of his own mausoleum.

"Just kidding."

And immediately, the house reappeared, graveyard gate and all. This time, however, Venus was amazed to see that the house lights were on and smoke was rising from the chimney. She spun around, eyes on Tommy, who was smiling wide.

"It's an illusion. A decoy to make sure no one else tries to buy the property."

Makes sense as to why I couldn't touch it, Venus thought. *It's not real.*

Berri spun to look at Tommy, eyes wide in wonder. "You *are* a zombie wizard!"

Tommy grimaced. "Please don't call me that."

"Why don't you want anyone to buy the property?" Venus asked, glancing between him and the now cozy looking house on the hill.

He made a face, disgust combined with something unrecognizable. "Are you kidding? I hate landlords." *Ah.* "Although the one thing that sucks about not having a caretaker?" He cast a look over the graveyard. "This place looks like a dump."

"Why don't you and the other residents clean it?"

He shrugged. "We're lazy."

Berri nudged Venus and when Venus turned to them, they were smiling wide. After a moment, it dawned on her and she too smiled. *It would be a waste if we loaded up all the equipment and didn't use it, right?*

"We can clean it for you, if you want." Berri said, beaming.

"Really?" Tommy sat up straight, eyeless chasms shining. "Do that, and I'll tell you everything you want to know, free of charge. I swear on my mausoleum. Scout's honor!"

Venus felt lighter, trying not to bounce on the balls of her feet. "Do you have a water pump or hose we can use?"

"Yeah, I think we might have one up front. For like, worship cleansing or whatever bullshit the original owners came up with." He smiled, as if remembering something fondly. "I ate their corpses first."

"Okay!" Venus said, good feeling gone. "We'll be right back with our equipment!"

Tommy nodded and waved his hand, the vines that had been binding Berri's hands flying up into the air and landing back between Tommy's teeth as a cigarette. *I guess that's what Cordelia meant when she said Tommy sold trick cigs.* Venus thought, linking arms with Berri as they wandered down the row of graves towards the car.

Venus took this as an opportunity and vaulted over the creaky gate, leaving Berri grumbling and struggling with the rusted handle as she unlocked the trunk. By the time Berri had managed to get through the gate, the trunk was shut and Venus had a washer in each hand.

"I'll take the heavy duty one," Berri said, smiling at their equipment. "I'll hook up the water if you get the gear situated?"

Venus nodded, walking through the gate that Berri held open for her. Berri grabbed the end of the hoses and Venus slowly uncoiled them as she backed down the row of headstones, towards the large mausoleums where Tommy was lounging. He was once again laying on the mausoleum across from his, the name *Skinner* carved onto the plaque. The first name had been rubbed away. Tommy followed her gaze and smiled.

"Death by frog, that one." He nodded, very solemnly. "Such a shame. She loved those things. Still does, but y'know, being dead does put a damper on things."

Is he joking? Venus shook her head, turning to face the mausoleum at hand. *Doesn't matter. I have a job to do.*

"Just yours?"

"Yep, couldn't care less about the rest of them." Out of the corner of her eye, Venus watched him leap to the ground, straightening with the fluidity of a cat. "You said you were on a deadline right? How tight are we talking?"

She screwed the white nozzle onto the washer, making sure it was tight. "Tonight, when the full moon is at its peak."

He whistled. "Then I'll talk while you wash. What do you need to know?"

Venus turned the machine on its side and pulled the trigger, letting the air stream out. "How do you prevent a ghost from consuming another ghost?"

"Wow, going straight for the dangerous one, eh?"

"The water is connected!" Berri shouted. "Start on the lowest setting!"

"Got it!" Venus called back, turning the dial and pressing the trigger again, water shooting out of the head, cutting a line in the dirt.

"Well, for a ghost to consume another ghost is no easy task! First they need to get the ghost into a contained space where they can't escape or are at a larger risk than their aggressor."

Venus raised the washer up to the top of the mausoleum, slicing through the layers of grime and dust that had been caked onto the granite. With each swipe of the water, another line of detailed stone was revealed.

"Then, they would need to be put into a position where they could be killed again. Yes, ghosts get to die twice if consumed! The energy that spills out has to be gathered in something so it isn't wasted, like a bowl or a bag."

An image popped into Venus's mind, a picture Lilly had taken and sent to the group chat, of an indentation in the ground with some black goop in it. "Does a ghost's dying energy have any physical appearance if wasted? Like, black goop?"

"I mean, I guess. Sometimes. The surviving ghost would eat this or absorb it, and the body of the ghost consumed would fade within minutes of separation from the energy."

Venus frowned, thinking back to the friendly faces of the girls in the warehouse, each one comfortable and happy with her friends. Footsteps approached on her right and she looked to see Berri wheeling the other machine over. They had put their corduroy jacket on.

"How do we stop that from happening?" Berri asked, flipping on their water pressure and quickly rinsing the front of the mausoleum.

"Well, it depends when you're interrupting. If you do it in the final stages, all you need to do is scoop up the essence of the ghost, which you won't absorb because you're human, and feed it back to the ghost it came from. But the most sure-fire way is to prevent the offending ghost from starting the kill."

Berri nodded at Venus and then nodded to the top of the mausoleum. Venus nodded back, biting back a smile. She loved climbing things.

"How do we do that, though?" Berri asked clearing out the top half of the mausoleum's front door of dirt, revealing the shimmering granite.

"First you have to find the ghost that's plotting to do the deed, and bind their soul to an object, preferably something flammable. It may seem cruel, but once you bind them to this object, you have to completely destroy it. It's rare, but in situations where multiple ghosts are at risk, it's the only fool proof option."

Venus shut off her water and looked over at Tommy.

"So we have to basically give out the ghost equivalent of the death penalty, which I am against, by the way, in order to protect the rest of the ghosts?" She let out a dry laugh. "I wonder how this'll go over with the rest of the group."

"Not well." Berri called out from around the corner of the mausoleum, having finished the front and moved on to the side.

Venus pointed at the low roof of the Skinner mausoleum. "Do you mind if I climb that?"

"Knock yourself out, she won't be back for a while." Tommy offered her his hand, which she took. "She's off visiting her husband, Chris. He doesn't reside very close by."

His hands were surprisingly warm, giving her the lift she needed to hop up on the tiled roof. "Thanks." He nodded. "How does one tie a ghost's spirit to an object?" She asked, backing up a few steps and making a few mental calculations.

Tommy huffed. "It's such a complicated procedure. First you have to open the object to the enchantment, then find some way to emotionally connect the spirit to the object, then tie them. Interrupting witches is so much easier! All you have to do is mess up their magic circle or interrupt them while they're chanting. It's almost ridiculously easy."

Venus dashed forward, her foot slipping on the last tile as she leapt into the air, crashing hard onto the other roof. Stars bloomed in her eyes. For several painfully long moments, she couldn't breathe.

"Would you mind explaining the ghost procedure?" Berri said, dialing down the pressure of their washer.

"Yeah, sure. So first-"

"Would you mind writing it down?" Venus wheezed. She had landed on her side, her ribs smacking hard onto the peak of the roof.

"Yeah, no prob. Do you have any paper?"

Venus sat up as Berri said: "I've got some in my coat pocket."

She watched as Tommy appeared next to Berri, who jumped, and reached into their pocket with his abnormally long fingers. He stepped away from Berri and his cigarette floated down into his hand as a ball-point pen.

"Do you want me to write what I said about the witches too? You never know when you need to beat up a witch who just happens to be a bit of a bitch, y'know?"

Venus nodded, knowing he wouldn't be able to see her. "Sure."

Washing the rest of the mausoleum took very little time, with Tommy quietly scratching away on his little notepad. *It probably says "How To Give A Ghost The Death Penalty" in neat cursive on the top,* she thought to herself, finally shutting off the pressure. *This is a pretty clean roof.* Venus had switched out the white nozzle for the green one, getting more grime and leaf litter out of nooks and crannies of the intricately carved roof tiles.

"You about done down there?" She called, leaning over the side to try and see where Berri had ended up.

"Yep!" Berri's head poked out from underneath the left eaves, smiling. "All done!"

"Catch!" Venus said, smiling as she dropped the washer over the side.

Berri's face fell as they scrambled to catch it, which they did. The air feeling lighter and cooler with every passing moment, Venus leapt from the roof, bending her knees to land on the grave stone to the right. She leapt from gravestone to gravestone, when suddenly, her foot slipped out from under her. Her heart sank, the familiar feeling of falling taking over. She braced for impact, but instead of crashing down onto stone and breaking her ass, she landed on something soft. That doesn't mean it was a comfortable landing, however. Looking down, she saw an indigo pillow beneath her.

"That's the closest to a thank you you're going to get from

me, so be grateful." Tommy said, turning his attention from her to the now shiny mausoleum. He was smiling wide. "It hasn't looked this nice since it was first built. I forgot about all of these beautiful details. Do you need to know anything else? I wrote the instructions for the binding down in full. Oh, and if any of you are performing a spell tonight, make sure to cast the appropriate energy circle, or the spell won't be as secure."

Venus stood up, rubbing her sore butt and nodding. "Noted."

"I have a question." Berri said, setting down their equipment and crossing their arms. "Is there any way to get back ghosts that have already been consumed?"

Tommy grimaced, gold eyebrows knitting above his eye sockets. "Not really. Once they've been consumed, they're gone, for good. With shadows, they can hold the memories in their filth, but with ghosts? Not happening."

Venus frowned, glancing around the graveyard. It felt safe, even though it was a bit off putting at first. "Why aren't there shadows here?"

"It's because I'm here. I eat the energy that would normally spill over and create the shades. "He nudged Berri. "See, we ghouls are more than just purple people eaters."

Berri nodded solemnly. "Yes, zombie wizards are more helpful than I first thought."

Venus smiled. Tommy's ears were twitching.

"Annoying comment aside, you two did a decent job. If you wanted to do this kind of thing professionally, I could send some work your way."

Berri beamed and Venus couldn't help but smile. "We'll think about it, Tommy. Thanks for your help."

"Anytime. Next time you come, you'll get a rib on the house." Tommy waved them off as they started down the path. "Good luck! You'll need it."

34

Jeannie

"So Tommy, a weird ghoul dude who sells his own ribs as food, said we have to kill this ghost for the sake of all the other ghosts?" Theodora rubbed her eyes as she held the steering wheel with one hand.

Jeannie half-smiled at Theo, whose expression was one of frustration, confusion, and exhaustion. She had gotten the front seat this time, after it was determined that Jaimie would rather sit in the third row than sit in anyone's lap to squeeze in. The many silver bracelets around Theo's wrists jangled, occasionally catching on the multitude of rings on his fingers. His black mesh shirt sleeves peeked out from beneath his oversized hockey jersey, tucked into black shorts. Spiderweb tights covered his brown legs and led into his boots, purple laces swinging as Theo pressed the gas.

"That's about right," Venus's voice came crackling through Jeannie's phone, which was hooked up to the speaker.

"Do we know which ghost it is?" Irsa asked.

Jeannie glanced at her through the rear-view mirror. She was sitting on the left side of the car, Lilly squished between her

241

and Acacia, tucking a stray hair into her black hijab. Her white turtleneck was bright underneath her black overalls, thick, fuzzy black tights stuffed into her sneakers. She had traded her usual turquoise glasses for contacts.

"I don't." Venus said.

"Me neither," Berri's voice cut in. "And I think we should figure that out first."

"Yeah, because we should be 100% sure before we murder someone in front of all of their friends, y'know?" Acacia chirped, crossing her arms in front of her.

She was wearing a gray sweatshirt with the words '*Horror movies and chill*' written across the front, three cute little ghosts embroidered underneath, each wearing a horror movie mask. Her jeans had candy corn spilling down the front that Jaimie had hand-painted for her so many Halloweens ago. Jeannie couldn't see her feet now, but she knew they were fuzzy and pumpkin covered.

"Obviously," Lillybelle said, pulling the sleeve of her orange cardigan down her prosthetic. She had swapped her usual turtleneck for a white v-neck tee, tucked into high-waisted black corduroy pants. "We should do some snooping and talk to the ghosts about what's going on."

"But let's make sure they don't know we suspect one of them, okay?" Jeannie said gently, eyes returning to the long road in front of them. "We don't want them going on high alert."

"I know it's not Quinn." Venus said, voice cutting out slightly as she spoke. "There would be no reason for her to take your stuff and get us to find them."

Jeannie nodded, crossing her off the mental list.

"Or Lori." Jaimie pitched in, sticking his tousled head out from behind Lilly's seat.

"Right, or Giorgia," Irsa said firmly. "They all seemed very upset about the disappearances, almost relieved that we were there."

"I doubt that it's Fiadh." Lilly said, softly. "She was so genuine. She really wants us to figure this out."

"Well, we're not going to solve this in the car, so we'll talk more when we park, okay?" Theo said, turning the car into the grass yard of the warehouse. "I can see you from here."

Venus waved at the group from the hood of her car, where Berri was leaning, smiling.

"And after this, we go to lunch, right?" Jaimie called, smiling sheepishly from the back as everyone laughed.

"Jaimie, how can you even be hungry?" Irsa asked, covering her smile with her hand. "You ate twelve pancakes, three of your veggie empanadas, and three plates of fruit!"

He groaned. "I'm a growing boy, Irsa! I can't help it."

Jeannie couldn't help smiling as she ended the call and got out of the car, Theo having safely parked next to the water pump. Her white sweater hung loosely off her arms, to the point where she could barely see her stained fingertips. She had brought thick rain boots, her long green pants tucked securely into them. Her backpack hung loosely from her shoulders, weighed down only by her phone and her flashlight.

She skipped over to Berri, who was leaning against Venus's car and smiling. "Hey Berri!"

They shot a glance at Venus. "Hey, Jeannie, how do you feel about my outfit?"

Jeannie took a moment to look them up and down, taking in the denim painted with mushrooms, the patterned socks, the corduroy jacket, green sweater vest, and the earrings. She frowned. "I mean, it's definitely your style. You look good!"

Berri laughed and stuck their tongue out at Venus, who groaned and put her face in her hands. *Oh, shoot.*

"You look good too, Venus," Jeannie said quickly, stepping towards her friend.

"It's not that, but thank you." She said, glaring at Berri through her fingers.

"She hates my shorts because they're denim-"

"No, I hate them because they are jorts! JORTS!" Venus said, hopping off the hood of her car, shaking her head.

"Hey, Berri!" Theo called, making their way over with the rest of the group. "Nice jorts!"

Venus looked as if her head was going to implode when Jaimie hopped in, wagging his sweatshirt sleeves between them. "We should probably head inside, y'know, solve the mysteries so that we can go to lunch?"

Jaimie led the way to the front of the building, where the front doors were cracked open. Jeannie frowned. "I thought we left these doors closed?"

"We did," Acacia said, pulling on the door handle. "I remember pushing them shut the other night."

Maybe it was just the wind? The door opened without issue, and they filed in, light spilling in through the clean windows and the small gaps in the ceiling. Shadows were relegated in their corners, still and soft, unmoving. Not at all like her dreams. Jeannie shook her head as they walked to where they knew the elevator was. *They're just dreams,* she chided herself. *Just silly nightmares. Silly detectives don't ponder nightmares and neither do silly security guards. So stop thinking about it!* Still, a writhing was growing in her stomach, skin on her hands tightening with each step.

Lillybelle pressed the elevator button with her finger, and the doors slid open, an orange light flickering.

"Does the elevator look different to anyone else?" Irsa said as Jeannie took a step forward.

A hot hand slammed her in the back, and she stumbled into the elevator.

"Hey-" she exclaimed, turning to see which of her friends had pushed her, when the doors slammed shut in her face. Jeannie grabbed the lattice of metal, trying to pull the doors open again. "What's happening?" She cried out, watching as

Venus and Jaimie struggled just as hard to wrench them apart on their side.

The elevator shook violently and she was thrown backwards as the elevator shot up at an incredible speed. Her ears rang as she tried to push herself to her feet, the shadows in the corners of the elevator lengthening towards her. As seconds passed, the elevator sped up, but the flashing number on the walls that sped past stayed the same:

4.

As the elevator passed the number each time, the room got darker and darker, the shadows dancing all around her, deepening and getting bigger. The rushing sound in her ears got louder and louder as she scrambled for her flashlight, the zipper on her backpack catching.

"You won't be needing that," A deep voice rumbled, sending a shiver down her spine. **"So we meet again, Jeannette."**

35

Lilly

Lillybelle's eyes were wide with shock, heartbeat loud in her chest as Venus threw herself at the lattice, which didn't budge. Jeannie had stumbled forward, whipped around as the doors slammed, and the elevator sped off. Berri arched their head to look up the elevator shaft as Venus swore violently.

"I can't even see the elevator!" They said, concern coating their voice.

"Maybe the ghosts needed to talk to her?" Irsa said nervously, picking at the hem of her hijab as Venus paced.

"What do we fucking do?" Jaimie hissed, glancing between the doors of the elevator and Venus.

"She's probably up on the seventh floor, we just need to, I guess, take the stairs?" Theo said, wringing their hands, eyes wide as they trembled.

"But why would they take her separately like that, hasn't she been through enough separated from the group?" Venus asked, eyes wild.

As Theo and Venus argued about the necessity of the ghosts

needing to talk to Jeannie alone, Lillyb noticed Acacia frowning and snapping next to her ears. "What's wrong?"

Acacia shook her head, leaning towards the far wall. "I think my cochlear is picking up something weird. Can you hear that?"

Lilly frowned and crossed to where Acacia was standing, focusing very hard. *What is that?* Under all of the clamor of voices, she could hear an extra one.

"Everyone shut up." Lilly said, quietly. Then again, when they didn't hear her: "Shut up, and listen!"

The rest of the group fell into a stunned silence, but she just put her finger over her lip, eyebrows knitting together. Another voice could be heard, muffled, but there. Acacia softly stepped towards the far wall, pressing herself up to the door, which was shut. Lilly followed slowly, putting her head next to Acacia's, using her free hand to beckon to the group.

A soft, feminine voice was chanting, words unintelligible and fluid. *It sounds kinda familiar.*

"What is that?" Berri whispered, eyes searching the ground.

"I don't know," Venus breathed, crouched beneath Berri.

"It's not spanish," Jaimie said quietly. "Not any kind I recognize anyway."

Irsa shushed them, shifting to listen closer. The voice rose and fell, the chanting rhythmic. Lillybelle leaned forward, resting her prosthetic against her chest. It slipped from her chest and hit the door, softly, but still a loud knock compared to the silence. The chanting stopped immediately. Venus swore.

"She stopped," Irsa said, frowning.

"How do we know it's a she?" Berri asked, still whispering.

"The only ghosts here are girls," Acacia said, smiling in sympathy at Lilly.

Berri nodded and Jaimie smiled, punching them in the arm. Venus smiled at Lilly, seemingly apologetic.

"What are you listening to?"

Lilly whipped around. A woman floated above them, almost

white eyes narrowed at the group. Her apron weighed down her flowing skirts, arms tightly crossed in front of her. She had a cold look, a dead expression engraved onto her features as she looked the group over. Her ratty blonde hair floated up around her in chunks, matted together. Something large had been tucked under the neckline of her dress, a small strip of leather stuck to the side of her neck.

"Nothing," blurted out Jaimie, and Lilly shot him a look.

The ghost tilted her head back, looking at them through singed eyelashes, before darting her eyes to the door behind them. "There's no one in that room." The spirit said, her body becoming more transparent as the seconds passed. "Anymore."

Within a blink of Lilly's eyes, the ghost had faded away from sight entirely, leaving only a sheen of mist in the air. *That's one of the powers that Dr. Frances was talking about. Has she eaten lately?* She blinked again. A ding rang out through the air, and turning, Lilly saw that the elevator doors had opened. It was empty.

36

Jeannie

Jeannie's heart beat was loud as she spun around, searching for the owner of the voice, which laughed all around her. *No no no no no no no no no no no no no no no no no. This can't be happening! I have to be dreaming, I can't be awake!*

"Oh, you're awake." The voice laughed, loud and heavy on her skin. **"Though, I'm glad you remember our conversation from last night."**

Last night? She thought, eyes searching the deepening shadows. *Oh.*

Her dreams from that night had been filled with darkness, the same laughter permeating her every movement, every breath. The memory of the seething heat wrapping itself thickly around her arms, holding her still as that voice had made that proposition.

'I've made a deal with someone,' *He had said, slowly circling her in the abyss of the warehouse in her mind.* **'But she has been... negligent, of her part of the deal. Her actions have proven her colleagues'**

thoughts about her to be true, as she is, indeed, as pathetic as they assume. I give her one task and she can't even do it.'

The voice had made a tutting sound.

"But you, my dearest Jeanette, have potential. You've proven yourself capable of many, many things. More capable than my current partner. She is weak, even with my help. But you and I? Together, we could be strong."

Jeannie shook her head violently, bringing her hands up to cover her face. Her hair whipped her in the face, the stench of motor oil and blood filling her nostrils and making her gag.

"Leave me the hell alone!"

The voice laughed, a sound that had replayed in her head over and over again, like a broken record connected directly to her brain.

"Have you thought about my proposition? I know you haven't been able to forget about me… You can feel me even now, can't you?" Her skin tightened and constricted, almost in response to his words. She gasped in pain, her hands squeezing together as if strings were trying to snap her wrist. **"It was me, who pushed you through the wall. It was me who grabbed you when you ran. It was me who held you hostage at the water pump. I've tainted you, don't you see? I've claimed you."**

The blackened skin twisted, making her scream out in pain as the shadows curled around her, licking up her boots and hanging from the ceiling in thick tendrils. The ones that were touching her burned, like boiling water poured on her skin.

"Get away from me!" She screamed, knees buckling as her fingers thrashed, bones cracking.

"You still don't get it, do you? That's fine." A

hand wrapped around her throat and someone she couldn't see raised her up against the ceiling. **"You'll understand soon enough."**

The hand fell away and she dropped to the ground, head spinning as she hit the concrete. A rush of voices clamored around her, and as she slowly opened her eyes, she could see the number on the wall, opposite the elevator shaft.

7.

Looking up, she made eye contact with Quinn, whose eyes were wide. *She knows.* Jeannie shook her head, only enough for Quinn to understand. Quinn's face fell but she nodded. A soft ding rang out.

"Jeannie!"

37

Is she okay?

Venus's heart dropped when she saw Jeannie on the ground, her body moving without thinking as she ran to her, immediately on her knees next to her friend. Jeannie was on all fours, forearms bracing on the floor, elbows scraped and arms shaking. Venus could hear everyone else exclaiming as they piled out of the elevator and towards them, but her attention was only on the girl trembling on the concrete.

"Jeannie, are you okay?" Her friend just nodded, blinking as she averted her gaze to the ground. Venus held out a hand to help her up, which Jeannie shakily took. "What happened?"

"I'm not sure," she said, standing with Venus and using her to steady herself. "I remember the doors slamming shut and then darkness."

Quinn floated closer, hands folded tightly in front of her apron. "We're not sure what happened either..."

"You mean you guys didn't take Jeannie in the elevator?" Irsa asked, eyes wide as she crossed between Quinn and Venus.

The ghost just shook her head. "We didn't send the elevator down until Olive came up and told us you were here."

Venus frowned, exchanging a glance with Lilly. "Who's Olive?"

Quinn turned her head to look back at the small group of ghosts on the far side of the building. The group looked smaller than usual. *Where's Lori?*

"Well, she isn't here right now, but she's really nice. A little shy, but very brave! She likes to venture out into the warehouse sometimes." Quinn shuddered. "I could never make myself do that again. It's just too risky."

"Have more people gone missing?" Lilly asked, and when she glanced over, she saw that Lilly's eyes were glued to the small group in the distance.

Quinn's face fell, eyes going to the ground. "Three. Lori disappeared the night you left. And we woke this morning to find Fiadh and Carmen were gone."

A strangled sound escaped Lilly, who cradled her prosthetic closer to her chest. Venus felt her own heart drop. *Lori's gone? But she was so sweet, so gentle! She ... And Fiadh... She begged us for help and now she's gone. They didn't deserve... None of them deserve this.* Her jaw set. *This needs to end.*

"Does Olive have blonde hair?" Venus asked, hooking an arm around Jeannie's waist

"And light eyes?" Jaimie added.

Jeannie frowned at this comment, leaning on Venus.

"That sounds like her!" Quinn said, hands relaxing. *She doesn't look scared.*

"Does she wear a pendant around her neck?" Venus asked, fingers curling around the page that felt like ice in her pocket.

"You mean, like a necklace?" Quinn nodded. "She does!"

The pendant of resilience, she thought to herself, tightening her hold on Jeannie. *It has to be Olive.*

"Do you mind if we ask around about some things?" Acacia asked, seemingly studying Quinn's expression.

Quinn's eyes widened and she seemed to perk up. "Are you close to figuring out what's happening?"

"Yes," Berri said, with more confidence than Venus felt.

"But we need to confirm some things before we can do anything," Theo said, tone reassuring, but firm.

Quinn nodded. "Sure, I'll take you over."

As they moved over the path that they had now traversed twice across the crumbling 7th floor, Jeannie stayed nearly glued to Venus's side, arm tightly wrapped around Venus's middle. She was close enough to probably hear Venus's heartbeat speeding up, and she took a breath, trying to calm herself a bit.

The rest of the ghosts were all huddled under the hole in the ceiling, sunlight spilling in. The mood was somber, the six ghosts left huddled in groups of two and three. And one. Giorgia was sitting by herself, waiting for Quinn. Her expression lacked the usual lightness she carried, almost cradling herself in her arms.

"No one really knows what to do, since Fiadh went missing. She always tries to keep our spirits up, so now everyone's lost hope." She turned to them, lips turning up. "But I know you can help us." Her eyes darted to Jeannie, and for a split-second, her expression changed. *Concern?* "I just know it."

She sank down next to Giorgia, who smiled softly at her friend returning. Giorgia turned her attention to the group, expression more serious than the first time they met.

"The shadows have been getting more vicious, on top of everything else. I almost got caught when I was going around the fifth floor. It's like they're, I don't know, agitated?"

"As if they're waiting for something?" Jeannie asked, her grip on Venus's waist loosening a bit.

"Yes, exactly!" Giorgia nodded. "As if they are waiting for something to happen."

Jeannie tensed, as if frozen in thought. Movement from behind Giorgia caught Venus's eye, and she looked to see one of the girls in the group of three perking up at the mention of the shadows. Slowly, Venus unhooked herself from Jeannie, who didn't seem to notice, and crossed around to her. The sound of footsteps and a glance over her shoulder told her that Theo had followed.

The girl that had attracted Venus's attention was very pretty, her hooked nose and smile lines giving her a very friendly face, though her expression was not one of joy. Her dark eyes darted between Venus and her friends, who looked a tad exasperated.

"I wanted to tell you something about the shadows, something I think you should know," She said, her voice lilting. Her companions rolled their eyes, and she sent them a pointed look. "They don't believe me, but I know that I'm right."

"About what?" Venus asked, tilting her head towards the girl. She was older than Venus, but she couldn't tell by how much.

"The spirits are being organized by something, I just know it. They used to behave differently. I liked to watch them from the light," she explained, making her reasonings very clear. "They used to be very erratic, very animalistic, but a little bit predictable. They had tells before they would attack, so you could almost bait them into attacking and easily avoid them. But then, they calmed down. They became unpredictable, almost behaved? It's like suddenly they were on a leash, being held back, but always on the edge of breaking free."

"When did that happen?" Theo asked, criss-crossing their legs and settling on the floor next to Venus's feet.

"I think during the last full moon? Usually, they are silent and fairly safe on the full moon, because they don't like the light, but this time it was if something was encouraging them, pushing them to get closer and closer."

One of her companions, with curly black hair and a freckled face, huffed. "Aster, you only think that because that's the night Siobhan went missing." The curly haired girl turned to the trio, almost as if she was lecturing them. "Aster has been obsessed with this theory, but there has been nothing to prove it!"

"Even Olive wouldn't believe that," said the third girl, tucking her hair into her headscarf.

"What do you mean?" Theo asked, beating Venus to it.

"Olive thinks something odd is happening with the shadows too," Aster said, throwing her hands into her lap.

"As if you even talk to Olive." The second girl rolled her eyes.

"Has Olive always been so..." Venus trailed off, searching for a word that would properly describe her feelings without offending the ghosts.

"Standoffish?" The third girl finished, a pitying look covering her sharp features. "Well, she was never super chatty, but she distanced herself from everyone the night Siobhan went missing."

"Siobhan was the first girl who disappeared," the second girl offered, face softening.

"Olive and Siobhan were really close. They would go off exploring together, fearlessly venturing out." Aster said, almost admiringly. "But she doesn't stick around much anymore, always going out alone. It's like, she felt guilty for some reason? I mean, it wasn't her fault that Siobhan disappeared."

The other two nodded in agreement, but Venus shot a look to Theo, who had looked up to meet her eyes, seeming to think the same thing. *Maybe she looked guilty because she was. Maybe Siobhan was her first victim.*

"Thanks for letting us know, Aster." Venus said, putting a

hand on Theo's shoulder. "We'll make sure we look into that, okay?"

Aster nodded gratefully as Theo stood and Venus led the way to two ghosts who they hadn't spoken to yet, although it seemed like Acacia and Jaimie had beat them to it. One of the girls was crying.

"I can't stand it!" she cried, tears running down her ghostly face. "I don't want to lose anyone else, we've already lost so many people!"

"I know," Jaimie said, on his knees next to her, tearing up too. *He's really good at connecting with people.* "We are working our hardest to make sure that we can stop what is happening, okay? You've gone through so much, but it's going to be over soon, okay?"

Acacia's expression was fierce. "I know it sucks right now, but you have to trust us, okay?" The ghost just shook her head, blubbering that she was scared to die again. "Hey, look at me." Acacia got on her level, leaning in close to her. "We will save everyone, I promise."

Venus felt the hair on the back of her neck prickle. Jaimie was notorious for making promises he couldn't keep, but Acacia always did her best to keep her word. In the entire time Venus had known Acacia, she had only broken one promise. *Just like her dad.*

Slowly, the ghost nodded, drying her tears. Acacia stood up and met Venus's gaze, and for a long moment, her face was unreadable. *She knows what this means, doesn't she?* The two groups crossed back to where Giorgia and Quinn were without a word. Jeannie was being held by Irsa, Lillybelle and Berri finishing their discussion with the two ghosts.

"We'll be back before the sun sets, to end this for good." Jeannie said, face serious as she looked Quinn in the eyes.

Quinn just nodded. "We trust you."

"And we'll see if we can do anything about the stairs,"

Giorgia added, seemingly connecting to a conversation the six had finished earlier. "So that you don't have to rely on us for the elevator all the time."

Berri smiled. "We appreciate it."

Waving goodbye, Venus made sure to be the one leading the group to the elevator, where she stepped in first. When the doors didn't slam shut, she ushered everyone else silently on to the elevator. A chill settled on her skin and she shuddered. Once everyone was inside, they shut the doors and they began their steady descent. Taking a deep breath, Venus opened her mouth, starting to say something when Lillybelle poked her in the arm.

Venus turned to see that she was holding up her phone, a message typed out into an unsent text bubble.

Say nothing, the text message read. *We're being watched.*

38

Lilly

Lillybelle could feel eyes burning into the back of her head as they left the building, only fading once the car had pulled away and sped down the road. No one said a word until the eight of them were completely settled in the corner booth at the *Circus Spoon Diner*, Venus's favorite restaurant in town. Funnily enough, it was a classic 50s diner, instead of the acrobatic theming the name implied.

The black and white checkered flooring reflected the neon lights that hung above, bouncing the neon blues and purples across the signature red leather seats. An almost ridiculously large jukebox was up against the wall, the pale blue paint chipping around the wooden frames that covered the wallpaper. Limp plastic menus lay flat on the table in front of each person, half remaining unopened.

Venus decided to interrupt the droning of Elvis and break the silence. "How did you know that we were being watched?"

Lilly met her eyes, slowly shaking her head. Venus was sitting on the edge of the booth, Irsa between her and Jeannie, Jaimie tucked in the corner with Berri.

259

"I had a bad feeling. I think Olive was lurking around, listening to see if we were onto her."

Lilly felt Theo release a breath next to her, their leg against hers. "So we are 100% sure it's her?"

"Who else would it be?" Berri asked, shaking their head as they thumbed through the two pages of the menu.

"No, I agree, I'm just making sure." Theo said, a bit defensively.

"There really isn't anyone else it could be." Acacia said. "The girls we were talking to said, that when they were talking about whether or not to ask for our help, Olive was the only one who was very against the idea."

"Apparently, she didn't think we would be able to help," Jaimie continued, eyes on the peeling corners of his menu. "So there was 'no point.'"

Lilly frowned. "She really didn't want us to interfere with her plan."

Theo crossed their arms. "And she apparently feels guilty about it all, distancing herself after killing her first friend."

Berri looked incredulous. "I would hope so!"

"She must be pretty desperate if she would rather kill all her friends than live trapped like that." Irsa said softly, eyes on the table.

"If she wants to escape so badly, why not just pass on?" Venus drummed her fingers on the table. "Like, move on from this plane permanently, like Cordelia's husband."

"Maybe she's scared of dying?" Acacia sighed. "Again."

"Maybe."

"I mean, if death didn't free her the first time, what's the guarantee that it would this time?" Acacia said, contemplatively tracing the edges of the menu.

"Well, regardless, if she's really that desperate as to kill and eat her friends of several decades, how do we know she'll wait until tonight to act?" Berri asked, gesturing out the window. "What if she does it now, while we're gone?"

"I doubt she would waste the opportunity to double the power." Lilly said, pulling her prosthetic into her lap.

"Plus, she can't get anyone away from each other now that everyone is on guard." Irsa added. "She has to wait until night fall, when everyone's guard is down from exhaustion."

Lilly's gaze darted to Jeannie, who had opened her mouth, as if she was about to say something, but when she didn't say anything, her hand darted to her throat. *Are her fingers twitching?* Lilly started to ask her what was wrong, but at that moment, someone came up to the table. A waiter in roller skates and a tiny teal apron had rolled up to the table, his white sleeves rolled up his thick arms. He was beefy, salt and pepper hair pinned behind his ears with comically colored barbell clips. His name tag said *Ivan*.

"Hello Venus, it's been a while!" He said, a hint of an accent coloring his voice.

Venus smiled. "Hey, Mr. V. Good to see you again."

"Are you ready to order? Or just drinks?"

Venus glanced around the table. "I think just drinks right now."

He nodded and as each person went around and said what they wanted, he jotted it down on his almost ridiculously small notepad. His pen had an elephant charm hanging off the end, swinging and glittering red in the neon lights. "So that is four soft drinks, one chocolate shake, one strawberry shake, one root beer float, and one tea, sweet not hot." At that last request, he shot a look at Theo, who smiled sheepishly. "I will be back." He skated off, almost too graceful for a man of his size.

"He's nice." Theo said, grinning widely. "Doesn't seem to like sweet tea, though."

Venus just laughed it off. "He works here with his fiance, who is also very nice. Cute couple, actually."

Theo nodded, but Lilly's eyes were back on Jeannie, who seemed to be preparing for something.

"What about the shadows?" She finally asked, as if choking out the words, glancing from person to person. "Everyone we've talked to has said something about the shadows and how they are a problem. Earlier, I heard the girl you guys were talking to," she gestured to Venus. "Say something about the shadows getting stronger. What if something was organizing the shadows, making them a big enough threat so that Olive can corner the other ghosts?"

Murmurs rose from the table and Lilly found herself slowly nodding. "Could be that the shadows are trying to feed off the power she's gaining and are helping her in exchange for power?"

"Yeah, like some sort of trade off." Theo said, sitting up a bit straighter. "They get to feed, and she gets enough power to escape."

"Maybe Olive teamed up with the shadows and she's the one controlling them? And she's consuming them, so that's why they can't be sensed? That pendant Venus told us about, that could be how she does it," Acacia said, brows furrowed as she brushed a vibrant blue strand of hair behind her hearing aids.

"But what about the shadow man that chased Jeannie?" Venus shook her head, hands splayed on the table. "He has to be involved here."

Jeannie reached down into her lap and pulled out a leather bound book, setting it gently on the table in front of her. *How long has she been holding that?* Her blackened fingers tapped the cover and she kept looking between Venus and Irsa, mouth a thin line. Lilly squinted, trying to read the cover from upside down. Venus sat straight up.

"What if it's a demon? This is the book about demon's that you got at Dr. Martin's shop, right Jeannie?" She nodded and Venus gasped. "Maybe it's a demon doing all of this! The pendant is involved with demonic magic, too, so it would make sense!"

The table got quiet. Irsa's eyes had been blown wide.

"Woah, okay, that changes things." Berri said, hands lacing in their hair as they leaned back against the booth wall.

"So, maybe Olive made a deal with the demon through the pendant in exchange for power?" Jaimie spun his knife on the table, finger on the dull end.

"And that's how she is going to get enough power to escape!" Theo slammed their hand on their leg, startling the few other customers in the diner. "The demon is consuming the ghosts as energy in exchange for her safe passage!"

"That would be why it only started recently. Maybe the demon only formed recently." Lilly said, mind going back to the darkness inside of the warehouse. *The dream.*

"Okay, guys!" Acacia said, gently tapping the table with her floppy menu. "How the fuck would we deal with a demon?"

"Well, it might not even be a demon, that's just a theory. An interesting theory, but one we can't confirm." Irsa said, picking nervously at the hem of her black hijab.

"Nor do we have the time to confirm it." Lilly said, glancing at her phone. *Only six hours until sunset.* "And even if it was, by stopping Olive, it would break the deal anyway," she said, taking a deep breath. "So, we can stick to the plan."

Venus sighed. "You're right, it was kinda farfetched."

Jeannie swallowed and stared down at her hands, almost deflating. Irsa leaned against Jeannie. "And what is the plan, exactly?"

Venus opened her mouth, but closed it and smiled as Ivan rolled up to the table, effortlessly balancing an overflowing tray on his palm. Quickly, he unloaded four glasses of ice in front of Berri, Irsa, Jeannie, and Lilly, setting a pitcher of Coke in the center of the table. A large beer glass was set down in front of Jaimie, two giant scoops of vanilla ice cream dripping into the root beer that filled the rest of the glass. A glass of iced tea was set in front of Theo, a slice of lemon sitting wedged onto the rim.

The presentation of the milkshakes themselves was impressive. Each shake came with a tall glass cup, ridged in the way only milkshake cups were. A thick rainbow straw poked out of a tower of whipped cream, a glistening maraschino cherry sitting on either side of the straw. A second, just as large, metal cup was set next to them, also full to the brim with milkshake. *Those look delicious.*

"That is what was left in the blender." He said, grinning at Acacia's expression of shock.

As Venus immediately put the straw between her lips, Lilly smiled. Her face lit up as the milkshake hit her tongue. *No wonder this is her favorite restaurant.*

"Before you order, are there dietary restrictions I need to know?" He asked, readying his silly little pen on the pad, expression serious.

After a few minutes of Ivan reassuring them that the french fries and beef products were halal and Theo's food would not be cross contaminated with nuts at any point, he skated away, notepad full of orders.

"I think we should split up," Venus said, turning her attention away from the delicious looking shake and to the piece of paper she had pulled from her pocket. "Some of us should go find out the truth about Adrienne's death, but the rest of us should work on destroying Olive and defending the rest of the ghosts."

"I am going to the school to do the spell for Adrienne, but it's okay if no one else wants to come." Lilly said, mind going to the book she had left in the front seat of the car.

"No, I'm coming too." Irsa said, sighing. "If it does turn out to be a demon, I do not want to be anywhere near it. No offense." She squeezed Jeannie's hand.

"I'll join you guys." Jaimie sighed. "If Scooby-Doo has taught me anything, it's that splitting up is bad, but if we can stay in larger groups, we should be fine."

"Ok good, we've got our teams then." Venus said, nodding to Lilly. "Then we need to figure out what we need to do. Tommy said that to get rid of a ghost, there are four main steps."

"Wait," Jeannie sat up in her seat. "Even if we destroy Olive, the shadows are still a major threat. I think that some of us should take care of Olive and some of us finish washing the building. Because then, it's safer for all of them and they won't be trapped."

"Okay, let's do both." Venus said, nodding at Jeannie, her gaze softening. *Does she.... It doesn't matter.*

"I would love to keep washing down the building, so I'm down for that." Berri said. "Though we would need to get a longer hose so that we could reach farther."

"We can go shopping for supplies after lunch," Theo said through the straw of her sweet tea. "I can imagine we need stuff for the ghosts and you guys probably need stuff for the spell, right Lilly?"

Lillybelle nodded. "The spell did have a couple of requirements so that it would work properly. I doubt my phone flashlight will work as a candle this time."

Jaimie looked confused at the statement, but said nothing as Venus began to explain the plan. She passed Tommy's instructions around the table for everyone to look at while they waited. Tommy's handwriting hadn't been the clearest, but the steps were simple, if not very specific.

1. *Find an object the ghost is connected to, as a ghost or alive. If as a ghost, any object that's been touched.*

"The knife," Jeannie reminded them. "She was holding a knife when I saw her."

"That could be what she's been using to kill the other ghosts and retrieve their life force," Berri said, chewing their finger.

1. *Write the ghosts full name on the object and seal it with ghost essence*

"Ghost essence?" Jaimie asked, exasperated.

"Could be the stuff we saw on the floor?" Lilly said, mind going back to the picture she had taken.

"Has to be," Venus replied, shaking her head at the air. "It's not like Tommy was very specific."

1. *Get the object in the same room as the ghost, alone so it doesn't get confused for others.*

"So, we get her alone?" Acacia asked, squinting down at the messy handwriting. "How are we supposed to get her by herself?"

"Well, she has to get one of the others by themselves to kill them right?" Berri said, using a fork and a knife to walk their fingers along the table. "What if we get one of the ghosts to lure her away and then get her that way?"

1. *Destroy the object (light it on fire)*

"Great," Theo scowled. "Anyone have a lighter and some lighter fluid?"

"We have to kill her the way she died before." Acacia looked unhappy at the thought.

"Maybe the fire will cleanse her, as she passes on permanently." Irsa said, hopeful.

As Venus started to hash out details with Berri and Acacia, Lilly's heartbeat loudened in her ears, thoughts drowning out their voices. She felt her chest tighten, guilt biting at her insides.

Is it really our right to decide who has to die? A wave of nausea washed over her. *What if we destroy her and she doesn't move on? What if we do this, but nothing changes? What if it's all for nothing?* Her breathing sped up and her mouth went dry. *Are we any better than her if we do this? What if we've been getting this all wrong? What if she isn't the one? What if they all die anyway? What if-*

A sharp jab in the ribs made her flinch, quickly turning to see Theo watching her, chin on the table. Theo was smiling, but it didn't reach their eyes.

"Lilly." He said, his voice painfully steady. "What are five things that you can see right now?"

"What?" Her voice came out slightly strangled, too quiet for the volume of the voices in her head.

"Give me your hand," Theo took her hand in theirs, holding up five fingers. "Five things you can see, right now. You don't have to say what they are, just when you have found them."

She swallowed, eyes darting around the table. *What can I see?* The matching ketchup and mustard bottles at the end of the table. Theo's car in the parking lot, out the window. Venus's ponytail coming loose as she absentmindedly pulled at the ribbon. The black-and-white tiles of the floor, worn in some places. The lights of the jukebox. "I found them."

Theo smiled, meeting Lilly's eyes. Theo pressed one of Lilly's finger in her palm. "Now four things you can hear."

Her chest vibrated as she took in a sharp breath. Berri's voice. Jaimie's nervous table tapping. The start of a Ray Charles song, piano a bit distorted by the speakers. Her own heart beat. "Done."

Another finger pressed down. Three left. "Three things you can feel."

The warmth of Theo's hands. The weight of her prosthetic pulling on her shoulder and the strap digging into her back. The uncomfortable leather of the seat pressing against her thighs. She nodded and Theo pushed another finger down.

"Two things you can smell."

Cheese, wafting from the kitchen. Theo's cologne.

"Now, take one deep breath with me."

After a moment of hesitation and a reassuring nod from Theo, she sucked in air through her nose until she couldn't any more, and let it out. Theo squeezed her hand, breathing with her.

"It'll be okay, Lilly. Whatever happens, we'll be okay."

Lilly felt herself nodding, the guilt that had been painfully digging into her now subsiding, still there, but smaller. Movement to her left told her that Ivan, the burly waiter, had silently skated up to them once again. This time, he carried a ridiculously large tray on his palm, setting it down on the edge of the table.

A kids grilled cheese and a side of onion rings was set in front of Berri, who grinned like the Cheshire cat and profusely thanked Ivan. Jaimie's meatless chicken tenders and mashed potatoes came next, the side of gravy steaming up next to the potato mound. Jeannie's chef salad was topped with grilled chicken slices and Acacia's hot dog with it's side of mac'n'cheese smelled delicious, the cheesy-meatiness wafting over to Lilly.

Theo only got a little bit of side eye from Acacia when his giant bowl of mac'n'cheese was placed down in front of him, Lilly's own club sandwich and fries set down immediately after. Venus got a double bacon cheeseburger with fries, which she immediately dipped in her milkshake.

"And last, but not least, a beef burger with halal french fries for our last little lady." Ivan said, placing the last plate in front of a beaming Irsa. "I can bring your chosen desserts after you finish."

"Sounds great, Mr. V." Venus said, visibly restraining herself from digging in.

"Thank you so much," Lilly added, her own stomach rumbling at the look of her sandwich.

A chorus of 'thank-you's rang out from the rest of the table and Ivan skated off, pleased. For several minutes, the table was quiet, only the sound of chewing and silverware heard. Of course, there was the obvious argument between Theo and Jaimie about whether or not ketchup belonged on mac'n'cheese, as a slightly horrified Acacia looked on. When they were most of the way done with their delicious food, Theo brought up the bill.

"Don't worry about cost, guys, I'll pay." Immediately, half the table broke into protesting, which Theo waved off. "Oh come on, it's no issue!"

"I can pay my part of the bill!" Berri cried, indignantly wiping mustard off of the corner of their mouth, brandishing an onion ring.

"It's only fair," Jeannie insisted, dumping the rest of her ranch on her salad. "I mean, we did stay at *your* house last night."

Theo just shook his head again. "It's no big deal! I mean, how many of you guys have a job?"

"I forget you had a job, actually." Acacia said, finishing off her side of mac.

Irsa frowned, placing her fork on her now clean plate, only a couple of fries left over.

"Where do you work again?"

"Zax." They said, taking a sip of their almost depleted sweet tea.

"You work at the Zax's Pies?" Venus asked, incredulous. Her burger was dripping from her fingers onto her shirt. "The house of chicken, bacon, and mixed meat pies?"

Jaimie laughed, using his fork to dip his vegan chicken into the mashed potato and gravy mixture he had made on his plate. "I thought you were a vegetarian too."

"I am." Theo said proudly, adding more ketchup to her mac'n'cheese mixture. "I refuse to eat anything that I can cuddle with."

"You won't eat meat, but you're fine working at a place that is practically a butchers shop?" Acacia smiled, taking a long sip of her strawberry milkshake. She had given all of the cherries to Jaimie already.

"Well, my manager told me that we get all of our meat from a farm that uses Zabiha practices, so I don't really feel any guilt."

"That's true, my parents do buy from that shop pretty often." Irsa nodded.

"See!"

"Anything you can cuddle with is off limits?" Jaimie asked, almost smirking. "So fish are fine?"

"You bet your ass fish are fine, I love sushi."

Lilly laughed, eating a piece of egg that had fallen from her sandwich when a thought popped in her head. She sat up straight, turning to Jaimie, who was trying to scoop the rest of the ice cream out of his root beer float with his spoon. "Will your mom be mad you aren't going to the Synagogue today?"

He shook his head, licking the ice cream from the spoon.

"Not really, she knows I prefer to do it my own way. Sometimes I go with her, though."

Venus groaned, as if remembering something. "I know my mom is going to be soo mad if I'm late for mass tomorrow, which I probably will be!"

"Sacrifices must be made." Jaimie said, solemnly nodding. There was whipped cream on his upper lip, giving him a wispy mustache.

"Speaking of, I'm going to go pray, so you guys keep talking." Irsa said, standing up after wiping her mouth with a napkin and placing it on her now empty plate. "Just fill me in when I get back. Is my travel rug in your car, Theo?"

"Yeah," they said through a bite of mac and cheese. "Take my keys."

Venus stood to let Irsa pass as Theo tossed her the car keys. As soon as she had walked away, Ivan skated up, setting down a banana split for Berri and a slice of chocolate chess pie in front of Lilly. Theo stood up.

"I'll go take care of the bill, just tell me what y'all talk about after, k?"

Lilly nodded, standing to let him through and sitting back down. Her fork pierced the tip of the pie and she lifted it to her mouth, the rich chocolate flavor exploding on her tongue. She smiled.

"I'm definitely ready to get back to the warehouse." Acacia said, wiping the grease from her food on her paper napkin. "I know we have a lot to do, but I'm ready to finish this."

Venus looked at her, concern painting her features. "Acacia, why did you make that promise?"

Lilly's eyebrows scrunched, confused. "What promise?"

Acacia said nothing, so Venus continued. "She promised the girls that we would protect them and save everyone."

Jeannie's jaw dropped, eyes serious. "Acacia, why would you promise that?"

"You never break a promise," Jaimie said, eyes wide in amazement.

Acacia gaze a sheepish smile that fell short of her eyes, ignoring the pained look Jeannie was giving her. "Because we can't break this promise. We have to save them. We just have to."

39

Venus

By the time the sun had set, Venus had accomplished everything she had needed to do in preparation. After the desserts had been finished, the bill paid, and Irsa's prayer rug rolled back up, they had split into their two groups. Theo had agreed to take Lilly's group where they needed to go and would meet them at the warehouse when the sun set, leaving Venus driving around everyone else.

The first stop was Theo's house, to grab everyone's stuff, but then it was the hardware store. The bill at checkout was almost painfully high, but between everyone's pocket money and Venus's membership discount, they were able to successfully pay for everything. Each person now had:

One (1) walkie talkie with a spare set of batteries,

One (1) heavy duty flashlight,

One (1) pocket knife, courtesy of Venus's personal stash,

One (1) set of heavy duty gloves

And one (1) pack of colored glow-sticks.

Jeannie now owned two 100-foot long hoses and several water guns. Berri had bought two step-ladders and Acacia was

272

the proud owner of rope, duct tape, and water balloons. Venus had changed into thicker boots, a poncho now replacing the flannel she had tied around her waist earlier. Acacia had tied her hair back and tucked it under her beanie and Berri's jacket was zipped all the way up. Theo had just gotten back from dropping the other group off at the school and had changed into taller boots, though their spiderweb leggings still left a lot of unprotected skin.

Jeannie was standing in the gravel lot in front of the warehouse, expression stoic, eyes on the windows of the seventh floor. Her flowy white sweater had been discarded, a long sleeve white shirt rolled up to her elbows. The stained skin only just ended where her shirt reached, the color rippling under her skin like waves of rot and ink. She had the length of hose wrapped around her shoulder, the wand of the washer gripped tightly in her hand. The water guns were strapped to her belt, her flashlight sticking out of her backpack. *She looks ready to go to war.*

"Here's the plan," Venus said, spreading out the pieces of paper that Lilly had given her: maps of the building, printed pictures she had taken, copies of Tommy's instructions. "Berri and Jeannie have volunteered to finish cleaning out the building with the power-washers. Acacia, you agreed to stay with the ghosts that are remaining while Theo and I corner and take care of Olive. Everyone keep your walkie's on channel 3 and keep them on."

"The last thing we want is to lose contact during the banishment." Theo said, nodding solemnly. *He's in full 'mom mode'.*

"Report anything suspicious." Jeannie nodded, grip on the washer never loosening.

Venus made sure to lead the way into the building, opening the door that they had closed last time. In every corner they passed, someone cracked a glow-stick and tossed it, marking what was already clean. The shadows shrank back, the little light it created barely making a dent on the ever growing darkness as the sun sank below the horizon.

Berri and Jeannie stopped on the first floor, right where the hoses had failed them the first night.

"When you get up there, can you send Quinn down?" Jeannie asked Acacia, pulling on her rubber gloves. "I wanted to ask her about something."

Acacia nodded, and the three continued on to where the elevator was. Acacia stepped into the elevator, closing the doors herself. With a hit of a button she was gone, slowly ascending to the upper floors. Venus turned to Theo, who had a step ladder in each hand.

"If the knife were to be anywhere, where would it be?"

Theo smiled. "I wonder."

The pair turned to the door that was on the wall opposite of the elevator, the one where they had heard the chanting earlier in the day. The handle was loose, but when she tried to push the door open, something was stopping it from opening. With two shoulders thrown against it, however, whatever it was fell away quickly, revealing a small, closet-like room. The window was broken, all of the glass completely gone. It had been swept into a pile in the corner and in the center of the room was a bowl, a small drum, and a silver knife.

Venus frowned as Theo picked up the drum, strumming her fingers across it. "Where would Olive have even gotten this stuff?"

Venus just shrugged. "Let's just get this over with. You have the name?"

Theo nodded, pulling a sharpie from his pocket. "Lilly said her name is Olive Marino." Theo wrote the name on the knife blade. "Done."

Venus took the knife back, holding it loosely in her left palm. "Let's go."

Once back in the hallway, they heard a blast of water from

their left. Jeannie and Berri had started up. Venus exchanged a look with Theo, who was once again carrying two of the step ladders. Venus herself was carrying one of them, but they had set them all down to open the door. The two made their way to the far stairwell, where they could see the open garage door in the distance. *I thought it closed behind Jeannie?* The shadows by the door seemed to writhe, hungrily.

Theo set down the step ladder at the base of the stairs, setting it up to make the gap easier to traverse. Earlier, they had decided that relying solely on ghost power to get up to the seventh floor was a bad idea, so the step ladders were there to make it a little bit safer. The stairs to the second and third floors were pretty safe, but there was something they needed to do before they could get any farther.

Setting the ladders against the wall, Venus made her way to the center of the building, Theo trailing behind. Just like in the picture, a small bowl shaped indent was in the floor, black goop sitting in the center. She frowned. There seemed to be more than was in the picture.

Theo, without hesitation, scooped some of it into their hands and motioned for Venus to take out the knife. Venus did, but not without shooting Theo a look of concern.

"Why would you just touch that?" Venus asked as Theo spread it on the flat side of the blade.

"I dunno know. It doesn't really feel like anything, though." When it was all on the knife, none of it was on Theo's hands, not even as a stain. The knife however, looked gross, the goop almost sizzling on the side.

"Step three, completed. Now, to find Olive." As she straightened up, both of their walkie talkie's crackled to life and Acacia's sweet voice came through.

"Hey Jeannie, Quinn is on her way down. Over."

A few seconds passed and it crackled to life again, this time Jeannie's voice coming through. "Got it."

Venus smiled and pressed the speak button. "You didn't say over. Over."

A beat. "Bitch. Over."

Theo burst out laughing and lead the way towards the stairwell. They started up the stairs and made it to the fourth floor without incident. Another flight and they found that the entrance to the fifth floor was blocked off by rubble, but the stairs themselves were fairly intact. When they reached the landing between the fifth and sixth floors, they were met with a gap between the second and the seventh step, the steps between having crumpled in the middle. Venus unfolded the ladder she was carrying to cover the gap, motioning for Theo to wait while she tested it out. The ladder held, so Theo passed the last step ladder up to her and crossed himself.

The sixth floor doorway was clear, but the stairwell had caved in above that point, making it impossible to continue. They stepped out onto the sixth floor, many gaps in the ceiling letting some light in. The moonlight shone through the many broken and smoke stained windows, casting thick shadows. A loud crackling from the walkie-talkies.

"I need to grab something from the car." Berri's voice broke through. "I'll be right back, over."

"Understood, over." Acacia's voice replied.

"Copy that." Venus said. "Over."

Theo tapped Venus on the shoulder and when Venus turned to look at them, pointed to the far end of the sixth floor. There, staring out the window, Olive floated, back to them. *I guess we don't need Quinn to lure her away.* Venus nodded at Theo, and she switched off her walkie. Theo did the same. *Don't want a stray voice giving us away.* Slowly, and as quietly as they could manage, they made their way across the floor, going around the broken and melted machinery. There were gaps in the ground, almost in a perfect circle around where Olive stood.

Venus pulled the knife out of her pocket, the goo almost sizzling on the blade, bubbling and writhing as if it were boiling. Quickly, Theo pulled out the lighter she had bought at the hardware store and flicked it on, bringing it towards Venus's blade. Olive spun around at the sound, pale eyes wide. Her gray eyes.

"What are you doing?" She cried, fear coursing through her voice as she darted towards them.

"I'm sorry Olive, but we can't let you do this anymore."

"No! It's not me!"

A cold feeling sunk in Venus's chest. *Something feels wrong.* Theo lit the blade and it instantly caught, the flame engulfing the blade and forcing Venus to drop it. Theo's brows were furrowed and he was biting his lip, as if he hadn't meant to do that yet. Olive screamed, a raw primal scream that seemed to echo in Venus's rib cage. A silver pendant tumbled from the neckline of her dress as her screams ricocheted across the building, a chorus of others joining her voice.

"Please! The necklace! You have to stop her! She's-"

Her body went stiff, hands clawing at her neck as she froze in the air. If she could've gone grayer, she would've but after a moment of still grayness, she melted away. Her features melted into a black smoke dissipating into the air. She was gone, haunting scream and expression gone with her. After Theo had finished stomping out the tall flame, Venus reached for her walkie-talkie, hands shaking.

"Did that feel wrong to you?" Theo asked, staring at the knife. *He felt it too.*

"Yeah, it did. What did she mean by 'it's not me'?"

Theo shrugged. "What necklace was she talking about? I mean, she was wearing the pendant, wasn't she?"

Venus shook her head and grabbed the walkie-talkie. *That didn't look like the pendant.* She switched it back on, ready to tell the team it had been done when screeching voices came from the talkie itself.

"-don't even know what the fuck happened!" Acacia was crying. "They're all gone, they just fucking disappeared-"

"Where are you guys?" Berri's voice shrieked.

What's going on? Quickly, Venus hit talk. "What's going on, what happened?"

"Where the fuck have you been we've been trying to reach you-"

"They're all gone!" Acacia cut in, voice ragged and high. "All of them, just disappeared like smoke!"

"What? What do you mean?" Theo cried, wrenching the walkie from Venus's hands.

"That's not the worst part!" Berri yelled. "Jeannie's gone!"

40

Jeannie

Jeannie had been peacefully cleaning the grime off the far wall when Quinn had appeared next to her. Quinn was quiet, smiling softly as Jeannie turned around and jumped nearly a foot in surprise.

"Sorry," she said, smile immediately falling to a look of concern. "I didn't want to interrupt your process, is all."

Jeannie nodded, tucking her hair back away from her face. "It's okay, I just didn't see you there. I've been kinda on edge."

"Is it because of the shadows?" Quinn asked, leaning forward as her feet floated off of the ground.

Jeannie shot a look at Berri, who was hopping along to a song quietly blasting from their phone as they cleaned the far wall. She switched her wand to a lower pressure level and turned back to Quinn.

"Yes," Her eyes went to her hands, the blackened skin looking almost diseased. "It's hot, like an iron is being pressed against my skin. Sometimes, it writhes underneath my skin, like a snake trying to strangle me from within."

Quinn's eyes squinted in sympathy. "I'm sorry, that sounds painful."

Jeannie nodded, letting out a shaky breath. "Not nearly as painful as it must be to lose so many of your friends."

"It does hurt." Quinn sank, feet back on the ground, but a pained smile formed on her face. "But the fire hurt more."

Jeannie felt her own face fall, shutting off her washer to get a good look at Quinn. She had crossed her arms, her dress sleeve falling away from her forearm and revealing bright, blistering burns.

"You remember how you died?"

Quinn cringed at the word, but nodded. "We don't talk about it a lot, but yes, we all do. I remember being in that elevator, the fire raging on above and beneath. The gears must have melted together, because they stopped between one of the floors. We couldn't get out. Fiadh's hands got stuck to the doors because she was trying to pull them open. I remember her screams as she couldn't pull them off. Olive, she and Siobhan were huddled in the middle. Siobhan was crying. Olive kept saying that she would protect her, she would make sure she got out." Quinn laughed, but there was no humor. "I guess she failed her twice."

Bile ate at the back of her throat, but she swallowed it down. "Quinn, that's what I wanted to talk to you about. I thought you deserved to know our plan."

"Have you figured out who's been doing this to us?" Quinn asked, hopeful.

Jeannie bit her lip. "We think so."

Jeannie's walkie talkie crackled to life and Berri's voice could be heard coming from it and from several feet away. She looked up and saw Berri looking at her, motioning to the front door.

"I need to grab something from the car." Berri said. "I'll be right back, over."

"Understood, over." Acacia's voice replied after a second.

"Copy that." Venus's voice broke through. "Over."

Jeannie nodded at Berri and watched as they crossed back through the building, past the heart Jeannie had left on the wall. She had carved it out to be slightly larger, but her own heart told her to leave it behind. She turned back to Quinn and took a deep breath.

"It's Olive."

Quinn's face dropped. "What."

"Olive has been the only one acting suspiciously, plus she's the only one who's been able to move around the building."

"No, it can't be Olive." Quinn said, moving closer to Jeannie. "It can't be."

"I know she's your friend, but it's her. The others say they have evidence that it's her and right now they're getting ready to stop her."

"No, you don't understand. It literally can't be her. I was with her the night that Siobhan went missing, that first night. She took me to the fourth floor, she was trying to show me the view from the windows. When we got back, Siobhan was gone. And I was with her when Lori went missing, I went to sleep holding her and woke up holding her. It's not her!"

Jeannie shook her head. "But, their description of her matches the woman I saw outside, the one with the knife. The one you saved me from. Blonde hair, blue eyes-"

"Olive has gray eyes!" Quinn hissed, nostrils flaring. "If that had been Olive, you wouldn't have been able to see her, I wouldn't have saved you from her, and I would have told you that was Olive! None of us can even go outside, that's why we're stuck!"

"But, if that wasn't Olive, who-"

"I don't know who! What are they going to do to Olive?"

"They said they were going to tie her to her knife, destroy it."

Quinn shook her head, relieved. "It won't work."

"Then who-"

"Quiet." Quinn's eyes were wide as she froze. "Someone is here."

"What do you mean?" Jeannie whispered, as Quinn ushered her against the wall.

"We can sense when someone is in the building, that's how we know when you guys are here. Someone else is here. And I think she's been here before"

Jeannie's eyes went wide with fear. "Who?"

A crash sounded to her right and before she could even move, Quinn had pushed her back. Instead of hitting the wall, she felt a wave of pressure wash through her and she couldn't move. *It's happened again.* She was in the wall. This time, however, she could see Quinn, pressed up against her, holding her tightly in the wall, face inches away from hers. The cold, transparent woman looked over her shoulder as Jeannie stood frozen behind her.

Unable to move or react, she was forced to watch in silence as the door Theo and Venus had searched was blown open. Out of the door, a woman strode out, blue eyes blown wide. She had a wild expression, ratty blonde hair, swept away from her face. She stalked towards Jeannie, eyes hungrily raking up and down the wall where she had disappeared. *Blue, blue, blue.*

As she approached, Jeannie felt a second set of hands wrapping around her waist, painfully familiar. A wave of revulsion washed over her, and if she could've moved, she would've gagged. Quinn's eyes went wide and Jeannie could hear Quinn's voice in her mind: *'It's you.'*

The woman stopped in front of Jeannie and her face split into a terrifying smile. A large black stone swung out from her hood as she leaned forward, hanging from a thin leather strap. It glowed.

"I've got you now." The woman said, voice familiar. *The phone call. The dream. It's been her every time.*

The next few moments felt as if they went by in slow motion. She thrust her hand forward, reaching into the wall. Quinn stared beyond Jeannie, behind Jeannie, *at him*, a million thoughts racing across her face.

'Protect her.' Jeannie heard Quinn say. The searing hands around her waist tightened, pulling her backwards as a familiar, haunting voice spilled into her mind. A pang of guilt rang through her, but it wasn't hers. *It's his.*

'You have my word.'

Satisfied, Quinn closed her eyes and let a tear run down her face, pushing Jeannie back as the woman's hand closed around her. Jeannie felt her soul scream as the woman's fingers twisted in Quinn and ripped her from the wall. A chorus of screams filled the air and the air turned to ice as the woman's eyes glowed black. Her mouth moved as if she was speaking, but it was drowned out by the blood curdling shrieks that reverberated across the building. Contorting and fading before Jeannie's eyes, Quinn dissipated into black smoke, pouring into black stone of the woman's necklace.

As quickly as the screaming had started, it abruptly cut off, black smoke seeping from the walls and ceiling and spilling into the stone. The woman shuddered, the power emanating from her in waves. When she opened her eyes again, they were a crystal blue. Her face split into a horrifying smile and she strode off towards the stairs, leaving Jeannie trembling within the wall.

Quinn's gone. And only the scalding shadow wrapped around her was left.

41

Lilly

Lilly took a deep breath of the crisp fall air, the wind whistling around the trio as they stood in front of the school. Theo's car had just pulled away, leaving Lilly, Irsa, and Jaimie to their mission, the chill of the evening settling in. Her bag was heavy and her wallet was light, all of the required materials piled in her tote. Once Irsa had finished her sunset prayer and rolled up her travel mat, Lilly led the way back to the greenhouse.

Jaimie was the first to go through the tile, Lilly following and helping Irsa through. The school halls were dark and the greenhouse door creaked as she pushed it open, a wave of humid air spilling over their skin and into the hallway. It clicked as Jaimie pushed it shut behind them, his footsteps a few steps behind Irsa and Lilly's. It took only minutes to reach the spot where Adrienne had been before.

"Adrienne!" Lilly quietly called out, setting her tote bag on the ground and sinking to her knees.

Irsa did the same, a few feet back. Jaimie sat directly next to Lilly, criss-cross apple sauce. He leaned towards her, pulling out the thick red tome that was at the top of the bag. Lilly took a deep breath and tried again. "Adrienne, are you here?"

Before Lilly had even finished speaking, a pale face appeared a few inches in front of her, making her jump back. Jaimie glanced at her, confused. Adrienne sat back, floating an inch or so off the ground, criss-cross like Jaimie.

"Always and forever!" she said, a smile on her pretty face.

Lilly glanced back at Irsa, who had tilted her head, frowning.

"Can they see you?" Lilly asked Adrienne, who smiled wider.

"Do you want them to?" she asked, throwing her head to the side.

Lilly nodded, then, after a moment, shook her head, gratefully taking the book from Jaimie. "It's your choice."

Adrienne bared her pearly white teeth and flipped back into the air. She winked.

"WoAH!" Jaimie's head snapped up towards Adrienne, mouth agape.

A gasp over her shoulder told Lilly that Irsa could see her too. Adrienne kicked her legs behind her, as if she were a schoolgirl laying on a bed at a slumber party.

"Hi!"

"Hello." Irsa squeaked, voice higher than normal. She scooted up closer, on Lilly's left. "You're Adrienne."

The ghost nodded. "It's nice to finally meet you, Irsa. You too, Jaimie."

Jaimie nodded, mouth still gaping.

"They've heard a lot about you." Lilly said, smiling as she flipped the pages until she reached the right one. "Okay, are you guys ready to do this?"

Jaimie shut his mouth and nodded again, turning to the bag.

"Do you mind if I just watch?" Irsa said, folding her hands in her lap.

Lilly nodded and then began to read. "'On this night of the High moon, the strongest moon for scrying and intuition, follow these steps to learn the full truth of a death.'" After receiving a nod of confirmation from the others, she continued. "'First cast a magic circle with your chosen deities as a form of protection. If you do not know how to cast a magic circle, consult the first pages or use a salt circle.'" She glanced over at Jaimie. "Can you grab the salt?"

Jaimie reached into the bag and grabbed a large container of cooking salt. Standing up, he poured a thick line of salt in a large circle around the four of them, Adrienne floating in the center of it. Salt circle complete, he sat back down and closed the container.

"'Next, place your white candle to the north, your blue candle to the west, your gray candle to the south, and your yellow candle to the east. One for guidance, one for discovery, one for perception, and one for truth.'"

Each candle was placed by Jaimie, with the help of Irsa's Qibla app. Lilly lit each candle with a long stemmed lighter, not wanting to burn her fingers. After ensuring all of the candles were properly lit and inscribed with their uses thanks to a pencil, she continued to read.

"'Put a piece of clear quartz and a piece of moonstone in the center of the circle.'"

Having found the crystals in a bin in a 'spiritual' shop, Jaimie placed them in the center of the circle.

"'Eat the almonds, celery, and grapes, one after the other, while visualizing your goal.'"

Jaimie exchanged a look with Lilly, but the slowly ate the almonds, two each. The celery was not nearly as enjoyable, but the tartness of the grapes helped to wash it away.

"'Now, as the taste lingers on the back of your tongue repeat the following.'"

Lilly set the book in front of her, letting both Jaimie and Irsa see it.

"Should we all read it at the same time?" Jaimie asked, looking between his friends.

Adrienne nodded."On the count of three?"

Lilly took a deep breath.

"One."

"Two."

"Three."

All together:

"Reveal to us the truth, reveal it to us soon, what happened to Adrienne Mills on this full moon. Reveal to us the truth, reveal it to us soon, reveal the death of Adrienne Mills on this full moon. Reveal to us the truth, reveal it to us soon, who killed Adrienne and led her to her doom?"

A gust of air blew out the candles and Adrienne screamed as everything went dark. The next time Lilly opened her eyes, she was watching Adrienne die.

42

Jeannie could feel herself vibrating, heart beating loudly in her chest as the woman that had destroyed Quinn turned the corner and disappeared. The tight grasp around her waist tightened and she felt herself pulled, backwards. Everything went black and she began to free fall.

She wasn't in a room, or in the wall. Her lungs burned as she inhaled, cold air hitting her once again. She was on her hands and knees for what felt like the millionth time in the past three days, no hands on her body. But the heat remained, imprinted in her skin. A sigh rose from the corner and she whipped around, searching the black for the voice.

"Why did you do that?" she asked, voice hoarse.

"Do what?" The voice asked, a forced nonchalance spilling like oil in her mind.

"Why would you do that?" She asked again, anger rising as her voice bounced in the corners of the void, ringing loudly in her own ears. "All you've done is make my life a living hell, torturing me, haunting my dreams, abusing my body! You've done everything you can to make me miserable, and then as soon as someone dies for me, you promise to protect me?"

Jeannie's voice hitched, mind replaying the way Quinn had disappeared, the pain in her face as she faded into nothingness.

"Why?" The voice echoed, circling around her. **"To show you that our deal could benefit you, if you choose. To show you that I'm on your side."**

"On my side?" she laughed, mirthlessly. "After everything that's happened, you're the only thing that's against me. You're the enemy!"

The voice made a tutting sound. **"If you really think that, than you're more lost than I thought you were."** A gust of air rushed at her, hot and in her face. **"She is the enemy, she has always been the enemy. If she hadn't shown up, the ghosts never would have started going missing. Did I help? Sure. But only while she was fulfilling her end of the deal. Now that I've got you, she means nothing."**

Jeannie closed her eyes, pressing her palms into her face. "Why are you doing this to me?"

"Why? I've told you why, Jeannette. I need some-one. Someone who can share. Someone who is strong enough to help me help them. All of this pain, this suffering, could end. You could end it. I could end it for you. I am choosing to show you what good could come from this. What good could come from me. Choose me, Jeannie. Choose you."

"Leave me alone."

The heat of the darkness rose up again and she cried out, her skin rippling as if it was being cooked off of her body.

"Let me remind you that while I'm asking you to

make a choice, I am also making a choice. I am
choosing patience. I could simply torture you until
your pathetic little mind becomes porridge and you
have no other thought in your mind but the word 'yes'.
You cannot get rid of me. I am a part of you. I will use
whatever methods it takes until you let. Me. In."

43

Lilly

Opening her eyes, Lilly knew she was about to watch Adrienne die. For starters, it was still sunny out the large windows and she was floating in the air. Looking to her left, Jaimie was floating next to her, eyes wide. Irsa was to the right and she opened her mouth to say something, but no sound came out. The three of them were transparent.

We're not real, she realized, looking down the hallway. The clock read 5:00 and a fading calendar that hung on a teachers door showed that it was March 22nd, a Tuesday. *We're in the past. Adrienne dies today.*

Almost as if on cue, a dark-skinned boy with a short afro and a patterned shirt exited the classroom to her left, arm in arm with a red head wearing blue jeans and a colorful blouse. Right behind them, closing the door as they left, was Adrienne, her familiar blonde hair and red flannel shirt just as they saw her as a ghost. Now, her arms were filled with books and her feet had both boots on. She turned to the two who had stopped to wait for her.

"You guys are doing way better than you were last week, I know you're going to crush these exams!"

The guy nodded and smiled at her, punching her elbow. "See you in bio tomorrow, okay?"

She nodded and the couple walked off, leaving Adrienne alone in the hallway to pack her papers away in her bag. A purple butterfly clip fell to the ground and she picked it up, using the far window as a mirror to try and put it back into her hair. Something flashed out of the corner of Lilly's eye, and she turned to see a man coming down the hallway.

He had dark hair, hanging in greasy ringlets in front of his eyes. He was wearing a dark blue jumpsuit, top half unzipped to reveal a grimy white shirt. He had on thick black boots and was rolling a mop and bucket down the hallway. He was giving a nasty look to the teen couple as they passed him, but smiled when he saw Adrienne.

As he got closer, Lilly leaned forward and read the name off of his glinting metal name tag. *Trabazo.* He crossed the hallway, to walk right up to Adrienne. She didn't seem to notice him until he was standing right next to her. Lilly's stomach turned as Adrienne turned to him, beaming.

"Hello, Mr. Trabazo! Have you had a good day today?"

He smiled at her and Lilly's mind went back to the newspaper article. *He had said she 'always paid attention to the little guy.'*

"Better now that you're here." He said.

She just laughed and put her bag over her shoulder. "That's good."

"You're a nice kid, y'know." He gestured behind him, where the two students had disappeared. "Tutoring riff-raff, like that."

Adrienne's eye twitched, shoulders tense, but she kept smiling. "They're both good students, they just struggle with math a bit. I mean, Will has a higher gpa than me, he just hates Calculus," she said, laughing politely as she shifted backwards.

"Yeah, but still," he continued, leaning towards her. "Makes me glad the door locks behind 'em."

She cleared her throat and stepped back, tapping her finger absently on her arm. "You've locked up already?"

"Of course, Miss Mills. Got to make sure the school stays safe," he eyed her up and down, eyes hovering at her skirt. "You're a real pretty girl, Miss Mills."

Adrienne's eyes widened and she casually swung her bag off her shoulder, in front of her legs. "Thank you, Mr. Trabazo."

He licked his lips and scratched his crotch, leaning towards her as she stepped back. "I'm a lucky guy, working here. I get to see pretty girls like you all day. I'm real lucky that you girls develop early."

"I should probably get going," she swallowed hard, smile dropping. "My parents are expecting me." Adrienne took a step back and he took a step towards her.

"What's the rush? I could take a pretty girl like you out for a drink. I'm sure you'd like that."

"No, thank you," she said, taking another step back and holding her bag tightly in front of her. "I don't think my parents would be very happy if I missed the bus home."

He leered at her, taking several steps towards her as she backed up. "I could give you a ride home, Miss Mills."

"No thank you," she said firmly, quickly stepping around him to get to the other side of the hallway.

He turned and grabbed her arm, wrenching her back, whatever smile he had once gone. "Slow down, you uppity bitch. I just want to take you out to have a good time."

Lilly lurched forward and tried to grab him, but her hands went right through him and she tumbled to the other side. Adrienne's eyes were wide and she tore her wrist away.

"Leave me the hell alone!"

Without another second, she took off down the hallway, sprinting towards the front office. Lilly flew after her, watching in horror as Adrienne threw herself at the office doors. The lights were off. *No one's there. He's the only one here.* A glance down the hall way showed that the janitor was racing after her, having thrown the mop aside.

Irsa tried to push the doors open, but she went right through them. *Is all we can do is to watch?* The front doors were locked too and so Adrienne quickly ducked down a different hallway. By then, he had almost caught up to her. She threw her backpack at him and he stumbled, giving her enough time to duck into a classroom and slam the door behind her.

Pushing through the wall, Lilly saw her rush to the window, fumbling with the key lock as he slammed the door open. She shoved the window open and dove, leg getting caught on the frame. He grabbed her legs and dragged her back, her arms flailing as she screamed. He slammed her onto the ground and her head ricocheted off the floor.

Lilly wanted to scream as Adrienne's arms went limp, weakly trying to push back as Trabazo got on his knees between her legs, grinning. *GET UP! GET UP! GET UP!* Irsa was standing in the doorway, tears running down her face as she too tried to scream at Adrienne, but no sound would come out.

"See, you snobbish slut," Trabazo said, a sleazy smile covering his features as he slowly pulled her left boot. "All you had to do was cooperate. I'll show you a good time, I promise."

He started to pull off her sock, when her head snapped up and she slammed her right foot into his groin. Hard. He howled and fell backwards, and as he screeched, she jumped up, tearing across the classroom and out the door. Lilly wanted to cry in relief, but her stomach still twisted and turned. *It's not over.* After a moment of writhing on the ground, Trabazo stood, eyes red with rage. He glanced around the room and grabbed a large metal paper-weight off the desk.

Lilly tore out of the room, watching in horror as Adrienne sluggishly ducked into a janitorial closet, door clicking painfully loudly behind her as the janitor stumbled out into the hallway, paperweight clutched in his hands. Jaimie was on his knees in front of the closet door, shaking his head and speaking to no one. As Lilly approached him, she realized she knew the words he was mouthing. They were echoing in her own head the closer she got.

This is where. This is where. This is where. This is where. This is where. This is where. This is where. This is where. This is where. This is where. This is where. This is where. This is where. This is where. This is where. This is where. This is where. ThiS IS WHERE. THIS IS WHERE. THIS IS WHERE. THIS IS WHERE. THIS IS WHERE THIS IS-

Adrienne's gasping breaths were loud through the door, but you could tell she was trying to cover her mouth. Trabazo's eyes were wild as he turned to the janitors closet. Irsa stayed by the classroom door, shaking her head violently as she cried. Jaimie refused to move closer to the door. Lilly was the only one who would witness it. The only one who could.

Even though her entire body screamed at her not to, she went through the wall into the closet, to see Adrienne shaking, in a ball against the wall. She watched in slow motion as Trabazo burst through the door and Adrienne jumped back too slowly, the paper weight coming down on her head. If Lilly had actually been in the room, the blood would have splattered all over her, but instead it splattered across the walls.

Adrienne writhed on the floor and he hit her with it again. She weakly kicked at him, but he pushed her legs aside. He threw away the paper weight and grabbed her by the throat. Her hands flew to her neck, trying to peel his fingers away. He slammed her head against the floor. Again. And again. And again. And again. Until she stopped fighting back. And he kept squeezing her throat until she stopped moving entirely. Her blood coated the wall and the floor and his hands and his face and his teeth. He smiled.

Lilly blinked and she was back in the dark school hallway, sitting in a circle of salt. Irsa was sobbing, shaking next to her and Jaimie was cradling himself in his arms. Lilly's face was cold, hot tears streaking down her cheeks. She looked up at Adrienne, who looked resigned to the fact that she had just lived through her death again.

"Where is your body?" Lilly croaked, harshly wiping tears from her face with one hand. "Why didn't it show us what he did with you? Why didn't it show us how he got away with it?"

Adrienne's eyes were dead, and she slowly raised a hand to her throat.

"Lilly.." Irsa cried, but Lilly ignored her, staring directly up at Adrienne.

"Why didn't it let us see where you are? Why would it show us how he murdered you but not what he did with you? Tell me!"

"Lillybelle!" Irsa cried again. This time Lilly looked over at her. "The janitor, Trabazo... He still works here."

Lilly felt her blood run cold. "What?"

"He still works here." Adrienne's face was fierce as she sunk to their level, getting in Lilly's face. "I know what he did with my body, but that doesn't matter. He's here. He is in the building."

44

Venus

Venus felt her heart drop in her chest. Theo scrambled for the walkie, immediately pressing talk. "What the fuck do you mean she's gone!"

"She's not fucking here!" Berri's voice crackled. "I came back inside and she and Quinn are fucking gone, flashlight, knife, washer, everything just on the ground! I can't find her!"

"And the ghosts!" Acacia was near hysterics. "They're all gone! One second I was talking to them, then they all go stiff and poof! Black smoke, they're all gone!"

A chill ran up Venus's spine and she turned to the knife they had just stamped out. Her name was still on the blade, but now it was glowing, the goop still sizzling.

"The knife," Venus started, eyes glued to it. "We did the ritual, but the knife is still fully intact."

"Did the spell kill all of them? Did Tommy lie to us?" Acacia asked, voice quiet.

"No!" Berri protested. "He wouldn't've done that! Tommy had no reason to!"

"Something else is going on," Venus said, shaking her head as she picked up the knife.

Had the handle always been wrapped in leather? Had she not noticed? She frowned, turning it over in her hand. Her finger caught on a groove and she lifted it to eye level. A small symbol had been carved into the knife's hilt, a familiar symbol. She had seen it on a flyer.

"Acacia, come down here, there's no point in anyone being alone anymore. Berri, go outside and wait by the car, I don't want you going missing too."

Theo frowned at Venus. "What did you find?"

Venus shook her head. "The signs were everywhere. We just didn't know what we were looking for."

She thrust her hand into her pocket, searching for the flyer, but instead her fingers wrapped around an icy sheet of paper. *Of course, the pendant.*

"What are you talking about?"

Acacia's voice came through the walkie-talkie. "The stairs are all blocked off, how do I get down?"

"Come to the hole in the floor, the big one. We'll catch you."

Theo shot Venus a look that said 'the fuck?'

"I'm turning off my radio," Acacia said, in a whisper through the walkie-talkie. "I hear footsteps."

A minute or so later, Acacia's head peaked over the edge of the hole, where Venus and Theo were standing waiting. Her eyes were wide when she saw the drop, but she sat down on the edge and scooted closer down. The ceiling had partially collapsed, meaning a large portion of it was five feet lower than the rest. She, very quietly, made her way in a crab crawl across the lowered portion.

"Okay, Acia, here's what we're going to do." Venus said, stepping closer to her. "You are gonna grab the rebar on either side of you and try to lower yourself as far as you can, okay? Theo will grab your legs, and I'll catch you, okay?"

Acacia said nothing, just nodding as she turned around. Her hands wrapped around the rebar, but it was obvious that she was sweating. Shakily, she slid herself off of the edge, holding tightly onto the rough bars. Theo caught her by the calves and it became obvious how much Acacia was trembling.

"Okay, Acia?"

"Yeah," she said, voice unsteady.

"You trust me?" She nodded again. "Fall."

Venus bent her knees and held out her arms as Acacia took a deep breath and pushed off of the rebar. She was in free fall for a moment, but then her weight hit Venus's arms, who bent her legs to absorb the shock as the trio nearly crumpled. Acacia's eyes were closed when Venus looked down at her in her arms, trembling. Theo released her and slowly, Venus set her on the ground.

"You okay?"

After a deep breath, Acacia nodded again. "Just hate falling, y'know?"

Venus nodded. "I have a plan."

"So you know what's going on?" Theo asked, pulling the walkie talkie back up.

"Yes," she said, leaning over to the walkie. "Berri, I know what's happening."

"It's not the ghosts, obviously. Is it the shadows, like the ghosts thought? Or some demon?" They gasped. "Were you right about the demon?"

Almost. Venus laughed. "None of that. It's something none of us knew was real until yesterday." Acacia and Theo looked confused. "It's a witch."

45

Jeannie

Jeannie's heart beat loud in her ears as the shadows crept closer to her from the corners of the void, thicker and darker than the rest of the space. Her fingers burned as she curled them around the water gun, the plastic trigger biting into her skin. An oily laugh coated her ear drums.

"Do you really think that will do anything?"

She turned to where the sound had been strongest and sprayed the corner. The shadows melted away and he hissed, making her flinch.

"Soon, you'll run out of water, and you'll be left alone with me, completely defenseless. It's just a matter of time."

She reached into her pocket and cracked one of the glow-sticks, it lighting up green in her palm. The shades shrunk back from the light. She tossed it towards the corner she had sprayed. It disappeared after several minutes, getting too small to see. The green hue raced up the wall, like a water color sitting on top of black oil, reflective and slick. Jeannie swallowed and took a shaky breath, closing her eyes. Feeling in her pocket, she had two more glow-sticks. The water gun was already half-empty, but the demon couldn't know that.

"Why does it have to be me?" she asked.

The voice grumbled, swirling around her like a heavy cloud on a hot wind. **"What, want to know why you're so special?"** The heat rushed onto the back of her neck, as if he was breathing on her. **"You're different. You don't want anything. You're just curious and scared, but there's this deeper strength, a darker power within you. It's extremely… desirable."**

She shuddered and stepped away, raising the water gun again.

"That's why I pushed you in to the warehouse, chased you down, led you the wrong way. I led you into a trap and you didn't even notice!" He laughed, like he thought it was all a big joke. **"And when you escaped me, running to the arms of your precious little friends? That just sweetened the pot. They saw me, but you had no idea that I had already left my mark. No one escapes from my shadows that easily, not for long. So when you grabbed the water pump, I decided to give you a taste of what I could offer: control, for a price."**

The memory of being frozen came back to her like hitting a brick wall, the familiar feeling of the inky black tendrils making their way under her skin and down into her bones making her skin crawl.

"And when you got away again, before I could reach your heart? That irritated me, sure, but the more you struggled and the farther you got away, the more tangled you got in my web. The more I

wanted to taste what you could offer me. The markings on your skin, the piece of me in your hair, all to constantly remind you of what was now part of you. Because you are a rare one, not the kind of person we usually get in our world."

He laughed and she sprayed the gun again, but the shadows didn't falter as much this time. **"I knew that the spirits sensed it too, that's why they saved you from that witch, even if they didn't know what she was."**

Her stomach turned. "Witch?"

She pressed the trigger again, but only a bit of water dripped out of the nozzle. The shadows shot towards her, wrapping around her legs.

"Of course. No ghost wants to consume their friends, but a witch? She wants power. Those ghosts were not the brightest. Well, a few of them caught on, but they've since been disposed of."

A rising wave of disgust was washing over her, fear and anger mixed into the churning emotions. "What are you talking about?"

"Those ghosts, the ones you said you would protect? They're gone. Dead. Permanently."

Jeannie's head spun, vision beginning to blur. She felt like throwing up. *No.*

"Yes," the shadows tightened around her legs, more shooting down from the ceiling for her arms. **"I can't break a deal until a new one is made, so this is all your fault."**

No.

"Yes! You're the reason they're gone, the reason they watched their friends die. I killed them

because of you! Because you wouldn't make the deal!'

She shook her head, letting her knees buckle.

"I made it easy, though. Because I'm merciful. I could make your end merciful too." She could feel his breath on her ear. **"All you have to do is say yes."**

46

Lilly

Lillybelle stood, meeting Adrienne's fierce gaze. "What do you want us to do?"

Adrienne's chest was rising and falling rapidly. *Do ghosts hyperventilate?* "You need to find my body. I can lead you to it," she said, turning to lead them to the office. "But we have to move quickly, he just entered on the far side of the building."

Lilly helped Irsa stand as Jaimie led the way behind Adrienne. She was obviously restraining herself from flying there without them, wringing her hands over and over again. They turned when they reached the office, following a path they had just relived moments earlier. A gnawing grew in Lilly's stomach as they passed the classroom Adrienne had tried to escape in. The door was cracked open, but she refused to go near it. Finally, they reached the janitor's closet, the door behind which Adrienne had lost everything.

Adrienne threw out her hand and the door flew open, swinging inwards and revealing the dark closet. As they entered, Lilly glanced at the spot where Adrienne had been huddled in a ball, thirty years ago. The spot where her head had hit the concrete floor again and again. *Thank god it's clean.*

The ghost refused to look at the spot and instead turned to the wall on the left side of the door, tracing her hand along the grooves.

"He killed me in here," she said softly, staring at the wall. "He hid me here, too. In the wall. He cleaned everything up and then put me right here, beneath the plaster. For almost a decade, I remember there being a bookshelf full of supplies right here."

To hide her. There were mops and crates leaned up against most of the wall, but after a minute or so of lifting and pushing, the wall was clear. Irsa just stared between Adrienne and the wall.

"What do we do?"

"You have to break down the wall. It's thin, so it shouldn't take long."

Jaimie took a deep breath and raised one of the mop handles, as if about to spear it through the wall.

"Wait!" Irsa said, raising her hand in front of Jaimie's face. "Say this goes according to plan. We find your body. We call the police. We have no proof that Trabazo did this. I mean, we know he did, but the police have no evidence."

"Finger prints?" Jaimie asked.

"No guarantee there are any and DNA from the attack would be long gone."

Lilly frowned and Adrienne deflated. "So after everything, he'll still get away with it?" Lilly's heart sank and Jaimie lowered the mop.

"Hello?"

They all froze. A deep voice had just spoken from the hallway, muffled by the door, but echoing down the empty halls. A familiar voice.

"I know someone's here," he called again. "I saw your little devil circle."

Lilly's eyes went wide. *The salt circle and candles.* They were still out in the open. Adrienne had gone stock still. Speaking in almost a whisper, she said: "It's him."

Irsa shrank away from the door, but Lilly stepped towards it, an idea blooming in her mind. She reached for the door handle.

"What are you doing?" Irsa hissed, an incredulous look on her face.

Lilly just smiled. "Start on the wall. I'm going to get some evidence."

47

Venus

She nodded as Theo and Acacia looked at her with shock and confusion.

"A witch?" Theo asked, shaking their head. "What do you mean?"

"This symbol," she said, showing the knife to the duo. "Does it look familiar to you?"

Acacia squinted. "That was on the flyer Dr. Martins gave you in the night market."

"Exactly," Venus said, lowering the blade. "A poster calling for recruits for a coven. A coven! A witch coven looking for new members. This knife never belonged to Olive, Jeannie saw a witch! The witch was outside."

Theo nodded. "The witch is the one who brought the bowl and the drum and was leaving all of those food wrappers everywhere!"

Venus smiled, although a little sadly. *It was right in front of us the whole time. And now it might be too late.* "And the pendant that Jeannie said she was wearing? The Pendant of Resilience. It's how she captured the ghosts, and it's how she's organizing the shadows. She must have found it somewhere in the building."

"I'd be willing to bet she's using it to cast a spell by channeling their souls." Berri said through the walkie talkie. They'd been listening the whole time.

"Tommy did mention how any spells are stronger tonight, remember? The same reason Lilly's doing her spell right now."

Venus nodded, then remembered Berri couldn't see her. "And Tommy also told us how to break a witches spell, remember?"

Theo smiled."And I'm sure you have a daring plan on how to kick her witchy ass?"

Venus nodded again. "I need you two to help me climb up onto the seventh floor, and then you two go meet up with Berri to search for Jeannie. Got it?"

Theo narrowed their eyes and Acacia crossed her arms.

"So let me get this right, you want us to send you, alone, up to the seventh floor. The floor that has no way to safely get down and now has a witch wandering its length." As Acacia spoke, Theo was ticking off the steps on his fingers. "You want us to get out of harms way and look for our missing friend while you get yourself killed in multiple ways so that the rest of us remain unscathed."

Venus nodded for a minute. *Pretty much.* "You forgot some key elements, my dearest, Watson." *Acacia loves those books.* "Berri is injured, and therefore shouldn't risk even coming up to this floor, let alone the seventh. Theo, I love you, but you do not have the upper or lower body strength to safely make your way up or down this gap by yourself. Acacia, not only do you have an easily breakable piece of very expensive equipment attached to you at all times, you get scared of everything. Also," Venus continued, waving her hands around as Theo frowned and counted on his fingers. "Need I remind you, I do risky shit like this all the time, I have the most weapons on me, and I'm the only one of us that has the info to stop the witch."

Theo frowned at the number of fingers they were holding up and Acacia gave her a look.

"You have a point."

Theo nodded. "Several."

"We just want you to stay safe," Acacia said, patting Venus on the shoulder. "You don't have to protect everyone all the time, okay?"

Venus smiled, but a gnawing voice in her head objected. *But if I don't, who will?* A second voice spoke up, slimier than the first. *It's not like you've succeeded so far. How many people have gotten hurt because of you? How many times has Jeannie gotten hurt? Gone missing? It's your turn to take on the burden. It's the least you can do, after everything.*

"I know," she lied. "I'll stay as safe as I can."

After a bit more bickering, Theo and Acacia linked arms. With a push and a jump, they launched Venus far enough up to scramble up onto the lower ledge of the ceiling.

"Venus," Acacia started, but she paused, as if searching for what to say. "If you don't respond in ten minutes, we're calling for back-up."

Venus started to protest, but Theo cut her off. "You don't get to argue, you don't get to choose. You do what you think is right by making sure we're out of harms way, and I appreciate that. But we aren't going to hang you out to dry."

A smile spread across Venus's face. "Got it."

Theo smiled back. "Now go get our friends back."

48

Lilly

As Lillybelle stepped out into the hallway, she pressed the record button on her phone and slipped it into her pocket. The door clicked behind her and she crossed to the middle of the hallway, which was still empty. *He hasn't come this way yet.*

Quickly but quietly, Lilly made her way to the end of the hall, where the office intersected with the three main hallways. She could see the outline of an older man, standing at the far end of the hallway where they had done the spell. He had kicked over one of the candles and the salt was scattered, no longer in it's circle. Trying to ignore the volume of her heartbeat in her own ears, she stepped into the hallway, making her self loud enough for him to hear. *Let the act begin.*

"Hello?" she asked, forcing her voice to go higher than it naturally was.

The man whipped around, shining a flashlight in her face. She blinked at the light, seeing behind the beam was a familiar face. It was Richard Trabazo, still the same old face, but with more wrinkles and gray hair. He was wearing a thick coat and work pants, but his boots were familiar. *They're the same ones.* A rage flickered within her, but she tamped it down, keeping her face loose in shock.

"Jesus, you scared me kid! You're not supposed to be here! How did you even get in here?"

It took everything in her not to flinch when he started towards her, but she kept her eyes wide, dropping her mouth in a doe-like confusion. "The front door was unlocked."

He frowned. "No, it wasn't."

She shrugged. "It was when I got here."

"Is there anyone with you?"

She shook her head again, never taking her eyes off him. "No, I came alone. No one wanted to come with me."

He seemed to relax upon hearing that, shaking his head and continuing towards her. "You aren't supposed to be here."

"You're not supposed to be here, either. I'm a student here," she said, crossing her arms, each breath tremoring..

He slowed his step, raising a hairy eyebrow at her. "It's Saturday, young lady."

"Well, what are you doing here?" Lilly countered, taking a step towards him, though everything in her screamed not to.

"I work her," he said, slowing almost to a crawl as he approached the spilled salt circle.

"It's Saturday," she parroted, keeping her voice light as she smiled.

"What are you doing here?" He repeated, stepping on the first line of salt.

Lillybelle smiled sweetly. "I wanted to talk to Adrienne."

He stopped dead in his tracks. "Who?" His voice shook.

She tilted her head at him. "You seem to know exactly who I'm talking about, Mr. Trabazo."

His eyes darkened. "How do you know my name?"

"You said you work here. You're the janitor, right? Have been for thirty-five years."

He narrowed his eyes at her. "I know you. You're that girl whose in that weirdo club, with the ginger and the terrorist. Spend all your time in the library." He took a step towards her and she instinctively took a step back.

"Do you get to know all of your victims?"

Something flickered in his eyes. *He's afraid.*

"I don't know what you're talking about."

"You know exactly what I'm talking about. I mean, you knew a lot about Adrienne, that's why they interviewed you when she disappeared," Lilly laughed. "What was it? 'She was a nice girl, always looking out for the little guy?'"

"She was a nice girl," he said, face stiff and blank. "It's a shame they never found out what happened to her."

"She was too nice, wasn't she Mr. Trabazo?" Lilly took a step backwards, looking him up and down. "Is that why you killed her?"

His eyes widened and his mouth set in a harsh line. "You don't know what you're talking about. She went missing, no one ever saw her again."

"Of course no one ever saw her again, you were the last person to ever see her alive. You told the police that, you told her parents that, you told the newspaper that. Everyone knows that you were the last person to see her. They searched the entire school for her body, her backpack. They couldn't find anything. You must've been so proud of yourself when they didn't find anything."

He said nothing.

"Can you answer one question for me?" Lilly asked, taking a step towards him even though her legs shook. "What did you do with the paper weight? I mean, I know you kept her boot, but did you keep the paper weight that you killed her with?"

His face fell for a moment, but then a smile split onto his

face, unsettling and euphoric. "How did you know I kept her boot?"

Lilly smiled, heart pounding so loudly that it nearly drowned out her voice.

"I didn't. You just told me."

He laughed and took a step towards her. "Well, who are you going to tell? You're all alone."

She nodded and took a step back. "Are you going to kill me the way you killed her?"

He took a step towards her and she stepped back. "I might. It was fun wrapping my fingers around her throat. If she hadn't fought back so much, I wouldn't have smashed her head in against the concrete."

Lilly forced herself to smile, mouth going dry as she took another small step backwards. "I promise I won't fight back as much as she did," she said, holding up her prosthetic. "Are you going to put my body where you put hers?"

He tilted his head at her, looking her up and down as he advanced towards her.

"Depends. You're a lot prettier than she was."

"I doubt that," she said, stepping farther backwards.

"I could show you a good time, little lady."

Lilly frowned, swallowing down the disgust and rage that was on the verge of consuming her. "I would say no, but that's what got Adrienne killed, isn't it? She said no because a creep twice her age hit on her and then refused to let her go."

His face fell and he took another, long step towards her. "Don't make her mistakes, little lady."

As Lilly took another several steps back, she heard a slam ring out in the distance. *Shit,* she thought. *They're working on the wall.* His head whipped to the sound and he narrowed his eyes at her. "I thought you said you were alone."

She shrugged, keeping her face as calm as she could muster. "I thought I was. It would be really unfortunate for you if we weren't. I mean, there's only so much room in the wall, right?"

"How did you know that's where I hid her body?"

Lilly smiled as her back hit the office wall. "Because Adrienne told me. In fact," she pointed over his shoulder. "She's standing right behind you."

49

Venus

Venus watched as Theo and Acacia turned and walked to the stairwell, and only when they had disappeared down the stairs did she turn and crawl up to the seventh floor. It was almost silent, the darkness of the evening having been fully settled for a while now. The light from the full moon spilled into the side of the building the ghosts usually were found congregating, but another light joined it and sent a chill running down Venus's spine.

Floating in the center of a glowing, golden circle, was a woman, ratty blonde hair hovering around her like a mangled fishing net in water. She was wearing dark robes, blackened with dirt and ash. It looked as if she was kneeling in the air, arms held out in front of her in some sort of partial prayer. Her eyes were wide open, a black glow over taking her vision and pouring from her mouth and nose. The darkness writhed around, the hot of the shadows shrinking away from the icy center of the circle.

Every atom in her body was screaming at her to back away. Venus stepped forward, making sure to keep low to the ground.

The closer she got to the witch, the clearer she saw that the light seemed to circle around the woman, rising through the air like a golden barrier. *Mierda, I guess I can't touch her. Think, Venus, think.* A few more steps closer and her skin was pinching with cold, pressing her tongue to the roof of her mouth to stop her teeth from chattering.

As she shivered with every step forward, Venus glanced at the ground, where the gold circle was brightest. Making up the circle were four assorted objects. To the North, was a large white crystal. To the East, a paper fan. To the South, a small incense burner sat smoking away, and to the West, a familiar wooden bowl, now full of water.

The witch was speaking, words Venus couldn't begin to understand filling the air alongside the smoke that poured from her mouth. She thought back to what Tommy had off-handedly said about witches that morning. *'All you have to do is mess up their magic circle or interrupt them while they're chanting.'* Venus took a deep breath. *Tommy, you had better be right about this.*

She lunged, fingers outstretched as she reached for the bowl, golden light filling her vision. Venus shrieked, hand bouncing off of the golden barrier, skin recoiling as if she had slammed into the side of a glacier. As she ricocheted and slammed into the ground, the muttering stopped, and as she slowly looked up, the witch's glowing black eyes were staring down at her. *Mierda.*

"Who are you? What are you doing here?" The witch thundered, voice amplified in the dilapidated room.

Think Venus, for the love of everything, think!

"I..." She could hear herself say, mind drawing a blank. "I'm sorry. Do you have a permit?"

The witch blinked, black smoke dissipating and golden glow slowly fading as her blonde brows knitted together. "What?"

"Do you have a permit?" Venus asked again, steadying her

voice as she watched the golden glow of the barrier sink. "Because if you don't, you'll have to move your spell."

The witch snickered, the black glow of the necklace dampening.

"What authority do you have over me, child?"

Venus stood slowly, wiping bits of gravel off of her pants. *If I can get her guard down, I can knock over the bowl.* She swallowed.

"Actually, miss ma'am, I'm from the local magical zoning committee, and this space hasn't been registered for any large summonings as of late."

The witch narrowed her eyes. "You're silly rules do not affect me, mortal. But you don't need to be mixed up in this. Be gone, before I remove you myself."

"Miss, as far as I'm aware, a witch still qualifies as a mortal," Venus said, inching to the right of the witch, eyes darting between the gold barrier and the bowl of water that lay on the floor. "and your coven does need to follow the rules of the magical zoning committee in order to avoid a fine."

"Coven?" The witch laughed and rose in the air, thick, black smoke pouring from her eyes and pendant. "I have no coven. Those pathetic wretches treated me like dirt. Like garbage! But now? I have the power to destroy them and everything they care for. And no thanks to that demon who traded me for some teenage skank."

Venus stumbled back as black shot from her hands and a section of the roof crumbled, sending chunks of concrete raining down. The barrier glowed brightly, strengthening in front of her as the air grew icy, shadows writhing violently all around them. *Fuck.*

"Is that why you did all of this? Just to get some revenge?"

The building shook as the witch stretched out her arms and shadows shot to her, wrapping around her like thick, black eels. Venus winced as the cold bit into her, ground breaking apart under her feet. She leapt to the side as a stroke of the witch's hand sent a fissure ripping across the floor. The witch smirked.

"Revenge is nothing compared to the sweet satisfaction of power. I will rip them limb from limb, boil their blood from the insides out and mutilate everyone they have ever loved."

Venus felt her mouth going dry as she clutched the ground, the chunk of concrete she was standing on, rising from the ground. The circle of magic the witch was in also was rising apart in chunks and she watched as the wooden bowl floated by her, the barrier stretching to accommodate the changes in shape. *I can almost reach it. Fuck, how do I get her to calm down?* Venus stopped. *Did she say demon?*

"But how can you claim to be so powerful? You haven't even cast the spell? Maybe it's because you're so pathetic, not even a demon wanted to be around you!"

"What did you say?" The witch roared, voice distorting with anger. For a moment, the barrier thinned, almost a golden smoke instead of a wall. *Bingo.* "You know not of what you speak, trespasser."

"Don't I?" Venus leapt from one hovering chunk of concrete to another, trying to avoid the parts of the ceiling that were falling in sprinklings of debris. "It's taken you over a month to siphon away, what, thirty ghosts? And you couldn't even do that by yourself! You had to wait until a full moon to get even this powerful. So why would they treat you like you're any better than trash?"

"Careful, child!' The witch snapped, the glow fading from her eyes as she sunk towards the concrete. *It's working.* "I have no qualms about killing a little girl first. And anyone else who dares to get in my way."

"Oh, right, I'm so scared!' Venus said, trying to keep her voice from trembling. She was only a foot away from the bowl. "Look, you couldn't even convince a demon, someone who preys on the weak, to stick around."

"Shut your mouth, you cretin! I will skin you!" The witch shrieked, gold light pulsing.

Venus's pulse was loud in her ears as the barrier thinned. She smiled. "I'll let you in on a little secret: I'm not even a part of the magical zoning committee."

A feral scream filled the air and the witch lunged for her as Venus leapt forward, outstretched hands aiming for the dissolved barrier. Her fingers made contact with the bowl and it went flying, water spraying everywhere. In the seconds the barrier was broken, everything fell. The chunks of concrete that had been suspended, crashed to the ground, along with parts of the ceiling. Venus slammed into the floor, the heat of the fall air immediately filling what had been an icy abyss seconds earlier.

Her arms ached and her head was spinning, but a smile settled on her lips. The water had spilled across the cracked concrete, the incense had been doused, and the fan had been torn in the crash. The gold barrier dissipated like smoke and the dark shadows fell away, writhing like hot tendrils in the corners. The witch was on her hands and knees, arms trembling. *It's over,* Venus thought to herself, pushing herself off the ground. She stood and began to turn back towards the hole in the ground that was across the building when a harsh sound hit her ears. Laughter.

"You nosy little bitch!" The witch spat and Venus turned to see her slowly standing, eyes crazed as she pushed her matted blonde hair out of her face. "I searched for months for this spell, dug through rubble and filth for this fucking pendant. I came here night after night, week after week, toiling away just for you to come waltzing in here with your little friends and ruin everything!"

Venus stumbled back as something long and silver flashed in her hands. *Oh fuck.* She turned run, but a black glow sent a wall of concrete up in front of her, stopping her in her tracks. The witch's hands were glowing.

"Maybe that demon thinks I'm worthless, but maybe I can get him back. Maybe by gutting you and spilling your filthy blood across my useless hands, I can prove that I don't fucking need him." The witch stepped forward, bleeding lips splitting into a smile. "I'm going to fucking kill you. And I'm going to enjoy every second."

50

Lilly

As the old janitor turned to look at nothing, Lillybelle took off running. Her heartbeat thundered in her ribcage, blood rushing in her ears. Her shoes slapped the floor with such intensity she thought her feet were going to come flying off. She didn't stop to see if he was chasing her until she reached the end of the hallway farthest from where she started. Her back was pressed against the door that lead to a different building as she took in deep, gulping breaths.

There was a janitorial closet to her left, a few doors down, and she crossed to it. It was locked. After a moment of consideration, she kicked the door handle, hard. The weak wood splintered loudly and the door burst open. *Now he knows where I am. The farther he is from them, the better.*

There was a light switch on the wall, but she ignored it, instead searching in the darkness for anything that stuck out. A large object glinted in the corner and she picked it up with her right hand. It was a spare pipe, probably for one of the frequently breaking bathrooms. But whatever it was for, today it had one job: self defense.

As she hovered by the door, pipe in hand, she heard the familiar sound of heavy boots slowly thunking down the hall. *Closer, closer. Closer... Swing!*

Just as he swung into the doorway, the pipe collided with his legs, sweeping him to the floor in a groaning pile. She hopped over him and darted out into the hallway. Watching him as he got up, she began to quickly back away. His gaze was murderous. She brandished the pipe, letting all of her rage spill out.

"Richard Trabazo! Did you murder Adrienne Mills?" she shouted, her own voice echoing off the walls.

He sneered at her, taking a step towards her as he wiped blood from his crushed nose."I squeezed her pretty little neck until she stopped moving and I watched her die!"

"Did you enjoy it, you sick fuck?"

Blood trickled into his teeth as he smiled at her. "Every second of it." She swung the pipe at him again, but this time he caught it. Wrapping his grimy fingers around it, he yanked it towards him, pulling her closer. "And I'll enjoy killing you just as much."

Her eyes went wide and she stumbled back. He dropped the pipe on the floor and advanced towards her. Without a second thought, she ran. This time, she could hear he was hot on her tail. She soon found herself in front of a familiar classroom door and she shoved herself through the door. It was, after all, unlocked. *It's repeating itself.*

She sprinted to behind the desk, the farthest from the door, with many pieces of furniture between herself and him. Once he got to the doorway, he stopped, glaring at her as he clenched his fists.

"This is where she tried to run, right?" she said, between shaky breaths. "She ran to the window and as she was escaping, you grabbed her and threw her on the ground. You tried to undress her."

He stepped into the room, expression cold. "She was a snobbish bitch who thought she was too good for someone like me. She got what she deserved."

"And she kicked you in the balls, which was better than you deserved."

He lunged for her across the room and she ducked around the desk, skirting around the edge of the classroom. Right as she reached the door, something yanked her backwards by the head. His hand was wrapped around her hair and he threw her to the ground.

Her ears rang as she felt herself slam into the floor, her head spinning. Before she could register what was happening, she felt a hand at the base of her scalp as he lifted her by the hair and banged her head into the side of a desk. She screamed in pain as stars bloomed in her eyes. He flipped her over, and as his fingers wrapped around her throat, all she could see was his leering face.

51

Pain speared through Jeannie as the heat became nearly unbearable, but even as she writhed, her resolve stayed the same. She could feel it's displeasure.

"Maybe I can motivate you." He rumbled, the heat dying away.

Her voice was dry and weak when she spoke. "Torture me all you want, I will never say yes. I know you can't kill me, so your threats are weak."

"You're right, I can torture you all I want, but I can't kill you." He sighed and one could almost hear the cogs turning in its brain. **"That would defeat the point. But what about... your friends? You care about them, don't you?"**

Her eyes went wide. "You wouldn't."

"You're right! *I.* **Wouldn't."** He laughed. **"But I'm not the one that's after them."**

She shook her head, trying to clear it from the nonsense it

was clearly spouting. *He's just trying to mess with my head.* "What are you talking about?"

"Do you want to see? See what I'm protecting you from? I can show you *exactly* what I mean."

On either side of her, the shadows seemed to part, each showing a window into the world instead of an abyss of black. On the left, a darkened classroom. On the right, the seventh floor of the warehouse. Each window zoomed closer, and a struggle was visible in each. Jeannie gasped.

The left window was of Lillybelle, writhing on the floor between classroom desks as an old man pinned her to the ground, hands wrapped around her throat. He looked gleeful as he pressed down, and he was saying something she couldn't make out. Blood was dripping from his face onto hers and she was crying out, her prosthetic twisted underneath her.

The right window was Venus, grappling with the witch Jeannie had been threatened by so many times before. The witch was slashing at Venus, the shining knife getting closer and closer with every swipe as Venus stumbled from concrete obstacles, thrown around as if they were made of paper. Venus was shaking and with each passing second, the blade got closer to slicing her skin as she jumped back a second too late every time.

"Lillybelle and Venus, your closest, most beloved friends, I can feel them! On the edge, their souls teetering over death. Lillybelle being strangled by a murderer who isn't ready to go to jail. And Venus? Chased by that knife wielding witch who was just denied the power of thirty souls at once."

Jeannie felt her heart sink as Lilly's eyes were wide, her fingers weakly trying to pry his iron grip off of her. Her feet were kicking underneath him, but it didn't deter him. Jeannie's chest grew constricted the longer she watched, but when she averted her gaze all she could see was the giant knife getting closer and closer to Venus's bruised skin, Venus getting slower and slower in her movements.

"I can make you feel what she's feeling right now. Hands wrapped around her throat, knife about to buried in hers- or maybe you don't need to feel it. It seems like the knowledge is enough. Because you and I both know that when he is finished strangling Lillybelle to death, he'll go to put her in the wall too." The left image flashed to Jaimie and Irsa kneeling next to a wall in a closet, slowly breaking it down.

"And he'll find Jaimie and Irsa waiting and he'll beat them to death. That wall will get mighty cramped. And the witch? Once Venus is dead on the floor, she'll go downstairs and gut the rest of them. Because *you* let her get that powerful by pushing me out again and again. You could've ended this days ago. But now all of your friends will die. And you will have to live the rest of your life knowing that it was all because you didn't care enough to save them."

"No!" Jeannie cried out, her chest aching. Hot tears streamed down her face. "That's not true!"

"With one word, just one, you save everyone. One tiny word, one little sacrifice, everyone lives. Are you really that selfish? So what's it gonna be? Because you- no... They are running out of time."

Jeannie dropped to her knees, hands curling painfully into her. "Please! I'll do anything! Anything you want, I'll do! Please..."

The shadow demon made a sound of disgust. **"Don't beg.**

It makes you look pathetic. And you are anything but pathetic." Jeannie swallowed and nodded, as the voice continued. **"Take a breath, close your eyes. It might... sting."**

As she closed her eyes, she felt a heat engulf her entirely, and she gasped. Every part of her body was screaming at the pain of the heat, but she couldn't say a word. *This is how I die.* And then it all went dark.

52

Lilly

Black spots were bursting like anti-fireworks behind Lillybelle's eyes, lungs constricting as his thick fingers pressed down on her neck. Darkness seemed to creep over her, pain exploding in her head as he laughed in her face. Hot blood dripped down from his smashed nose, stinging her eyes and wetting her cheeks. Her fingers felt leaden as she weakly tried to scrape him off of her. The shadows of the room seemed to creep closer, but it wasn't because of her blurring vision.

A dark warmth ran over her body and his face screwed up in confusion as his fingers lifted off of her neck, but he was still caged around her. ***Your pocket knife,*** a deep, yet somehow familiar voice said in her head. ***Use it.*** As the air rushed back into her lungs, she felt her finger tips tingling. Almost as if they were being guided, they flew from her neck to her right pants pocket, where the knife had laid forgotten. A small button that she hadn't known about opened it in seconds, the switch blade light in her palm.

A flashing light and an ear-destroying screech filled the air, red light flaring from the ceiling. In the seconds it took for him to react to the fire-alarm, she pulled the knife from her pocket. She plunged it into the side of his head, the blade sinking into the top of his ear. He screamed and fell backwards, hands immediately clutching his head, blood gushing from between his fingers.

Now run.

Without a second thought to the voice that had saved her life, Lilly scrambled to her feet, taking what felt like ages to get out of the door, knife still in hand. Her vision swayed as she fled in slow-motion into the hallway, towards the janitors closet where her friends were waiting. Her heart pounded in her chest, stumbling as the flashing lights and screaming alarm sent her spiraling the wrong direction. Her feet were heavy, the tingling in her hand fading as her lungs fought to expand against her ribs.

Hands landed on her shoulders and she panicked, swinging her knife weakly behind her. Irsa jumped back, eyes wide and Lilly dropped the knife, letting it clatter to the floor.

"Lilly, are you okay?!?" Lillybelle opened her mouth to speak, but her throat burned and nothing came out. She shook her head."Don't worry, help is coming. I pulled the fire alarm!"

Lilly blinked, confused. "What?" She managed to croak, voice barely audible under the screeching fire alarm.

Irsa frowned. "We're at a high school, so it auto contacts the fire department. Someone is coming for us!"

Thank god. Lilly closed her eyes against the flashing lights, head pounding. She began to sway and Irsa caught her by the arms, grabbing her shoulder instead of her prosthetic.

"We found her, Lilly. We found Adrienne."

She opened her eyes and a smile creeped onto her face, but it quickly fell again when she heard someone staggering behind them. She turned around and saw that Trabazo had gotten back up and was livid, scarlet soaking the side of his face. His hands were covered in blood and his eyes held only hate.

Fuck.

53

Venus ducked as the witch threw herself at her, the blade only barely avoiding slicing her throat as the woman spun around. As she turned to run, the knife came hurtling at her face again, the room molding at the will of the witch to stop her every escape. She cried out, the blade slicing across her palm viciously as she threw her hands in front of her face. Venus tumbled backwards, clutching her hand as the blonde lifted the knife to her mouth and licked the blood.

"You're a fucking psycho, bitch!" Venus yelled, backing up as she pressed the bleeding hand to her stomach.

The witch let her lids drop, the knife falling to her side. "I'm a witch!

"No, no," Venus insisted, eyes wide as the woman stepped towards her. "I think we've realized you're both!"

The witch snarled and lunged forwards, and Venus defensively threw up her hands again, bracing for the cold impact, but it never came. Both stared as the knife blackened and crumbled to ash in her hand. A deep voice, unfamiliar and unwelcome, whispered into her mind.

The pendant.

Venus stared at it, glittering black in the low light. Moving on instinct alone, she lunged forward and her fingers wrapped around the black stone. It felt as if she had just grabbed hot ice. Shrieking in pain, she dropped the stone and it hit the ground. It shattered on impact. Immediately, black shadows shot out of it, consuming not only the shards of the necklace, but everything it could touch.

Run.

Not wanting to ignore such generous instructions, Venus bolted, leaping over holes in the ground and ducking behind rubble, the landscape in front of her rapidly moving to block her path. She could hear the screaming of the crazy woman behind her but she refused to turn around, breeze rushing in her ears as she ran. Holes filled as she reached them and pieces of the ceiling dropped inches from her face, shards of rebar spearing the floor underneath her shoes as she danced around the debris. *Thank fuck for fast reflexes.*

In the near distance she saw the hole in the floor that she had climbed through and almost felt herself float with relief, yet a nugget of dread stuck in her throat. As she quickly approached, her feet bounced off the hard concrete, but a hot feeling on the back of her neck told her to **duck** and she hit the ground. Hard.

A flash of light soared over her head and slammed into the hole. Her palms were bleeding worse than before but when she looked through the smoke, she saw that a giant piece of melted metal and concrete had filled the hole. *Mierda, mierda, mierda.* Venus's eyes went wide and she turned over her shoulder to see the witch's hands smoking as well, eyes glowing gold.

Fuck! Venus thought, scrambling to her feet, eyes wide. Ignoring the dull pain in her hands, she searched the darkness for some other way out as the witch began muttering again.

Something writhed underneath her and she watched as a black path carved itself out in front of her, the shadows congregating and leading towards the end of the building, to a familiar corner. In the distance, near the opposite stairwell, was the section of wall where the delivery chutes were open.

Feeling her heart rising in her ribcage, Venus ran. She ran as if she had been set on fire, because she knew, if she didn't reach those chutes in time, she would be next in the rubble pile. The black path was hot, steam seemingly rising from her shoes as she soared through the air. The building golden light of the psycho's next spell cast her in shadow, yet her destination had never been so clear.

Dive.

Her feet left the ground as she felt the cold approach of the magic blast, the hot shadows stretching towards her. Her hands touched the metal and in an instant she was within the delivery chutes, tumbling downwards into a hot, black void.

54

Lillybelle took a reflexive step back and Irsa stepped in front of her, holding her hand tightly behind her. Trabazo took a step forward and leered at the two girls, gesturing towards them as he smiled. His teeth were smeared with blood.

"You told me you were alone, miss," he gazed at them through lowered lids, giving an eerie depth to his face. "You lied."

"You lied too," Irsa said over the screeching alarms, holding Lilly firmly behind her. "You said you would take Adrienne home. You never did."

He sneered, wiping his bloody hands on his pants. "I made her a new home."

"I don't think a layer of drywall in a high school closet counts as a home," Irsa shot back, shrugging. "But neither does the place you're going."

The smell of iron was filling Lilly's nostrils. *Where's the smell coming from?* Her head spun, and she clutched on Irsa's shoulders. Trabazo laughed, taking a step towards them, cracking his knuckles.

"And where will that be?"

Irsa smiled at him, but there was no kindness in her eyes. "Federal prison."

His face dropped, and for the first time all night, Lilly saw real fear in his soulless eyes. "Oh no, I'm not going anywhere. Because no one is going to know about this and no one is going to know about you. I will kill you like I killed that bimbo bitch thirty years ago, and just like thirty years ago, no one will know what happened to you. And I will go about my life as I have."

Lilly smiled. She opened her mouth to say something, but stopped. Something was glinting in the corner of her eye.

"What? Cat got your tongue?" he laughed, flexing his fingers as he took another step. "Something steal your breath?"

She shook her head. "You forgot something," she croaked, pulling Irsa back next to her.

He rolled his head, eyes on her like a snake's on a mouse. "What's that?"

"It's not the 90s anymore. There are cameras everywhere, and," her voice was weak as she took a breath and reached into her pocket, pulling out her phone, which was still recording. "I have your confession right here. On recording, right now."

Baring his teeth in anger, he rushed forward. Lillybelle and Irsa stumbled back quickly, alarmed. Suddenly, Trabazo froze, eyes wide. He crumpled to the ground like a large sack of potatoes and standing behind him, holding a very familiar pipe, was Jaimie.

"Holy shit!" He squeaked, voice unbelievably high against the screaming fire alarm. "Are you guys okay?"

Irsa smiled and nodded. "Let's go, Lilly."

Irsa stepped over the unconscious janitor, holding Lillybelle in her arms as she did, but Lilly stopped. She smiled at the man laying at the floor and spit on his face. Then, she nodded, and continued after Jaimie. The wailing sirens were quickly approaching.

55

If Venus could compare the delivery chutes to anything, she would have to describe them as a very uncomfortable, sweaty, and bumpy slide that felt like it would never end. The pitch black darkness and claustrophobia of the chutes themselves did not make it a more enjoyable experience, but after what felt like an eternity, a light flashed in her eyes and she was shot out of a chute. She landed hard on the concrete ground, but when she looked around, there wasn't a chute in sight.

Instead, she was sitting next to the open garage door that Jeannie had come running out of what felt like ages ago. Standing, she quickly made her way outside, into the crisp air. It only took a couple of minutes to make her way around the side of the building, but every second alone in the dark made her skin crawl. When she heard a clamor of voices, relief washed over her and she ran around the side of the building.

Acacia, Theo, and Berri were talking to several older women, each clad in shimmering silver robes. On seeing her, Berri ran over and threw their arms around her.

"Thank goodness you're okay!" They said, holding her in a tight hug. "What the hell happened?"

Venus shook her head. "I stopped her spell and pissed her off, so she attacked me with a knife." *No need to mention the human sacrifice threat.*

Venus showed Beri her palms and Berri yelped. "Fuck! You need to go to a hospital, like, now!"

One of the older women seemed to perk up immediately upon hearing the word hospital and she quickly bustled over. Upon seeing the wound, she tutted and frowned. "I'm so sorry this all happened! Let me fix you right up, dearie."

She closed her eyes and held her fingers over Venus's, green light pouring out onto her wound. Right before her eyes, Venus watched as the wound cleaned up and closed itself, healing instantly. The blood remained, but other than that, her skin was unharmed. Venus's eyes were wide and she thought Berri's might pop out of their head.

"I might need some of that too." Berri rolled up their pant leg to show off the injury from the days prior.

"Thank you, but who are you?" Venus asked, rubbing her finger over the small white scar that had been bleeding only seconds earlier, as the woman did the same for Berri.

The woman smiled, her bright green eyes shimmering brilliantly in the low light. "I'm sorry, dearie, I forgot to introduce myself. My name is Catarina, I'm a member of the coven."

"I called the witch related hotline that was on the coven poster," Acacia said, walking over and smiling. "Theo insisted we call them as soon as you left, but I gave you the five minute benefit-of-the-doubt."

Catarina nodded. "Yes, it seems that one of our newest recruits, Brooklyn, got it into her head that we thought she was weak. In reality, she was a legacy recruit who refused to attend any meetings or undertake any training. A bit unstable, that one."

No shit. The other witches nodded. The one with the golden brooch stepped forward, curly red hair spilling out from under her hood. "Two of our members are going in to restrain her as we speak. She will then be stripped of her coven status and all of her magical involvement. Because she attempted to harm other members of the Underworld, she will be blacklisted permanently."

Venus nodded. "What about the ghosts? Are they going to come back?"

The two witches exchanged a look.

"Unfortunately, that is outside of our realm," Katarina's colleague said, not unkindly. "The pendant, though usually tracked by witches, is created with demonic magic. We have no way of accessing anything it consumed. Brooklyn will be heavily punished, but there is little we can do for the victims."

Venus felt her heart deflate. "So, after everything we did, all of the injuries, the work we did... We still failed them?"

56

Jeannie

Jeannie's body felt different, but it didn't, not truly. Everything about her was the same.

'Almost everything,' *the familiar deep voice said.*

Jeannie was no longer in the void. Instead, she was standing in the first room of the building, the first room they had cleaned, several days before. *Has it only been days?* The door into the building stood open, and the double doors outside also stood open. The cold air of the evening was refreshing on her skin, the darkness all around her still uncomfortable and unsettling.

But the thing that she was most aware of, at almost all times, was her heart beat. It was so much louder than before, so much slower. It felt heavier in her chest, slowly pounding away at her ribcage, as if trying to break free from a box too small for what it could do.

Get out, she said to the voice. *Get out of my skin.*

'As you wish,' he replied. She could feel his smile against her. **'I'll be close.'**

A clatter to her right made her jump. The witch she had hidden from too many times was being led out of the warehouse in thick magic cuffs, red light circling her body. Upon seeing Jeannie, she lunged at her, but Jeannie barely flinched.

"You! You're the one who took him from me! Why would he choose you over me?!?" The ratty haired witch screeched. "You stole everything from me! I'll gut you, you skank!"

Jeannie said nothing as the girl was wrenched past her and put in the car that was outside. She just shook her head violently, chest constricted as she tried to breathe. *This is all your fault*, she thought. There was no response.

After a deep breath, Jeannie stepped out into the evening air. Immediately, eyes were on her. Familiar and unfamiliar, but one set was loving, gentle. The hug she got from her, not so gentle.

Venus hugged her as if she was never going to let go. Jeannie was okay with that. She hugged back, just as tightly. It felt like it lasted forever, but as she was letting go, she wished it had lasted longer. Venus gripped her by the forearms, blood on her fingers as she held her, green eyes piercing her soul in an unfamiliar, yet painfully intimate way. A look that begged the truth. Her question made Jeannie want to break into a million pieces.

"Jeannie, where were you?"

Her throat went dry as she opened her mouth. **'That's a good question Jeannie,'** his voice whispered. **'Where were you?'**

"I'm not sure," Jeannie said, not untruthfully. "It was just, darkness." Jeannie ignored the laughter that echoed cruelly in her skull.

"Okay, I'm just glad you're safe"

Jeannie nodded. "Me too."

Acacia rubbed Jeannie's arm affectionately, but her expression didn't match her tone. "It's all over." Her eyes were watery.

Jeannie's stomach dropped. "The ghosts?"

Acacia just shook her head. Jeannie's hands went limp and she felt her shoulders slump. *After everything*, she thought. *It wasn't enough?* Heat ran over her hands, down her spine, and through her feet.

A cry behind her made her jump and she spun around. Her heart soared. Kneeling on the ground, was Quinn, tears dripping down her face as if she had been unfrozen in time. Immediately, she put her hands on her chest, as if feeling to make sure she was real. She looked up, a grin forming underneath her tears. Behind her, more gasps and cries rang out as one by one, the ghosts began to reappear, each still mid cry from their disappearance. Lori and Giorgia were hugging, and Fiadh was smiling as each of her friends appeared from the shadows one by one. There were nearly two dozen ghosts all congregated, exclaiming at each others appearances, some happy, some in tears.

A blonde ghost reappeared screaming, gray eyes searching the others. *Olive.* The woman they had almost framed looked relieved to be back, but as soon as she realized what was happening, another wave of panic over took her. She began to search through the ghosts, as if looking for someone specific. After a moment, she froze as someone called out.

"Olive?" The blonde ghost shook as the voice called out again. "Olive, where are you?"

A dark skinned ghost, shoved her way out from the back of the group, a brightly colored head scarf wrapped around her hair. On seeing each other, the two women froze, but then broke down, tears and cries of joy filling the air as she threw herself at the blonde. Olive kissed the new ghost over and over again, holding her in a very familiar embrace.

"Siobhan! Siobhan, I love you so much. Siobhan, never leave me again, promise me!"

"I promise, Olive! I promise, I love you. Olive, I love you so much."

Good friends, was it? As Olive and Siobhan wept and kissed, Quinn and the ghost Venus had talked to earlier, Aster, came up to Acacia, who was shaking next to Jeannie. Aster leaned towards her, smiling through her own tears of relief.

"You did it. You saved us. You saved every one of us, just like you promised. Thank you, so much." Acacia was sobbing, her face in her hands, but she nodded. Quinn smiled at Jeannie.

"Looks like she's not the only one who kept her promise."

Jeannie nodded, mouth pressed tight in a line. "I'm safe, as promised." Jeannie said, shaking her head as Quinn smiled. "Why did you do that?"

Quinn folded her hands in her skirt, smiling, before turning over her shoulder and looking at her friends. "Because I knew you could do this. I knew you could set us free. Jeannie, look," She gestured towards the women. "I knew you were special, because you got us all back, but you also got us outside. Jeannie, we haven't been outside in fifty years. And you set us free."

Jeannie looked around at the ghosts, at the cold wind that rustled the tree branches, at the gravel parking lot that was overgrown with weeds. At the wide world that these women hadn't been able to see since they had died. As she was looking around, she saw something she hadn't seen before.

Leaning against the corner of the building, hands in pockets, was a man. A man made of shadows. There was no telling where one part of him ended and another part began, but she could see him clearly, as if she were looking at a drawing underwater. He smiled at her.

'I'm not evil, Jeannette,' His voice rumbled inside of her chest. **'I can do good things too. Keep that in mind.'**

She nodded and Quinn smiled at her again.

"We have the whole world to explore thanks to you. Remember to enjoy it, while you're still alive."

Epilogue

Lilly

"So, they arrested Trabazo, right? Like, you gave them your evidence and showed them the body and he got arrested right?"

Theo was dismembering a slice of pizza as they talked, the plasticky-cheese hanging off their fingers like zombie-flesh. Irsa was shaking her head, smiling widely as Jeannie picked at her sandwich next to her, fingers tremoring. The blackened skin peeked out through a tiny tear in the gardening gloves she has started wearing. *To avoid the questions.*

"Yes, like we told you!" Irsa said, laughing. "After they put him in the squad car, we showed him where Adrienne's body was, in the closet. Lilly gave them her phone and showed them her injuries, and they took the security camera footage."

"How did he not realize that there were cameras everywhere?" Venus asked, shaking her head. "Seems like a rookie move, to be honest."

Lilly nudged Acacia, before quickly one-handed signing what she wanted to say.

"She says he was the type of person who was stuck in the past. Mentally, anyway." Acacia translated, eyes on Lilly's fingers. "He was reliving what he felt were his 'glory days,' whatever that means."

"They say he's pleading innocent," Jaimie said through a bite of sandwich, nodding at Theo's inquiring gaze. "Which is typical, based on what I saw of him."

Lilly couldn't help but smile at them. Swallowing still hurt, but at least her turtleneck covered the bandages. Berri turned to her, tapping their blunted nails on the table.

"What did your parents say when they got to the hospital?"

Lilly shuddered. The disinfectant smell she knew so well still hung on her, like a shitty perfume that would haunt her nightmares. *The nurses were glad I was there for a new reason, at least. Relieved I wouldn't need physical therapy again.*

"They were not happy, obviously," she said, voice strained. "I got a whole lecture on personal safety, but as soon as the other was out of the room, they each congratulated me on, and I quote, 'catching the bad guy.'"

"I mean, at least they're both proud of you?" Acacia laughed.

"My parents were kinda similar," Jaimie nodded, shrugging. "Even though I didn't do much."

Irsa punched his arm. "You saved us from that creep! My parents were gushing about how you are such a good friend, protecting us from that guy. Of course, I'm grounded for the next two months," She waved her hand in the air. "But they'll get over it."

Lilly felt a pair of eyes on her, and as she turned, she saw the green eyed perpetrator averting her gaze, turning cheeks reddening. "I can't believe you went after that bitch- sorry, witch- alone, V," Lilly said, smiling at her friend.

Venus shrugged. "I knew I could handle it," she said nonchalantly, but as she moved her shoulders, Lilly could see that familiar twinge of pain. *From what they were talking about earlier, she was a psycho. I'm glad she's okay.*

"But can we talk about the ghosts for a second?" Berri cut in, fingers splayed on the table. Their neon green fingernails were barely green anymore, because of how badly they were chipped and they had obviously clipped the length of the acrylic themself. "They all came back, all were fine, and they want us to come back and wash the rest of the building! And, they said they'd pay us!"

Venus laughed. "With what? Ghost money?"

"Money is money, man."

"Rewind to how they came back, please." Jaimie said, looking between his friends. "Like, I'm still confused on what happened."

Acacia laughed. "It wasn't Olive, obviously. Apparently, the reason she was acting so weird is because she always felt when the witch was in the building. Because Siobhan, her girlfriend, was taken first, she could feel her moving through the building while trapped in the pendant."

Jaimie nodded solemnly. "Makes sense. And how did the witch put the ghosts in the necklace?"

Venus just shrugged. "I don't know exactly, but I read a bit about how witches can, like, channel energy through objects? The pendant could capture souls to channel, I guess? I do know that as soon as I broke it, the ghosts were free to find their way back from whatever darkness they were trapped in."

Lilly nodded and sipped a spoonful of soup out of her thermos, throat aching at the swallowing. *No more solid foods for me. Just pudding and soup for the next few weeks.* While Theo cleaned their fingers of pizza sauce and Jaimie laced his fingers with Acacia's, Jeannie leaned forward.

"I think we should do it." After getting a look, she continued. "The job, I mean. The building is safe now, so it should be no problem."

"Do we know it's 100% safe, though?" Jaimie asked, fingers drumming against Acacia's.

"Yes!" Jeannie said, quickly adding: "I mean, the witch problem is solved, and if we wash it down, the shadows should be completely gone! I was talking to Quinn and she said that, now that they can move around, they would gladly get us some business in the Underworld. After Siobhan and Olive's wedding, of course."

"Which apparently we're invited to?" Acacia added, looking a little baffled.

Berri's eyes went wide and Lilly tilted her head at Jeannie, warmth spreading across her chest. *It's good to see Jeannie back to herself. Well, somewhat back to herself anyway.*

"That sounds amazing!" Berri said. "We could have a whole business!"

Jeannie smiled back, catching Lilly's eye. "That's what I said, and when she asked how she should recommend us, I kinda already gave her a company name."

Irsa leaned forward, the corners of her lips quirking up. "What'd you say?"

"Don't hate me, it's a work-shoppable name." The beaming look on her face said it wasn't. "I said that we were called the Paranormal Powerwashers."

* * *

Thank you for reading The Paranormal Powerwashers and the Missing Ghosts! If you liked this book, you'll love the next book in the series where the gang is hired by a werewolf and encounter a haunted hotel!

* * *

Also by Jules King

The Paranormal Powerwashers and the Missing Ghosts

The Paranormal Powerwashers and the Werewolf's Promise

The Paranormal Powerwashers and the Homecoming Haunting

About the Author

Jules King has been a life long fan of the paranormal. Her influences include *Scooby-Doo, Supernatural,* and a host of video games ranging from *Powerwash Simulator* to *Five Nights at Freddy's.* From North Carolina, Jules started this novel when she was sixteen and will be entering her freshman year of college in the fall of 2024. When not writing, she can be found petting her cats, enjoying a brownie, or driving around in her heavily decorated car, Ethel.